THE NEW HUGO WINNERS

VOLUME IV

D1173209

THE NEW HUGO WINNERS

VOLUME IV

PRESENTED BY
GREGORY BENFORD

THE NEW HUGO WINNERS, VOLUME IV

A Baen Books Original

Baen Publishing Enterprises
P.O. Box 1403
Riverdale, NY 10471

ISBN: 0-671-87852-2

Cover art by Bob Eggleton

First printing, November 1997

Distributed by Simon & Schuster
1230 Avenue of the Americas
New York, NY 10020

Printed in the United States of America

Contents

Credits

1992
50th Convention
Orlando

A Walk in the Sun
by Geoffrey Landis

Gold
by Isaac Asimov

Beggars in Spain
by Nancy Kress

Hard science fiction proceeds from a fidelity to both the facts and attitudes of science, into the murkier landscape of the human soul. In this crisply constructed story, Landis hedges his hero in with inescapable constraints, then demands that solution come from facing the hard facts of the airless moon. His way out demands an extreme of endurance and cleverness, but all along the game is played fairly—no miracles pop out of hats.

Geoff Landis is uniquely qualified to play this exacting game, for he is a trained physicist working for NASA. His career is built on solidly made short stories, making him a member of a small band, perhaps no more than thirty, who make up the hard sf community.

I have sat in convention bars and tossed ideas back and forth with Geoff for hours, and always found his instincts for technical matters on the mark. You will find this tale of adroitly conceived constraint up to his highest standard, and richly deserving its award. A tale of survival in desperate, strange circumstances, it stands in a long sf tradition, and quite matches the classics.

A Walk In The Sun
by Geoffrey A. Landis

The pilots have a saying: a good landing is any landing you can walk away from.

Perhaps Sanjiv might have done better, if he'd been alive. Trish had done the best she could. All things considered, it was a far better landing than she had any right to expect.

Titanium struts, pencil-slender, had never been designed to take the force of a landing. Paper-thin pressure walls had buckled and shattered, spreading wreckage out into the vacuum and across a square kilometer of lunar surface. An instant before impact she remembered to blow the tanks. There was no explosion, but no landing could have been gentle enough to keep *Moonshadow* together. In eerie silence, the fragile ship had crumpled and ripped apart like a discarded aluminum can.

The piloting module had torn open and broken loose from the main part of the ship. The fragment settled against a crater wall. When it stopped moving, Trish unbuckled the straps that held her in the pilot's seat and fell slowly to the ceiling. She oriented herself to the unaccustomed gravity, found an undamaged EVA pack and plugged it into her suit, then crawled out into the sunlight through the jagged hole where the living module had been attached.

She stood on the grey lunar surface and stared. Her shadow reached out ahead of her, a pool of inky black in the shape of a fantastically stretched man. The landscape was rugged and utterly barren, painted in stark shades of grey and black. "Magnificent desolation," she whispered. Behind her, the sun hovered just over the mountains, glinting off shards of titanium and steel scattered across the cratered plain.

Patricia Jay Mulligan looked out across the desolate moonscape and tried not to weep.

First things first. She took the radio out from the shattered crew compartment and tried it. Nothing. That was no surprise; Earth was over the horizon, and there were no other ships in cislunar space.

After a little searching she found Sanjiv and Theresa. In the low gravity they were absurdly easy to carry. There was no use in burying them. She sat them in a niche between two boulders, facing the sun, facing west, toward where the Earth was hidden behind a range of black mountains. She tried to think of the right words to say, and failed. Perhaps as well; she wouldn't know the proper service for Sanjiv anyway. "Goodbye, Sanjiv. Goodbye, Theresa. I wish—I wish things would have been different. I'm sorry." Her voice was barely more than a whisper. "Go with God."

She tried not to think of how soon she was likely to be joining them.

She forced herself to think. What would her sister have done? Survive. Karen would survive. First: inventory your assets. She was alive, miraculously unhurt. Her vacuum suit was in serviceable condition. Life-support was powered by the suit's solar arrays; she had air and water for as long as the sun continued to shine. Scavenging the wreckage yielded plenty of unbroken food packs; she wasn't about to starve.

Second: call for help. In this case, the nearest help was a quarter of a million miles over the horizon. She would need a high-gain antenna and a mountain peak with a view of Earth.

In its computer, *Moonshadow* had carried the best maps of the moon ever made. Gone. There had been other maps on the ship; they were scattered with the wreckage. She'd managed to find a detailed map of Mare Nubium—useless—and a small global map meant to be used as an index. It would have to do. As near as she could tell, the impact site was just over the eastern edge of Mare Smythii—"Smith's Sea." The mountains in the distance should mark the edge of the sea, and, with luck, have a view of Earth.

She checked her suit. At a command, the solar arrays spread out to their full extent like oversized dragonfly wings and glinted in prismatic colors as they rotated to face the sun. She verified that the suit's systems were charging properly, and set off.

Close up, the mountain was less steep than it had looked from the crash site. In the low gravity, climbing was hardly more difficult than walking, although the two-meter dish made her balance awkward. Reaching the ridgetop, Trish was rewarded with the sight of a tiny sliver of blue on the horizon. The mountains on the far side of the valley were still in darkness. She hoisted the radio higher up on her shoulder and started across the next valley.

From the next mountain peak the Earth edged over the horizon, a blue and white marble half-hidden by black mountains. She unfolded the tripod for the antenna and carefully sighted along the feed. "Hello? This is Astronaut Mulligan from *Moonshadow*. Emergency. Repeat, this is an emergency. Does anybody hear me?"

She took her thumb off the *transmit* button and waited for a response, but heard nothing but the soft whisper of static from the sun.

"This is Astronaut Mulligan from *Moonshadow*. Does anybody hear me?" She paused again. "*Moonshadow, calling anybody. Moonshadow*, calling anybody. This is an emergency."

"—shadow, *this is Geneva control. We read you faint but clear. Hang on, up there.*" She released her breath in a sudden gasp. She hadn't even realized she'd been holding it.

After five minutes the rotation of the Earth had taken the ground antenna out of range. In that time after they had gotten over their surprise that there was a survivor of the *Moonshadow*—she learned the parameters of the problem. Her landing had been close to the sunset terminator: the very edge of the illuminated side of the moon. The moon's rotation is slow, but inexorable. Sunset would arrive in three days. There was no shelter on the moon, no place to wait out the fourteen-day-long lunar night. Her solar cells needed sunlight to keep her air fresh. Her search of the wreckage had yielded no unruptured storage tanks, no batteries, no means to lay up a store of oxygen.

And there was no way they could launch a rescue mission before nightfall.

Too many "no"s.

She sat silent, gazing across the jagged plain toward the slender blue crescent, thinking.

After a few minutes the antenna at Goldstone rotated into range, and the radio crackled to life. "Moonshadow, *do you read me? Hello*, Moonshadow, *do you read me?*"

"*Moonshadow* here."

She released the transmit button and waited in long silence for her words to be carried to Earth.

"*Roger*, Moonshadow. *We confirm the earliest window for a rescue mission is thirty days from now. Can you hold on that long?*"

She made her decision and pressed the transmit button. "Astronaut Mulligan for *Moonshadow*. I'll be here waiting for you. One way or another."

She waited, but there was no answer. The receiving antenna at Goldstone couldn't have rotated out of range so quickly. She checked the radio. When she took the cover off, she could see that the printed circuit board on the power supply had been slightly cracked from the crash, but she couldn't see any broken leads or components clearly out of place. She banged on it with her fist—Karen's first rule of electronics: if it doesn't work, hit it—and re-aimed the antenna, but it didn't help. Clearly something in it had broken.

What would Karen have done? Not just sit here and die, that was certain. Get a move on, kiddo. When sunset catches you, you'll die.

They had heard her reply. She had to believe they heard her reply and would be coming for her. All she had to do was survive.

The dish antenna would be too awkward to carry with her. She could afford nothing but the bare necessities. At sunset her air would be gone. She put down the radio and began to walk.

Mission Commander Stanley stared at the X-rays of his engine. It was four in the morning. There would be no more sleep for him that night; he was scheduled to fly to Washington at six to testify to Congress.

"Your decision, Commander," the engine technician said. "*We* can't find any flaws in the X-rays we took of the flight engines, but it could be hidden. The nominal flight profile doesn't take the engines to a hundred twenty, so the blades should hold even if there is a flaw."

"How long a delay if we yank the engines for inspection?"

"Assuming they're okay, we lose a day. If not, two, maybe three."

Commander Stanley drummed his fingers in irritation. He hated to be forced into hasty decisions. "Normal procedure would be?"

"Normally we'd want to reinspect."

"Do it."

He sighed. Another delay. Somewhere up there, somebody was counting on him to get there on time. If she was still alive. If the cut-off radio signal didn't signify catastrophic failure of other systems.

If she could find a way to survive without air.

On Earth it would have been a marathon pace. On the moon it was an easy lope. After ten miles the trek fell into an easy rhythm: half a walk, half like jogging, and half bounding like a slow-motion kangaroo. Her worst enemy was boredom.

Her comrades at the academy—in part envious of the top scores that had made her the first of their class picked for a mission—had ribbed her mercilessly about flying a mission that would come within a few kilometers of the moon without landing. Now she had a chance to see more of the moon up close than anybody in history. She wondered what her classmates were thinking now. She would have a tale to tell—if only she could survive to tell it.

The warble of the low voltage warning broke her out of her reverie. She checked her running display as she started down the maintenance checklist. Elapsed EVA time, eight point three hours. System functions, nominal, except that the solar array current was way below norm. In a few moments she found the trouble: a thin layer of dust on her solar array. Not a serious problem; it could be brushed off. If she couldn't find a pace that would avoid kicking dust on the arrays, then she would have to break every few hours to housekeep. She rechecked the array and continued on.

With the sun unmoving ahead of her and nothing but the hypnotically blue crescent of the slowly rotating Earth creeping imperceptibly off the horizon, her attention wandered. *Moonshadow* had been tagged as an easy mission, a low-orbit mapping flight to scout sites for the future moonbase. *Moonshadow* had never been intended to land, not on the moon, not anywhere.

She'd landed it anyway; she'd had to.

Walking west across the barren plain, Trish had nightmares of blood and falling, Sanjiv dying beside her; Theresa already dead in the lab module; the moon looming huge, spinning at a crazy angle in the viewports. Stop the spin, aim for the terminator at low sun angles, the illumination makes it easier to see the roughness of the surface. Conserve fuel, but remember to blow the tanks an instant before you hit to avoid explosion.

That was over. Concentrate on the present. One foot in front of the other. Again. Again.

The undervoltage alarm chimed again. Dust, already?

She looked down at her navigation aid and realized with a shock that she had walked a hundred and fifty kilometers.

Time for a break anyway. She sat down on a boulder, fetched a snack-pack out of her carryall, and set a timer for fifteen minutes. The airtight quick-seal on the food pack was designed to mate to the matching port in the lower part of her faceplate. It would be important to keep the seal free of grit. She verified the vacuum seal twice before opening the pack into the suit, then pushed the food bar in so she could turn her head and gnaw off pieces. The bar was hard and slightly sweet.

She looked west across the gently rolling plain. The horizon looked flat, unreal; a painted backdrop barely out of reach. On the moon, it should be easy to keep up a pace of fifteen or even twenty miles an hour—counting time out for sleep, maybe ten. She could walk a long, long way.

Karen would have liked it; she'd always liked hiking in

desolate areas. "Quite pretty, in its own way, isn't it, Sis?" Trish said. "Who'd have thought there were so many shadings of grey? Plenty of uncrowded beach. Too bad it's such a long walk to the water."

Time to move on. She continued on across terrain that was generally flat, although everywhere pocked with craters of every size. The moon is surprisingly flat; only one percent of the surface has a slope of more than fifteen degrees. The small hills she bounded over easily; the few larger ones she detoured around. In the low gravity this posed no real problem to walking. She walked on. She didn't feel tired, but when she checked her readout and realized that she had been walking for twenty hours, she forced herself to stop.

Sleeping was a problem. The solar arrays were designed to be detached from the suit for easy servicing, but had no provision to power the life-support while detached. Eventually she found a way to stretch the short cable out far enough to allow her to prop up the array next to her so she could lie down without disconnecting the power. She would have to be careful not to roll over. That done, she found she couldn't sleep. After a time she lapsed into a fitful doze, dreaming not of the *Moonshadow* as she'd expected, but of her sister, Karen, who—in the dream— wasn't dead at all, but had only been playing a joke on her, pretending to die.

She awoke disoriented, muscles aching, then suddenly remembered where she was. The Earth was a full handspan above the horizon. She got up, yawned, and jogged west across the gunpowder-grey sandscape.

Her feet were tender where the boots rubbed. She varied her pace, changing from jogging to skipping to a kangaroo bounce. It helped some; not enough. She could feel her feet starting to blister, but knew that there was no way to take off her boots to tend, or even examine, her feet.

Karen had made her hike on blistered feet, and had had no patience with complaints or slacking off. She should have broken her boots in before the hike. In the one-sixth gee, at least the pain was bearable.

After a while her feet simply got numb.

Small craters she bounded over; larger ones she detoured around; larger ones yet she simply climbed across. West of Mare Smythii she entered a badlands and the terrain got bumpy. She had to slow down. The downhill slopes were in full sun, but the crater bottoms and valleys were still in shadow.

Her blisters broke, the pain a shrill and discordant singing in her boots. She bit her lip to keep herself from crying and continued on. Another few hundred kilometers and she was in Mare Spumans—"Sea of Froth"—and it was clear trekking again. Across Spumans, then into the north lobe of Fecundity and through to Tranquility. Somewhere around the sixth day of her trek she must have passed Tranquility Base; she carefully scanned for it on the horizon as she traveled but didn't see anything. By her best guess she missed it by several hundred kilometers; she was already deviating toward the north, aiming for a pass just north of the crater Julius Caesar into Mare Vaporum to avoid the mountains. The ancient landing stage would have been too small to spot unless she'd almost walked right over it.

"Figures," she said. "Come all this way, and the only tourist attraction in a hundred miles is closed. That's the way things always seem to turn out, eh, Sis?"

There was nobody to laugh at her witticism, so after a moment she laughed at it herself.

Wake up from confused dreams to black sky and motionless sunlight, yawn, and start walking before you're completely awake. Sip on the insipid warm water, trying not to think about what it's recycled from. Break, cleaning your solar arrays, your life, with exquisite care. Walk. Break. Sleep again, the sun nailed to the sky in the same position it was in when you awoke. Next day do it all over. And again. And again.

The nutrition packs are low-residue, but every few days you must still squat for nature. Your life support can't recycle solid waste, so you wait for the suit to desiccate the waste and then void the crumbly brown powder to vacuum. Your trail is marked by your powdery deposits, scarcely distinguishable from the dark lunar dust.

Walk west, ever west, racing the sun.

Earth was high in the sky; she could no longer see it without craning her neck way back. When the Earth was directly overhead she stopped and celebrated, miming the opening of an invisible bottle of champagne to toast her imaginary traveling companions. The sun was well above the horizon now. In six days of travel she had walked a quarter of the way around the moon.

She passed well south of Copernicus, to stay as far out of the impact rubble as possible without crossing mountains. The terrain was eerie, boulders as big as houses, as big as shuttle tanks. In places the footing was treacherous where the grainy regolith gave way to jumbles of rock, rays thrown out by the cataclysmic impact billions of years ago. She picked her way as best she could. She left her radio on and gave a running commentary as she moved. "Watch your step here, footing's treacherous. Coming up on a hill; think we should climb it or detour around?"

Nobody voiced an opinion. She contemplated the rocky hill. Likely an ancient volcanic bubble, although she hadn't realized that this region had once been active. The territory around it would be bad. From the top she'd be able to study the terrain for a ways ahead. "Okay, listen up, everybody. The climb could be tricky here, so stay close and watch where I place my feet. Don't take chances better slow and safe than fast and dead. Any questions?" Silence; good. "Okay, then. We'll take a fifteen minute break when we reach the top. Follow me."

Past the rubble of Copernicus, Oceanus Procellarum was smooth as a golf course. Trish jogged across the sand with a smooth, even glide. Karen and Dutchman seemed to always be lagging behind or running up ahead out of sight. Silly dog still followed Karen around like a puppy, even though Trish was the one who fed him and refilled his water dish every day since Karen went away to college. The way Karen wouldn't stay close behind her annoyed Trish. Karen had *promised* to let her be the leader this time—but she kept her feelings to herself. Karen had called her a bratty little pest, and she was determined to show she could act like an adult. Anyway, she was the one with the map. If Karen got lost, it would serve her right.

She angled slightly north again to take advantage of the map's promise of smooth terrain. She looked around to see if Karen was there, and was surprised to see that the Earth was a gibbous ball low down on the horizon. Of course, Karen wasn't there. Karen had died years ago. Trish was alone in a spacesuit that itched and stank and chafed her skin nearly raw across the thighs. She should have broken it in better, but who would have expected she would want to go jogging in it?

It was unfair how she had to wear a spacesuit and Karen didn't. Karen got to do a lot of things that she didn't, but how come she didn't have to wear a spacesuit? *Everybody* had to wear a spacesuit. It was the rule. She turned to Karen to ask. Karen laughed bitterly. "I don't have to wear a spacesuit, my bratty little sister, because I'm *dead*. Squished like a bug and buried, remember?"

Oh, yes, that was right. Okay, then, if Karen was dead, then she didn't have to wear a spacesuit. It made perfect sense for a few more kilometers, and they jogged along together in companionable silence until Trish had a sudden thought. "Hey, wait—if you're dead, then how can you be here?"

"Because I'm not here, silly. I'm a fig-newton of your overactive imagination."

With a shock, Trish looked over her shoulder. Karen wasn't there. Karen had never been there.

"I'm sorry. Please come back. Please?"

She stumbled and fell headlong, sliding in a spray of dust down the bowl of a crater. As she slid she frantically twisted to stay face-down, to keep from rolling over on the fragile solar wings on her back. When she finally slid to a stop, the silence echoing in her ears, there was a long scratch like a badly healed scar down the glass of her helmet. The double reinforced faceplate had held, fortunately, or she wouldn't be looking at it.

She checked her suit. There were no breaks in the integrity, but the titanium strut that held out the left wing of the solar array had buckled back and nearly broken. Miraculously there had been no other damage. She pulled off the array and studied the damaged strut. She bent it back into position as best she could, and splinted the joint with a mechanical pencil tied on with two short lengths of wire. The pencil had been only extra weight anyway; it was lucky she hadn't thought to discard it. She tested the joint gingerly. It wouldn't take much stress, but if she didn't bounce around too much it should hold. Time for a break anyway.

When she awoke she took stock of her situation. While she hadn't been paying attention, the terrain had slowly turned mountainous. The next stretch would be slower going than the last bit.

"About time you woke up, sleepyhead," said Karen. She yawned, stretched, and turned her head to look back at the line of footprints. At the end of the long trail, the Earth showed as a tiny blue dome on the horizon, not very far away at all, the single speck of color in a landscape of uniform grey. "Twelve days to walk halfway around the moon," she said. "Not bad, kid. Not great, but not bad. You training for a marathon or something?"

Trish got up and started jogging, her feet falling into rhythm automatically as she sipped from the suit recycler, trying to wash the stale taste out of her mouth. She called out to Karen behind her without turning around. "Get a move on, we got places to go. You coming, or what?"

In the nearly shadowless sunlight the ground was washed-out, two-dimensional. Trish had a hard time finding footing, stumbling over rocks that were nearly invisible against the flat landscape. One foot in front of the other. Again. Again.

The excitement of the trek had long ago faded, leaving behind a relentless determination to prevail, which in turn had faded into a kind of mental numbness. Trish spent the time chatting with Karen, telling the private details of her life, secretly hoping that Karen would be pleased, would say something telling her she was proud of her. Suddenly she noticed that Karen wasn't listening; had apparently wandered off on her sometime when she hadn't been paying attention.

She stopped on the edge of a long, winding rille. It looked like a riverbed just waiting for a rainstorm to fill it, but Trish knew it had never known water. Covering the bottom was only dust, dry as powdered bone. She slowly picked her way to the bottom, careful not to slip again and risk damage to her fragile life-support system. She looked up at the top. Karen was standing on the rim waving at her. "Come *on!* Quit *dawdling,* you slowpoke—you want to stay here *forever?*"

"What's the hurry? We're ahead of schedule. The sun is high up in the sky, and we're halfway around the moon. We'll make it, no sweat."

Karen came down the slope, sliding like a skier in the powdery dust. She pressed her face up against Trish's helmet and stared into her eyes with a manic intensity that almost frightened her. "The hurry, my lazy little sister, is that you're halfway around the moon, you've finished with the easy part and it's all mountains and badlands from here on, you've got six thousand kilometers to walk in a broken spacesuit, and if you slow down and let the sun get ahead of you, and then run into one more teensy little problem, just one, you'll be dead, dead, dead, just like me. You wouldn't like it, trust me. Now get your pretty little lazy butt into gear and *move!*"

And, indeed, it was slow going. She couldn't bound down slopes as she used to, or the broken strut would fail and she'd have to stop for painstaking repair. There were no more level plains; it all seemed to be either boulder fields, crater walls, or mountains. On the eighteenth day she came to a huge natural arch. It towered over her head, and she gazed up at it in awe, wondering how such a structure could have been formed on the moon.

"Not by wind, that's for sure," said Karen. "Lava, I'd figure. Melted through a ridge and flowed on, leaving the hole; then over the eons micrometeoroid bombardment ground off the rough edges. Pretty, though, isn't it?"

"Magnificent."

Not far past the arch she entered a forest of needle-thin crystals. At first they were small, breaking like glass under her feet, but then they soared above her, six-sided spires and minarets in fantastic colors. She picked her way in silence between them, bedazzled by the forest of light sparkling between the sapphire spires. The crystal jungle finally thinned out and was replaced by giant crystal boulders, glistening iridescent in the sun. Emeralds? Diamonds?

"I don't know, kid. But they're in our way. I'll be glad when they're behind us."

And after a while the glistening boulders thinned out as well, until there were only a scattered few glints of color on the slopes of the hills beside her, and then at last the rocks were just rocks, craggy and pitted.

Crater Daedalus, the middle of the lunar farside. There was no celebration this time. The sun had long ago stopped its lazy rise, and was imperceptibly dropping toward the horizon ahead of them.

"It's a race against the sun, kid, and the sun ain't making any stops to rest. You're losing ground."

"I'm tired. Can't you see I'm tired? I think I'm sick. I hurt all over. Get off my case. Let me rest. Just a few more minutes? Please?"

"You can rest when you're dead." Karen laughed in a strangled, high-pitched voice. Trish suddenly realized that she was on the edge of hysteria. Abruptly she stopped laughing. "Get a move on, kid. Move!"

The lunar surface passed under her, an irregular grey treadmill.

Hard work and good intentions couldn't disguise the fact that the sun was gaining. Every day when she woke up the sun was a little lower down ahead of her, shining a little more directly in her eyes.

Ahead of her, in the glare of the sun she could see an oasis, a tiny island of grass and trees in the lifeless desert. She could already hear the croaking of frogs: *braap*, *braap*, *BRAAP!*

No. That was no oasis; that was the sound of a malfunction alarm. She stopped, disoriented. Overheating. The suit air conditioning had broken down. It took her half a day to find the clogged coolant valve and another three hours soaked in sweat to find a way to unclog it without letting the precious liquid vent to space. The sun sank another handspan toward the horizon.

The sun was directly in her face now. Shadows of the rocks stretched toward her like hungry tentacles, even the smallest looking hungry and mean. Karen was walking beside her again, but now she was silent, sullen.

"Why won't you talk to me? Did I do something? Did I say something wrong? Tell me."

"I'm not here, little sister, I'm dead. I think it's about time you faced up to that."

"Don't say that. You can't be dead."

"You have an idealized picture of me in your mind. Let me go. *Let me go!*"

"I can't. Don't go. Hey—do you remember the time we saved up all our allowances for a year so we could buy a horse? And we found a stray kitten that was real sick, and we took the shoebox full of our allowance and the kitten to the vet, and he fixed the kitten but wouldn't take any money?"

"Yeah, I remember. But somehow we still never managed to save enough for a horse." Karen sighed. "Do you think it was easy growing up with a bratty little sister dogging my footsteps, trying to imitate everything I did?"

"I wasn't either bratty."

"You were too."

"No, I wasn't. I adored you." Did she? "I *worshipped* you."

"I know you did. Let me tell you, kid, that didn't make it any easier. Do you think it was easy being worshipped? Having to be a paragon all the time? Christ, all through high school, when I wanted to get high, I had to sneak away and do it in private, or else I knew my damn kid sister would be doing it too."

"You didn't. You never."

"Grow up, kid. Damn right I did. You were always right behind me. Everything I did, I knew you'd be right there doing it next. I had to struggle like hell to keep ahead of you, and you, damn you, followed effortlessly. You were smarter than me—you know that, don't you?—and how do you think that made me feel?"

"Well, what about me? Do you think it was easy for *me*? Growing up with a dead sister—everything I did, it was 'Too bad you can't be more like Karen' and 'Karen wouldn't have done it that way' and 'If only Karen had. . . .' How do you think that made *me* feel, huh? You had it easy—I was the one who had to live up to the standards of a goddamn *angel.*"

"Tough breaks, kid. Better than being dead."

"Damn it, Karen, I loved you. I love you. Why did you have to go away?"

"I know that, kid. I couldn't help it. I'm sorry. I love you too, but I have to go. Can you let me go? Can you just be yourself now, and stop trying to be me?"

"I'll . . . I'll try."

"Goodbye, little sister."

"Goodbye, Karen."

She was alone in the settling shadows on an empty, rugged plain. Ahead of her, the sun was barely kissing the ridgetops. The dust she kicked up was behaving strangely; rather than falling to the ground, it would hover half a meter off the ground. She puzzled over the effect, then saw that all around her, dust was silently rising off the ground. For a moment she thought it was another hallucination, but then realized it was some kind of electrostatic charging effect. She moved forward again through the rising fog of moondust. The sun reddened, and the sky turned a deep purple.

The darkness came at her like a demon. Behind her only the tips of mountains were illuminated, the bases disappearing into shadow. The ground ahead of her was covered with pools of ink that she had to pick her way around. Her radio locator was turned on, but receiving only static. It could only pick up the locator beacon from the *Moonshadow* if she got in line of sight of the crash site. She must be nearly there, but none of the landscape looked even slightly familiar. Ahead was that the ridge she'd climbed to radio Earth? She couldn't tell. She climbed it, but didn't see the blue marble. The next one?

The darkness had spread up to her knees. She kept

tripping over rocks invisible in the dark. Her footsteps struck sparks from the rocks, and behind her footprints glowed faintly. Triboluminescent glow, she thought nobody has *ever* seen that before. She couldn't die now, not so close. But the darkness wouldn't wait. All around her the darkness lay like an unsuspected ocean, rocks sticking up out of the tidepools into the dying sunlight. The undervoltage alarm began to warble as the rising tide of darkness reached her solar array. The crash site had to be around here somewhere, it had to. Maybe the locator beacon was broken? She climbed up a ridge and into the light, looking around desperately for clues. Shouldn't there have been a rescue mission by now?

Only the mountaintops were in the light. She aimed for the nearest and tallest mountain she could see and made her way across the darkness to it, stumbling and crawling in the ocean of ink, at last pulling herself into the light like a swimmer gasping for air. She huddled on her rocky island, desperate as the tide of darkness slowly rose about her. Where were they? *Where were they?*

Back on Earth, work on the rescue mission had moved at a frantic pace. Everything was checked and triple-checked in space, cutting corners was an invitation for sudden death, but still the rescue mission had been dogged by small problems and minor delays, delays that would have been routine for an ordinary mission, but loomed huge against the tight mission deadline.

The scheduling was almost impossibly tight—the mission had been set to launch in four months, not four weeks. Technicians scheduled for vacations volunteered to work overtime, while suppliers who normally took weeks to deliver parts delivered overnight. Final integration for the replacement for *Moonshadow*, originally to be called *Explorer* but now hastily re-christened *Rescuer*, was speeded up, and the transfer vehicle launched to the Space

Station months ahead of the original schedule, less than two weeks after the *Moonshadow* crash. Two shuttle-loads of propellant swiftly followed, and the transfer vehicle was mated to its aeroshell and tested. While the rescue crew practiced possible scenarios on the simulator, the lander, with engines inspected and replaced, was hastily modified to accept a third person on ascent, tested, and then launched to rendezvous with *Rescuer*. Four weeks after the crash the stack was fueled and ready, the crew briefed, and the trajectory calculated. The crew shuttle launched through heavy fog to join their *Rescuer* in orbit.

Thirty days after the unexpected signal from the moon had revealed a survivor of the *Moonshadow* expedition, *Rescuer* left orbit for the moon.

From the top of the mountain ridge west of the crash site, Commander Stanley passed his searchlight over the wreckage one more time and shook his head in awe. "An amazing job of piloting," he said. "Looks like she used the TEI motor for braking, and then set it down on the RCS verniers."

"Incredible," Tanya Nakora murmured. "Too bad it couldn't save her."

The record of Patricia Mulligan's travels was written in the soil around the wreck. After the rescue team had searched the wreckage, they found the single line of footsteps that led due west, crossed the ridge, and disappeared over the horizon. Stanley put down the binoculars. There was no sign of returning footprints. "Looks like she wanted to see the moon before her air ran out," he said. Inside his helmet he shook his head slowly. "Wonder how far she got?"

"Could she be alive somehow?" asked Nakora. "She was a pretty ingenious kid."

"Not ingenious enough to breathe vacuum. Don't fool yourself—this rescue mission was a political toy from the start. We never had a chance of finding anybody up here still alive."

"Still, we had to try, didn't we?"

Stanley shook his head and tapped his helmet. "Hold on a sec, my damn radio's acting up. I'm picking up some kind of feedback—almost sounds like a voice."

"I hear it too, Commander. But it doesn't make any sense."

The voice was faint in the radio. "Don't turn off the lights. Please, please, don't turn off your light. . . ."

Stanley turned to Nakora. "Do you . . . ?"

"I hear it, Commander . . . but I don't believe it."

Stanley picked up the searchlight and began sweeping the horizon. "Hello? *Rescuer* calling Astronaut Patricia Mulligan. Where the hell are you?"

The spacesuit had once been pristine white. It was now dirty grey with moondust, only the ragged and bent solar array on the back carefully polished free of debris. The figure in it was nearly as ragged.

After a meal and a wash, she was coherent and ready to explain.

"It was the mountaintop. I climbed the mountaintop to stay in the sunlight, and I just barely got high enough to hear your radios."

Nakora nodded. "That much we figured out. But the rest—the last month—you really walked all the way around the moon? Eleven thousand kilometers?"

Trish nodded. "It was all I could think of. I figured, about the distance from New York to LA and back—people have walked that and lived. It came to a walking speed of just under ten miles an hour. Farside was the hard part— turned out to be much rougher than nearside. But strange and weirdly beautiful, in places. You wouldn't believe the things I saw."

She shook her head, and laughed quietly. "I don't believe

some of the things I saw. The immensity of it—we've barely scratched the surface. I'll be coming back, Commander. I promise you."

"I'm sure you will," said Commander Stanley. "I'm sure you will."

As the ship lifted off the moon, Trish looked out for a last view of the surface. For a moment she thought she saw a lonely figure standing on the surface, waving her goodbye. She didn't wave back.

She looked again, and there was nothing out there but magnificent desolation.

Isaac Asimov introduced earlier collections of Hugo winners with his jovial authority. This story carries forward effortlessly, gliding on his unique gift for quick narration and darting ideas. Isaac was a genius at the apparently simple. Anyone who thinks that writing about complex ideas, including both modern science and the human heart, with clarity and simplicity, is welcome to try; if so, take Asimov as your model. Like Arthur Clarke, his method is deceptively transparent; indeed, readers typically remark of them both, as I heard a fan put it, "They have no style, they just write."

Ah, the depths of admirable innocence behind that phrase. For it is best if a reader does not see the furniture moving around behind a thin curtain, while reading a story. The events of the imagined world should be real, manufactured by the reader himself in that theatre of the mind which words excite. Reading is an intellectually demanding amusement, for it calls upon us to take symbols and make of them pictures, sights, sounds, to conjure up people and emotions with our mental machinery. How much more difficult to do this if the devices of the author peek into the mental field of vision, destroying the fleeting sense of real events unfolding. So it is with style, I think, for most readers. They do not want to see style so much as feel it. They desire to be propelled through events and sensations and ideas which unfurl effortlessly, as though ordained, and they do not wish to feel any intrusion. The author's voice does this task best when it is transparent, seemingly "natural," inevitable.

Isaac had that gift. Of course, what style appears invisible yet effective depends upon the taste of the reader. For a huge readership, Isaac's worked that wonder. He is the only author represented with a book in each classification of the Dewey Decimal System in the Library of Congress. Not only did he write compulsively, he did it well. I have known only two writers who truly enjoyed the sheer process of writing—from the deep concentration through the mechanical details of hammering out thoughts on a keyboard, through (in Isaac's case) the tedium of making up cards for each important word in a book, to create its Index. (The other is Dean Koontz, whose work methods are quite different, but inner demons seem similar at least in their incessant energies.)

Alas, we shall have no more of Isaac's limpid prose. I was so struck by his death that when his widow, Janet, proposed to me in 1995 that I write a novel set in his Foundation, I at first declined. My first thought was, how could I echo that style? Isaac wrote much of his fiction in a way he termed "direct and spare," though in the later works he relaxed this constraint a bit. For the Foundation novels he used a particularly bare-boards approach, with virtually no background descriptions or novelistic details. I found that I had to explore Asimovian ideas my own way, so the resulting book, *Foundation's Fear*, is not an imitation Asimov novel, but a Benford novel using Asimov's basic ideas and backdrop.

I recall my last conversation with him, only months before he died. His prodigious memory had failed and he could again read favorite mysteries, not knowing how they would turn out. An oblique blessing indeed. He told me how his memory once had organized each scrap of new information, filing it properly under instinctive headings for instant recovery. "It saved time looking things up," he said. I once tested this filing system by demanding that he immediately tell me a joke with a camel in it. Without blinking, he did. Okay, I said, now another. He delivered just as quickly. I wondered how many more camel jokes he had and he shot back, "Three."

His books were filled with such almost offhand intelligence and knowledge. Readers flocked to them. Such is the continuing impact of probably the most influential sf novelist since Wells. For a memorable lingering moment with him, "Gold" give us Isaac still at his peak.

Gold
by Isaac Asimov

Jonas Willard looked from side to side and tapped his baton on the stand before him.

He said, "Understood now? This is just a practice scene, designed to find out if we know what we're doing. We've gone through this enough times so that I expect a professional performance now. Get ready. All of you get ready."

He looked again from side to side. There was a person at each of the voice-recorders, and there were three others working the image projection. A seventh was for the music and an eighth for the all-important background. Others waited to one side for their turn.

Willard said, "All right now. Remember this old man has spent his entire adult life as a tyrant. He is accustomed to having everyone jump at his slightest word, to having everyone tremble at his frown. That is all gone now but he doesn't know it. He faces his daughter whom he thinks of only as a bent-headed obsequious girl who will do anything he says, and he cannot believe that it is an imperious queen that he now faces. So let's have the King."

Lear appeared. Tall, white hair and beard, somewhat disheveled, eyes sharp and piercing.

Willard said, "Not bent. Not bent. He's eighty years old but he doesn't think of himself as old. Not now. Straight.

Every inch a king." The image was adjusted. "That's right. And the voice has to be strong. No quavering. Not now. Right?"

"Right, chief," said the Lear voice-recorder, nodding.

"All right. The Queen."

And there she was, almost as tall as Lear, standing straight and rigid as a statue, her draped clothing in fine array, nothing out of place. Her beauty was as cold and unforgiving as ice.

"And the Fool."

A little fellow, thin and fragile, like a frightened teenager but with a face too old for a teenager and with a sharp look in eyes that seemed so large that they threatened to devour his face.

"Good," said Willard. "Be ready for Albany. He comes in pretty soon. Begin the scene." He tapped the podium again, took a quick glance at the marked-up play before him and said, "Lear!" and his baton pointed to the Lear voice-recorder, moving gently to mark the speech cadence that he wanted created.

Lear says, "How now, daughter? What makes that frontlet on? Methinks you are too much o' late i' th' frown."

The Fool's thin voice, fifelike, piping, interrupts, "Thou wast a pretty fellow when thou hadst no need to care for her frowning—"

Goneril, the Queen, turns slowly to face the Clown as he speaks, her eyes turning momentarily into balls of lurid light—doing it so momentarily that those watching caught the impression rather than viewed the fact. The Fool completes his speech in gathering fright and backs his way behind Lear in a blind search for protection against the searing glance.

Goneril proceeds to tell Lear the facts of life and there is the faint crackling of thin ice as she speaks, while the music plays in soft discords, barely heard.

Nor are Goneril's demands so out of line, for she wants

an orderly court and there couldn't be one as long as Lear still thought of himself as tyrant. But Lear is in no mood to recognize reason. He breaks into a passion and begins railing.

Albany enters. He is Goneril's consort—round-faced, innocent, eyes looking about in wonder. What is happening? He is completely drowned out by his dominating wife and by his raging father-in-law. It is at this point that Lear breaks into one of the great piercing denunciations in all of literature. He is overreacting. Goneril has not as yet done anything to deserve *this*, but Lear knows no restraint. He says:

> "Hear, Nature, hear dear goddess, hear!
> Suspend thy purpose, if thou didst intend
> To make this creature fruitful.
> Into her womb convey sterility;
> Dry up in her the organs of increase;
> And from her derogate body never spring
> A babe to honour her! If she must teem,
> Create her child of spleen, that it may live
> And be a thwart disnatur'd torment to her.
> Let it stamp wrinkles in her brow of youth,
> With cadent tears fret channels in her cheeks,
> Turn all her mother's pains and benefits
> To laughter and contempt, that she may feel
> How sharper than a serpent's tooth, it is
> To have a thankless child!"

The voice-recorder strengthened Lear's voice for this speech, gave it a distant hiss, his body became taller and somehow less substantial as though it had been converted into a vengeful Fury.

As for Goneril, she remained untouched throughout, never flinching, never receding, but her beautiful face, without any change that could be described, seemed to accumulate evil so that by the end of Lear's curse, she had the appearance of an archangel still, but an archangel ruined. All possible pity had been wiped out of the countenance, leaving behind only a devil's dangerous magnificence.

The Fool remained behind Lear throughout, shuddering. Albany was the very epitome of confusion, asking useless questions, seeming to want to step between the two antagonists and clearly afraid to do so.

Willard tapped his baton and said, "All right. It's been recorded and I want you all to watch the scene." He lifted his baton high and the synthesizer at the rear of the set began what could only be called the instant replay.

It was watched in silence, and Willard said, "It was good, but I think you'll grant it was not good enough. I'm going to ask you all to listen to me, so that I can explain what we're trying to do. Computerized theater is not new, as you all know. Voices and images have been built up to beyond what human beings can do. You don't have to break your speechifying in order to breathe; the range and quality of the voices are almost limitless; and the images can change to suit the words and action. Still, the technique has only been used, so far, for childish purposes. What we intend now is to make the first serious compu-drama the world has ever seen, and nothing will do—for me, at any rate—but to start at the top. I want to do the greatest play written by the greatest playwright in history: *King Lear* by William Shakespeare.

"I want not a word changed. I want not a word left out. I don't want to modernize the play. I don't want to remove the archaisms, because the play, *as written,* has its glorious music and any change will diminish it. But in that case, how do we have it reach the general public? I don't mean the students, I don't mean the intellectuals, I mean *everybody.* I mean people who've never watched Shakespeare before and whose idea of a good play is a slapstick musical. This play *is* archaic in spots, and people don't talk in iambic pentameter. They are not even accustomed to hearing it on the stage.

"So we're going to have to translate the archaic and the unusual. The voices, more than human, will, just by their timbre and changes, interpret the words. The images will shift to reinforce the words.

"Now Goneril's change in appearance as Lear's curse proceeded was good. The viewer will gauge the devastating effect it has on her even though her iron will won't let it show in words. The viewer will therefore feel the devastating effect upon himself, too, even if some of the words Lear uses are strange to him.

"In that connection, we must remember to make the Fool look older with every one of his appearances. He's a weak, sickly fellow to begin with, broken-hearted over the loss of Cordelia, frightened to death of Goneril and Regan, destroyed by the storm from which Lear, his only protector, can't protect him—and I mean by that the storm of Lear's daughter's as well as of the raging weather. When he slips out of the play in Act III, Scene VI, it must be made plain that he is about to die. Shakespeare doesn't say so, so the Fool's face must say so.

"However, we've got to do something about Lear. The voice-recorder was on the right track by having a hissing sound in the voice-track. Lear is spewing venom; he is a man who, having lost power, has no recourse but vile and extreme words. He is a cobra who cannot strike. But I don't want the hiss noticeable until the right time. What I am more interested in is the background."

The woman in charge of background was Meg Cathcart. She had been creating backgrounds for as long as the compu-drama technique had existed.

"What do you want in background?" Cathcart asked, coolly.

"The snake motif," said Willard. "Give me some of that

and there can be less hiss in Lear's voice. Of course, I don't want you to show a snake. The too obvious doesn't work. I want a snake there that people can't see but that they can *feel* without quite noting *why* they feel. I want them to know a snake is there without really knowing it is there, so that it will chill them to the bone, as Lear's speech should. So when we do it over, Meg, give us a snake that is not a snake."

"And how do I do that, Jonas?" said Cathcart, making free with his first name. She knew her worth and how essential she was.

He said, "I don't know. If I did I'd be a backgrounder instead of a lousy director. I only know what I want. You've got to supply it. You've got to supply sinuosity, the impression of scales. Until we get to one point. Notice when Lear says, 'How sharper than a serpent's tooth it is to have a thankless child.' That is *power*. The whole speech leads up to that and it is one of the most famous quotes in Shakespeare. And it is *sibilant*. There is the 'sh,' the three s's in 'serpent's' and in 'thankless,' and the two unvoiced 'th's in 'tooth' and 'thankless.' *That* can be hissed. If you keep down the hiss as much as possible in the rest of the speech, you can hiss here, and you should zero in to his face and make it venomous. And for background, the serpent—which, after all, is now referred to in the words—can make its appearance in background. A flash of an open mouth and fangs, fangs— We must have the momentary appearance of fangs as Lear says, 'a serpent's tooth.' "

Willard felt very tired suddenly. "All right. We'll try again tomorrow. I want each one of you to go over the entire scene and try to work out the strategy you intend to use. Only please remember that you are not the only ones involved. What you do must match the others, so I'll encourage you to talk to each other about this—and, most of all, to listen to *me* because I have no instrument to handle and I alone can see the play as a whole. And if I seem as tyrannical as Lear at his worst in spots, well, that's my job."

Willard was approaching the great storm scene, the most difficult portion of this most difficult play, and he felt wrung out. Lear has been cast out by his daughters into a raging storm of wind and rain, with only his Fool for company, and he has gone almost mad at this mistreatment. To him, even the storm is not as bad as his daughters.

Willard pointed his baton and Lear appeared. A point in another direction and the Fool was there clinging, disregarded, to Lear's left leg. Another point and the background, came in, with its impression of a storm, of a howling wind, of driving rain, of the crackle of thunder and the flash of lightning.

The storm took over, a phenomenon of nature, but even as it did so, the image of Lear extended and became what seemed mountain-tall. The storm of his emotions matched the storm of the elements, and his voice gave back to the wind every last howl. His body lost substance and wavered with the wind as though he himself were a storm cloud, contending on an equal basis with the atmospheric fury. Lear, having failed with his daughters, defied the storm to do its worst. He called out in a voice that was far more than human:

> "Blow, winds, and crack your cheeks! rage!
>   blow!
> You cataracts and hurricanoes, spout
> Till you have drench'd our steeples, drown'd the
>   cocks!
> You sulph'rous and thought-executing fires.
> Vaunt-couriers to oak-cleaving thunderbolts,
> Singe my white head! And thou, all-shaking
>   thunder,

> *Strike flat the thick rotundity o' th' world.*
> *Crack Nature's moulds, all germains spill at*
>   *once.*
> *That make ingrateful man."*

The Fool interrupts, his voice shrilling, and making Lear's defiance the more heroic by contrast. He begs Lear to make his way back to the castle and make peace with his daughters, but Lear doesn't even hear him. He roars on:

> *"Rumble thy bellyful! Spit, fire! spout, rain!*
> *Nor rain, wind, thunder, fire are my daughters.*
> *I tax not you, you elements, with unkindness.*
> *I never gave you kingdom, call'd you children,*
> *You owe me no subscription. Then let fall*
> *Your horrible pleasure. Here I stand your slave,*
> *A poor, infirm, weak, and despis'd old man . . ."*

The Duke of Kent, Lear's loyal servant (though the King in a fit of rage has banished him) finds Lear and tries to lead him to some shelter. After an interlude in the castle of the Duke of Gloucester, the scene returns to Lear in the storm, and he is brought, or rather dragged, to a hovel.

And then, finally, Lear learns to think of others. He insists that the Fool enter first and then he lingers outside to think (undoubtedly for the first time in his life) of the plight of those who are not kings and courtiers.

His image shrank and the wildness of his face smoothed out. His head was lifted to the rain, and his words seemed detached and to be coming not quite from him, as though he were listening to someone else read the speech. It was, after all, not the old Lear speaking, but a new and better Lear, refined and sharpened by suffering. With an anxious Kent watching, and striving to lead him into the hovel, and with Meg Cathcart managing to work up an impression of beggars merely by producing the fluttering of rags, Lear says:

> *"Poor naked wretches, wheresoe'er you are,*
> *That bide the pelting of this pithess storm.*
> *How shall your houseless heads and unfed sides,*
> *Your loop'd and window'd raggedness, defend*
>   *you*
> *From seasons such as these? O, I have ta'en*
> *Too little care of this! Take physic, pomp;*
> *Expose thyself to feel what wretches feel,*
> *That thou mayst shake the superflux to them*
> *And show the heavens more just."*

"Not bad," said Wilbur, eventually. "We're getting the idea. Only, Meg, rags aren't enough. Can you manage an impression of hollow eyes? Not blind ones. The eyes are there, but sunken in."

"I think I can do that," said Cathcart.

It was difficult for Willard to believe. The money spent was greater than expected. The time it had taken was considerably greater than had been expected. And the general weariness was far greater than had been expected. Still, the project was coming to an end.

He had the reconciliation scene to get through—so simple that it would require the most delicate touches. There would be no background, no souped-up voices, no images, for at this point Shakespeare became simple. Nothing beyond simplicity was needed.

Lear was an old man, just an old man. Cordelia, having found him, was a loving daughter, with none of the majesty of Goneril, none of the cruelty of Regan, just softly endearing.

Lear, his madness burned out of him, is slowly beginning to understand the situation. He scarcely recognizes

Cordelia at first and thinks he is dead and she is a heavenly spirit. Nor does he recognize the faithful Kent.

When Cordelia tries to bring him back the rest of the way to sanity, he says:

> *"Pray, do not mock me.*
> *I am a very foolish fond old man.*
> *Fourscore and upward, not an hour more nor*
>   *less.*
> *And, to deal plainly,*
> *I fear I am not in my perfect mind.*
> *Methinks I should know you, and know this*
>   *man;*
> *Yet I am doubtful; for I am mainly ignorant*
> *What place this is; and all the skills I have*
> *Remembers not these garments; nor I know not*
> *Where I did lodge last night. Do not laugh at*
>   *me;*
> *For (as I am a man) I think this lady*
> *To be my child Cordelia."*

Cordelia tells him she is and he says:

> *"Be your tears wet? Yes, faith. I pray weep not.*
> *If you have poison for me, I will drink it.*
> *I know you do not love me; for your sisters*
> *Have, as I do remember, done me wrong.*
> *You have some cause, they have not."*

All poor Cordelia can say is "No cause, no cause."

And eventually, Willard was able to draw a deep breath and say, "We've done all we can do. The rest is in the hands of the public."

It was a year later that Willard, now the most famous man in the entertainment world, met Gregory Laborian.

It had come about almost accidentally and largely because of the activities of a mutual friend. Willard was not grateful.

He greeted Laborian with what politeness he could manage and cast a cold eye on the time-strip on the wall.

He said, "I don't want to seem unpleasant or inhospitable, Mr.—uh—but I'm really a very busy man, and don't have much time."

"I'm sure of it, but that's why I want to see you. Surely, you want to do another compu-drama."

"Surely I intend to, but," and Willard smiled dryly, "*King Lear* is a hard act to follow and I don't intend to turn out something that will seem like trash in comparison."

"But what if you never find anything that can match *King Lear*?"

"I'm sure I never will, but I'll find *something*."

"I *have* something."

"Oh?"

"I have a story, a novel, that could be made into a compu-drama."

"Oh, well. I can't really deal with items that come in over the transom."

"I'm not offering you something from a slush pile. The novel has been published and it has been rather highly thought of."

"I'm sorry. I don't want to be insulting. But I didn't recognize your name when you introduced yourself."

"Laborian. Gregory Laborian."

"But I still don't recognize it. I've never read anything by you. I've never heard of you."

Laborian sighed. "I wish you were the only one, but you're not. Still, I could give you a copy of my novel to read."

Willard shook his head. "That's kind of you, Mr. Laborian, but I don't want to mislead you. I have no time to read it. And even if I had the time—I just want you to understand—I don't have the inclination."

"I could make it worth your while, Mr. Willard."

"In what way?"

"I could pay you. I wouldn't consider it a bribe, merely an offer of money that you would well deserve if you worked with my novel."

"I don't think you understand, Mr. Laborian, how much money it takes to make a first-class compu-drama. I take it you're not a multimillionaire."

"No, I'm not, but I can pay you a hundred thousand globo-dollars."

"If that's a bribe, at least it's a totally ineffective one. For a hundred thousand globo-dollars, I couldn't do a single scene."

Laborian sighed again. His large brown eyes looked soulful. "I understand, Mr. Willard, but if you'll just give me a few more minutes—" (for Willard's eyes were wandering to the time-strip again.)

"Well, five more minutes. That's all I can manage really."

"It's all I need. I'm not offering the money for making the compu-drama. You know, and I know, Mr. Willard, that you can go to any of a dozen people in the country and say you are doing a compu-drama and you'll get all the money you need. After *King Lear*, no one will refuse you anything, or even ask you what you plan to do. I'm offering you one hundred thousand globo-dollars for your own use."

"Then it *is* a bribe, and that won't work with me. Good-bye, Mr. Laborian."

"Wait. I'm not offering you an electronic switch. I don't suggest that I place my financial card into a slot and that you do so, too, and that a hundred thousand globo-dollars be transferred from my account to yours. I'm talking *gold*, Mr. Willard."

Willard had risen from his chair, ready to open the door and usher Laborian out, but now he hesitated. "What do you mean, gold?"

"I mean that I can lay my hands on a hundred thousand

globo-dollars of gold, about fifteen pounds' worth, I think. I may not be a multimillionaire, but I'm quite well off and I wouldn't be stealing it. It would be my own money and I am entitled to draw it in gold. There is nothing illegal about it. What I am offering you is a hundred thousand globo-dollars in five-hundred globo-dollar pieces—two hundred of them. *Gold,* Mr. Willard."

Gold! Willard was hesitating. Money, when it was a matter of electronic exchange, meant nothing. There was no feeling of either wealth or of poverty above a certain level. The world was a matter of plastic cards (each keyed to a nucleic acid pattern) and of slots, and all the world transferred, transferred, transferred.

Gold was different. It had a feel. Each piece had a weight. Piled together it had a gleaming beauty. It was wealth one could appreciate and experience. Willard had never even seen a gold coin, let alone felt or hefted one. Two hundred of them!

He didn't need the money. He was not so sure he didn't need the gold.

He said, with a kind of shamefaced weakness. "What kind of a novel is it that you are talking about?"

"Science fiction."

Willard made a face. "I've never read science fiction."

"Then it's time you expanded your horizons, Mr. Willard. Read mine. If you imagine a gold coin between every two pages of the book, you will have your two hundred."

And Willard, rather despising his own weakness, said, "What's the name of your book?"

"*Three in One.*"

"And you have a copy?"

"I brought one with me."

And Willard held out his hand and took it.

That Willard was a busy man was by no means a lie. It took him better than a week to find the time to read the book, even with two hundred pieces of gold glittering, and luring him on.

Then he sat a while and pondered. Then he phoned Laborian.

The next morning, Laborian was in Willard's office again.

Willard said, bluntly, "Mr. Laborian, I have read your book."

Laborian nodded and could not hide the anxiety in his eyes. "I hope you like it, Mr. Willard."

Willard lifted his hand and rocked it right and left. "So-so. I told you I have not read science fiction, and I don't know how good or bad it is of its kind—"

"Does it matter, if you liked it?"

"I'm not sure if I liked it. I'm not used to this sort of thing. We are dealing in this novel with three sexes."

"Yes."

"Which you call a Rational, an Emotional, and a Parental."

"Yes."

"But you don't describe them?"

Laborian looked embarrassed. "I didn't describe them, Mr. Willard, because I couldn't. They're alien creatures, really alien. I didn't want to pretend they were alien by simply giving them blue skins or a pair of antennae or a third eye. I *wanted* them indescribable, so I didn't describe them, you see."

"What you're saying is that your imagination failed."

"N—no. I wouldn't say that. It's more like not having that *kind* of imagination. I don't describe anyone. If I were to write a story about you and me, I probably wouldn't bother describing either one of us."

Willard stared at Laborian without trying to disguise his contempt. He thought of himself. Middle-sized, soft about the middle, needed to reduce a bit, the beginnings of a double chin, and a mole on his right wrist. Light brown hair, dark blue eyes, bulbous nose. What was so hard to describe? Anyone could do it. If you had an imaginary character, think of someone real—and describe.

There was Laborian, dark in complexion, crisp curly black hair, looked as though he needed a shave, probably looked that way all the time, prominent Adam's apple, small scar on the right cheek, dark brown eyes rather large, and his only good feature.

Willard said, "I don't understand you. What kind of writer are you if you have trouble describing things? What do you write?"

Laborian said, gently, somewhat as though this was not the first time he had had to defend himself along those lines, "You've read *Three in One.* I've written other novels and they're all in the same style. Mostly conversation. I don't see things when I write; I *hear*, and for most part, what my characters talk about are ideas—competing ideas. I'm strong on that and my readers like it."

"Yes, but where does that leave *me?* I can't devise a compu-drama based on conversation alone. I have to create sight and sound and subliminal messages, and you leave me nothing to work on."

"Are you thinking of doing *Three in One*, then?"

"Not if you give me nothing to work on. Think, Mr. Laborian, think! This Parental. He's the dumb one."

"Not dumb," said Laborian, frowning. "Single-minded. He only has room in his mind for children, real and potential."

"Blockish! If you didn't use that actual word for the Parental in the novel, and I don't remember offhand whether you did or not, it's certainly the impression I got. Cubical. Is that what he is?"

"Well, simple. Straight lines. Straight planes. Not cubical. Longer than he is wide."

"How does he move? Does he have legs?"

"I don't know. I honestly never gave it any thought."

"Hmp. And the Rational. He's the smart one and he's smooth and quick. What is he? Egg-shaped?"

"I'd accept that. I've never given that any thought, either, but I'd accept that."

"And no legs?"

"I haven't described any."

"And how about the middle one. Your 'she' character—the other two being 'he's.' "

"The Emotional."

"That's right. The Emotional. You did better on her."

"Of course. I did most of my thinking about her. She was trying to save the alien intelligences—us—of an alien world, Earth. The reader's sympathy must be with her, even though she fails."

"I gather she was more like a cloud, didn't have any firm shape at all, could attenuate and tighten."

"Yes, yes. That's exactly right."

"Does she flow along the ground or drift through the air?"

Laborian thought, then shook his head. "I don't know. I would say you would have to suit yourself when it came to that."

"I see. And what about the sex?"

Laborian said, with sudden enthusiasm, "That's a crucial point. I never have any sex in my novels beyond that which is absolutely necessary and then I manage to refrain from describing it—"

"You don't like sex?"

"I like sex fine, thank you. I just don't like it in my novels. Everyone else puts it in and, frankly, I think that readers find its absence in my novels refreshing; at least, my readers do. And I must explain to you that my books do very well. I wouldn't have a hundred thousand dollars to spend if they didn't."

"All right. I'm not trying to put you down."

"However, there are always people who say I don't include sex because I don't know how, so—out of vainglory, I suppose—I wrote this novel just to show that I *could* do it. The entire novel deals with sex. Of course, it's alien sex, not at all like ours."

"That's right. That's why I have to ask you about the mechanics of it. How does it work?"

Laborian looked uncertain for a moment. "They melt."

"I know that that's the word you use. Do you mean they come together? Superimpose?"

"I suppose so."

Willard sighed. "How can you write a book without knowing anything about so fundamental a part of it?"

"I don't have to describe it in detail. The reader gets the impression. With subliminal suggestion so much a part of the compu-drama, how can you ask the question?"

Willard's lips pressed together. Laborian had him there. "Very well. They superimpose. What do they look like after they have superimposed?"

Laborian shook his head. "I avoided that."

"You realize, of course, that I can't."

Laborian nodded. "Yes."

Willard heaved another sigh and said, "Look, Mr. Laborian, assuming that I agree to do such a compu-drama—and I have not yet made up my mind on the matter—I would have to do it entirely my way. I would tolerate no interference from you. You have ducked so many of your own responsibilities in writing the book that I can't allow you to decide suddenly that you want to participate in my creative endeavors."

"That's quite understood, Mr. Willard. I only ask that you keep my story and as much of my dialogue as you can. All of the visual, sonic, and subliminal aspects I am willing to leave entirely in your hands."

"You understand that this is not a matter of a verbal agreement which someone in our industry, about a century and a half ago, described as not worth the paper it was written on. There will have to be a written contract made firm by my lawyers that will exclude you from participation."

"My lawyers will be glad to look over it, but I assure you I am not going to quibble."

"*And*," said Willard severely, "I will want an advance on the money you offered me. I can't afford to have you change your mind on me and I am not in the mood for a long lawsuit."

At this, Laborian frowned. He said, "Mr. Willard, those who know me *never* question my financial honesty. You don't know me, so I'll permit the remark, but please don't repeat it. How much of an advance do you wish?"

"Half," said Willard, briefly.

Laborian said, "I will do better than that. Once you have obtained the necessary commitments from those who will be willing to put up the money for the compu-drama and once the contract between us is drawn up, then I will give you every cent of the hundred thousand dollars even before you begin the first scene of the book."

Willard's eyes opened wide and he could not prevent himself from saying, "Why?"

"Because I want to urge you on. What's more, if the compu-drama turns out to be too hard to do, if it won't work, or if you turn out something that will not do—my hard luck—you can keep the hundred thousand. It's a risk I'm ready to take."

"Why? What's the catch?"

"No catch. I'm gambling on immortality. I'm a popular writer but I have never heard anyone call me a great one. My books are very likely to die with me. Do *Three in One* as a compu-drama and do it well and that at least might live on, and make my name ring down through the ages," he smiled ruefully, "or at least some ages. However—"

"Ah," said Willard. "Now we come to it."

"Well, yes. I have a dream that I'm willing to risk a great deal for, but I'm not a complete fool. I will give you the hundred thousand I promised before you start and if the thing doesn't work out you can keep it, but the payment will be electronic. *If,* however, you turn out a product that satisfies me, then you will return the electronic gift and I will give you the hundred thousand globo-dollars in gold pieces. You have nothing to lose except that to an artist like yourself, gold must be more dramatic and worthwhile than blips in a finance-card." And Laborian smiled gently.

Willard said, "Understand, Mr. Laborian! I would be taking a risk, too. I risk losing a great deal of time and effort that I might have devoted to a more likely project. I risk producing a docu-drama that will be a failure and that will tarnish the reputation I have built up with *Lear.* In my business, you're only as good as your most recent product. I will consult various people—"

"On a confidential basis, please."

"Of course! And I will do a bit of deep consideration. I am willing to go along with your proposition for now, but you mustn't think of it as a definite commitment. Not yet. We will talk further."

Jonas Willard and Meg Cathcart sat together over lunch in Meg's apartment. They were at their coffee when Willard said, with apparent reluctance as one who broaches a subject he would rather not, "Have you read the book?"

"Yes, I have."

"And what did you think?"

"I don't know," said Cathcart peering at him from under the dark, reddish hair she wore clustered over her forehead. "At least not enough to judge."

"You're not a science fiction buff either, then?"

"Well, I've read science fiction, mostly sword and sorcery, but nothing like *Three in One.* I've heard of Laborian, though. He does what they call 'hard science fiction.' "

"It's hard enough. I don't see how I can do it. That book, whatever its virtues, just isn't me."

Cathcart fixed him with a sharp glance. "How do you know it isn't you?"

"Listen, it's important to know what you can't do."

"And you were born knowing you can't do science fiction?"

"I have an instinct in these things."

"So you say. Why don't you think what you might do with those three undescribed characters, and what you would want subliminally, before you let your instinct tell you what you can and can't do. For instance, how would you do the Parental, who is referred to constantly as 'he' even though it's the Parental who bears the children? That struck me as jackassy, if you must know."

"No, no," said Willard, at once. "I accept the 'he.' Laborian might have invented a third pronoun, but it would have made no sense and the reader would have gagged on it. Instead, he reserved the pronoun, 'she,' for the Emotional. She's the central character, differing from the other two enormously. The use of 'she' for her and only for her focuses the reader's attention on her, and it's on her that the reader's attention *must* focus. What's more, it's on her that the viewer's attention *must* focus in the compu-drama."

"Then you *have* been thinking of it." She grinned, impishly. "I wouldn't have known if I hadn't needled you."

Willard stirred uneasily. "Actually, Laborian said something of the sort, so I can't lay claim to complete creativity here. But let's get back to the Parental. I want to talk about these things to you because everything is going to depend on subliminal suggestion, if I do try to do this thing. The Parental is a block, a rectangle."

"A right parallelepiped, I think they would call it in solid geometry."

"Come on. I don't care what they call it in solid geometry. The point is we can't just have a block. We have to give it personality. The Parental is a 'he' who bears children, so we have to get across an epicene quality. The voice has to be neither clearly masculine nor feminine. I'm not sure that I have in mind exactly the timbre and sound I will need, but that will be for the voice-recorder and myself to work out by trial and error, I think. Of course, the voice isn't the only thing."

"What else?"

"The feet. The Parental moves about, but there is no description of any limbs. He has to have the equivalent of arms; there are things he does. He obtains an energy source that he feeds the Emotional, so we'll have to evolve arms that are alien but that are arms. And we need legs. And a number of sturdy, stumpy legs that move rapidly."

"Like a caterpillar? Or a centipede?"

Willard winced. "Those aren't pleasant comparisons, are they?"

"Well, it would be my job to sublimate, if I may use the expression, a centipede, so to speak, without showing one. Just the notion of a series of legs, a double fading row of parentheses, just on and off as a kind of visual leitmotiv for the Parental, whenever he appears."

"I see what you mean. We'll have to try it out and see what we can get away with. The Rational is ovoid. Laborian admitted it might be egg-shaped. We can imagine him progressing by rolling but I find that completely inappropriate. The Rational is mind-proud, dignified. We can't make him do anything laughable, and rolling would be laughable."

"We could have him with a flat bottom slightly curved, and he could slide along it, like a penguin belly-whopping."

"Or like a snail on a layer of grease. No. That would be just as bad. I had thought of having three legs extrude. In other words, when he is at rest, he would be smoothly ovoid and proud of it, but when he is moving three stubby legs emerge and he can walk on them."

"Why three?"

"It carries on the three motif; three sexes, you know. It could be a kind of hopping run. The foreleg digs in and holds firm and the two hind legs come along on each side."

"Like a three-legged kangaroo?"

"Yes! Can you subliminate a kangaroo?"

"I can try."

"The Emotional, of course, is the hardest of the three. What can you do with something that may be nothing but a coherent cloud of gas?"

Cathcart considered. "What about giving the impression of draperies containing nothing. They would be moving about wraith-like, just as you presented *Lear* in the storm scene. She would be wind, she would be air, she would be the filmy, foggy draperies that would represent that."

Willard felt himself drawn to the suggestion. "Hey, that's not bad, Meg. For the subliminal effect, could you do Helen of Troy?"

"Helen of Troy?"

"Yes! To the Rational and Parental, the Emotional is the most beautiful thing ever invented. They're crazy about her. There's this strong, almost unbearable sexual attraction—their kind of sex—and we've got to make the audience aware of it in *their* terms. If you can somehow get across a statuesque Greek woman, with bound hair and draperies—the draperies would exactly fit what we're imagining for the Emotional—and make it look like the paintings and sculptures everyone is familiar with, that would be the Emotional's leitmotiv."

"You don't ask simple things. The slightest intrusion of a human figure will destroy the mood."

"You don't intrude a human figure. Just the suggestion of one. It's important. A human figure, in actual fact, may destroy the mood, but we'll have to *suggest* human figures throughout. The audience has to think of these odd things as human beings. No mistake."

"I'll think about it," said Cathcart, dubiously.

"Which brings us to another thing. The melting. The
triple-sex of these things. I gather they superimpose. I
gather from the book that the Emotional is the key to that.
The Parental and Rational can't melt without her. She's
the essential part of the process. But, of course, that fool,
Laborian, doesn't describe it in detail. Well, we can't have
the Rational and Parental running toward the Emotional
and jumping on her. That would kill the drama at once
no matter what else we might do."

"I agree."

"What we must do, then, and this is off the top of my
head, is to have the Emotional expand, the draperies move
out and enswathe (if that's the word) both Parental and
Rational. They are obscured by the draperies and we don't
see exactly how it's done but they get closer and closer
until they superimpose."

"We'll have to emphasize the drapery," said Cathcart.
"We'll have to make it as graceful as possible in order to
get across the beauty of it, and not just the eroticism. We'll
have to have music."

"*Not* the Romeo and Juliet overture, please. A slow
waltz, perhaps, because the melting takes a long time. And
not a familiar one. I don't want the audience humming
along with it. In fact, it would be best if it comes in
occasional bits so that the audience gets the impression
of a waltz, rather than actually hearing it."

"We can't see how to do it, until we try it and see what
works."

"Everything I say now is a first-order suggestion that
may have to be yanked about this way and that under the
pressure of actual events. And what about the orgasm?
We'll have to indicate that somehow."

"Color."

"Hmm."

"Better than sound, Jonas. You can't have an explosion.

I wouldn't want some kind of eruption, either. Color. Silent color. That might do it."

"What color? I don't want a blinding flash, either."

"No. You might try a delicate pink, very slowly darkening, and then toward the end suddenly becoming a deep, deep red."

"I'm not sure. We'll have to try it out. It must be unmistakable and moving and not make the audience giggle or feel embarrassed. I can see ourselves running through every color change in the spectrum, and, in the end, finding that it will depend on what you do subliminally. And that brings us to the triple-beings."

"The what?"

"You know. After the last melting, the superimposition remains permanent and we have the adult form that is all three components together. There, I think, we'll have to make them more human. Not human, mind you. Just more human. A faint suggestion of human form, not just subliminal, either. We'll need a voice that is somehow reminiscent of all three, and I don't know how the recorder can make that work. Fortunately, the triple-beings don't appear much in the story."

Willard shook his head. "And that brings us to the rough fact that the compu-drama might not be a possible project at all."

"Why not? You seem to have been offering potential solutions of all kinds for the various problems."

"Not for the essential part. Look! In *King Lear,* we had human characters, *more* than human characters. You had searing emotions. What have we got here? We have funny little cubes and ovals and drapery. Tell me how my *Three in One* is going to be different from an animated cartoon?"

"For one thing, an animated cartoon is two-dimensional. Even with elaborate animation it is flat, and its coloring is without shading. It is invariably satirical—"

"I know all that. That's not what I want you to tell me. You're missing the important point. What a compu-drama has, that a mere animated cartoon does not, are subliminal suggestions such as can only be created by a complex computer in the hands of an imaginative genius. What my compu-drama has that an animated cartoon doesn't is *you*, Meg."

"Well, I was being modest."

"Don't be. I'm trying to tell you that everything— *everything*—is going to depend on you. We have a story here that is dead serious. Our Emotional is trying to save Earth out of pure idealism; it's not her world. And she doesn't succeed, and she won't succeed in my version, either. No cheap, happy ending."

"Earth isn't exactly destroyed."

"No, it isn't. There's still time to save it if Laborian ever gets around to doing a sequel, but in *this* story the attempt fails. It's a tragedy and I want it treated as one—as tragic as *Lear*. No funny voices, no humorous actions, no satirical touches. Serious. Serious. Serious. And I'm going to depend on you to make it so. It will be you who makes sure that the audience reacts to the Rational, the Emotional, the Parental, as though they were human beings. All their peculiarities will have to melt away and they'll have to be recognized as intelligent beings on a par with humanity, if not ahead of it. Can you do it?"

Cathcart said dryly, "It looks as though you will insist I can."

"I do so insist."

"Then you had better see about getting the ball rolling, and you leave me alone while you're doing it. I need time to think. Lots of time."

The early days of the shooting were an unmitigated disaster. Each member of the crew had his copy of the book, carefully, almost surgically trimmed, but with no scenes entirely omitted.

"We're going to stick to the course of the book as closely as we can, and improve it as we go along just as much as we can," Willard had announced confidently. "And the first thing we do is get a hold on the triple-beings."

He turned to the head voice-recorder. "How have you been working on that?"

"I've tried to fuse the three voices."

"Let's hear. All right, everyone quiet."

"I'll give you the Parental first," said the recorder. There came a thin, tenor voice, out of key with the blockish figure that the Image man had produced. Willard winced slightly at the mismatch, but the Parental *was* mismatched—a masculine mother. The Rational, rocking slowly back and forth, had a somewhat self-important voice; enunciation over-careful, and it was a light baritone.

Willard interrupted. "Less rocking in the Rational. We don't want the audience to become seasick. He rocks when he is deep in thought, and not all the time."

He then nodded his head at Dua's draperies, which seemed quite successful, as did her clear and infinitely sweet soprano voice.

"She must never shriek," said Willard, severely, "not even when she is in a passion."

"She won't," said the recorder. "The trick is, though, to blend the voices in setting up the triple-being, in having each one distantly identifiable."

All three voices sounded softly, the words not clear. They seemed to melt into each other and then the voice could be heard enunciating.

Willard shook his head in immediate discontent. "No, that won't do at all. We can't have three voices in a kind of intimate patchwork. We'd be making the triple-being a figure of fun. We need one voice which somehow suggests all three."

The voice-recorder was clearly offended. "It's easy to say that. How do you suggest we do it?"

"I do it," said Willard, brutally, "by ordering you to do it. I'll tell you when you have it. And Cathcart—where is Cathcart?"

"Here I am," she said, emerging from behind her instrumentation. "Where I'm supposed to be."

"I don't like the sublimination, Cathcart. I gather you tried to give the impression of cerebral convolutions."

"For intelligence. The triple-beings represent the intelligence-peak of these aliens."

"Yes, I understand, but what you managed to do was to give the impression of worms. You'll have to think of something else. And I don't like the appearance of the triple-being, either. He looks just like a big Rational."

"He *is* like a big Rational," said one of the imagists.

"Is he described in the book that way?" asked Willard, sharply.

"Not in so many words, but the impression I get—"

"Never mind your impression. I'll make the decisions."

Willard grew fouler-tempered as the day wore on. At least twice he had difficulty controlling his passion, the second time coming when he happened to notice someone watching the proceedings from a spot at one edge of the lot.

He strode toward him angrily. "What are you doing here?"

It was Laborian, who answered quietly, "Watching."

"Our contract states—"

"That I am to interfere in the proceedings in no way. It does not say I cannot watch quietly."

"You'll get upset if you do. This is the way preparing a compu-drama works. There are lots of glitches to overcome and it would be upsetting to the company to have the author watching and disapproving."

"I'm not disapproving. I'm here only to answer questions if you care to ask them."

"Questions? What kind of questions?"

Laborian shrugged. "I don't know. Something might puzzle you and you might want a suggestion."

"I see," said Willard, with heavy irony, "so you can teach me my business."

"No, so I can answer your questions."

"Well, I have one."

"Very well," and Laborian produced a small cassette recorder. "If you'll just speak into this and say that you are asking me a question and wish me to answer without prejudicing the contract, we're in business."

Willard paused for a considerable time, staring at Laborian as though he suspected trickery of some sort, then he spoke into the cassette.

"Very well." said Laborian. "What's your question?"

"Did you have anything in mind for the appearance of the triple-being in the book?"

"Not a thing," said Laborian, cheerfully.

"How could you do that?" Willard's voice trembled as though he were holding back a final "you idiot" by main force.

"Easily. What I don't describe, the reader supplies in his own mind. Each reader does it differently to suit himself, I presume. That's the advantage of writing. A compu-drama would have an enormously larger audience than a book could have, but you must pay for that by having to present an image."

"I understand that," said Willard. "So much for the question, then."

"Not at all. I have a suggestion."

"Like what?"

"Like a head. Give the triple-being a head. The Parental has no head, nor the Rational, nor the Emotional, but all three look up to the triple-beings as creatures of intelligence beyond their own. That is the entire difference between the triple-beings and the three Separates. Intelligence."

"A head?"

"Yes. We associate intelligence with heads. The head contains the brain, it contains the sense organs. Omit the head and we cannot believe in intelligence. The headless oysters or clams are mollusks that seem no more intelligent to us than a spring of grass would be, but the related octopus, also a mollusk, we accept as possibly intelligent because it has a head—and eyes. Give the triple-being eyes, too."

Work had, of course, ceased on the set. Everyone had gathered in as closely as they thought judicious to listen to the conversation between director and author.

Willard said, "What kind of head?"

"Your choice. All you need is a bulge *suggesting* a head. And eyes. The viewer is sure to get the idea."

Willard turned away, shouting, "Well, get back to work. Who called a vacation? Where are the imagists? Back to the machine and begin trying out heads."

He turned suddenly and said, in an almost surly fashion, to Laborian. "Thank you!"

"Only if it works," said Laborian, shrugging.

The rest of the day was spent in testing heads, searching for one that was not a humorous bulge, and not an unimaginative copy of the human head, and eyes that were not astonished circles or vicious slits. Then, finally, Willard called a halt and growled, "We'll try again tomorrow. If anyone gets any brilliant thoughts overnight, give them to Meg Cathcart. She'll pass on to me any that are worth it." And he added, in an annoyed mutter, "I suppose she'll have to remain silent."

Willard was right and wrong. He was right. There were no brilliant ideas handed to him, but he was wrong for he had one of his own.

He said to Cathcart, "Listen, can you get across a top hat?"

"A what?"

"The sort of thing they wore in Victorian times. Look, when the Parental invades the lair of the triple-beings to steal an energy source, he's not an impressive sight in himself, but you told me you could just get across the idea of a helmet and a long line that will give the notion of a spear. He'll be on a knightly quest."

"Yes, I know," she said, "but it might not work. We'll have to try it out."

"Of course, but that points the direction. If you have just a suggestion of a top hat, it will give the impression of the triple-being as an aristocrat. The exact shape of the head and eyes becomes less crucial in that case. Can it be done?"

"Anything can be done. The question is: will it work?"

"We'll try it."

And as it happened, one thing led to another. The suggestion of the top hat caused the voice-recorder to say, "Why not give the triple-being a British accent?"

Willard was caught off-guard. "Why?"

"Well, the British have a language with more tones than we do. At least, the upper classes do. The American version of English tends to be flat, and that's true of the Separates, too. If the triple-being spoke British rather than English, his voice could rise and fall with the words—tenor and baritone and even an occasional soprano squeak. That's what we would want to indicate with the three voices out of which his voice was formed."

"Can you do that?" said Willard.

"I think so."

"Then we'll try. Not bad—if it works."

It was interesting to see how the entire group found themselves engaged in the Emotional.

The scene in particular where the Emotional was fleeing across the face of the planet, where she had her brief set-to with the other Emotionals caught at everyone.

Willard said tensely, "This is going to be one of the great dramatic scenes. We'll put it out as widely as we can. It's going to be draperies, draperies, draperies, but they must not be entangled one with the other. Each one must be distinct. Even when you rush the Emotionals in toward the audience I want each set of draperies to be a different off-white. And I want Dua's drapery to be distinct from all of them. I want her to glitter a little, just to be different, and because she's *our* Emotional. Got it?"

"Got it," said the leading imagist. "We'll handle it."

"And another thing. All the other Emotionals twitter. They're birds. Our Emotional *doesn't* twitter, and she despises the rest because she's more intelligent than they are and she knows it. And when she's fleeing—" he paused, and brooded a bit. "Is there any way we can get away from the 'Ride of the Valkyries'?"

"We don't want to," said the soundman promptly. "Nothing better for the purpose has ever been written."

Cathcart said, "Yes, but we'll only have snatches of it now and then. Hearing a few bars has the effect of the whole, and I can insert the hint of tossing manes."

"Manes?" said Willard, dubiously.

"Absolutely. Three thousand years of experience with horses has pinned us down to the galloping stallion as the epitome of wild speed. All our mechanical devices are too static, however fast they go. And I can arrange to have the manes just match, emphasize, and punctuate the flowing of the draperies."

"That sounds good. We'll try it."

Willard knew where the final stumbling block would be found. The last melting. He called the troupe together to lecture them, partly to make sure they understood what it was they were all doing now, partly to put off the time of reckoning when they would actually try to put it all into sound, image, and sublimation.

He said, "All right, the Emotional's interest is in saving the other world—Earth—only because she can't bear the thought of the meaningless destruction of intelligent beings. She knows the triple-beings are carrying through a scientific project, necessary for the welfare of *her* world and caring nothing for the danger into which it puts the alien world—us.

"She tries to warn the alien world and fails. She knows, at last, that the whole purpose of melting is to produce a new set of Rational, Emotional and Parental, and then, with that done, there is a final melting that would turn the original set into a triple-being. Do you have that? It's a sort of larval form of Separates and an adult form of triples.

"But the Emotional doesn't want to melt. She doesn't want to produce the new generation. Most of all, she doesn't want to become a triple-being and participate in what she considers their work of destruction. She is, however, tricked into the final melt and realizes too late that she is not only going to be a triple-being but a triple-being who will be, more than any other, responsible for the scientific project that will destroy the other world.

"All this Laborian could describe in words, words, words, in his book, but we've got to do it more immediately and more forcefully, in images and sublimination as well. That's what we're now going to try to do."

They were three days in the trying before Willard was satisfied.

The weary Emotional, uncertain, stretching outward, with Cathcart's sublimination instilling the feeling of not-sure, not-sure. The Rational and Parental enfolded and coming together, more rapidly than on previous occasions—hurrying for the superimposition before it might be stopped—and the Emotional realizing too late the significance of it all and struggling—struggling—

And failure. The drenching feeling of failure as a new triple-being stepped out of the superimposition, more nearly human than anyone else in the compu-drama—proud, indifferent.

The scientific procedure would go on. Earth would continue the downward slide.

And somehow this was it—this was the nub of everything that Willard was trying to do—that within the new triple-being the Emotional still existed in part. There was just the wisping of drapery and the viewer was to know that the defeat was not final after all.

The Emotional would, somehow, still try, lost though it was in a greater being.

They watched the completed compu-drama, all of them, seeing it for the first time as a whole and not as a collection of parts, wondering if there were places to edit, to reorder. (Not now, thought Willard, not now. Afterwards, when he had recovered and could look at it more objectively.)

He sat in his chair, slumped. He had put too much of himself into it. It had seemed to him that it contained everything he wanted it to contain; that it did everything he wanted to have done; but how much of that was merely wishful thinking?

When it was over and the last tremulous, subliminal cry of the defeated-but-not-yet-defeated Emotional faded, he said, "Well."

And Cathcart said, "That's almost as good as your *King Lear* was, Jonas."

There was a general murmur of agreement and Willard cast a cynical eye about him. Wasn't that what they would be bound to say, no matter what?

His eye caught that of Gregory Laborian. The writer was expressionless, said nothing.

Willard's mouth tightened. There at least he could expect an opinion that would be backed, or not backed, by gold. Willard had his hundred thousand. He would see now whether it would stay electronic.

He said, and his own uncertainty made him sound imperious, "Laborian. I want to see you in my office."

They were together alone for the first time since well before the compu-drama had been made.

"Well?" said Willard. "What do you think, Mr. Laborian?"

Laborian smiled. "That woman who runs the subliminal background told you that it was almost as good as your *King Lear* was, Mr. Willard."

"I heard her."

"She was quite wrong."

"In your opinion?"

"Yes. My opinion is what counts right now. She was quite wrong. Your *Three in One* is much better than your *King Lear*."

"Better?" Willard's weary face broke into a smile.

"Much better. Consider the material you had to work with in doing *King Lear*. You had William Shakespeare, producing words that sang, that were music in themselves; William Shakespeare producing characters who, whether for good or evil, whether strong or weak, whether shrewd or foolish, whether faithful or traitorous, were all larger than life; William Shakespeare, dealing with two overlapping plots, reinforcing each other and tearing the viewers to shreds.

"What was your contribution to *King Lear*? You added dimensions that Shakespeare lacked the technological knowledge to deal with, that he couldn't dream of; but the fanciest technologies and all that your people and your own talents could do could only build somewhat on the greatest literary genius of all time, working at the peak of his power.

"But in *Three in One*, Mr. Willard, you were working with *my* words which didn't sing; *my* characters, which weren't great; *my* plot which tore at no one. You dealt with *me*, a run-of-the-mill writer and you produced something great, something that will be remembered long after I am dead. One book of mine, anyway, will live on because of what you have done.

"Give me back my electronic hundred thousand, Mr. Willard, and I will give you this."

The hundred thousand was shifted back from one financial card to the other and, with an effort, Laborian then pulled his fat briefcase onto the table and opened it. From it, he drew out a box, fastened with a small hook. He unfastened it carefully, and lifted the top. Inside it glittered the gold pieces, each one marked with the planet Earth, the western hemisphere on one side, the eastern on the other. Large gold pieces, two hundred of them, each worth five hundred globo-dollars.

Willard, awed, plucked out one of the gold pieces. It weighed about one and a quarter ounces. He threw it up in the air and caught it.

"Beautiful," he said.

"It's yours, Mr. Willard," said Laborian. "Thank you for doing the compu-drama for me. It is worth every piece of that gold."

Willard stared at the gold and said, "You made me do the compu-drama of your book with your offer of this gold. To get this gold, I forced myself beyond my talents. Thank you for that, and you are right. It was worth every piece of that gold."

He put the gold piece back in the box and closed it. Then he lifted the box and handed it back to Laborian.

I first met Nancy Kress amid the swirl of a world science fiction convention. She looked quite out of place, neatly and stylishly dressed and mannerly, polite, her sentences archly sophisticated and rendered in an accent I spotted as typical of upstate New York; I had heard similar ones while at Cornell University as a postdoctoral fellow. So I mistook her for a "civilian", an otherwise ordinary person who had mistakenly wandered into our tribal ceremonies.

Big mistake. She quickly put me right: she was so a science fiction person and a writer, too. Then she quite quickly told me three generic jokes, all "How many X does it take to screw in a light bulb?" with variations I had not heard before, including one science fictional one. (Mercifully, I do not have the trademark memory of Isaac Asimov, and so can't remember them. They were undoubtedly politically incorrect, anyway.)

At least I was right about the accent. She was born in Buffalo and now resides with her family in Brockport. Her stories were from the first elegant and insightful, spare where they could afford to be, lush where they needed to be—a writer's writer. Early on she won a Nebula for "Out of All Them Bright Stars," which hints at her signature approach: she asks how technology affects ordinary people, not just technophiles and the usual elite classes.

This novelette was striking, popular, and spawned novels based on its central idea, which Kress spun froth in dizzying detail. She has always had a fine ear for social unease and unforeseen consequences. This tale may well stir you to follow the later novel of the same title, and then the equally powerful Beggars and Choosers.

Beggars In Spain
by Nancy Kress

With energy and sleepless vigilance go forward and give
us victories.

—Abraham Lincoln,
to Major General Joseph Hooker, 1863

1

They sat stiffly on his antique Eames chairs, two people
who didn't want to be here, or one person who didn't want
to and one who resented the other's reluctance. Dr. Ong
had seen this before. Within two minutes he was sure: the
woman was the silently furious resister. She would lose.
The man would pay for it later, in little ways, for a long
time.

"I presume you've performed the necessary credit
checks already," Roger Camden said pleasantly, "*so* let's
get right on to details, shall we, doctor?"

"Certainly," Ong said. "Why don't we start by your telling
me all the genetic modifications you're interested in for
the baby."

The woman shifted suddenly on her chair. She was in
her late twenties—clearly a second wife—but already had

a faded look, as if keeping up with Roger Camden was
wearing her out. Ong could easily believe that. Mrs.
Camden's hair was brown, her eyes were brown, her skin
had a brown tinge that might have been pretty if her cheeks
had had any color. She wore a brown coat, neither
fashionable nor cheap, and shoes that looked vaguely
orthopedic. Ong glanced at his records for her name:
Elizabeth. He would bet people forgot it often.

Next to her, Roger Camden radiated nervous vitality,
a man in late middle age whose bullet-shaped head did
not match his careful haircut and Italian-silk business suit.
Ong did not need to consult his file to recall anything about
Camden. A caricature of the bullet-shaped head had been
the leading graphic of yesterday's on-line edition of the
Wall Street Journal: Camden had led a major coup in cross-
border data-atoll investment. Ong was not sure what cross-
border data-atoll investment was.

"A girl," Elizabeth Camden said. Ong hadn't expected
her to speak first. Her voice was another surprise: upper-
class British. "Blonde. Green eyes. Tall. Slender."

Ong smiled. "Appearance factors are the easiest to
achieve, as I'm sure you already know. But all we can do
about 'slenderness' is give her a genetic disposition in that
direction. How you feed the child will naturally—"

"Yes, yes," Roger Camden said, "that's obvious. Now:
intelligence. *High* intelligence. And a sense of daring."

"I'm sorry, Mr. Camden—personality factors are not yet
understood well enough to allow genet—"

"Just testing," Camden said, with a smile that Ong
thought was probably supposed to be light-hearted.

Elizabeth Camden said, "Musical ability."

"Again, Mrs. Camden, a disposition to be musical is all
we can guarantee."

"Good enough," Camden said. "The full array of corrections for any potential gene-linked health problem, of
course."

"Of course," Dr. Ong said. Neither client spoke. So far theirs was a fairly modest list, given Camden's money; most clients had to be argued out of contradictory genetic tendencies, alteration overload, or unrealistic expectations. Ong waited. Tension prickled in the room like heat.

"And," Camden said, "no need to sleep."

Elizabeth Camden jerked her head sideways to look out the window.

Ong picked a paper magnet off his desk. He made his voice pleasant. "May I ask how you learned whether that genetic-modification program exists?"

Camden grinned. "You're not denying it exists. I give you full credit for that, Doctor."

Ong held onto his temper. "May I ask how you learned whether the program exists?"

Camden reached into an inner pocket of his suit. The silk crinkled and pulled; body and suit came from different social classes. Camden was, Ong remembered, a Yagaiist, a personal friend of Kenzo Yagai himself. Camden handed Ong hard copy: program specifications.

"Don't bother hunting down the security leak in your data banks, Doctor, you won't find it. But if it's any consolation, neither will anybody else. Now." He leaned suddenly forward. His tone changed. "I know that you've created twenty children so far who don't need to sleep at all. That so far nineteen are healthy, intelligent, and psychologically normal. In fact, better than normal— they're all unusually precocious. The oldest is already four years old and can read in two languages. I know you're thinking of offering this genetic modification on the open market in a few years. All I want is a chance to buy it for my daughter *now*. At whatever price you name."

Ong stood. "I can't possibly discuss this with you unilaterally, Mr. Camden. Neither the theft of our data—"

"Which wasn't a theft—your system developed a spon-

taneous bubble regurgitation into a public gate, have a hell
of a time proving otherwise—"

"—*nor* the offer to purchase this particular genetic
modification lies in my sole area of authority. Both have
to be discussed with the Institute's Board of Directors."

"By all means, by all means. When can I talk to them,
too?"

"You?"

Camden, still seated, looked up at him. It occurred to
Ong that there were few men who could look so confident
eighteen inches below eye level. "Certainly. I'd like the
chance to present my offer to whoever has the actual
authority to accept it. That's only good business."

"This isn't solely a business transaction, Mr. Camden."

"It isn't solely pure scientific research, either," Camden
retorted. "You're a for-profit corporation here. *With* certain
tax breaks available only to firms meeting certain fair-
practice laws."

For a minute Ong couldn't think what Camden meant.
"Fair-practice laws . . ."

". . . are designed to protect minorities who are suppliers.
I know, it hasn't ever been tested in the case of customers,
except for red-lining in Y-energy installations. But it could
be tested, Doctor Ong. Minorities are entitled to the same
product offerings as non-minorities. I know the Institute
would not welcome a court case, Doctor. None of your
twenty genetic beta-test families are either Black or
Jewish."

"A court . . . but you're not Black or Jewish!"

"I'm a different minority. Polish-American. The name
was Kaminsky." Camden finally stood. And smiled warmly.
"Look, it is preposterous. You know that, and I know that,
and we both know what a grand time journalists would
have with it anyway. And you know that I don't want to
sue you with a preposterous case, just to use the threat
of premature and adverse publicity to get what I want. I

don't want to make threats at all, believe me I don't. I just want this marvelous advancement you've come up with for my daughter." His face changed, to an expression Ong wouldn't have believed possible on those particular features: wistfulness. "Doctor—do you know how much more I could have accomplished if I hadn't had to *sleep* all my life?"

Elizabeth Camden said harshly, "You hardly sleep now."

Camden looked down at her as if he had forgotten she was there. "Well, no, my dear, not now. But when I was young . . . college, I might have been able to finish college and still support . . . well. None of that matters now. What matters, Doctor, is that you and I and your Board come to an agreement."

"Mr. Camden, please leave my office now."

"You mean before you lose your temper at my presumptuousness? You wouldn't be the first. I'll expect to have a meeting set up by the end of next week, whenever and wherever you say, of course. Just let my personal secretary, Diane Clavers, know the details. Anytime that's best for you."

Ong did not accompany them to the door. Pressure throbbed behind his temples. In the doorway Elizabeth Camden turned. "What happened to the twentieth one?"

"What?"

"The twentieth baby. My husband said nineteen of them are healthy and normal. What happened to the twentieth?"

The pressure grew stronger, hotter. Ong knew that he should not answer; that Camden probably already knew the answer even if his wife didn't; that he, Ong, was going to answer anyway; that he would regret the lack of self-control, bitterly, later.

"The twentieth baby is dead. His parents turned out to be unstable. They separated during the pregnancy, and his mother could not bear the twenty-four-hour crying of a baby who never sleeps."

Elizabeth Camden's eyes widened. "She killed it?"

"By mistake," Camden said shortly. "Shook the little thing too hard." He frowned at Ong. "Nurses, Doctor. In shifts. You should have picked only parents wealthy enough to afford nurses in shifts."

"That's horrible!" Mrs. Camden burst out, and Ong could not tell if she meant the child's death, the lack of nurses, or the Institute's carelessness. Ong closed his eyes.

When they had gone, he took ten milligrams of cyclobenzaprine-III. For his back—it was solely for his back. The old injury hurting again. Afterward he stood for a long time at the window, still holding the paper magnet, feeling the pressure recede from his temples, feeling himself calm down. Below him Lake Michigan lapped peacefully at the shore; the police had driven away the homeless in another raid just last night, and they hadn't yet had time to return. Only their debris remained, thrown into the bushes of the lakeshore park: tattered blankets, newspapers, plastic bags like pathetic trampled standards. It was illegal to sleep in the park, illegal to enter it without a resident's permit, illegal to be homeless and without a residence. As Ong watched, uniformed park attendants began methodically spearing newspapers and shoving them into clean self-propelled receptacles.

Ong picked up the phone to call the President of Biotech Institute's Board of Directors.

Four men and three women sat around the polished mahogany table of the conference room. *Doctor, lawyer, Indian chief,* thought Susan Melling, looking from Ong to Sullivan to Camden. She smiled. Ong caught the smile and looked frosty. Pompous ass. Judy Sullivan, the Institute lawyer, turned to speak in a low voice to Camden's lawyer, a thin nervous man with the look of being owned. The owner, Roger Camden, the Indian chief himself, was the happiest-looking person in the room. The lethal little man—what did it take to become that rich, starting from nothing? She, Susan, would certainly never know—radiated excitement. He beamed, he glowed, so unlike the usual parents-to-be that Susan was intrigued. Usually the prospective daddies and mommies—especially the daddies—sat there looking as if they were at a corporate merger. Camden looked as if he were at a birthday party.

Which, of course, he was. Susan grinned at him, and was pleased when he grinned back. Wolfish, but with a sort of delight that could only be called innocent—what would he be like in bed? Ong frowned majestically and rose to speak.

"Ladies and gentlemen, I think we're ready to start. Perhaps introductions are in order. Mr. Roger Camden, Mrs. Camden, are of course our clients. Mr. John Jaworski, Mr. Camden's lawyer. Mr. Camden, this is Judith Sullivan, the Institute's head of Legal; Samuel Krenshaw, representing Institute Director Dr. Brad Marsteiner, who unfortunately couldn't be here today; and Dr. Susan Melling, who developed the genetic modification affecting sleep. A few legal points of interest to both parties—"

"Forget the contracts for a minute," Camden interrupted. "Let's talk about the sleep thing. I'd like to ask a few questions."

Susan said, "What would you like to know?" Camden's eyes were very blue in his blunt-featured face; he wasn't what she had expected. Mrs. Camden, who apparently lacked both a first name and a lawyer, since Jaworski had been introduced as her husband's but not hers, looked either sullen or scared. It was difficult to tell which.

Ong said sourly, "Then perhaps we should start with a short presentation by Dr. Melling."

Susan would have preferred a Q&A, to see what Camden would ask. But she had annoyed Ong enough for one session. Obediently she rose.

"Let me start with a brief description of sleep. Researchers have known for a long time that there are actually three kinds of sleep. One is 'slow-wave sleep,' characterized on an EEG by delta waves, One is 'rapid-eye-movement sleep,' or REM sleep, which is much lighter sleep and contains most dreaming. Together these two make up 'core sleep.' The third type of sleep is 'optional sleep,' so-called because people seem to get along without it with no ill effects, and some short sleepers don't do it at all, sleeping naturally only 3 or 4 hours a night."

"That's me," Camden said. "I trained myself into it. Couldn't everybody do that?"

Apparently they were going to have a Q&A after all. "No. The actual sleep mechanism has some flexibility, but not the same amount for every person. The raphe nuclei on the brain stem—"

Ong said, "I don't think we need that level of detail, Susan. Let's stick to basics."

Camden said, "The raphe nuclei regulate the balance among neurotransmitters and peptides that lead to a pressure to sleep, don't they?"

Susan couldn't help it; she grinned. Camden, the laser-sharp ruthless financier, sat trying to look solemn, a third-grader waiting to have his homework praised. Ong looked sour. Mrs. Camden looked away, out the window.

"Yes, that's correct, Mr. Camden. You've done your research."

Camden said, "This is my *daughter*," and Susan caught her breath. When was the last time she had heard that note of reverence in anyone's voice? But no one in the room seemed to notice.

"Well, then," Susan said, "you already know that the reason people sleep is because a pressure to sleep builds up in the brain. Over the last twenty years, research has determined that's the *only* reason. Neither slow-wave sleep nor REM sleep serve functions that can't be carried on while the body and brain are awake. A lot goes on during sleep, but it can go on awake just as well, if other hormonal adjustments are made.

"Sleep once served an important evolutionary function. Once Clem Pre-Mammal was done filling his stomach and squirting his sperm around, sleep kept him immobile and away from predators. Sleep was an aid to survival. But now it's a left-over mechanism, like the appendix. It switches on every night, but the need is gone. So we turn off the switch at its source, in the genes."

Ong winced. He hated it when she oversimplified like that. Or maybe it was the light-heartedness he hated. If Marsteiner were making this presentation, there'd be no Clem Pre-Mammal.

Camden said, "What about the need to dream?"

"Not necessary. A left-over bombardment of the cortex to keep it on semi-alert in case a predator attacked during sleep. Wakefulness does that better."

"Why not have wakefulness instead then? From the start of the evolution?"

He was testing her. Susan gave him a full, lavish smile, enjoying his brass. "I told you. Safety from predators. But when a modern predator attacks—say, a cross-border data-atoll investor—it's safer to be awake."

Camden shot at her, "What about the high percentage of REM sleep in fetuses and babies?"

"Still an evolutionary hangover. Cerebrum develops perfectly well without it."

"What about neural repair during slow-wave sleep?"

"That does go on. But it can go on during wakefulness, if the DNA is programmed to do so. No loss of neural efficiency, as far as we know."

"What about the release of human growth enzyme in such large concentrations during slow-wave sleep?"

Susan looked at him admiringly. "Goes on without the sleep. Genetic adjustments tie it to other changes in the pineal gland."

"What about the—"

"The *side effects*?" Mrs. Camden said. Her mouth turned down. "What about the bloody side effects?"

Susan turned to Elizabeth Camden. She had forgotten she was there. The younger woman stared at Susan, mouth turned down at the corners.

"I'm glad you asked that, Mrs. Camden. Because there *are* side effects." Susan paused; she was enjoying herself. "Compared to their age mates, the non-sleep children—who have *not* had IQ genetic manipulation—are more intelligent, better at problem-solving, and more joyous."

Camden took out a cigarette. The archaic, filthy habit surprised Susan. Then she saw that it was deliberate: Roger Camden drawing attention to an ostentatious display to draw attention away from what he was feeling. His cigarette lighter was gold, monogrammed, innocently gaudy.

"Let me explain," Susan said. "REM sleep bombards the cerebral cortex with random neural firings from the brainstem; dreaming occurs because the poor besieged cortex tries so hard to make sense of the activated images and memories. It spends a lot of energy doing that. Without that energy expenditure, non-sleep cerebrums save the wear-and-tear and do better at coordinating real-life input. Thus greater intelligence and problem-solving.

"Also, doctors have known for sixty years that anti-depressants, which lift the mood of depressed patients, also suppress REM sleep entirely. What they have proved in the last ten years is that the reverse is equally true: suppress REM sleep and people don't *get* depressed. The non-sleep kids are cheerful, outgoing . . . *joyous*. There's no other word for it."

"At what cost?" Mrs. Camden said. She held her neck rigid, but the corners of her jaw worked.

"No cost. No negative side effects at all."

"So far," Mrs. Camden shot back.

Susan shrugged. "So far."

"They're only four years old! At the most!"

Ong and Krenshaw were studying her closely. Susan saw the moment the Camden woman realized it; she sank back into her chair, drawing her fur coat around her, her face blank.

Camden did not look at his wife. He blew a cloud of cigarette smoke. "Everything has costs, Dr. Melling."

She liked the way he said her name. "Ordinarily, yes. Especially in genetic modification. But we honestly have not been able to find any here, despite looking." She smiled directly into Camden's eyes. "Is it too much to believe that just once the universe has given us something wholly good, wholly a step forward, wholly beneficial? Without hidden penalties?"

"Not the universe. The intelligence of people like you," Camden said, surprising Susan more than anything else that had gone before. His eyes held hers. She felt her chest tighten.

"I think," Dr. Ong said dryly, "that the philosophy of the universe may be beyond our concerns here. Mr. Camden, if you have no further medical questions, perhaps we can return to the legal points Ms. Sullivan and Mr. Jaworski have raised. Thank you, Dr. Melling."

Susan nodded. She didn't look again at Camden. But she knew what he said, how he looked, that he was there.

The house was about what she had expected, a huge mock Tudor on Lake Michigan north of Chicago. The land heavily wooded between the gate and the house, open between the house and the surging water. Patches of snow dotted the dormant grass. Biotech had been working with the Camdens for four months, but this was the first time Susan had driven to their home.

As she walked toward the house, another car drove up

behind her. No, a truck, continuing around the curved driveway to a service entry at the side of the house. One man rang the service bell; a second began to unload a plastic-wrapped playpen from the back of the truck. White, with pink and yellow bunnies. Susan briefly closed her eyes.

Camden opened the door himself. She could see the effort not to look worried. "You didn't have to drive out, Susan—I'd have come into the city!"

"No, I didn't want you to do that, Roger. Mrs. Camden is here?"

"In the living room." Camden led her into a large room with a stone fireplace. English country-house furniture; prints of dogs or boats, all hung eighteen inches too high: Elizabeth Camden must have done the decorating. She did not rise from her wing chair as Susan entered.

"Let me be concise and fast," Susan said, "I don't want to make this any more drawn-out for you than I have to. We have all the amniocentesis, ultrasound, and Langston test results. The fetus is fine, developing normally for two weeks, no problems with the implant on the uterus wall. But a complication has developed."

"What?" Camden said. He took out a cigarette, looked at his wife, put it back unlit.

Susan said quietly, "Mrs. Camden, by sheer chance both your ovaries released eggs last month. We removed one for the gene surgery. By more sheer chance the second fertilized and implanted. You're carrying two fetuses."

Elizabeth Camden grew still. "Twins?"

"No," Susan said. Then she realized what she had said. "I mean, yes. They're twins, but non-identical. Only one has been genetically altered. The other will be no more similar to her than any two siblings. It's a so-called 'normal' baby. And I know you didn't want a so-called normal baby."

Camden said, "No. I didn't."

Elizabeth Camden said, "I did."

Camden shot her a fierce look that Susan couldn't read. He took out the cigarette again, lit it. His face was in profile to Susan, thinking intently; she doubted he knew the cigarette was there, or that he was lighting it. "Is the baby being affected by the other one's being there?"

"No," Susan said. "No, of course not. They're just . . . co-existing."

"Can you abort it?"

"Not without risk of aborting both of them. Removing the unaltered fetus might cause changes in the uterus lining that could lead to a spontaneous miscarriage of the other." She drew a deep breath. "There's that option, of course. We can start the whole process over again. But as I told you at the time, you were very lucky to have the in vitro fertilization take on only the second try. Some couples take eight or ten tries. If we started all over, the process could be a lengthy one."

Camden said, "Is the presence of this second fetus harming my daughter? Taking away nutrients or anything? Or will it change anything for her later on in the pregnancy?"

"No. Except that there is a chance of premature birth. Two fetuses take up a lot more room in the womb, and if it gets too crowded, birth can be premature. But the—"

"How premature? Enough to threaten survival?"

"Most probably not."

Camden went on smoking. A man appeared at the door. "Sir, London calling. James Kendall for Mr. Yagai."

"I'll take it." Camden rose. Susan watched him study his wife's face. When he spoke, it was to her. "All right, Elizabeth. All right." He left the room.

For a long moment the two women sat in silence. Susan was aware of disappointment; this was not the Camden she had expected to see. She became aware of Elizabeth Camden watching her with amusement.

"Oh, yes, Doctor. He's like that."

Susan said nothing.

"Completely overbearing. But not this time." She laughed softly, with excitement. "Two. Do you . . . do you know what sex the other one is?"

"Both fetuses are female."

"I wanted a girl, you know. And now I'll have one."

"Then you'll go ahead with the pregnancy."

"Oh, yes. Thank you for coming, Doctor."

She was dismissed. No one saw her out. But as she was getting into her car, Camden rushed out of the house, coatless. "Susan! I wanted to thank you. For coming all the way out here to tell us yourself."

"You already thanked me."

"Yes. Well. You're sure the second fetus is no threat to my daughter?"

Susan said deliberately, "Nor is the genetically altered fetus a threat to the naturally conceived one."

He smiled. His voice was low and wistful. "And you think that should matter to me just as much. But it doesn't. And why should I fake what I feel? Especially to you?"

Susan opened her car door. She wasn't ready for this, or she had changed her mind, or something. But then Camden leaned over to close the door, and his manner held no trace of flirtatiousness, no smarmy ingratiation. "I better order a second playpen."

"Yes."

"And a second car seat."

"Yes."

"But not a second night-shift nurse."

"That's up to you."

"And you." Abruptly he leaned over and kissed her, a kiss so polite and respectful that Susan was shocked. Neither lust nor conquest would have shocked her; this did. Camden didn't give her a chance to react; he closed the car door and turned back toward the house. Susan drove toward the gate, her hands shaky on the wheel until amusement replaced shock: It *had* been a deliberately distant, respectful kiss, an engineered enigma. And nothing else could have guaranteed so well that there would have to be another.

She wondered what the Camdens would name their daughters.

Dr. Ong strode the hospital corridor, which had been dimmed to half-light. From the nurse's station in Maternity a nurse stepped forward as if to stop him—it was the middle of the night, long past visiting hours—got a good look at his face, and faded back into her station. Around a corner was the viewing glass to the nursery. To Ong's annoyance, Susan Melling stood pressed against the glass. To his further annoyance, she was crying.

Ong realized that he had never liked the woman. Maybe not any women. Even those with superior minds could not seem to refrain from being made damn fools by their emotions.

"Look," Susan said, laughing a little, swiping at her face. "Doctor—*look*."

Behind the glass Roger Camden, gowned and masked, was holding up a baby in white undershirt and pink blanket. Camden's blue eyes—theatrically blue, a man really should not have such garish eyes—glowed. The baby had a head covered with blond fuzz, wide eyes, pink skin. Camden's eyes above the mask said that no other child had ever had these attributes.

Ong said, "An uncomplicated birth?"

"Yes," Susan Melling sobbed. "Perfectly straightforward. Elizabeth is fine. She's asleep. Isn't she beautiful? He has the most adventurous spirit I've ever known." She wiped her nose on her sleeve; Ong realized that she was drunk. "Did I ever tell you that I was engaged once? Fifteen years ago, in med school? I broke it off because he grew to seem so ordinary, so boring. Oh, God, I shouldn't be telling you all this I'm sorry I'm sorry."

Ong moved away from her. Behind the glass Roger
Camden laid the baby in a small wheeled crib. The
nameplate said BABY GIRL CAMDEN #1. 5.9 POUNDS.
A night nurse watched indulgently.

Ong did not wait to see Camden emerge from the
nursery or to hear Susan Melling say to him whatever she
was going to say. Ong went to have the OB paged. Melling's
report was not, under the circumstances, to be trusted.
A perfect, unprecedented chance to record every detail
of gene-alteration with a non-altered control, and Melling
was more interested in her own sloppy emotions. Ong
would obviously have to do the report himself after talking
to the OB. He was hungry for every detail. And not just
about the pink-cheeked baby in Camden's arms. He
wanted to know everything about the birth of the child
in the other glass-sided crib: BABY GIRL CAMDEN #2.
5.1 POUNDS. The dark-haired baby with the mottled red
features, lying scrunched down in her pink blanket, asleep.

2

Leisha's earliest memory was of flowing lines that were
not there. She knew they were not there because when
she reached out her fist to touch them, her fist was empty.
Later she realized that the flowing lines were light:
sunshine slanting in bars between curtains in her room,
between the wooden blinds in the dining room, between
the criss-cross lattices in the conservatory. The day she
realized the golden flow was light she laughed out loud
with the sheer joy of discovery, and Daddy turned from
putting flowers in pots and smiled at her.

The whole house was full of light. Light bounded off
the lake, streamed across the high white ceilings, puddled
on the shining wooden floors. She and Alice moved

continually through light, and sometimes Leisha would stop and tip back her head and let it flow over her face. She could feel it, like water.

The best light, of course, was in the conservatory. That's where Daddy liked to be when he was home from making money. Daddy potted plants and watered trees, humming, and Leisha and Alice ran between the wooden tables of flowers with their wonderful earthy smells, running from the dark side of the conservatory where the big purple flowers grew to the sunshine side with sprays of yellow flowers, running back and forth, in and out of the light. "Growth," Daddy said to her, "flowers all fulfilling their promise. Alice, be careful! You almost knocked over that orchid!" Alice, obedient, would stop running for a while. Daddy never told Leisha to stop running.

After a while the light would go away. Alice and Leisha would have their baths, and then Alice would get quiet, or cranky. She wouldn't play nice with Leisha, even when Leisha let her choose the game or even have all the best dolls. Then Nanny would take Alice to "bed," and Leisha would talk with Daddy some more until Daddy said he had to work in his study with the papers that made money. Leisha always felt a moment of regret that he had to go do that, but the moment never lasted very long because Mamselle would arrive and start Leisha's lessons, which she liked. Learning things was so interesting! She could already sing twenty songs and write all the letters in the alphabet and count to fifty. And by the time lessons were done, the light had come back, and it was time for breakfast.

Breakfast was the only time Leisha didn't like. Daddy had gone to the office, and Leisha and Alice had breakfast with Mommy in the big dining room. Mommy sat in a red robe, which Leisha liked, and she didn't smell funny or talk funny the way she would later in the day, but still breakfast wasn't fun. Mommy always started with The Question. "Alice, sweetheart, how did you sleep?"

"Fine, Mommy."

"Did you have any nice dreams?"

For a long time Alice said no. Then one day she said, "I dreamed about a horse. I was riding him." Mommy clapped her hands and kissed Alice and gave her an extra sticky bun. After that Alice always had a dream to tell Mommy.

Once Leisha said, "I had a dream, too. I dreamed light was coming in the window and it wrapped all around me like a blanket and then it kissed me on my eyes."

Mommy put down her coffee cup so hard that coffee sloshed out of it. "Don't lie to me, Leisha. You did not have a dream."

"Yes, I did," Leisha said.

"Only children who sleep can have dreams. Don't lie to me. You did not have a dream."

"Yes I did! I did!" Leisha shouted. She could see it, almost: the light streaming in the window and wrapping around her like a golden blanket.

"I will not tolerate a child who is a liar! Do you hear me, Leisha—I won't tolerate it!"

"You're a liar!" Leisha shouted, knowing the words weren't true, hating herself because they weren't true but hating Mommy more and that was wrong, too, and there sat Alice stiff and frozen with her eyes wide. Alice was scared and it was Leisha's fault.

Mommy called sharply, "Nanny! Nanny! Take Leisha to her room at once. She can't sit with civilized people if she can't refrain from telling lies!"

Leisha started to cry. Nanny carried her out of the room. Leisha hadn't even had her breakfast. But she didn't care about that; all she could see while she cried was Alice's eyes, scared like that, reflecting broken bits of light.

But Leisha didn't cry long. Nanny read her a story, and then played Data Jump with her, and then Alice came up and Nanny drove them both into Chicago to the zoo where there were wonderful animals to see, animals Leisha could not have dreamed—nor Alice *either*. And by the time they came back Mommy had gone to her room and Leisha knew that she would stay there with the glasses of funny-smelling stuff the rest of the day and Leisha would not have to see her.

But that night, she went to her mother's room.

"I have to go to the bathroom," she told Mamselle. Mamselle said, "Do you need any help?" maybe because Alice still needed help in the bathroom. But Leisha didn't, and she thanked Mamselle. Then she sat on the toilet for a minute even though nothing came, so that what she had told Mamselle wouldn't be a lie.

Leisha tiptoed down the hall. She went first into Alice's room. A little light in a wall socket burned near the "crib." There was no crib in Leisha's room. Leisha looked at her sister through the bars. Alice lay on her side, with her eyes closed. The lids of the eyes fluttered quickly, like curtains blowing in the wind. Alice's chin and neck looked loose.

Leisha closed the door very carefully and went to her parents' room.

They didn't "sleep" in a crib but in a huge enormous "bed," with enough room between them for more people. Mommy's eyelids weren't fluttering; she lay on her back making a hrrr-hrrr sound through her nose. The funny smell was strong on her. Leisha backed away and tiptoed over to Daddy. He looked like Alice, except that his neck and chin looked even looser, folds of skin collapsed like the tent that had fallen down in the backyard. It scared Leisha to see him like that. Then Daddy's eyes flew open so suddenly that Leisha screamed.

Daddy rolled out of bed and picked her up, looking quickly at Mommy. But she didn't move. Daddy was wearing only his underpants. He carried Leisha out into the hall, where Mamselle came rushing up saying, "Oh, sir, I'm sorry, she just said she was going to the bathroom—"

"It's all right," Daddy said. "I'll take her with me."

"No!" Leisha screamed, because Daddy was only in his underpants and his neck had looked all funny and the room smelled bad because of Mommy. But Daddy carried her into the conservatory, set her down on a bench, wrapped himself in a piece of green plastic that was supposed to cover up plants, and sat down next to her.

"Now, what happened, Leisha? What were you doing?"

Leisha didn't answer.

"You were looking at people sleeping, weren't you?" Daddy said, and because his voice was softer Leisha mumbled, "Yes." She immediately felt better; it felt good not to lie.

"You were looking at people sleeping because you don't sleep and you were curious, weren't you? Like Curious George in your book?"

"Yes," Leisha said. "I thought you said you made money in your study all night!"

Daddy smiled. "Not all night. Some of it. But then I sleep, although not very much." He took Leisha on his lap. "I don't need much sleep, so I get a lot more done at night than most people. Different people need different amounts of sleep. And a few, a very few, are like you. You don't need any."

"Why not?"

"Because you're special. Better than other people. Before you were born, I had some doctors help make you that way."

"Why?"

"So you could do anything you want to and make manifest your own individuality."

Leisha twisted in his arms to stare at him; the words meant nothing. Daddy reached over and touched a single flower growing on a tall potted tree. The flower had thick white petals like the cream he put in coffee, and the center was a light pink.

"See, Leisha—this tree made this flower. Because it *can*. Only this tree can make this kind of wonderful flower. That plant hanging up there can't, and those can't either. Only this tree. Therefore the most important thing in the world for this tree to do is grow this flower. The flower is the tree's individuality—that means just *it*, and nothing else—made manifest. Nothing else matters."

"I don't understand, Daddy."

"You will. Someday."

"But I want to understand *now*," Leisha said, and Daddy laughed with pure delight and hugged her. The hug felt good, but Leisha still wanted to understand.

"When you make money, is that your indiv . . . that thing?"

"Yes," Daddy said happily.

"Then nobody else can make money? Like only that tree can make that flower?"

"Nobody else can make it just the ways I do."

"What do you do with the money?"

"I buy things for you. This house, your dresses, Mamselle to teach you, the car to ride in."

"What does the tree do with the flower?"

"Glories in it," Daddy said, which made no sense. "Excellence is what counts, Leisha. Excellence supported by individual effort. And that's *all* that counts."

"I'm cold, Daddy."

"Then I better bring you back to Mamselle."

Leisha didn't move. She touched the flower with one finger. "I want to sleep, Daddy."

"No, you don't, sweetheart. Sleep is just lost time, wasted life. It's a little death."

"Alice sleeps."

"Alice isn't like you."

"Alice isn't special?"

"No. You are."

"Why didn't you make Alice special, too?"

"Alice made herself. I didn't have a chance to make her special."

The whole thing was too hard, Leisha stopped stroking the flower and slipped off Daddy's lap. He smiled at her. *"My* little questioner. When you grow up, you'll find your own excellence, and it will be a new order, specialness the world hasn't ever seen before. You might even be like Kenzo Yagai. He made the Yagai generator that powers the world."

"Daddy, you look funny wrapped in the flower plastic." Leisha laughed. Daddy did, too. But then she said, "When I grow up, I'll make my specialness find a way to make Alice special, too," and Daddy stopped laughing.

He took her back to Mamselle, who taught her to write her name, which was so exciting she forgot about the puzzling talk with Daddy. There were six letters, all different, and together they were her *name.* Leisha wrote it over and over, laughing, and Mamselle laughed too. But later, in the morning, Leisha thought again about the talk with Daddy. She thought of it often, turning the unfamiliar words over and over in her mind like small hard stones, but the part she thought about most wasn't a word. It was the frown on Daddy's face when she told him she would use her specialness to make Alice special, too.

Every week Dr. Melling came to see Leisha and Alice, sometimes alone, sometimes with other people. Leisha and Alice both liked Dr. Melling, who laughed a lot and whose eyes were bright and warm. Often Daddy was there, too. Dr. Melling played games with them, first with Alice and Leisha separately and then together. She took their pictures and weighed them. She made them lie down on a table and stuck little metal things to their temples, which sounded scary but wasn't because there were so many machines to watch, all making interesting noises, while you were lying there. Dr. Melling was as good at answering questions as Daddy. Once Leisha said, "Is Dr. Melling a special person? Like Kenzo Yagai?" And Daddy laughed and glanced at Dr. Melling and said, "Oh, yes, indeed."

When Leisha was five she and Alice started school. Daddy's driver took them every day into Chicago. They were in different rooms, which disappointed Leisha. The kids in Leisha's room were all older. But from the first day she adored school, with its fascinating science equipment and electronic drawers full of math puzzlers and other children to find countries on the map with. In half a year she had been moved to yet a different room, where the kids were still older, but they were nonetheless nice to her. Leisha started to learn Japanese. She loved drawing the beautiful characters on thick white paper. "The Sauley School was a good choice," Daddy said.

But Alice didn't like the Sauley School. She wanted to go to school on the same yellow bus as Cook's daughter. She cried and threw her paints on the floor at the Sauley School. Then Mommy came out of her room—Leisha hadn't seen her for a few weeks, although she knew Alice had—and threw some candlesticks from the mantlepiece on the floor. The candlesticks, which were china, broke. Leisha ran to pick up the pieces while Mommy and Daddy screamed at each other in the hall by the big staircase.

"She's my daughter, too! And I say she can go!"

"You don't have the right to say anything about it! A weepy drunk, the most rotten role model possible for both of them . . . and I thought I was getting a fine English aristocrat!"

"You got what you paid for! Nothing! Not that you ever needed anything from me or anybody else!"

"Stop it!" Leisha cried. "Stop it!" and there was silence in the hall. Leisha cut her fingers on the china; blood streamed onto the rug. Daddy rushed in and picked her up. "Stop it," Leisha sobbed, and didn't understand when Daddy said quietly, "*You* stop it, Leisha. Nothing *they* do should touch you at all. You have to be at least that strong."

Leisha buried her head in Daddy's shoulder. Alice transferred to Carl Sandburg Elementary School, riding there on the yellow school bus with Cook's daughter.

A few weeks later Daddy told them that Mommy was going away for a few weeks to a hospital, to stop drinking so much. When Mommy came out, he said, she was going to live somewhere else for a while. She and Daddy were not happy. Leisha and Alice would stay with Daddy and they would visit Mommy sometimes. He told them this very carefully, finding the right words for truth. Truth was very important, Leisha already knew. Truth was being true to your self, your specialness. Your individuality. An individual respected facts, and so always told the truth.

Mommy, Daddy did not say but Leisha knew, did not respect facts.

"I don't want Mommy to go away," Alice said. She started to cry. Leisha thought Daddy would pick Alice up, but he didn't. He just stood there looking at them both.

Leisha put her arms around Alice. "It's all right, Alice. It's all right! We'll make it all right! I'll play with you all the time we're not in school so you don't miss Mommy!"

Alice clung to Leisha. Leisha turned her head so she didn't have to see Daddy's face.

3

Kenzo Yagai was coming to the United States to lecture. The title of his talk, which he would give in New York, Los Angeles, Chicago, and Washington, with a repeat in Washington as a special address to Congress, was "The Further Political Implications of Inexpensive Power." Leisha Camden, eleven years old, was going to have a private introduction after the Chicago talk, arranged by her father.

She had studied the theory of cold fusion at school, and her Global Studies teacher had traced the changes in the world resulting from Yagai's patented, low-cost applications of what had, until him, been unworkable theory. The rising prosperity of the Third World, the last death throes of the old communist systems, the decline of the oil states, the renewed economic power of the United States. Her study group had written a script, filmed with the school's professional-quality equipment, about how a 1985 American family lived with expensive energy costs and a belief in tax-supported help, while a 2019 family lived with cheap energy and a belief in the contract as the basis of civilization. Parts of her own research puzzled Leisha.

"Japan thinks Kenzo Yagai was a traitor to his own country," she said to Daddy at supper.

"No," Camden said. "*Some* Japanese think that. Watch out for generalizations, Leisha. Yagai patented and marketed Y-energy first in the United States because here there were at least the dying embers of individual enterprise. Because of his invention, our entire country has slowly swung back toward an individual meritocracy, and Japan has slowly been forced to follow."

"Your father held that belief all along," Susan said. "Eat your peas, Leisha." Leisha ate her peas. Susan and Daddy had only been married less than a year; it still felt a little strange to have her there. But nice. Daddy said Susan was a valuable addition to their household, intelligent, motivated, and cheerful. Like Leisha herself.

"Remember, Leisha," Camden said, "a man's worth to society and to himself doesn't rest on what he thinks other people should do or be or feel, but on himself. On what he can actually do, and do well. People trade what they do well, and everyone benefits. The basic tool of civilization is the contract. Contracts are voluntary and mutually beneficial. As opposed to coercion, which is wrong."

"The strong have no right to take anything from the weak

by force," Susan said. "Alice, eat your peas, too, honey."

"Nor the weak to take anything by force from the strong," Camden said. "That's the basis of what you'll hear Kenzo Yagai discuss tonight, Leisha."

Alice said, "I don't like peas."

Camden said, "Your body does. They're good for you."

Alice smiled. Leisha felt her heart lift; Alice didn't smile much at dinner any more. "My body doesn't have a contract with the peas."

Camden said, a little impatiently, "Yes, it does. Your body benefits from them. Now eat."

Alice's smile vanished. Leisha looked down at her plate. Suddenly she saw a way out. "No, Daddy—look, Alice's body benefits, but the peas don't! It's not a mutually beneficial consideration—so there's no contract! Alice is right!"

Camden let out a shout of laughter. To Susan he said, "Eleven years old . . . *eleven*." Even Alice smiled, and Leisha waved her spoon triumphantly, light glinting off the bowl and dancing silver on the opposite wall.

But even so, Alice did not want to go hear Kenzo Yagai. She was going to sleep over at her friend Julie's house; they were going to curl their hair together. More surprisingly, Susan wasn't coming either. She and Daddy looked at each other a little funny at the front door, Leisha thought, but Leisha was too excited to think about this. She was going to hear *Kenzo Yagai*.

Yagai was a small man, dark and slim. Leisha liked his accent. She liked, too, something about him that took her a while to name. "Daddy," she whispered in the half-darkness of the auditorium, "he's a joyful man."

Daddy hugged her in the darkness.

Yagai spoke about spirituality and economics. "A man's spirituality—which is only his dignity as a man—rests on his own efforts. Dignity and worth are not automatically conferred by aristocratic birth—we have only to look at history to see that. Dignity and worth are not automatically conferred by inherited wealth—a great heir may be a thief, a wastrel, cruel, an exploiter, a person who leaves the world much poorer than he found it. Nor are dignity and worth automatically conferred by existence itself—a mass murderer exists, but is of negative worth to his society and possesses no dignity in his lust to kill.

"No, the only dignity, the only spirituality, rests on what a man can achieve with his own efforts. To rob a man of the chance to achieve, and to trade what he achieves with others, is to rob him of his spiritual dignity as a man. This is why communism has failed in our time. *All* coercion—all force to take from a man his own efforts to achieve—causes spiritual damage and weakens a society. Conscription, theft, fraud, violence, welfare, lack of legislative representation *all* rob a man of his chance to choose, to achieve on his own, to trade the results of his achievement with others. Coercion is a cheat. It produces nothing new. Only freedom—the freedom to achieve, the freedom to trade freely the results of achievement—creates the environment proper to the dignity and spirituality of man."

Leisha applauded so hard her hands hurt. Going backstage with Daddy, she thought she could hardly breathe. Kenzo Yagai!

But backstage was more crowded than she had expected. There were cameras everywhere. Daddy said, "Mr. Yagai, may I present my daughter Leisha," and the cameras moved in close and fast—on *her*. A Japanese man whispered something in Kenzo Yagai's ear, and he looked more closely at Leisha. "Ah, yes."

"Look over here, Leisha," someone called, and she did. A robot camera zoomed so close to her face that Leisha stepped back, startled. Daddy spoke very sharply to someone, then to someone else. The cameras didn't move. A woman suddenly knelt in front of Leisha and thrust a microphone at her. "What does it feel like to never sleep, Leisha?"

"What?"

Someone laughed. The laugh was not kind. "Breeding geniuses . . ."

Leisha felt a hand on her shoulder. Kenzo Yagai gripped her very firmly, pulled her away from the cameras. Immediately, as if by magic, a line of Japanese men formed behind Yagai, parting only to let Daddy through. Behind the line, the three of them moved into a dressing room, and Kenzo Yagai shut the door.

"You must not let them bother you, Leisha," he said in his wonderful accent. "Not ever. There is an old Oriental proverb: 'The dogs bark but the caravan moves on.' You must never let your individual caravan be slowed by the barking of rude or envious dogs."

"I won't," Leisha breathed, not sure yet what the words really meant, knowing there was time later to sort them out, to talk about them with Daddy. For now she was dazzled by Kenzo Yagai, the actual man himself who was changing the world without force, without guns, with trading his special individual efforts. "We study your philosophy at my school, Mr. Yagai."

Kenzo Yagai looked at Daddy. Daddy said, "A private school. But Leisha's sister also studies it, although cursorily, in the public system. Slowly, Kenzo, but it comes. It comes." Leisha noticed that he did not say why Alice was not here tonight with them.

Back home, Leisha sat in her room for hours, thinking over everything that had happened. When Alice came home from Julie's the next morning, Leisha rushed toward her. But Alice seemed angry about something.

"Alice—what is it?"

"Don't you think I have enough to put up with at school already?" Alice shouted. "Everybody knows, but at least when you stayed quiet it didn't matter too much! They'd stopped teasing me! Why did you have to do it?"

"Do what?" Leisha said, bewildered.

Alice threw something at her: a hard-copy morning paper, on newsprint flimsier than the Camden system used. The paper dropped open at Leisha's feet. She stared at her own picture, three columns wide, with Kenzo Yagai. The headline said YAGAI AND THE FUTURE: ROOM FOR THE REST OF US? Y-ENERGY INVENTOR CONFERS WITH 'SLEEP-FREE' DAUGHTER OF MEGA-FINANCIER ROGER CAMDEN.

Alice kicked the paper. "It was on TV last night too—*on TV*. I work hard not to look stuck-up or creepy, and you go and do this! Now Julie probably won't even invite me to her slumber party next week!" She rushed up the broad curving stairs toward her room.

Leisha looked down at the paper. She heard Kenzo Yagai's voice in her head: "The dogs bark but the caravan moves on." She looked at the empty stairs. Aloud she said, "Alice—your hair looks really pretty curled like that."

4

"I want to meet the rest of them," Leisha said. "Why have you kept them from me this long?"

"I haven't kept them from you at all," Camden said. "Not offering is not the same as denial. Why shouldn't you be the one to do the asking? You're the one who now wants it."

Leisha looked at him. She was 15, in her last year at the Sauley School. "Why didn't you offer?"

"Why should I?"

"I don't know," Leisha said. "But you gave me everything else."

"Including the freedom to ask for what you want."

Leisha looked for the contradiction, and found it. "Most things that you provided for my education I didn't ask for, because I didn't know enough to ask and you, as the adult, did. But you've never offered the opportunity for me to meet any of the other sleepless mutants—"

"Don't use that word," Camden said sharply.

"—so you must either think it was not essential to my education or else you had another motive for not wanting me to meet them."

"Wrong," Camden said. "There's a third possibility. That I think meeting them is essential to your education, that I do want you to, but this issue provided a chance to further the education of your self-initiative by waiting for *you* to ask."

"All right," Leisha said, a little defiantly; there seemed to be a lot of defiance between them lately, for no good reason. She squared her shoulders. Her new breasts thrust forward. "I'm asking. How many of the Sleepless are there, who are they, and where are they?"

Camden said, "If you're using that term—'the Sleepless'— you've already done some reading on your own. So you probably know that there are 1,082 of you so far in the United States, a few more in foreign countries, most of them in major metropolitan areas. Seventy-nine are in Chicago, most of them still small children. Only nineteen anywhere are older than you."

Leisha didn't deny reading any of this. Camden leaned forward in his study chair to peer at her. Leisha wondered if he needed glasses. His hair was completely gray now, sparse and stiff, like lonely broomstraws. The *Wall Street Journal* listed him among the hundred richest men in America; *Women's Wear Daily* pointed out that he was the only billionaire in the country who did not move in the society of international parties, charity balls, and personal jets. Camden's jet ferried him to business meetings around the world, to the chairmanship of the Yagai Economics Institute, and to very little else. Over the years he had grown richer, more reclusive, and more cerebral. Leisha felt a rush of her old affection.

She threw herself sideways into a leather chair, her long slim legs dangling over the arm. Absently she scratched a mosquito bite on her thigh. "Well, then, I'd like to meet Richard Keller." He lived in Chicago and was the beta-test Sleepless closest to her own age. He was 17.

"Why ask me? Why not just go?"

Leisha thought there was a note of impatience in his voice. He liked her to explore things first, then report on them to him later. Both parts were important.

Leisha laughed. "You know what, Daddy? You're predictable."

Camden laughed, too. In the middle of the laugh Susan came in. "He certainly is not. Roger, what about that meeting in Buenos Aires Thursday? Is it on or off?." When he didn't answer, her voice grew shriller. "Roger? I'm talking to you!"

Leisha averted her eyes. Two years ago Susan had finally left genetic research to run Camden's house and schedule; before that she had tried hard to do both. Since she had left Biotech, it seemed to Leisha, Susan had changed. Her voice was tighter. She was more insistent that Cook and the gardener follow her directions exactly, without deviation. Her blonde braids had become stiff sculptured waves of platinum.

"It's on," Roger said.

"Well, thanks for at least answering. Am I going?"

"If you like."

"I like."

Susan left the room. Leisha rose and stretched. Her long legs rose on tiptoe. It felt good to reach, to stretch, to feel sunlight from the wide windows wash over her face. She smiled at her father, and found him watching her with an unexpected expression. "Leisha—"

"What?"

"See Keller. But be careful."

"Of what?"

But Camden wouldn't answer.

❖   ❖   ❖

The voice on the phone had been noncommittal. "Leisha Camden? Yes, I know who you are. Three o'clock on Thursday?" The house was modest, a thirty-year-old Colonial on a quiet suburban street where small children on bicycles could be watched from the front window. Few roofs had more than one Y-energy cell. The trees, huge old sugar maples, were beautiful.

"Come in," Richard Keller said.

He was no taller than she, stocky, with a bad case of acne. Probably no genetic alterations except sleep, Leisha guessed. He had thick dark hair, a low forehead, and bushy black brows. Before he closed the door Leisha saw his stare at her car and driver, parked in the driveway next to a rusty ten-speed bike.

"I can't drive yet," she said. "I'm still fifteen."

"It's easy to learn," Keller said. "So, you want to tell me why you're here?"

Leisha liked his directness. "To meet some other Sleepless."

"You mean you never have? Not any of us?"

"You mean the rest of you know each other?" She hadn't expected that.

"Come to my room, Leisha."

She followed him to the back of the house. No one else seemed to be home. His room was large and airy, filled with computers and filing cabinets. A rowing machine sat in one corner. It looked like a shabbier version of the room of any bright classmate at the Sauley School, except there was more space without a bed. She walked over to the computer screen.

"Hey—you working on Boesc equations?"

"On an application of them."

"To what?"

"Fish migration patterns."

Leisha smiled. "Yeah that would work. I never thought of that."

Keller seemed not to know what to do with her smile. He looked at the wall, then at her chin. "You interested in Gaea patterns? In the environment?"

"Well, no," Leisha confessed. "Not particularly. I'm going to study politics at Harvard. Pre-law. But of course we had Gaea patterns at school."

Keller's gaze finally came unstuck from her face. He ran a hand through his dark hair. "Sit down, if you want."

Leisha sat, looking appreciatively at the wall posters, shifting green on blue, like ocean currents. "I like those. Did you program them yourself?"

"You're not at all what I pictured," Keller said.

"How did you picture me?"

He didn't hesitate. "Stuck-up. Superior. Shallow, despite your IQ."

She was more hurt than she had expected to be.

Keller blurted, "You're the only one of the Sleepless who's really rich. But you already know that."

"No, I don't. I've never checked."

He took the chair beside her, stretching his stocky legs straight in front of him, in a slouch that had nothing to do with relaxation. "It makes sense, really. Rich people don't have their children genetically modified to be superior—they think any offspring of theirs is already superior. By their values. And poor people can't afford it. We Sleepless are upper-middle class, no more. Children of professors, scientists, people who value brains and time."

"My father values brains and time," Leisha said. "He's the biggest supporter of Kenzo Yagai."

"Oh, Leisha, do you think I don't already know that? Are you flashing me or what?"

Leisha said with great deliberateness, "I'm *talking* to you." But the next minute she could feel the hurt break through on her face.

"I'm sorry," Keller muttered. He shot off his chair and

paced to the computer, back. "I am sorry. But I don't . . .
I don't understand what you're doing here."

"I'm lonely," Leisha said, astonished at herself. She
looked up at him. "It's true. I'm lonely. I am. I have friends
and Daddy and Alice—but no one really knows, really
understands—what? I don't know what I'm saying."

Keller smiled. The smile changed his whole face, opened
up its dark planes to the light. "I do. Oh, do I. What do
you do when they say, 'I had such a dream last night!'?"

"Yes!" Leisha said. "But that's even really minor—it's
when I say 'I'll look that up for you tonight' and they get
that funny look on their face that means 'She'll do it while
I'm asleep.' "

"But that's even really minor," Keller said. "It's when
you're playing basketball in the gym after supper and then
you go to the diner for food and then you say 'Let's have
a walk by the lake' and they say 'I'm really tired. I'm going
home to bed now.' "

"But that's really minor," Leisha said, jumping up. "It's
when you really are absorbed by the movie and then you
get the point and it's so goddamn beautiful you leap up
and say 'Yes! Yes!' and Susan says 'Leisha, really—you'd
think nobody but you ever enjoyed anything before.' "

"Who's Susan?" Keller said.

The mood was broken. But not really; Leisha could say
"my stepmother" without much discomfort over what Susan
had promised to be and what she had become. Keller stood
inches from her, smiling that joyous smile, understanding,
and suddenly relief washed over Leisha so strong that she
walked straight into him and put her arms around his neck,
only tightening them when she felt his startled jerk. She
started to sob—she, Leisha, who never cried.

"Hey," Richard said. "Hey."

"Brilliant," Leisha said, laughing. "Brilliant remark."

She could feel his embarrassed smile. "Wanta see my
fish migration curves instead?"

"No," Leisha sobbed, and he went on holding her, patting her back awkwardly, telling her without words that she was home.

Camden waited up for her, although it was past midnight. He had been smoking heavily. Through the blue air he said quietly, "Did you have a good time, Leisha?"

"Yes."

"I'm glad," he said, and put out his last cigarette, and climbed the stairs—slowly, stiffly, he was nearly seventy now—to bed.

They went everywhere together for nearly a year: swimming, dancing, to the museums, the theater, the library. Richard introduced her to the others, a group of twelve kids between fourteen and nineteen, all of them intelligent and eager. All Sleepless.

Leisha learned.

Tony's parents, like her own, had divorced. But Tony, fourteen, lived with his mother, who had not particularly wanted a Sleepless child, while his father, who had, acquired a red hovercar and a young girlfriend who designed ergonomic chairs in Paris. Tony was not allowed to tell anyone—relatives, schoolmates—that he was Sleepless. "They'll think you're a freak," his mother said, eyes averted from her son's face. The one time Tony disobeyed her and told a friend that he never slept, his mother beat him. Then she moved the family to a new neighborhood. He was nine years old.

Jeanine, almost as long-legged and slim as Leisha, was training for the Olympics in ice skating. She practiced twelve hours a day, hours no Sleeper still in high school could ever have. So far the newspapers had not picked up the story. Jeanine was afraid that, if they did, they would somehow not let her compete.

Jack, like Leisha, would start college in September. Unlike Leisha, he had already started his career. The practice of law had to wait for law school; the practice of investment required only money. Jack didn't have much, but his precise financial analyses parlayed $600 saved from summer jobs to $3000 through stock-market investing, then to $10,000, and then he had enough to qualify for information-fund speculation. Jack was fifteen, not old enough to make legal investments; the transactions were all in the name of Kevin Baker, the oldest of the Sleepless, who lived in Austin. Jack told Leisha, "When I hit 84 per cent profit over two consecutive quarters, the data analysts logged onto me. They were just sniffing. Well, that's their job, even when the overall amounts are actually small. It's the patterns they care about. If they take the trouble to cross-reference data banks and come up with the fact that Kevin is a Sleepless, will they try to stop us from investing somehow?"

"That's paranoid," Leisha said.

"No, it's not," Jeanine said. "Leisha, you don't *know*."

"You mean because I've been protected by my father's money and caring," Leisha said. No one grimaced; all of them confronted ideas openly, without shadowy allusions. Without dreams.

"Yes," Jeanine said. "Your father sounds terrific. And he raised you to think that achievement should not be fettered—Jesus Christ, he's a Yagaiist. Well, good. We're glad for you." She said it without sarcasm. Leisha nodded. "But the world isn't always like that. They hate us."

"That's too strong," Carol said. "Not hate."

"Well, maybe," Jeanine said. "But they're different from us. We're better, and they naturally resent that."

"I don't see what's natural about it," Tony said. "Why shouldn't it be just as natural to admire what's better? We do. Does any one of us resent Kenzo Yagai for his genius? Or Nelson Wade, the physicist? Or Catherine Raduski?"

"We don't resent them because we *are* better," Richard said. "Q.E.D."

"What we should do is have our own society," Tony said.

"Why should we allow their regulations to restrict our natural, honest achievements? Why should Jeanine be barred from skating against them and Jack from investing on their same terms just because we're Sleepless? Some of them are brighter than others of them. Some have greater persistence. Well, we have greater concentration, more biochemical stability, and more time. All men are not created equal."

"Be fair, Jack—no one has been barred from anything yet," Jeanine said.

"But we will be."

"*Wait*," Leisha said. She was deeply troubled by the conversation. "I mean, yes, in many ways we're better. But you quoted out of context, Tony. The Declaration of Independence doesn't say all men are created equal in ability. It's talking about rights and power—it means that all are created equal *under the law*. We have no more right to a separate society or to being free of society's restrictions than anyone else does. There's no other way to freely trade one's efforts, unless the same contractual rules apply to all."

"Spoken like a true Yagaiist," Richard said, squeezing her hand.

"That's enough intellectual discussion for me," Carol said, laughing. "We've been at this for hours. We're at the beach, for Chrissake. Who wants to swim with me?"

"I do," Jeanine said. "Come on, Jack."

All of them rose, brushing sand off their suits, discarding sunglasses. Richard pulled Leisha to her feet. But just before they ran into the water, Tony put his skinny hand on her arm. "One more question, Leisha. Just to think about. If we achieve better than most other people, and we trade with the Sleepers when it's mutually beneficial, making no distinction there between the strong and the weak—what obligation do we have to those so weak they don't have anything to trade with us? We're already going to give more than we get—do we have to do it when we get nothing at all? Do we have to take care of their deformed and handicapped and sick and lazy and shiftless with the products of our work?"

"Do the Sleepers have to?" Leisha countered.

"Kenzo Yagai would say no. He's a Sleeper."

"He would say they would receive the benefits of contractual trade even if they aren't direct parties to the contract. The whole world is better-fed and healthier because of Y-energy."

"Come on!" Jeanine yelled. "Leisha, they're dunking me! Jack, you stop that! Leisha, help me!"

Leisha laughed. Just before she grabbed for Jeanine, she caught the look on Richard's face, on Tony's: Richard frankly lustful, Tony angry. At her. But why? What had she done, except argue in favor of dignity and trade?

Then Jack threw water on her, and Carol pushed Jack into the warm spray, and Richard was there with his arms around her, laughing.

When she got the water out of her eyes, Tony was gone.

Midnight. "Okay," Carol said. "Who's first?"

The six teenagers in the brambled clearing looked at each other. A lamp, kept on low for atmosphere, cast weird shadows across their faces and over their bare legs. Around the clearing Roger Camden's trees stood thick and dark, a wall between them and the closest of the estate's outbuildings. It was very hot. August air hung heavy, sullen. They had voted against bringing an air-conditioned Y-field because this was a return to the primitive, the dangerous; let it be primitive.

Six pairs of eyes stared at the glass in Carol's hand.

"Come *on*," she said. "Who wants to drink up?" Her voice was jaunty, theatrically hard. "It was difficult enough to get this."

"How *did* you get it?" said Richard, the group member—

except for Tony—with the least influential family contacts, the least money. "In a drinkable form like that?"

"My cousin Brian is a pharmaceutical supplier to the Biotech Institute. He's curious." Nods around the circle; except for Leisha, they were Sleepless precisely because they had relatives somehow connected to Biotech. And everyone was curious. The glass held interleukin-1, an immune system booster, one of many substances which as a side effect induced the brain to swift and deep sleep.

Leisha stared at the glass. A warm feeling crept through her lower belly, not unlike the feeling when she and Richard made love.

Tony said, "Give it to me!"

Carol did. "Remember—you only need a little sip."

Tony raised the glass to his mouth, stopped, looked at them over the rim from his fierce eyes. He drank.

Carol took back the glass. They all watched Tony. Within a minute he lay on the rough ground; within two, his eyes closed in sleep.

It wasn't like seeing parents sleep, siblings, friends. It was Tony. They looked away, didn't meet each other's eyes. Leisha felt the warmth between her legs tug and tingle, faintly obscene.

When it was her turn, she drank slowly, then passed the glass to Jeanine. Her head turned heavy, as if it were being stuffed with damp rags. The trees at the edge of the clearing blurred. The portable lamp blurred, too—it wasn't bright and clean anymore but squishy, blobby; if she touched it, it would smear. Then darkness swooped over her brain, taking it away: *Taking away her mind.* "Daddy!" She tried to call, to clutch for him, but then the darkness obliterated her.

Afterward, they all had headaches. Dragging themselves back through the woods in the thin morning light was torture, compounded by an odd shame. They didn't touch each other. Leisha walked as far away from Richard as she could. It was a whole day before the throbbing left the base of her skull, or the nausea her stomach.

There had not even been any dreams.

"I want you to come with me tonight," Leisha said, for the tenth or twelfth time. "We both leave for college in just two days; this is the last chance. I really want you to meet Richard."

Alice lay on her stomach across her bed. Her hair, brown and lusterless, fell around her face. She wore an expensive yellow jumpsuit, silk by Ann Patterson, which rucked up in wrinkles around her knees.

"Why? What do you care if I meet Richard or not?"

"Because you're my sister," Leisha said. She knew better than to say "my twin." Nothing got Alice angry faster.

"I don't want to." The next moment Alice's face changed. "Oh, I'm sorry, Leisha—I didn't mean to sound so snotty. But . . . but I don't want to."

"It won't be all of them. Just Richard. And just for an hour or so. Then you can come back here and pack for Northwestern."

"I'm not going to Northwestern."

Leisha stared at her.

Alice said, "I'm pregnant."

Leisha sat on the bed. Alice rolled onto her back, brushed the hair out of her eyes, and laughed. Leisha's ears closed against the sound. "Look at you," Alice said. "You'd think it was you who was pregnant. But you never would be, would you, Leisha? Not until it was the proper time. Not you."

"How?" Leisha said. "We both had our caps put in . . ."

"I had the cap removed," Alice said.

"You wanted to get pregnant?"

"Damn flash I did. And there's not a thing Daddy can do about it. Except, of course, cut off all credit completely, but I don't think he'll do that, do you?" She laughed again. "Even to me?"

"But Alice . . . why? Not just to anger Daddy!"

"No," Alice said. "Although you would think of that, wouldn't you? Because I want something to love. Something of my *own*. Something that has nothing to do with this house."

Leisha thought of her and Alice running through the conservatory, years ago, her and Alice darting in and out of the sunlight. "It hasn't been so bad growing up in this house."

"Leisha, you're stupid. I don't know how anyone so smart can be so stupid. Get out of my room! Get out!"

"But Alice . . . a *baby* . . ."

"Get out!" Alice shrieked. "Go to Harvard! Go be successful! Just get out!"

Leisha jerked off the bed. "Gladly! You're irrational, Alice! You don't think ahead, you don't plan, a *baby* . . ." But she could never sustain anger. It dribbled away, leaving her mind empty. She looked at Alice, who suddenly put out her arms. Leisha went into them.

"You're the baby," Alice said wonderingly. "You *are*. You're so . . . I don't know what. You're a baby."

Leisha said nothing. Alice's arms felt warm, felt whole, felt like two children running in and out of sunlight. "I'll help you, Alice. If Daddy won't."

Alice abruptly pushed her away. "I don't need your help."

Alice stood. Leisha rubbed her empty arms, fingertips scraping across opposite elbows. Alice kicked the empty, open trunk in which she was supposed to pack for Northwestern, and then abruptly smiled, a smile that made Leisha look away. She braced herself for more abuse. But what Alice said, very softly, was, "Have a good time at Harvard."

5

She loved it.

From the first sight of Massachusetts Hall, older than the United States by a half century, Leisha felt something that had been missing in Chicago: Age. Roots. Tradition. She touched the bricks of Widener Library, the glass cases in the Peabody Museum, as if they were the grail. She had never been particularly sensitive to myth or drama; the anguish of Juliet seemed to her artificial, that of Willy Loman merely wasteful. Only King Arthur, struggling to create a better social order, had interested her. But now, walking under the huge autumn trees, she suddenly caught a glimpse of a force that could span generations, fortunes left to endow learning and achievement the benefactors would never see, individual effort spanning and shaping centuries to come. She stopped, and looked at the sky through the leaves, at the buildings solid with purpose. At such moments she thought of Camden, bending the will of an entire genetic research Institute to create her in the image he wanted.

Within a month, she had forgotten all such mega-musings.

The work load was incredible, even for her. The Sauley School had encouraged individual exploration at her own pace; Harvard knew what it wanted from her, at its pace. In the last twenty years, under the academic leadership of a man who in his youth had watched Japanese economic domination with dismay, Harvard had become the controversial leader of a return to hard-edged learning of facts, theories, applications, problem-solving, intellectual efficiency. The school accepted one out of every two hundred applications from around the world. The daughter of England's Prime Minister had flunked out her first year and been sent home.

Leisha had a single room in a new dormitory, the dorm because she had spent so many years isolated in Chicago and was hungry for people, the single so she would not disturb anyone else when she worked all night. Her second day a boy from down the hall sauntered in and perched on the edge of her desk.

"So you're Leisha Camden."

"Yes."

"Sixteen years old."

"Almost seventeen."

"Going to out-perform us all, I understand, without even trying."

Leisha's smile faded. The boy stared at her from under lowered downy brows. He was smiling, his eyes sharp. From Richard and Tony and the others Leisha had learned to recognize the anger that presented itself as contempt.

"Yes," Leisha said coolly, "I am."

"Are you sure? With your pretty little-girl hair and your mutant little-girl brain?"

"Oh, leave her alone, Hannaway," said another voice. A tall blond boy, so thin his ribs looked like ripples in brown sand, stood in jeans and bare feet, drying his wet hair. "Don't you ever get tired of walking around being an asshole?"

"Do you?" Hannaway said. He heaved himself off the desk and started toward the door. The blond moved out of his way. Leisha moved into it.

"The reason I'm going to do better than you," she said evenly, "is because I have certain advantages you don't. Including sleeplessness. And then after I 'out-perform' you, I'll be glad to help you study for your tests so that you call pass, too."

The blond, drying his ears, laughed. But Hannaway stood still, and into his eyes came an expression that made Leisha back away. He pushed past her and stormed out.

"Nice going, Camden," the blond said. "He deserved that."

"But I meant it," Leisha said. "I will help him study."

The blond lowered his towel and stared. "You did, didn't you? You meant it."

"Yes! Why does everybody keep questioning that?"

"Well," the boy said, "I don't. You can help me if I get into trouble." Suddenly he smiled. "But I won't."

"Why not?"

"Because I'm just as good at anything as you are, Leisha Camden."

She studied him. "You're not one of us. Not Sleepless."

"Don't have to be. I know what I can do. Do, be, create, trade."

She said, delighted, "You're a Yagaiist!"

"Of course." He held out his hand. "Stewart Sutter. How about a fish-burger in the Yard?"

"Great," Leisha said. They walked out together, talking excitedly. When people stared at her, she tried not to notice. She was here. At Harvard. With space ahead of her, time to learn, and with people like Stewart Sutter who accepted and challenged her.

All the hours he was awake.

She became totally absorbed in her classwork. Roger Camden drove up once, walking the campus with her, listening, smiling. He was more at home than Leisha would have expected: He knew Stewart Sutter's father, Kate Addams' grandfather. They talked about Harvard, business, Harvard, the Yagai Economics Institute, Harvard. "How's Alice?" Leisha asked once, but Camden said that he didn't know, she had moved out and did not want to see him. He made her an allowance through his attorney. While he said this, his face remained serene.

Leisha went to the Homecoming Ball with Stewart, who was also majoring in pre-law but was two years ahead of

Leisha. She took a weekend trip to Paris with Kate Addams and two other girlfriends, taking the Concorde III. She had a fight with Stewart over whether the metaphor of superconductivity could apply to Yagaiism, a stupid fight they both knew was stupid but had anyway, and afterward they became lovers. After the fumbling sexual explorations with Richard, Stewart was deft, experienced, smiling faintly as he taught her how to have an orgasm both by herself and with him. Leisha was dazzled. "It's so *joyful*," she said, and Stewart looked at her with a tenderness she knew was part disturbance but didn't know why.

At mid-semester she had the highest grades in the freshman class. She got every answer right on every single question on her mid-terms. She and Stewart went out for a beer to celebrate, and when they came back Leisha's room had been destroyed. The computer was smashed, the data banks wiped, hardcopies and books smoldered in a metal wastebasket. Her clothes were ripped to pieces, her desk and bureau hacked apart. The only thing untouched, pristine, was the bed.

Stewart said, "There's no way this could have been done in silence. Everyone on the floor—hell, on the floor *below*—had to know. Someone will talk to the police." No one did. Leisha sat on the edge of the bed, dazed, and looked at the remnants of her Homecoming gown. The next day Dave Hannaway gave her a long, wide smile.

Camden flew east again, taut with rage. He rented her an apartment in Cambridge with E-lock security and a bodyguard named Toshio. After he left, Leisha fired the bodyguard but kept the apartment. It gave her and Stewart more privacy, which they used to endlessly discuss the situation. It was Leisha who argued that it was an aberration, an immaturity.

"There have always been haters, Stewart. Hate Jews, hate Blacks, hate immigrants, hate Yagaiists who have more initiative and dignity than you do. I'm just the latest object of hatred. It's not new, it's not remarkable. It doesn't mean any basic kind of schism between the Sleepless and Sleepers."

Stewart sat up in bed and reached for the sandwiches on the night stand. "Doesn't it? Leisha, you're a different kind of person entirely. More evolutionarily fit, not only to survive but to prevail. Those other 'objects of hatred' you cite, except Yagaiists—they were all powerless in their societies. They occupied *inferior* positions. You, on the other hand—all three Sleepless in Harvard Law are on the *Law Review*. All of them. Kevin Baker, your oldest, has already founded a successful bio-interface software firm and is making money, a lot of it. Every Sleepless is making superb grades, none have psychological problems, all are healthy—and most of you aren't even adults yet. How much hatred do you think you're going to encounter once you hit the big-stakes world of finance and business and scarce endowed chairs and national politics?"

"Give me a sandwich," Leisha said. "Here's my evidence you're wrong: You yourself. Kenzo Yagai. Kate Addams. Professor Lane. My father. Every Sleeper who inhabits the world of fair trade, mutually beneficial contracts. And that's most of you, or at least most of you who are worth considering. You believe that competition among the most capable leads to the most beneficial trades for everyone, strong and weak. Sleepless are making real and concrete contributions to society, in a lot of fields. That has to outweigh the discomfort we cause. We're *valuable* to you. You know that."

Stewart brushed crumbs off the sheets. "Yes. I do. Yagaiists do."

"Yagaiists run the business and financial and academic worlds. Or they will. In a meritocracy, they *should*. You underestimate the majority of people, Stew. Ethics aren't confined to the ones out front."

"I hope you're right," Stewart said. "Because, you know, I'm in love with you."

Leisha put down her sandwich.

"Joy," Stewart mumbled into her breasts, "you are joy."

When Leisha went home for Thanksgiving, she told Richard about Stewart. He listened, tight-lipped.

"A Sleeper."

"A *person*," Leisha said. "A good, intelligent, achieving person!"

"Do you know what your good intelligent achieving Sleepers have done, Leisha? Jeanine has been barred from Olympic skating. 'Genetic alteration, analogous to steroid abuse to create an unsportsmanlike advantage.' Chris Devereaux's left Stanford. They trashed his laboratory, destroyed two years' work in memory formation proteins. Kevin Baker's software company is fighting a nasty advertising campaign, all underground of course, about kids using software designed by 'non-human minds.' Corruption, mental slavery, satanic influences: the whole bag of witch-hunt tricks. Wake up, Leisha!"

They both heard his words. Moments dragged by. Richard stood like a boxer, forward on the balls of his feet, teeth clenched. Finally he said, very quietly, "Do you love him?"

"Yes," Leisha said. "I'm sorry."

"Your choice," Richard said coldly. "What do you do while he's asleep? Watch?"

"You make it sound like a perversion!"

Richard said nothing. Leisha drew a deep breath. She spoke rapidly but calmly, a controlled rush: "While Stewart is asleep I work. The same as you do. Richard—don't do this. I didn't mean to hurt you. And I don't want to lose the group. I believe the Sleepers are the same species as we are—are you going to punish me for that? Are you going to *add* to the hatred? Are you going to tell me that I can't belong to a wider world that includes all honest, worthwhile people whether they sleep or not? Are you going to tell me that the most important division is by genetics and not by economic spirituality? Are you going to force me into an artificial choice, 'us' or 'them'?"

Richard picked up a bracelet. Leisha recognized it: She had given it to him in the summer. His voice was quiet. "No. It's not a choice. He played with the gold links a minute, then looked up at her. "Not yet."

By spring break, Camden walked more slowly. He took medicine for his blood pressure, his heart. He and Susan, he told Leisha, were getting a divorce. "She changed, Leisha, after I married her. You saw that. She was independent and productive and happy, and then after a few years she stopped all that and became a shrew. A whining shrew." He shook his head in genuine bewilderment. "You saw the change."

Leisha had. A memory came to her: Susan leading her and Alice in "games" that were actually controlled cerebral-performance tests, Susan's braids dancing around her sparkling eyes. Alice had loved Susan, then, as much as Leisha had.

"Dad, I want Alice's address."

"I told you up at Harvard, I don't have it," Camden said. He shifted in his chair, the impatient gesture of a body that never expected to wear out. In January Kenzo Yagai had died of pancreatic cancer; Camden had taken the news hard. "I make her allowance through an attorney. By her choice."

"Then I want the address of the attorney."

The attorney, however, refused to tell Leisha where Alice was. "She doesn't want to be found, Ms. Camden. She wanted a complete break."

"Not from me," Leisha said.

"Yes," the attorney said, and something flickered behind his eyes, something she had last seen in Dave Hannaway's face.

She flew to Austin before returning to Boston, making her a day late for classes. Kevin Baker saw her instantly, canceling a meeting with IBM. She told him what she needed, and he set his best data-net people on it, without telling them why. Within two hours she had Alice's address from the attorney's electronic files. It was the first time, she realized, that she had ever turned to one of the Sleepless for help, and it had been given instantly. Without trade.

Alice was in Pennsylvania. The next weekend Leisha rented a hovercar and driver—she had learned to drive, but only groundcars as yet—and went to High Ridge, in the Appalachian Mountains.

It was an isolated hamlet, twenty-five miles from the nearest hospital. Alice lived with a man named Ed, a silent carpenter twenty years older than she, in a cabin in the woods. The cabin had water and electricity but no news net. In the early spring light the earth was raw and bare, slashed with icy gullies. Alice and Ed apparently worked at nothing. Alice was eight months pregnant.

"I didn't want you here," she said to Leisha. "So why are you?"

"Because you're my sister."

"God, look at you. Is that what they're wearing at Harvard? Boots like that? When did you become fashionable, Leisha? You were always too busy being intellectual to care."

"What's this all about, Alice? Why here? What are you doing?"

"Living," Alice said. "Away from dear Daddy, away from Chicago, away from drunken broken Susan—did you know she drinks? Just like Mom. He does that to people. But not to me. I got out. I wonder if you ever will."

"Got out? To this?"

"I'm happy," Alice said angrily. "Isn't that what it's supposed to be about? Isn't that the aim of your great

Kenzo Yagai—happiness through individual effort?"

Leisha thought of saying that Alice was making no efforts that she could see. She didn't say it. A chicken ran through the yard of the cabin. Behind, the mountains rose in layers of blue haze. Leisha thought what this place must have been like in winter: cut off from the world where people strived towards goals, learned, changed.

"I'm glad you're happy, Alice."

"Are you?"

"Yes."

"Then I'm glad, too," Alice said, almost defiantly. The next moment she abruptly hugged Leisha, fiercely, the huge hard mound of her belly crushed between them. Alice's hair smelled sweet, like fresh grass in sunlight.

"I'll come see you again, Alice."

"Don't," Alice said.

6

SLEEPLESS MUTIÉ BEGS FOR REVERSAL OF GENE TAMPERING, screamed the headline in the Food Mart. "PLEASE LET ME SLEEP LIKE REAL PEOPLE!" CHILD PLEADS.

Leisha typed in her credit number and pressed the news kiosk for a printout, although ordinarily she ignored the electronic tabloids. The headline went on circling the kiosk. A Food Mart employee stopped stacking boxes on shelves and watched her. Bruce, Leisha's bodyguard, watched the employee.

She was twenty-two, in her final year at Harvard Law, editor of the *Law Review*, ranked first in her class. The next three were Jonathan Cocchiara, Len Carter, and Martha Wentz. All Sleepless.

In her apartment she skimmed the print-out. Then she

accessed the Groupnet run from Austin. The files had more news stories about the child, with comments from other Sleepless, but before she could call them up Kevin Baker came on-line himself, on voice.

"Leisha. I'm glad you called. I was going to call you."

"What's the situation with this Stella Bevington, Kev? Has anybody checked it out?"

"Randy Davies. He's from Chicago but I don't think you've met him, he's still in high school. He's in Park Ridge, Stella's in Skokie. Her parents wouldn't talk to him—were pretty abusive, in fact—but he got to see Stella face-to-face anyway. It doesn't look like an abuse case, just the usual stupidity: parents wanted a genius child, scrimped and saved, and now they can't handle that she is one. They scream at her to sleep, get emotionally abusive when she contradicts them, but so far no violence."

"Is the emotional abuse actionable?"

"I don't think we want to move on it yet. Two of us will keep in close touch with Stella—she does have a modem, and she hasn't told her parents about the net—and Randy will drive out weekly."

Leisha bit her lip. "A tabloid shitpiece said she's seven years old."

"Yes."

"Maybe she shouldn't be left there. I'm an Illinois resident, I can file an abuse grievance from here if Candy's got too much in her briefcase . . . ."

Seven years old.

"No. Let it sit a while. Stella will probably be all right. You know that."

She did. Nearly all of the Sleepless stayed "all right," no matter how much opposition came from the stupid segment of society. And it was only the stupid segment, Leisha argued, a small if vocal minority. Most people could, and would, adjust to the growing presence of the Sleepless, when it became clear that that presence included not only growing power but growing benefits to the country as a whole.

Kevin Baker, now twenty-six, had made a fortune in micro-chips so revolutionary that Artificial Intelligence, once a debated dream, was yearly closer to reality. Carolyn Rizzolo had won the Pulitzer Prize in drama for her play *Morning Light*. She was twenty-four. Jeremy Robinson had done significant work in superconductivity applications while still a graduate student at Stanford. William Thaine, *Law Review* editor when Leisha first came to Harvard, was now in private practice. He had never lost a case. He was twenty-six, and the cases were becoming important. His clients valued his ability more than his age.

But not everyone reacted that way.

Kevin Baker and Richard Keller had started the datanet that bound the Sleepless into a tight group, constantly aware of each other's personal fights. Leisha Camden financed the legal battles, the educational costs of Sleepless whose parents were unable to meet them, the support of children in emotionally bad situations. Rhonda Lavelier got herself licensed as a foster mother in California, and whenever possible the Group maneuvered to have small Sleepless who were removed from their homes assigned to Rhonda. The Group now had three ABA lawyers; within the next year they would gain four more, licensed to practice in five different states.

The one time they had not been able to remove an abused Sleepless child legally, they kidnapped him.

Timmy DeMarzo, four years old. Leisha had been opposed to the action. She had argued the case morally and pragmatically—to her they were the same thing—thus: If they believed in their society, in its fundamental laws and in their ability to belong to it as free-trading productive individuals, they must remain bound by the society's contractual laws. The Sleepless were, for the most part, Yagaiists. They should already know this. And if the FBI caught them, the courts and press would crucify them.

They were not caught.

Timmy DeMarzo—not even old enough to call for help on the datanet, they had learned of the situation through the automatic police-record scan Kevin maintained through his company—was stolen from his own backyard in Wichita. He had lived the last year in an isolated trailer in North Dakota; no place was too isolated for a modem. He was cared for by a legally irreproachable foster mother who had lived there all her life. The foster mother was second cousin to a Sleepless, a broad cheerful woman with a much better brain than her appearance indicated. She was a Yagaiist. No record of the child's existence appeared in any data bank: not the IRS, not any school's, not even the local grocery store's computerized check-out slips. Food specifically for the child was shipped in monthly on a truck owned by a Sleepless in State College, Pennsylvania. Ten of the Group knew about the kidnapping, out of the total 3,428 born in the United States. Of that total, 2,691 were part of the Group via the net. Another 701 were as yet too young to use a modem. Only 36 Sleepless, for whatever reason, were not part of the Group.

The kidnapping had been arranged by Tony Indivino.

"It's Tony I wanted to talk to you about," Kevin said to Leisha. "He's started again. This time he means it. He's buying land."

She folded the tabloid very small and laid it carefully on the table. "Where?"

"Allegheny Mountains. In southern New York State. A lot of land. He's putting in the roads now. In the spring, the first buildings."

"Jennifer Sharifi still financing it?" She was the American-born daughter of an Arab prince who had wanted a Sleepless child. The prince was dead and Jennifer, dark-eyed and multilingual, was richer than Leisha would one day be.

"Yes. He's starting to get a following, Leisha."

"I know."

"Call him."

"I will. Keep me informed about Stella."

She worked until midnight at the *Law Review*, then until four A.M. preparing her classes. From four to five she handled legal matters for the Group. At five A.M. she called Tony, still in Chicago. He had finished high school, done one semester at Northwestern, and at Christmas vacation he had finally exploded at his mother for forcing him to live as a Sleeper. The explosion, it seemed to Leisha, had never ended.

"Tony? Leisha."

"The answers are yes, yes, no, and go to hell."

Leisha gritted her teeth. "Fine. Now tell me the questions."

"Are you really serious about the Sleepless withdrawing into their own self-sufficient society? Is Jennifer Sharifi willing to finance a project the size of building a small city? Don't you think that's a cheat of all that can be accomplished by patient integration of the Group into the mainstream? And what about the contradictions of living in an armed restricted city and still trading with the Outside?"

"I would never tell you to go to hell."

"Hooray for you," Tony said. After a moment he added, "I'm sorry. That sounds like one of them."

"It's wrong for us, Tony."

"Thanks for not saying I couldn't pull it off."

She wondered if he could. "We're not a separate species, Tony."

"Tell that to the Sleepers."

"You exaggerate. There are haters out there, there are always haters, but to give up . . ."

"We're not giving up. Whatever we create can be freely traded: software, hardware, novels, information, theories, legal counsel. We can travel in and out. But we'll have a safe place to return to. Without the leeches who think we owe them blood because we're better than they are."

"It isn't a matter of owing."

"Really?" Tony said. "Let's have this out, Leisha. All the way. You're a Yagaiist—what do you believe in?"

"Tony . . ."

"*Do it*," Tony said, and in his voice she heard the fourteen-year-old Richard had introduced her to. Simultaneously, she saw her father's face: not as he was now, since the by-pass, but as he had been when she was a little girl, holding her on his lap to explain that she was special.

"I believe in voluntary trade that is mutually beneficial. That spiritual dignity comes from supporting one's life through one's own efforts, and trading the results of those efforts in mutual cooperation throughout the society. That the symbol of this is the contract. And that we need each other for the fullest, most beneficial trade."

"Fine," Tony bit off. "Now what about the beggars in Spain?"

"The what?"

"You walk down a street in a poor country like Spain and you see a beggar. Do you give him a dollar?"

"Probably."

"Why? He's trading nothing with you. He has nothing to trade."

"I know. Out of kindness. Compassion."

"You see six beggars. Do you give them all a dollar?"

"Probably," Leisha said.

"You would. You see a hundred beggars and you haven't got Leisha Camden's money—do you give them each a dollar?"

"No."

"Why not?"

Leisha reached for patience. Few people could make her want to cut off a comm link; Tony was one of them. "Too draining on my own resources. My life has first claim on the resources I earn."

"All right. Now consider this. At Biotech Institute—where you and I began, dear pseudo-sister—Dr. Melling has just yesterday—"

"*Who?*"

"Dr. Susan Melling. Oh, God, I completely forgot—she used to be married to your father!"

"I lost track of her," Leisha said. "I didn't realize she'd gone back to research. Alice once said . . . never mind. What's going on at Biotech?"

"Two crucial items, just released. Carla Dutcher has had first-month fetal genetic analysis, Sleeplessness is a dominant gene. The next generation of the Group won't sleep either."

"We all knew that," Leisha said. Carla Dutcher was the world's first pregnant Sleepless. Her husband was a Sleeper. "The whole world expected that."

"But the press will have a windfall with it anyway. Just watch. Muties Breed! New Race Set To Dominate Next Generation of Children!"

Leisha didn't deny it. "And the second item?"

"It's sad, Leisha. We've just had our first death."

Her stomach tightened. "Who?"

"Bernie Kuhn. Seattle." She didn't know him. "A car accident. It looks pretty straightforward—he lost control on a steep curve when his brakes failed. He had only been driving a few months. He was seventeen. But the significance here is that his parents have donated his brain and body to Biotech, in conjunction with the pathology department at the Chicago Medical School. They're going to take him apart to get the first good look at what prolonged sleeplessness does to the body and brain."

"They should," Leisha said. "That poor kid. But what are you so afraid they'll find?"

"I don't know. I'm not a doctor. But whatever it is, if the haters can use it against us, they will."

"You're paranoid, Tony."

"Impossible. The Sleepless have personalities calmer and more reality-oriented than the norm. Don't you read the literature?"

"Tony—"

"What if you walk down that street in Spain and a hundred beggars each want a dollar and you say no and they have nothing to trade you but they're so rotten with anger about what you have that they knock you down and grab it and then beat you out of sheer envy and despair?"

Leisha didn't answer.

"Are you going to say that's not a human scenario, Leisha? That it never happens?"

"It happens," Leisha said evenly. "But not all that often."

"Bullshit. Read more history. Read more *newspapers*. But the point is: What do you owe the beggars then? What does a good Yagaiist who believes in mutually beneficial contracts do with people who have nothing to trade and can only take?"

"You're not—"

"*What*, Leisha? In the most objective terms you can manage, what do we owe the grasping and non-productive needy?"

"What I said originally. Kindness. Compassion."

"Even if they don't trade it back? Why?"

"Because . . ." She stopped.

"Why? Why do law-abiding and productive human beings owe anything to those who neither produce very much nor abide by laws? What philosophical or economic or spiritual justification is there for owing them anything? Be as honest as I know you are."

Leisha put her head between her knees. The question gaped beneath her, but she didn't try to evade it. "I don't know. I just know we do."

"*Why?*"

She didn't answer. After a moment, Tony did. The intellectual challenge was gone from his voice. He said, almost tenderly, "Come down in the spring and see the site for Sanctuary. The buildings will be going up then."

"No," Leisha said.

"I'd like you to."

"No. Armed retreat is not the way."

Tony said, "The beggars are getting nastier, Leisha. As the Sleepless grow richer. And I don't mean in money."

"Tony—" she said, and stopped. She couldn't think what to say.

"Don't walk down too many streets armed with just the memory of Kenzo Yagai."

In March, a bitterly cold March of winds whipping down the Charles River, Richard Keller came to Cambridge. Leisha had not seen him for four years. He didn't send her word on the Groupnet that he was coming. She hurried up the walk to her townhouse, muffled to the eyes in a red wool scarf against the snowy cold, and he stood there blocking the doorway. Behind Leisha, her bodyguard tensed.

"Richard! Bruce, it's all right, this is an old friend."

"Hello, Leisha."

He was heavier, sturdier-looking, with a breadth of shoulder she didn't recognize. But the face was Richard's, older but unchanged: dark low brows, unruly dark hair. He had grown a beard.

"You look beautiful," he said.

She handed him a cup of coffee. "Are you here on business?" From the Groupnet she knew that he had finished his Master's and had done outstanding work in marine biology in the Caribbean, but had left that a year ago and disappeared from the net.

"No. Pleasure." He smiled suddenly, the old smile that opened up his dark face. "I almost forgot about that for a long time. Contentment, yes, we're all good at the contentment that comes from sustained work, but pleasure? Whim? Caprice? When was the last time you did something silly, Leisha?"

She smiled. "I ate cotton candy in the shower."

"Really? Why?"

"To see if it would dissolve in gooey pink patterns."

"Did it?"

"Yes. Lovely ones."

"And that was your last silly thing? When was it?"

"Last summer," Leisha said, and laughed.

"Well, mine is sooner than that. It's now. I'm in Boston for no other reason than the spontaneous pleasure of seeing you."

Leisha stopped laughing. "That's an intense tone for a spontaneous pleasure, Richard."

"Yup," he said, intensely. She laughed again. He didn't.

"I've been in India, Leisha. And China and Africa. Thinking, mostly. Watching. First I traveled like a Sleeper, attracting no attention. Then I set out to meet the Sleepless in India and China. There are a few, you know, whose parents were willing to come here for the operation. They pretty much are accepted and left alone. I tried to figure out why desperately poor countries—by our standards anyway; over there Y-energy is mostly available only in big cities—don't have any trouble accepting the superiority of Sleepless, whereas Americans, with more prosperity than any time in history, build in resentment more and more."

Leisha said, "Did you figure it out?"

"No. But I figured out something else, watching all those communes and villages and kampongs. We are too individualistic."

Disappointment swept Leisha. She saw her father's face: *Excellence is what counts, Leisha. Excellence supported by individual effort. . . .* She reached for Richard's cup. "More coffee?"

He caught her wrist and looked up into her face. "Don't

misunderstand me, Leisha. I'm not talking about work. We are too much individuals in the rest of our lives. Too emotionally rational. Too much alone. Isolation kills more than the free flow of ideas. It kills joy."

He didn't let go of her wrist. She looked down into his eyes, into depths she hadn't seen before: It was the feeling of looking into a mine shaft, both giddy and frightening, knowing that at the bottom might be gold or darkness. Or both.

Richard said softly, "Stewart?"

"Over long ago. An undergraduate thing." Her voice didn't sound like her own.

"Kevin?"

"No, never—we're just friends."

"I wasn't sure. Anyone?"

"No."

He let go of her wrist. Leisha peered at him timidly. He suddenly laughed. "Joy, Leisha." An echo sounded in her mind, but she couldn't place it and then it was gone and she laughed too, a laugh airy and frothy as pink cotton candy in summer.

"Come home, Leisha. He's had another heart attack."

Susan Melling's voice on the phone was tired. Leisha said, "How bad?"

"The doctors aren't sure. Or say they're not sure. He wants to see you. Can you leave your studies?"

It was May, the last push toward her finals. The *Law Review* proofs were behind schedule. Richard had started a new business, marine consulting to Boston fishermen plagued with sudden inexplicable shifts in ocean currents, and was working twenty hours a day. "I'll come," Leisha said.

Chicago was colder than Boston. The trees were half-budded. On Lake Michigan, filling the huge east windows of her father's house, whitecaps tossed up cold spray.

Leisha saw that Susan was living in the house: her brushes on Camden's dresser, her journals on the credenza in the foyer.

"Leisha," Camden said. He looked old. Gray skin, sunken cheeks, the fretful and bewildered look of men who accepted potency like air, indivisible from their lives. In the corner of the room, on a small eighteenth-century slipper chair, sat a short, stocky woman with brown braids.

"*Alice.*"

"Hello, Leisha."

"*Alice.* I've looked for you. . . ." The wrong thing to say. Leisha had looked, but not very hard, deterred by the knowledge that Alice had not wanted to be found. "How are you?"

"I'm fine," Alice said. She seemed remote, gentle, unlike the angry Alice of six years ago in the raw Pennsylvania hills. Camden moved painfully on the bed. He looked at Leisha with eyes which, she saw, were undimmed in their blue brightness.

"I asked Alice to come. And Susan. Susan came a while ago. I'm dying, Leisha."

No one contradicted him. Leisha, knowing his respect for facts, remained silent. Love hurt her chest.

"John Jaworski has my will, None of you can break it. But I wanted to tell you myself what's in it. The last few years I've been selling, liquidating. Most of my holdings are accessible now. I've left a tenth to Alice, a tenth to Susan, a tenth to Elizabeth, and the rest to you, Leisha, because you're the only one with the individual ability to use the money to its full potential for achievement."

Leisha looked wildly at Alice, who gazed back with her strange remote calm. "Elizabeth? My . . . mother? Is alive?"

"Yes," Camden said.

"You told me she was dead! Years and years ago!"

"Yes. I thought it was better for you that way. She didn't like what you were, was jealous of what you could become.

And she had nothing to give you. She would only have caused you emotional harm."

Beggars in Spain . . .

"That was wrong, Dad. You were wrong. She's my *mother* . . ." She couldn't finish the sentence.

Camden didn't flinch. "I don't think I was. But you're an adult now. You can see her if you wish."

He went on looking at her from his bright, sunken eyes, while around Leisha the air heaved and snapped. Her father had lied to her. Susan watched her closely, a small smile on her lips. Was she glad to see Camden fall in his daughter's estimation? Had she all along been that jealous of their relationship, of Leisha . . .

She was thinking like Tony.

The thought steadied her a little. But she went on staring at Camden, who went on staring implacably back, unbudged, a man positive even on his death bed that he was right.

Alice's hand was on her elbow, Alice's voice so soft that no one but Leisha could hear. "He's done now, Leisha. And after a while you'll be all right."

Alice had left her son in California with her husband of two years, Beck Watrous, a building contractor she had met while waitressing in a resort on the Artificial Islands. Beck had adopted Jordan, Alice's son.

"Before Beck there was a real bad time," Alice said in her remote voice. "You know, when I was carrying Jordan I actually used to dream that he would be Sleepless? Like you. Every night I'd dream that, and every morning I'd wake up and have morning sickness with a baby that was only going to be a stupid nothing like me. I stayed with Ed in Pennsylvania, remember? You came to see me there once—for two more years. When he beat me, I was glad. I wished Daddy could see. At least Ed was touching me."

Leisha made a sound in her throat.

"I finally left because I was afraid for Jordan. I went to California, did nothing but eat for a year. I got up to 190 pounds." Alice was, Leisha estimated, five-foot-four. "Then I came home to see Mother."

"You didn't tell me," Leisha said "You knew she was alive and you didn't tell me."

"She's in a drying-out tank half the time," Alice said, with brutal simplicity. "She wouldn't see you if you wanted to. But she saw me, and she fell slobbering all over me as her 'real' daughter, and she threw up on my dress. And I backed away from her and looked at the dress and knew it *should* be thrown up on, it was so ugly. Deliberately ugly. She started screaming how Dad had ruined her life, ruined mine, all for you. And do you know what I did?"

"What?" Leisha said. Her voice was shaky.

"I flew home, burned all my clothes, got a job, started college, lost fifty pounds, and put Jordan in play therapy."

The sisters sat silent. Beyond the window the lake was dark, unlit by moon or stars. It was Leisha who suddenly shook, and Alice who patted her shoulder.

"Tell me . . ." Leisha couldn't think what she wanted to be told, except that she wanted to hear Alice's voice in the gloom, Alice's voice as it was now, gentle and remote, without damage any more from the damaging fact of Leisha's existence. Her very existence as damage. ". . . tell me about Jordan. He's five now? What's he like?"

Alice turned her head to look levelly into Leisha's eyes. "He's a happy, ordinary little boy. Completely ordinary."

Camden died a week later. After the funeral, Leisha tried to see her mother at the Brookfield Drug and Alcohol Abuse Center. Elizabeth Camden, she was told, saw no one except her only child, Alice Camden Watrous.

Susan Melling, dressed in black, drove Leisha to the airport. Susan talked deftly, determinedly, about Leisha's studies, about Harvard, about the *Review*. Leisha answered in monosyllables but Susan persisted, asking questions, quietly insisting on answers: When would Leisha take her bar exams? Where was she interviewing for jobs? Gradually Leisha began to lose the numbness she had felt since her father's casket was lowered into the ground. She realized that Susan's persistent questioning was a kindness.

"He sacrificed a lot of people," Leisha said suddenly.

"Not me," Susan said. She pulled the car into the airport parking lot. "Only for a while there, when I gave up my work to do his. Roger didn't respect sacrifice much."

"Was he wrong?" Leisha said. The question came out with a kind of desperation she hadn't intended.

Susan smiled sadly. "No. He wasn't wrong. I should never have left my research. It took me a long time to come back to myself after that."

He does that to people, Leisha heard inside her head. Susan? Or Alice? She couldn't, for once, remember clearly. She saw her father in the old conservatory, potting and repotting the dramatic exotic flowers he had loved.

She was tired. It was muscle fatigue from stress, she knew; twenty minutes of rest would restore her. Her eyes burned from unaccustomed tears. She leaned her head back against the car seat and closed them.

Susan pulled the car into the airport parking lot and turned off the ignition. "There's something I want to tell you, Leisha."

Leisha opened her eyes. "About the will?"

Susan smiled tightly. "No. You really don't have any problems with how he divided the estate, do you? It seems to you reasonable. But that's not it. The research team from Biotech and Chicago Medical has finished its analysis of Bernie Kuhn's brain."

Leisha turned to face Susan. She was startled by the complexity of Susan's expression. Determination, and satisfaction, and anger, and something else Leisha could not name.

Susan said, "We're going to publish next week, in the *New England Journal of Medicine*. Security has been unbelievably restricted—no leaks to the popular press. But I want to tell you now, myself, what we found. So you'll be prepared."

"Go on," Leisha said. Her chest felt tight.

"Do you remember when you and the other Sleepless kids took interleukin-1 to see what sleep was like? When you were sixteen?"

"How did you know about that?"

"You kids were watched a lot more closely than you think. Remember the headache you got?"

"Yes." She and Richard and Tony and Carol and Jeanine . . . after her rejection by the Olympic Committee, Jeanine had never skated again. She was a kindergarten teacher in Butte, Montana.

"Interleukin-1 is what I want to talk about. At least partly. It's one of a whole group of substances that boost the immune system. They stimulate the production of antibodies, the activity of white blood cells, and a host of other immunoenhancements. Normal people have surges of IL-1 released during the slow-wave phases of sleep. That means that they—we—are getting boosts to the immune system during sleep. One of the questions we researchers asked ourselves twenty-eight years ago was: Will Sleepless kids who don't get those surges of IL-1 get sick more often?"

"I've never been sick," Leisha said.

"Yes, you have. Chicken pox and three minor colds by the end of your fourth year," Susan said precisely. "But in general you were all a very healthy lot. So we researchers were left with the alternate theory of sleep-driven immunoenhancement: that the burst of immune activity existed as a counterpart to a greater vulnerability of the body in sleep to disease, probably in some way connected to the fluctuations in body temperature during REM sleep. In other words, sleep caused the immune vulnerability that endogenous pyrogens like IL-1 counteract. Sleep was the problem, immune system enhancements were the solution. Without sleep, there would be no problem. Are you following this?"

"Yes."

"Of course you are. Stupid question." Susan brushed her hair off her face. It was going gray at the temples. There was a tiny brown age spot beneath her right ear.

"Over the years we collected thousands—maybe hundreds of thousands—of Single Photon Emission Tomography scans of you and the other kids' brains, plus endless EEG's, samples of cerebrospinal fluid, and all the rest of it. But we couldn't really see inside your brains, really know what's going on in there. Until Bernie Kuhn hit that embankment."

"Susan," Leisha said, "give it to me straight. Without more build-up."

"You're not going to age."

"What?"

"Oh, cosmetically, yes. Gray hair, wrinkles, sags. But the absence of sleep peptides and all the rest of it affects the immune and tissue-restoration systems in ways we don't understand. Bernie Kuhn had a perfect liver. Perfect lungs, perfect heart, perfect lymph nodes, perfect pancreas, perfect medulla oblongata. Not just healthy, or young—*perfect*. There's a tissue regeneration enhancement that clearly derives from the operation of the immune system but is radically different from anything we ever suspected. Organs show no wear and tear—not even the minimal amount expected in a seventeen-year-old. They just repair themselves, perfectly, on and on . . . and on."

"For how long?" Leisha whispered.

"Who the hell knows? Bernie Kuhn was young—maybe there's some compensatory mechanism that cuts in at some point and you'll all just collapse, like an entire fucking gallery of Dorian Grays. But I don't think so. Neither do I think it can go on forever; no tissue regeneration can do that. But a long, long time."

Leisha stared at the blurred reflections in the car windshield. She saw her father's face against the blue satin of his casket, banked with white roses. His heart, unregenerated, had given out.

Susan said, "The future is all speculative at this point. We know that the peptide structures that build up the pressure to sleep in normal people resemble the components of bacterial cell walls. Maybe there's a connection between sleep and pathogen receptivity. We don't know. But ignorance never stopped the tabloids. I wanted to prepare you because you're going to get called supermen, *homo perfectus*, who-all-knows-what. Immortal."

The two women sat in silence. Finally Leisha said, "I'm going to tell the others. On our datanet. Don't worry about the security. Kevin Baker designed Groupnet; nobody knows anything we don't want them to."

"You're that well organized already?"

"Yes."

Susan's mouth worked. She looked away from Leisha. "We better go in. You'll miss your flight."

"Susan . . ."

"What?"

"Thank you."

"You're welcome," Susan said, and in her voice Leisha heard the thing she had seen before in Susan's expression and not been able to name: It was longing.

Tissue regeneration. A long, long time, sang the blood in Leisha's ears on the flight to Boston. *Tissue regeneration*. And, eventually: *Immortal*. No, not that, she told herself severely. Not that. The blood didn't listen.

"You sure smile a lot," said the man next to her in first

class, a business traveler who had not recognized Leisha. "You coming from a big party in Chicago?"

"No. From a funeral."

The man looked shocked, then disgusted. Leisha looked out the window at the ground far below. Rivers like microcircuits, fields like neat index cards. And on the horizon, fluffy white clouds like masses of exotic flowers, blooms in a conservatory filled with light.

The letter was no thicker than any hard-copy mail, but hard-copy mail addressed by hand to either of them was so rare that Richard was nervous. "It might be explosive." Leisha looked at the letter on their hall credenza. MS. LIESHA CAMDEN. Block letters, misspelled.

"It looks like a child's writing," she said.

Richard stood with head lowered, legs braced apart. But his expression was only weary. "Perhaps deliberately like a child's. You'd be more open to a child's writing, they might have figured."

" 'They'? Richard, are we getting that paranoid?"

He didn't flinch from the question. "Yes. For the time being."

A week earlier the *New England Journal of Medicine* had published Susan's careful, sober article. An hour later the broadcast and datanet news had exploded in speculation, drama, outrage, and fear. Leisha and Richard, along with all the Sleepless on the Groupnet, had tracked and charted each of four components, looking for a dominant reaction: speculation ("The Sleepless may live for centuries, and this might lead to the following events . . ."); drama ("If a Sleepless marries only Sleepers, he may have lifetime enough for a dozen brides—and several dozen children, a bewildering blended family. . . ."); outrage ("Tampering with the law of nature has only brought among us unnatural so-called people who will live with the unfair advantage of time: time to accumulate more kin, more power, more property than the rest of us could ever know. . . ."); and fear ("How soon before the Super-race takes over?")

"They're all fear, of one kind or another," Carolyn Rizzolo finally said, and the Groupnet stopped their differentiated tracking.

Leisha was taking the final exams of her last year of law school. Each day comments followed her to the campus, along the corridors and in the classroom; each day she forgot them in the grueling exam sessions, all students reduced to the same status of petitioner to the great university. Afterward, temporarily drained, she walked silently back home to Richard and the Groupnet, aware of the looks of people on the street, aware of her bodyguard Bruce striding between her and them.

"It will calm down," Leisha said. Richard didn't answer.

The town of Salt Springs, Texas, passed a local ordinance that no Sleepless could obtain a liquor license, on the grounds that civil rights statutes were built on the "all men were created equal" clause of the Constitution, and Sleepless clearly were not covered. There were no Sleepless within a hundred miles of Salt Springs and no one had applied for a new liquor license there for the past ten years, but the story was picked up by United Press and by Datanet News, and within twenty-four hours heated editorials appeared, on both sides of the issue, across the nation.

More local ordinances appeared. In Pollux, Pennsylvania, the Sleepless could be denied apartment rental on the grounds that their prolonged wakefulness would increase both wear-and-tear on the landlord's property and utility bills. In Cranston Estates, California, Sleepless were barred from operating twenty-four-hour businesses: "unfair competition." Iroquois County, New York, barred them from serving on county juries, arguing that a jury containing Sleepless, with their skewed idea of time, did not constitute "a jury of one's peers."

"All those statutes will be thrown out in superior courts,"

Leisha said. "But God! The waste of money and docket time to do it!" A part of her mind noticed that her tone as she said this was Roger Camden's.

The state of Georgia, in which some sex acts between consenting adults were still a crime, made sex between a Sleepless and a Sleeper a third-degree felony, classing it with bestiality.

Kevin Baker had designed software that scanned the newsnets at high speed, flagged all stories involving discrimination or attacks on Sleepless, and categorized them by type. The files were available on Groupnet. Leisha read through them, then called Kevin. "Can't you create a parallel program to flag defenses of us? We're getting a skewed picture."

"You're right," Kevin said, a little startled. "I didn't think of it."

"Think of it," Leisha said, grimly. Richard, watching her, said nothing.

She was most upset by the stories about Sleepless children. Shunning at school, verbal abuse by siblings, attacks by neighborhood bullies, confused resentment from parents who had wanted an exceptional child but had not bargained on one who might live centuries. The school board of Gold River, Iowa, voted to bar Sleepless children from conventional classrooms because their rapid learning "created feelings of inadequacy in others, interfering with their education." The board made funds available for Sleepless to have tutors at home. There were no volunteers among the teaching staff. Leisha started spending as much time on Groupnet with the kids, talking to them all night long, as she did studying for her bar exams, scheduled for July.

Stella Bevington stopped using her modem.

Kevin's second program catalogued editorials urging fairness towards Sleepless. The school board of Denver set aside funds for a program in which gifted children, including the Sleepless, could use their talents and build teamwork through tutoring even younger children. Rive Beau, Louisiana, elected Sleepless Danielle du Cherney to the City Council, although Danielle was twenty-two and technically too young to qualify. The prestigious medical research firm of Halley-Hall gave much publicity to their hiring of Christopher Amren, a Sleepless with a Ph.D. in cellular physics.

Dora Clarq, a Sleepless in Dallas, opened a letter addressed to her and a plastic explosive blew off her arm.

Leisha and Richard stared at the envelope on the hall credenza. The paper was thick, cream-colored, but not expensive: the kind of paper made of bulky newsprint dyed the shade of vellum. There was no return address. Richard called Liz Bishop, a Sleepless who was majoring in Criminal Justice in Michigan. He had never spoken with her before—neither had Leisha—but she came on Groupnet immediately and told them how to open it, or she could fly up and do it if they preferred. Richard and Leisha followed her directions for remote detonation in the basement of the townhouse. Nothing blew up. When the letter was open, they took it out and read it:

Dear Ms. Camden,

You been pretty good to me and I'm sorry to do this but I quit. They are making it pretty hot for me at the union not officially but you know how it is. If I was you I wouldn't go to the union for another bodyguard I'd try to find one privately. But be careful. Again I'm sorry but I have to live too.

Bruce

"I don't know whether to laugh or cry," Leisha said. "The two of us getting all this equipment, spending hours on this set-up so an explosive won't detonate . . ."

"It's not as if I at least had a whole lot else to do," Richard said. Since the wave of anti-Sleepless sentiment, all but two of his marine-consultant clients, vulnerable to the marketplace and thus to public opinion, had canceled their accounts.

Groupnet, still up on Leisha's terminal, shrilled in emergency override. Leisha got there first. It was Tony.

"Leisha. I'll need your legal help, if you'll give it. They're trying to fight me on Sanctuary. Please fly down here."

Sanctuary was raw brown gashes in the late-spring earth. It was situated in the Allegheny Mountains of southern New York State, old hills rounded by age and covered with pine and hickory. A superb road led from the closest town, Belmont, to Sanctuary. Low, maintenance-free buildings, whose design was plain but graceful, stood in various stages of completion. Jennifer Sharifi, looking strained, met Leisha and Richard. "Tony wants to talk to you, but first he asked me to show you both around."

"What's wrong?" Leisha asked quietly. She had never met Jennifer before but no Sleepless looked like that—pinched, spent, *weary*—unless the stress level was enormous.

Jennifer didn't try to evade the question. "Later. First look at Sanctuary. Tony respects your opinion enormously, Leisha; he wants you to see everything."

The dormitories each held fifty, with communal rooms for cooking, dining, relaxing, and bathing, and a warren of separate offices and studios and labs for work. "We're calling them 'dorms' anyway, despite the etymology," Jennifer said, trying to smile. Leisha glanced at Richard. The smile was a failure.

She was impressed, despite herself, with the completeness of Tony's plans for lives that would be both communal and intensely private. There was a gym, a small hospital—"By the end of next year, we'll have eighteen AMA-certified doctors, you know, and four are thinking of coming here"—a daycare facility, a school, an intensive-crop farm. "Most of our food will come in from the outside, of course. So will most people's jobs, although they'll do as much of them as possible from here, over datanets. We're not cutting ourselves off from the world—only creating a safe place from which to trade with it." Leisha didn't answer.

Apart from the power facilities, self-supported Y-energy, she was most impressed with the human planning. Tony had Sleepless interested from virtually every field they would need both to care for themselves and to deal with the outside world. "Lawyers and accountants come first," Jennifer said. "That's our first line of defense in safeguarding ourselves. Tony recognizes that most modern battles for power are fought in the courtroom and boardroom."

But not all. Last, Jennifer showed them the plans for physical defense. She explained them with a mixture of defiance and pride: Every effort had been made to stop attackers without hurting them. Electronic surveillance completely circled the 150 square miles Jennifer had purchased—some *counties* were smaller than that, Leisha thought, dazed. When breached, a force field a half-mile within the E-gate activated, delivering electric shocks to anyone on foot—"But only on the *outside* of the field. We don't want any of our kids hurt." Unmanned penetration by vehicles or robots was identified by a system that located all moving metal above a certain mass within Sanctuary. Any moving metal that did not carry a special signaling device designed by Donna Pospula, a Sleepless who had patented important electronic components, was suspect.

"Of course, we're not set up for an air attack or an outright army assault," Jennifer said. "But we don't expect that. Only the haters in self-motivated hate." Her voice sagged.

Leisha touched the hard-copy of the security plans with

one finger. They troubled her. "If we can't integrate ourselves into the world . . . free trade should imply free movement."

"Yeah. Well," Jennifer said, such an uncharacteristic Sleepless remark—both cynical and inarticulate—that Leisha looked up. "I have something to tell you, Leisha."

"What?"

"Tony isn't here."

"Where is he?"

"In Allegheny County jail. It's true we're having zoning battles about Sanctuary—zoning! In this isolated spot! But this is something else, something that just happened this morning. Tony's been arrested for the kidnapping of Timmy DeMarzo."

The room wavered. "FBI?"

"Yes."

"How . . . how did they find out?"

"Some agent eventually cracked the case. They didn't tell us how. Tony needs a lawyer, Leisha. Dana Monteiro has already agreed, but Tony wants you."

"Jennifer—I don't even take the bar exams until July!"

"He says he'll wait. Dana will act as his lawyer in the meantime. Will you pass the bar?"

"Of course. But I already have a job lined up with Morehouse, Kennedy, & Anderson in New York—" She stopped. Richard was looking at her hard, Jennifer gazing down at the floor. Leisha said quietly, "What will he plead?"

"Guilty," Jennifer said, "with—what is it called legally?— extenuating circumstances."

Leisha nodded. She had been afraid Tony would want to plead not guilty: more lies, subterfuge, ugly politics. Her mind ran swiftly over extenuating circumstances, precedents, tests to precedents. They could use *Clements v. Voy* . . .

"Dana is at the jail now," Jennifer said. "Will you drive in with me?"

"Yes."

In Belmont, the county seat, they were not allowed to see Tony. Dana Monteiro, as his attorney, could go in and out freely. Leisha, not officially an attorney at all, could go nowhere. This was told them by a man in the D.A.'s office whose face stayed immobile while he spoke to them, and who spat on the ground behind their shoes when they turned to leave, even though this left him with a smear of spittle on his courthouse floor.

Richard and Leisha drove their rental car to the airport for the flight back to Boston. On the way Richard told Leisha he was leaving her. He was moving to Sanctuary, now, even before it was functional, to help with the planning and building.

She stayed most of the time in her townhouse, studying ferociously for the bar exams or checking on the Sleepless children through Groupnet. She had not hired another bodyguard to replace Bruce, which made her reluctant to go outside very much; the reluctance in turn made her angry with herself. Once or twice a day she scanned Kevin's electronic news clippings.

There were signs of hope. The New York Times ran an editorial, widely reprinted on the electronic news services:

PROSPERITY AND HATRED: A LOGIC CURVE WE'D RATHER NOT SEE

The United States has never been a country that much values calm, logic, rationality. We have, as a people, tended to label these things "cold." We have, as a people, tended to admire feeling and action: We exalt in our stories and our memorials not the creation of the Constitution but its defense at Iwo Jima; not the intellectual achievements of a Stephen Hawking but the heroic passion of a Charles Lindbergh; not the inventors of the monorails and computers that unite us but the composers of the angry songs of rebellion that divide us.

A peculiar aspect of this phenomenon is that it grows stronger in times of prosperity. The better off our citizenry, the greater their contempt for the calm reasoning that got them there, and the more passionate their indulgence in emotion. Consider, in the last century, the gaudy excesses of the Roaring Twenties and the anti-establishment contempt of the sixties. Consider, in our own century, the unprecedented prosperity brought, about by Y-energy—and then consider that Kenzo Yagai, except to his followers, was seen as a greedy and bloodless logician, while our national adulation goes to neo-nihilist writer Stephen Castelli, to "feelie" actress Brenda Foss, and to daredevil gravity-well diver Jim Morse Luter.

But most of all, as you ponder this phenomenon in your Y-energy houses, consider the current outpouring of irrational feeling directed at the "Sleepless" since the publication of the joint findings of the Biotech Institute and the Chicago Medical School concerning Sleepless tissue regeneration.

Most of the Sleepless are intelligent. Most of them are calm, if you define that much-maligned word to mean directing one's energies into solving problems rather than to emoting about them. (Even Pulitzer Prize winner Carolyn Rizzolo gave us a stunning play of ideas, not of passions run amuck.) All of them show a natural bent toward achievement, a bent given a decided boost by the one-third more time in their days to achieve in. Their achievements lie, for the most part, in logical fields rather than emotional ones: Computers. Law.

Finance. Physics. Medical research. They are rational, orderly, calm, intelligent, cheerful, young, and possibly very long-lived.

And, in our United States of unprecedented prosperity, increasingly hated.

Does the hatred that we have seen flower so fully over the last few months really grow, as many claim, from the "unfair advantage" the Sleepless have over the rest of us in securing jobs, promotions, money, success? Is it really envy over the Sleepless' good fortune? Or does it come from something more pernicious, rooted in our tradition of shoot-from-the-hip American action: Hatred of the logical, the calm, the considered? Hatred in fact of the superior mind?

If so, perhaps we should think deeply about the founders of this country: Jefferson, Washington, Paine, Adams—inhabitants of the Age of Reason, all. These men created our orderly and balanced system of laws precisely to protect the property and achievements created by the individual efforts of balanced and rational minds. The Sleepless may be our severest internal test yet of our own sober belief in law and order. No, the Sleepless were not "created equal," but our attitudes toward them should be examined with a care equal to our soberest jurisprudence. We may not like what we learn about our own motives, but our credibility as a people may depend on the rationality and intelligence of the examination.

Both have been in short supply in the public reaction to last month's research findings.

Law is not theater. Before we write laws reflecting gaudy and dramatic feelings, we must be very sure we understand the difference.

Leisha hugged herself, gazing in delight at the screen, smiling. She called the New York *Times*: Who had written the editorial? The receptionist, cordial when she answered the phone, grew brusque. The *Times* was not releasing that information, "prior to internal investigation."

It could not dampen her mood. She whirled around the apartment, after days of sitting at her desk or screen. Delight demanded physical action. She washed dishes, picked up books. There were gaps in the furniture patterns where Richard had taken pieces that belonged to him; a little quieter now, she moved the furniture to close the gaps.

Susan Melling called to tell her about the *Times* editorial; they talked warmly for a few minutes. When Susan hung up, the phone rang again.

"Leisha? Your voice still sounds the same. This is Stewart Sutter."

"Stewart." She had not seen him for years. Their romance had lasted two years and then dissolved, not from any painful issue so much as from the press of both their studies. Standing by the comm terminal, hearing his voice, Leisha suddenly felt again his hands on her breasts in the cramped dormitory bed: All those years before she had found a good use for a bed. The phantom hands became Richard's hands, and a sudden pain pierced her.

"Listen," Stewart said, "I'm calling because there's some information I think you should know. You take your bar exams next week, right? And then you have a tentative job with Morehouse, Kennedy, & Anderson."

"How do you know all that, Stewart?"

"Men's room gossip. Well, not as bad as that. But the New York legal community—that part of it, anyway—is smaller than you think. And, you're a pretty visible figure."

"Yes," Leisha said neutrally.

"Nobody has the slightest doubt you'll be called to the bar. But there is some doubt about the job with

Morehouse, Kennedy. You've got two senior partners, Alan Morehouse and Seth Brown, who have changed their minds since this . . . flap. 'Adverse publicity for the firm,' 'turning law into a circus,' blah blah blah. You know the drill. But you've also got two powerful champions, Ann Carlyle and Michael Kennedy, the old man himself. He's quite a mind. Anyway, I wanted you to know all this so you can recognize exactly what the situation is and know whom to count on in the infighting."

"Thank you," Leisha said. "Stew . . . why do you care if I get it or not? Why should it matter to you?"

There was a silence on the other end of the phone. Then Stewart said, very low, "We're not all noodleheads out here, Leisha. Justice does still matter to some of us. So does achievement."

Light rose in her, a bubble of buoyant light.

Stewart said, "You have a lot of support here for that stupid zoning fight over Sanctuary, too. You might not realize that, but you do. What the Parks Commission crowd is trying to pull is . . . but they're just being used as fronts. You know that. Anyway, when it gets as far as the courts, you'll have all the help you need."

"Sanctuary isn't my doing. At all."

"No? Well, I meant the plural you."

"Thank you. I mean that. How are you doing?"

"Fine. I'm a daddy now."

"Really! Boy or girl?"

"Girl. A beautiful little bitch, drives me crazy. I'd like you to meet my wife sometime, Leisha."

"I'd like that," Leisha said.

She spent the rest of the night studying for her bar exams. The bubble stayed with her. She recognized exactly what it was: joy.

It was going to be all right. The contract, unwritten, between her and her society—Kenzo Yagai's society, Roger

Camden's society—would hold. With dissent and strife and yes, some hatred: She suddenly thought of Tony's beggars in Spain, furious at the strong because they themselves were not. Yes. But it would hold.

She believed that.

She did.

7

Leisha took her bar exams in July. They did not seem hard to her. Afterward three classmates, two men and a woman, made a fakely casual point of talking to Leisha until she had climbed safely into a taxi whose driver obviously did not recognize her, or stop signs. The three were all Sleepers. A pair of undergraduates, clean-shaven blond men with the long faces and pointless arrogance of rich stupidity, eyed Leisha and sneered. Leisha's female classmate sneered back.

Leisha had a flight to Chicago the next morning. Alice was going to join her there. They had to clean out the big house on the lake, dispose of Roger's personal property, put the house on the market. Leisha had had no time to do it earlier.

She remembered her father in the conservatory, wearing an ancient flat-topped hat he had picked up somewhere, potting orchids and jasmine and passion flowers.

When the doorbell rang she was startled; she almost never had visitors. Eagerly, she turned on the outside camera—maybe it was Jonathan or Martha, back in Boston to surprise her, to celebrate. Why hadn't she thought before about some sort of celebration?

Richard stood gazing up at the camera. He had been crying.

She tore open the door. Richard made no move to come

in. Leisha saw that what the camera had registered as grief was actually something else: tears of rage.

"Tony's dead."

Leisha put out her hand, blindly. Richard did not take it.

"They killed him in prison. Not the authorities—the other prisoners. In the recreation yard. Murderers, rapists, looters, scum of the earth—and they thought they had the right to kill him because he was different."

Now Richard did grab her arm, so hard that something, some bone, shifted beneath the flesh and pressed on a nerve. "Not just different—*better*. Because he was better, because we all are, we goddamn just don't stand up and shout it, out of some misplaced feeling for *their* feelings . . . God!"

Leisha pulled her arm free and rubbed it, numb, staring at Richard's contorted face.

"They beat him to death with a lead pipe. No one even knows how they got a lead pipe. They beat him on the back of the head and they rolled him over and—"

"Don't!" Leisha said. It came out a whimper.

Richard looked at her. Despite his shouting, his violent grip on her arm, Leisha had the confused impression that this was the first time he had actually seen her. She went on rubbing her arm, staring at him in terror.

He said quietly, "I've come to take you to Sanctuary, Leisha. Dan Walcott and Vernon Bulriss are in the car outside. The three of us will carry you out, if necessary. But you're coming. You see that, don't you? You're not safe here, with your high profile and your spectacular looks—you're a natural target if anyone is. Do we have to force you? Or do you finally see for yourself that we have no choice— the bastards have left us no choice except Sanctuary?"

Leisha closed her eyes. Tony, at fourteen, at the beach. Tony, his eyes ferocious and alight, the first to reach out his hand for the glass of interleukin-1. Beggars in Spain.

"I'll come."

❖   ❖   ❖

She had never known such anger. It scared her, coming in bouts throughout the long night, receding but always returning again. Richard held her in his arms, sitting with their backs against the wall of her library, and his holding made no difference at all. In the living room Dan and Vernon talked in low voices.

Sometimes the anger erupted in shouting, and Leisha heard herself and thought *I don't know you.* Sometimes it became crying, sometimes talking about Tony, about all of them. Not the shouting nor the crying nor the talking eased her at all.

Planning did, a little. In a cold dry voice she didn't recognize, Leisha told Richard about the trip to close the house in Chicago. She had to go; Alice was already there. If Richard and Dan and Vernon put Leisha on the plane, and Alice met her at the other end with union bodyguards, she should be safe enough. Then she would change her return ticket from Boston to Belmont and drive with Richard to Sanctuary.

"People are already arriving," Richard said. "Jennifer Sharifi is organizing it, greasing the Sleeper suppliers with so much money they can't resist. What about this townhouse here, Leisha? Your furniture and terminal and clothes?"

Leisha looked around her familiar office. Law books lined the walls, red and green and brown, although most of the same information was on-line. A coffee cup rested on a print-out on the desk. Beside it was the receipt she had requested from the taxi driver this afternoon, a giddy souvenir of the day she had passed her bar exams; she had thought of having it framed. Above the desk was a holographic portrait of Kenzo Yagai.

"Let it rot," Leisha said.

Richard's arm tightened around her.

"I've never seen you like this," Alice said, subdued. "It's more than just clearing out the house, isn't it?"

"Let's get on with it," Leisha said. She yanked a suit from her father's closet. "Do you want any of this stuff for your husband?"

"It wouldn't fit."

"The hats?"

"No," Alice said. "Leisha—what is it?"

"Let's just *do* it!" She yanked all the clothes from Camden's closet, piled them on the floor, scrawled FOR VOLUNTEER AGENCY on a piece of paper and dropped it on top of the pile. Silently, Alice started adding clothes from the dresser, which already bore a taped paper scrawled ESTATE AUCTION.

The curtains were already down throughout the house; Alice had done that yesterday. She had also rolled up the rugs. Sunset glared redly on the bare wooden floors.

"What about your old room?" Leisha said. "What do you want there?"

"I've already tagged it," Alice said. "A mover will come Thursday."

"Fine. What else?"

"The conservatory. Sanderson has been watering everything, but he didn't really know what needed how much, so some of the plants are—"

"Fire Sanderson," Leisha said curtly. "The exotics can die. Or have them sent to a hospital, if you'd rather. Just watch out for the ones that are poisonous. Come on, let's do the library."

Alice sat slowly on a rolled-up rug in the middle of Camden's bedroom. She had cut her hair; Leisha thought it looked ugly, jagged brown spikes around her broad face. She had also gained more weight. She was starting to look like their mother.

Alice said, "Do you remember the night I told you I was pregnant? Just before you left for Harvard?"

"Let's do the library!"

"Do you?" Alice said. "For God's sake, can't you just once

listen to someone else, Leisha? Do you have to be so much like Daddy every single minute?"

"I'm not like Daddy!"

"The hell you're not. You're exactly what he made you. But that's not the point. Do you remember that night?"

Leisha walked over the rug and out the door. Alice simply sat. After a minute Leisha walked back in. "I remember."

"You were near tears," Alice said implacably. Her voice was quiet. "I don't even remember exactly why. Maybe because I wasn't going to college after all. But I put my arms around you, and for the first time in years—years, Leisha— I felt you really were my sister. Despite all of it—the roaming the halls all night and the show-off arguments with Daddy and the special school and the artificially long legs and golden hair—all that crap. You seemed to need me to hold you. You seemed to need me. You seemed to *need*."

"What are you saying?" Leisha demanded. "That you can only be close to someone if they're in trouble and need you? That you can only be a sister if I was in some kind of pain, open sores running? Is that the bond between you Sleepers? 'Protect me while I'm unconscious, I'm just as crippled as you are'?"

"No," Alice said. "I'm saying that *you* could be a sister only if you were in some kind of pain."

Leisha stared at her. "You're stupid, Alice."

Alice said calmly, "I know that. Compared to you, I am. I know that." Leisha jerked her head angrily. She felt ashamed of what she had just said, and yet it was true, and they both knew it was true, and anger still lay in her like a dark void, formless and hot. It was the formless part that was the worst. Without shape, there could be no action; without action, the anger went on burning her, choking her.

Alice said, "When I was twelve Susan gave me a dress for our birthday. You were away somewhere, on one of those overnight field trips your fancy progressive school did all the time. The dress was silk, pale blue, with antique lace—very beautiful. I was thrilled, not only because it was beautiful but because Susan had gotten it for me and gotten software for you. The dress was mine. Was, I thought, *me*." In the gathering gloom Leisha could barely make out her broad, plain features. "The first time I wore it a boy said, 'Stole your sister's dress, Alice? Snitched it while she was *sleeping*?' Then he laughed like crazy, the way they always did.

"I threw the dress away. I didn't even explain to Susan, although I think she would have understood. Whatever was yours was yours, and whatever wasn't yours was yours, too. That's the way Daddy set it up. The way he hard-wired it into our genes."

"You, too?" Leisha said. "You're no different from the other envious beggars?"

Alice stood up from the rug. She did it slowly, leisurely, brushing dust off the back of her wrinkled skirt, smoothing the print fabric. Then she walked over and hit Leisha in the mouth.

"Now do you see me as real?" Alice asked quietly.

Leisha put her hand to her mouth. She felt blood. The phone rang, Camden's unlisted personal line. Alice walked over, picked it up, listened, and held it calmly out to Leisha. "It's for you."

Numb, Leisha took it.

"Leisha? This is Kevin. Listen, something's happened. Stella Bevington called me, on the phone not Groupnet, I think her parents took away her modem. I picked up the phone and she screamed, 'This is Stella! They're hitting me he's drunk—'and then the line went dead. Randy's gone to Sanctuary—hell, they've *all* gone. You're closest to her, she's still in Skokie. You better get there fast. Have you got bodyguards you trust?"

"Yes," Leisha said, although she hadn't. The anger—finally—took form. "I can handle it."

"I don't know how you'll get her out of there," Kevin said. "They'll recognize you, they know she called somebody, they might even have knocked her out . . ."

"I'll handle it," Leisha said.

"Handle what?" Alice said.

Leisha faced her. Even though she knew she shouldn't, she said, "What your people do. To one of ours. A seven-year-old kid who's getting beaten up by her parents because she's Sleepless—because she's *better* than you are—" She ran down the stairs and out to the rental car she had driven from the airport.

Alice ran right down with her. "Not your car, Leisha. They can trace a rental car just like that. My car."

Leisha screamed, "If you think you're—"

Alice yanked open the door of her battered Toyota, a model so old the Y-energy cones weren't even concealed but hung like drooping jowls on either side. She shoved Leisha into the passenger seat, slammed the door, and rammed herself behind the wheel. Her hands were steady. "Where?"

Blackness swooped over Leisha. She put her head down, as far between her knees as the cramped Toyota would allow. Two—no, three—days since she had eaten. Since the night before the bar exams. The faintness receded, swept over her again as soon as she raised her head.

She told Alice the address in Skokie.

"Stay way in the back," Alice said. "And there's a scarf in the glove compartment—put it on. Low, to hide as much of your face as possible."

Alice had stopped the car along Highway 42. Leisha said, "This isn't—"

"It's a union quick-guard place, We have to look like we have some protection, Leisha. We don't need to tell him anything. I'll hurry."

She was out in three minutes with a huge man in a cheap

dark suit. He squeezed into the front seat beside Alice and said nothing at all. Alice did not introduce him.

The house was small, a little shabby, with lights on downstairs, none upstairs. The first stars shone in the north, away from Chicago. Alice said to the guard, "Get out of the car and stand here by the car door—no, more in the light—and don't do anything unless I'm attacked in some way." The man nodded. Alice started up the walk. Leisha scrambled out of the back seat and caught her sister two-thirds of the way to the plastic front door.

"Alice, what the hell are you doing? *I* have to—"

"Keep your voice down," Alice said, glancing at the guard. "Leisha, *think*. You'll be recognized. Here, near Chicago, with a Sleepless daughter—these people have looked at your picture in magazines for years. They've watched long-range holovids of you. They know you. They know you're going to be a lawyer. Me they've never seen. I'm nobody."

"Alice—"

"For Chrissake, get back in the car!" Alice hissed, and pounded on the front door.

Leisha drew off the walk, into the shadow of a willow tree. A man opened the door. His face was completely blank. Alice said, "Child Protection Agency. We got a call from a little girl, this number. Let me in."

"There's no little girl here."

"This is an emergency, priority one," Alice said. "Child Protection Act 186. Let me in!"

The man, still blank-faced, glanced at the huge figure by the car. "You got a search warrant?"

"I don't need one in a priority-one child emergency. If you don't let me in, you're going to have legal snarls like you never bargained for."

Leisha clamped her lips together. No one would believe that, it was legal gobbledygook. . . . Her lip throbbed where Alice had hit her.

The man stood aside to let Alice enter.

The guard started forward. Leisha hesitated, then let him. He entered with Alice.

Leisha waited, alone, in the dark.

In three minutes they were out, the guard carrying a child. Alice's broad face gleamed pale in the porch light. Leisha sprang forward, opened the car door, and helped the guard ease the child inside. The guard was frowning, a slow puzzled frown shot with wariness.

Alice said, "Here. This is an extra hundred dollars. To get back to the city by yourself."

"Hey . . ." the guard said, but he took the money. He stood looking after them as Alice pulled away.

"He'll go straight to the police," Leisha said despairingly. "He has to, or risk his union membership."

"I know," Alice said. "But by that time we'll be out of the car."

"*Where?*"

"At the hospital," Alice said.

"Alice, we can't—" Leisha didn't finish. She turned to the back seat. "Stella? Are you conscious?"

"Yes," said the small voice.

Leisha groped until her fingers found the rear-seat illuminator. Stella lay stretched out on the back seat, her face distorted with pain. She cradled her left arm in her right. A single bruise colored her face, above the left eye.

"You're Leisha Camden," the child said, and started to cry.

"Her arm's broken," Alice said.

"Honey, can you . . ." Leisha's throat felt thick, she had trouble getting the words out ". . . can you hold on till we get you to a doctor?"

"Yes," Stella said. "Just don't take me back there!"

"We won't," Leisha said. "Ever." She glanced at Alice and saw Tony's face.

Alice said, "There's a community hospital about ten miles south of here."

"How do you know that?"

"I was there once. Drug overdose," Alice said briefly. She drove hunched over the wheel, with the face of someone thinking furiously. Leisha thought, too, trying to see a way around the legal charge of kidnapping. They probably couldn't say the child came willingly: Stella would undoubtedly cooperate but at her age and in her condition she was probably *non sui juris*, her word would have no legal weight . . .

"Alice, we can't even get her into the hospital without insurance information. Verifiable online."

"Listen," Alice said, not to Leisha but over her shoulder, toward the back seat, "here's what we're going to do, Stella. I'm going to tell them you're my daughter and you fell off a big rock you were climbing while we stopped for a snack at a roadside picnic area. We're driving from California to Philadelphia to see your grandmother. Your name is Jordan Watrous and you're five years old. Got that, honey?"

"I'm seven," Stella said. "Almost eight."

"You're a very large five. Your birthday is March 23. Can you do this, Stella?"

"Yes," the little girl said. Her voice was stronger.

Leisha stared at Alice. "Can *you* do this?"

"Of course I can," Alice said. "I'm Roger Camden's daughter."

Alice half-carried, half-supported Stella into the Emergency Room of the small community hospital. Leisha watched from the car: the short stocky woman, the child's thin body with the twisted arm. Then she drove Alice's car to the farthest corner of the parking lot, under the dubious cover of a skimpy maple, and locked it. She tied the scarf more securely around her face.

Alice's license plate number, and her name, would be in every police and rental-car databank by now. The medical banks were slower; often they uploaded from local precincts only once a day, resenting the governmental interference in what was still, despite a half-century of battle, a private-sector enterprise. Alice and Stella would probably be all right in the hospital. Probably. But Alice could not rent another car.

Leisha could.

But the data file that would flash to rental agencies on Alice Camden Watrous might or might not include that she was Leisha Camden's twin.

Leisha looked at the rows of cars in the lot. A flashy luxury Chrysler, an Ikeda van, a row of middle-class Toyotas and Mercedes, a vintage '99 Cadillac—she could imagine the owner's face if that were missing—ten or twelve cheap runabouts, a hovercar with the uniformed driver asleep at the wheel. And a battered farm truck.

Leisha walked over to the truck. A man sat at the wheel, smoking. She thought of her father.

"Hello," Leisha said.

The man rolled down his window but didn't answer. He had greasy brown hair.

"See that hovercar over there?" Leisha said. She made her voice sound young, high. The man glanced at it indifferently; from this angle you couldn't see that the driver was asleep. "That's my bodyguard. He thinks I'm in the hospital, the way my father told me to, getting this lip looked at." She could feel her mouth swollen from Alice's blow.

"So?"

Leisha stamped her foot. "So I don't want to be inside. He's a shit and so's Daddy. I want *out*. I'll give you four thousand bank credits for your truck. Cash."

The man's eyes widened. He tossed away his cigarette, looked again at the hovercar. The driver's shoulders were broad, and the car was within easy screaming distance.

"All nice and legal," Leisha said, and tried to smirk. Her knees felt watery.

"Let me see the cash."

Leisha backed away from the truck, to where he could not reach her. She took the money from her arm clip. She was used to carrying a lot of cash; there had always been Bruce, or someone like Bruce. There had always been safety.

"Get out of the truck on the other side," Leisha said, "and lock the door behind you. Leave the keys on the seat, where I can see them from here. Then I'll put the money on the roof where you can see it."

The man laughed, a sound like gravel pouring. "Regular little Dabney Engh, aren't you? Is that what they teach you society debs at your fancy schools?"

Leisha had no idea who Dabney Engh was. She waited, watching the man try to think of a way to cheat her, and tried to hide her contempt. She thought of Tony.

"All right," he said, and slid out of the truck.

"Lock the door!"

He grinned, opened the door again, locked it. Leisha put the money on the roof, yanked open the driver's door, clambered in, locked the door, and powered up the window. The man laughed. She put the key into the ignition, started the truck, and drove toward the street. Her hands trembled.

She drove slowly around the block twice. When she came back, the man was gone, and the driver of the hovercar was still asleep. She had wondered if the man would wake him, out of sheer malice, but he had not. She parked the truck and waited.

An hour and a half later, Alice and a nurse wheeled Stella out of the Emergency Entrance. Leisha leaped out of the truck and yelled, "Coming, Alice!" waving both her arms. It was too dark to see Alice's expression; Leisha could only hope that Alice showed no dismay at the battered truck, that she had not told the nurse to expect a red car.

Alice said, "This is Julie Bergadon, a friend that I called while you were setting Jordan's arm." The nurse nodded, uninterested. The two women helped Stella into the high truck cab; there was no back seat. Stella had a cast on her arm and looked drugged.

"How?" Alice said as they drove off.

Leisha didn't answer. She was watching a police hovercar land at the other end of the parking lot. Two officers got out and strode purposefully towards Alice's locked car under the skimpy maple.

"My God," Alice said. For the first time, she sounded frightened.

"They won't trace us," Leisha said. "Not to this truck. Count on it."

"Leisha." Alice's voice spiked with fear. "Stella's *asleep*."

Leisha glanced at the child, slumped against Alice's shoulder. "No, she's not. She's unconscious from painkillers."

"Is that all right? Normal? For . . . her?"

"We can black out. We can even experience substance-induced sleep." Tony and she and Richard and Jeanine in the midnight woods . . . "Didn't you know that, Alice?"

"No."

"We don't know very much about each other, do we?"

They drove south in silence. Finally Alice said, "Where are we going to take her, Leisha?"

"I don't know. Any one of the Sleepless would be the first place the police would check—"

"You can't risk it. Not the way things are," Alice said. She sounded weary. "But all my friends are in California. I don't think we could drive this rust bucket that far before getting stopped."

"It wouldn't make it anyway."

"What should we do?"

"Let me think."

At an expressway exit stood a pay phone. It wouldn't be data-shielded, as Groupnet was. Would Kevin's open line be tapped? Probably.

There was no doubt the Sanctuary line would be.

Sanctuary. All of them going there or already there,

Kevin had said. Holed up, trying to pull the worn Allegheny Mountains around them like a safe little den. Except for the children like Stella, who could not.

Where? With whom?

Leisha closed her eyes. The Sleepless were out; the police would find Stella within hours. Susan Melling? But she had been Alice's all-too-visible stepmother, and was co-beneficiary of Camden's will; they would question her almost immediately. It couldn't be anyone traceable to Alice. It could only be a Sleeper that Leisha knew, and trusted, and why should anyone at all fit that description? Why should she risk so much on anyone who did? She stood a long time in the dark phone kiosk. Then she walked to the truck. Alice was asleep, her head thrown back against the seat. A tiny line of drool ran down her chin. Her face was white and drained in the bad light from the kiosk. Leisha walked back to the phone.

"Stewart? Stewart Sutter?"

"Yes?"

"This is Leisha Camden. Something has happened." She told the story tersely, in bald sentences. Stewart did not interrupt.

"Leisha—" Stewart said, and stopped.

"I need help, Stewart." *'I'll help you, Alice.' 'I don't need your help.'* A wind whistled over the dark field beside the kiosk and Leisha shivered. She heard in the wind the thin keen of a beggar. In the wind, in her own voice.

"All right," Stewart said, "this is what we'll do. I have a cousin in Ripley, New York, just over the state line from Pennsylvania on the route you'll be driving east. It has to be in New York, I'm licensed in New York. Take the little girl there. I'll call my cousin and tell her you're coming. She's an elderly woman, was quite an activist in her youth, her name is Janet Patterson. The town is—"

"What makes you so sure she'll get involved? She could go to jail. And so could you."

"She's been in jail so many times you wouldn't believe it. Political protests going all the way back to Vietnam. But no one's going to jail. I'm now your attorney of record, I'm privileged. I'm going to get Stella declared a ward of the state. That shouldn't be too hard, with the hospital records you established in Skokie. Then she can be transferred to a foster home in New York, I know just the place, people who are fair and kind. Then Alice—"

"She's resident in Illinois. You can't—"

"Yes, I can. Since those research findings about the Sleepless life span have come out, legislators have been railroaded by stupid constituents scared or jealous or just plain angry. The result is a body of so-called 'law' riddled with contradictions, absurdities, and loopholes. None of it will stand in the long run—or at least I hope not—but in the meantime it can all be exploited. I can use it to create the most goddamn convoluted case for Stella that anybody ever saw, and in meantime she won't be returned home. But that won't work for Alice—she'll need an attorney licensed in Illinois."

"We have one," Leisha said. "Candace Holt."

"No, not a Sleepless. Trust me on this, Leisha. I'll find somebody good. There's a man in—are you crying?"

"No," Leisha said, crying.

"Ah, God," Stewart said. "Bastards. I'm sorry all this happened, Leisha."

"Don't be," Leisha said.

When she had directions to Stewart's cousin, she walked back to the truck. Alice was still asleep, Stella still unconscious. Leisha closed the truck door as quietly as possible. The engine balked and roared, but Alice didn't wake. There was a crowd of people with them in the narrow and darkened cab: Stewart Sutter, Tony Indivino, Susan Melling, Kenzo Yagai, Roger Camden.

To Stewart Sutter she said, You called to inform me about the situation at Morehouse, Kennedy. You are risking your career and your cousin for Stella. And you stand to gain nothing. Like Susan telling me in advance about Bernie Kuhn's brain. Susan, who lost her life to Daddy's dream and regained it by her own strength. A contract without consideration for each side is not a contract: Every first-year student knows that.

To Kenzo Yagai she said, Trade isn't always linear. You missed that. If Stewart gives me something, and I give Stella something, and ten years from now Stella is a different person because of that and gives something to someone else as yet unknown—it's an ecology. An *ecology* of trade, yes, each niche needed, even if they're not contractually bound. Does a horse need a fish? *Yes.*

To Tony she said, Yes, there are beggars in Spain who trade nothing, give nothing, do nothing. But there are *more* than beggars in Spain. Withdraw from the beggars, you withdraw from the whole damn country. And you withdraw from the possibility of the ecology of help. That's what Alice wanted, all those years ago in her bedroom. Pregnant, scared, angry, jealous, she wanted to help me, and I wouldn't let her because I didn't need it. But I do now. And she did then. Beggars need to help as well as be helped.

And finally, there was only Daddy left. She could see him, bright-eyed, holding thick-leaved exotic flowers in his strong hands. To Camden she said, You were wrong. Alice *is* special. Oh, Daddy—the specialness of Alice! You were *wrong*.

As soon as she thought this, lightness filled her. Not the buoyant bubble of joy, not the hard clarity of examination, but something else: sunshine, soft through the conservatory glass, where two children ran in and out. She suddenly felt light herself, not buoyant but translucent, a medium for the sunshine to pass clear through, on its way to somewhere else.

She drove the sleeping woman and the wounded child through the night, east, toward the state line.

1993
51st Convention
San Francisco

Even the Queen
by Connie Willis

The Nutcracker Coup
by Janet Kagan

Barnacle Bill The Spacer
by Lucius Shepard

Connie Willis has received far more awards in the genre than any other writer. Why could Asimov and Clarke, Heinlein and Herbert, not equal her mark? Because she is a master of the short, memorable, witty short story.

This one is typical. Only Connie would have thought of taking "women's troubles," as they used to be called, and making it the pivot of a story. Or if they did, they would not have had the lightness of touch to render it all in terms of a rather dotty cross-talk scene. If you frown, wondering if such a significant change in human control of physiology could leave so much else in women's lives untouched, perhaps you would rather like a different sort of sf story— one more linear, extrapolative. But that story would probably not have the grace and wit of this one, which we are lucky to have.

Even The Queen
by Connie Willis

The phone sang as I was looking over the defense's motion to dismiss. "It's the universal ring," my law clerk Bysshe said, reaching for it. "It's probably the defendant. They don't let you use signatures from jail."

"No, it's not," I said. "It's my mother."

"Oh." Bysshe reached for the receiver. "Why isn't she using her signature?"

"Because she knows I don't want to talk to her. She must have found out what Perdita's done."

"Your daughter Perdita?" he asked, holding the receiver against his chest. "The one with the little girl?"

"No, that's Viola. Perdita's my younger daughter. The one with no sense."

"What's she done?"

"She's joined the Cyclists."

Bysshe looked enquiringly blank, but I was not in the mood to enlighten him. Or in the mood to talk to Mother. "I know exactly what Mother will say," I said. "She'll ask me why I didn't tell her, and then she'll demand to know what I'm going to do about it, and there is nothing I can do about it, or I obviously would have done it already."

Bysshe looked bewildered. "Do you want me to tell her you're in court?"

"No." I reached for the receiver. "I'll have to talk to her

167

sooner or later." I took it from him. "Hello, Mother," I said.

"Traci," Mother said dramatically, "Perdita has become a Cyclist."

"I know."

"Why didn't you tell me?"

"I thought Perdita should tell you herself."

"Perdita!" She snorted. "She wouldn't tell me. She knows what I'd have to say about it. I suppose you told Karen."

"Karen's not here. She's in Iraq." The only good thing about this whole debacle was that thanks to Iraq's eagerness to show it was a responsible world community member and its previous penchant for self-destruction, my mother-in-law was in the one place on the planet where the phone service was bad enough that I could claim I'd tried to call her but couldn't get through, and she'd have to believe me.

The Liberation has freed us from all sorts of indignities and scourges, including Iraq's Saddams, but mothers-in-law aren't one of them, and I was almost happy with Perdita for her excellent timing. When I didn't want to kill her.

"What's Karen doing in Iraq?" Mother asked.

"Negotiating a Palestinian homeland."

"And meanwhile her granddaughter is ruining her life," she said irrelevantly. "Did you tell Viola?"

"I *told* you, Mother. I thought Perdita should tell all of you herself."

"Well, she didn't. And this morning one of my patients, Carol Chen, called me and demanded to know what I was keeping from her. I had no idea what she was talking about."

"How did Carol Chen find out?"

"From her daughter, who almost joined the Cyclists last year. *Her* family talked her out of it," she said accusingly. "Carol was convinced the medical community had discovered some terrible side-effect of ammenerol and were covering it up. I cannot believe you didn't tell me, Traci."

And I cannot believe I didn't have Bysshe tell her I was

in court, I thought. "I told you, Mother. I thought it was
Perdita's place to tell you. After all, it's her decision."

"Oh, Traci!" Mother said. "You cannot mean that!"

In the first fine flush of freedom after the Liberation,
I had entertained hopes that it would change everything—
that it would somehow do away with inequality and
matriarchal dominance and those humorless women
determined to eliminate the word "manhole" and third-
person singular pronouns from the language.

Of course it didn't. Men still make more money,
"herstory" is still a blight on the semantic landscape, and
my mother can still say, "Oh, *Traci!*" in a tone that reduces
me to pre-adolescence.

"Her decision!" Mother said. "Do you mean to tell me
you plan to stand idly by and allow your daughter to make
the mistake of her life?"

"What can I do? She's twenty-two years old and of sound
mind."

"If she were of sound mind she wouldn't be doing this.
Didn't you try to talk her out of it?"

"Of course I did, Mother."

"And?"

"And I didn't succeed. She's determined to become a
Cyclist."

"Well, there must be something we can do. Get an
injunction or hire a deprogrammer or sue the Cyclists for
brainwashing. You're a judge, there must be some law you
can invoke—"

"The law is called personal sovereignty, Mother, and
since it was what made the Liberation possible in the first
place, it can hardly be used against Perdita. Her decision
meets all the criteria for a case of personal sovereignty:
it's a personal decision, it was made by a sovereign adult,
it affects no one else—"

"What about my practice? Carol Chen is convinced
shunts cause cancer."

"Any effect on your practice is considered an indirect effect. Like secondary smoke. It doesn't apply. Mother, whether we like it or not, Perdita has a perfect right to do this, and we don't have any right to interfere. A free society has to be based on respecting others' opinions and leaving each other alone. We have to respect Perdita's right to make her own decisions."

All of which was true. It was too bad I hadn't said any of it to Perdita when she called. What I had said, in a tone that sounded exactly like my mothers, was "Oh, Per*dita*!"

"This is all your fault, you know," Mother said. "I *told* you you shouldn't have let, her get that tattoo over her shunt. And don't tell me it's a free society. What good is a free society when it allows my granddaughter to ruin her life?" She hung up.

I handed the receiver back to Bysshe.

"I really liked what you said about respecting your daughter's right to make her own decisions," he said. He held out my robe. "And about not interfering in her life."

"I want you to research the precedents on deprogramming for me," I said, sliding my arms into the sleeves. "And find out if the Cyclists have been charged with any free-choice violations—brainwashing, intimidation, coercion."

The phone sang, another universal. "Hello, who's calling?" Bysshe said cautiously. His voice became suddenly friendlier. "Just a minute." He put his hand over the receiver. "It's your daughter Viola."

I took the receiver. "Hello, Viola."

"I just talked to Grandma," she said. "You will not believe what Perdita's done now. She's joined the Cyclists."

"I know," I said.

"You *know*? And you didn't tell me? I can't believe this. You never tell me anything."

"I thought Perdita should tell you herself," I said tiredly.

"Are you kidding? She never tells me anything either.

That time she had eyebrow implants she didn't tell me for three weeks, and when she got the laser tattoo she didn't tell me at all. *Twidge* told me. You should have called me. Did you tell Grandma Karen?"

"She's in Baghdad," I said.

"I know," Viola said. "I called her."

"Oh, Viola, you didn't!"

"Unlike you, Mom, I believe in telling members of our family about matters that concern them."

"What did she say?" I asked, a kind of numbness settling over me now that the shock had worn off.

"I couldn't get through to her. The phone service over there is terrible. I got somebody who didn't speak English, and then I got cut off, and when I tried again they said the whole city was down."

Thank you, I breathed silently. Thank you, thank you, thank you.

"Grandma Karen has a right to know, Mother. Think of the effect this could have on Twidge. She thinks Perdita's wonderful. When Perdita got the eyebrow implants, Twidge glued LED's to hers, and I almost never got them off. What if Twidge decides to join the Cyclists, too?"

"Twidge is only nine. By the time she's supposed to get her shunt, Perdita will have long since quit." I hope, I added silently. Perdita had had the tattoo for a year and a half now and showed no signs of tiring of it. Besides, Twidge has more sense."

"It's true. Oh, Mother, how *could* Perdita do this? Didn't you tell her about how awful it was?"

"Yes," I said. "And inconvenient. And unpleasant and unbalancing and painful. None of it made the slightest impact on her. She told me she thought it would be fun."

Bysshe was pointing to his watch and mouthing, "Time for court."

"Fun!" Viola said. "When she saw what I went through that time? Honestly, Mother, sometimes I think she's completely brain-dead. Can't you have her declared incompetent and locked up or something?"

"No," I said, trying to zip up my robe with one hand. "Viola, I have to go. I'm late for court. I'm afraid there's nothing we can do to stop her. She's a rational adult."

"Rational!" Viola said. "Her eyebrows light up, Mother. She has Custer's Last Stand lased on her arm."

I handed the phone to Bysshe. "Tell Viola I'll talk to her tomorrow." I zipped up my robe. "And then call Baghdad and see how long they expect the phones to be out." I started into the courtroom. "And if there are any more universal calls, make sure they're local before you answer."

Bysshe couldn't get through to Baghdad, which I took as a good sign, and my mother-in-law didn't call. Mother did, in the afternoon, to ask if lobotomies were legal.

She called again the next day. I was in the middle of my Personal Sovereignty class, explaining the inherent right of citizens in a free society to make complete jackasses of themselves. They weren't buying it.

"I think it's your mother," Bysshe whispered to me as he handed me the phone. "She's still using the universal. But it's local. I checked."

"Hello, Mother," I said.

"It's all arranged," Mother said. "We're having lunch with Perdita at McGregor's. It's on the corner of Twelfth Street and Larimer."

"I'm in the middle of class," I said.

"I know. I won't keep you. I just wanted to tell you not to worry. I've taken care of everything."

I didn't like the sound of that. "What have you done?"

"Invited Perdita to lunch with us. I told you. At McGregor's."

"Who is 'us,' Mother?"

"Just the family," she said innocently. "You and Viola."

Well, at least she hadn't brought in the deprogrammer. Yet. "What are you up to, Mother?"

"Perdita said the same thing. Can't a grandmother ask her granddaughters to lunch? Be there at twelve-thirty."

"Bysshe and I have a court calendar meeting at three."

"Oh, we'll be done by then. And bring Bysshe with you. He can provide a man's point of view."

She hung up.

"You'll have to go to lunch with me, Bysshe," I said. "Sorry."

"Why? What's going to happen at lunch?"

"I have no idea."

On the way over to McGregor's, Bysshe told me what he'd found out about the Cyclists. "They're not a cult. There's no religious connection. They seem to have grown out of a pre-Liberation women's group," he said, looking at his notes, "although there are also links to the pro-choice movement, the University of Wisconsin, and the Museum of Modern Art."

"What?"

"They call their group leaders 'docents.' Their philosophy seems to be a mix of pre-Liberation radical feminism and the environmental primitivism of the eighties. They're floratarians and they don't wear shoes."

"Or shunts," I said. We pulled up in front of McGregor's and got out of the car. "Any mind control convictions?" I asked hopefully.

"No. A bunch of suits against individual members, all of which they won."

"On grounds of personal sovereignty."

"Yeah. And a criminal one by a member whose family tried to deprogram her. The deprogrammer was sentenced to twenty years, and the family got twelve."

"Be sure to tell Mother about that one," I said, and opened the door to McGregor's.

It was one of those restaurants with a morning glory vine twining around the *maitre d*'s desk and garden plots between the tables.

"Perdita suggested it," Mother said, guiding Bysshe and me past the onions to our table. "She told me a lot of the Cyclists are floratarians."

"Is she here?" I asked, sidestepping a cucumber frame.

"Not yet." She pointed past a rose arbor. "There's our table."

Our table was a wicker affair under a mulberry tree. Viola and Twidge were seated on the far side next to a trellis of runner beans, looking at menus.

"What are you doing here, Twidge?" I asked. "Why aren't you in school?"

"I am," she said, holding up her LCD slate. "I'm remoting today."

"I thought she should be part of this discussion," Viola said. "After all, she'll be getting her shunt soon."

"My friend Kensy says she isn't going to get one, like Perdita," Twidge said.

"I'm sure Kensy will change her mind when the time comes," Mother said. "Perdita will change hers, too. Bysshe, why don't you sit next to Viola?"

Bysshe slid obediently past the trellis and sat down in the wicker chair at the far end of the table. Twidge reached across Viola and handed him a menu. "This is a great restaurant," she said. "You don't have to wear shoes." She held up a bare foot to illustrate. "And if you get hungry while you're waiting, you can just pick something." She twisted around in her chair, picked two of the green beans, gave one to Bysshe, and bit into the other one. "I bet she doesn't. Kensy says a shunt hurts worse than braces."

"It doesn't hurt as much as not having one," Viola said, shooting me a Now-Do-You-See-What-My-Sister's-Caused? look.

"Traci, why don't you sit across from Viola?" Mother said

to me. "And we'll put Perdita next to you when she comes."

"If she comes," Viola said.

"I told her one o'clock," Mother said, sitting down at the near end. "So we'd have a chance to plan our strategy before she gets here. I talked to Carol Chen—"

"Her daughter nearly joined the Cyclists last year," I explained to Bysshe and Viola.

"*She* said they had a family gathering, like this, and simply talked to her daughter, and she decided she didn't want to be a Cyclist after all." She looked around the table. "So I thought we'd do the same thing with Perdita. I think we should start by explaining the significance of the Liberation and the days of dark oppression that preceded it—"

"*I* think," Viola interrupted, "we should try to talk her into just going off the ammenerol for a few months instead of having the shunt removed. If she comes. Which she won't."

"Why not?"

"Would you? I mean, it's like the Inquisition. Her sitting here while all of us 'explain' at her. Perdita may be crazy, but she's not stupid."

"It's hardly the Inquisition," Mother said. She looked anxiously past me toward the door. "I'm sure Perdita—" She stopped, stood up, and plunged off suddenly through the asparagus.

I turned around, half-expecting Perdita with light-up lips or a full-body tattoo, but I couldn't see through the leaves. I pushed at the branches.

"Is it Perdita?" Viola said, leaning forward.

I peered around the mulberry bush. "Oh, my God," I said.

It was my mother-in-law, wearing a black abayah and a silk yarmulke. She swept toward us through a pumpkin patch, robes billowing and eyes flashing. Mother hurried in her wake of trampled radishes, looking daggers at me.

I turned them on Viola. "It's your grandmother Karen," I said accusingly. "You told me you didn't get through to her."

"I didn't," she said. "Twidge, sit up straight. And put your slate down."

There was an ominous rustling in the rose arbor, as of leaves shrinking back in terror, and my mother-in-law arrived.

"Karen!" I said, trying to sound pleased. "What on earth are you doing here? I thought you were in Baghdad."

"I came back as soon as I got Viola's message," she said, glaring at everyone in turn. "Who's this?" she demanded, pointing at Bysshe. "Viola's new livein?"

"No!" Bysshe said, looking horrified.

"This is my law clerk, Mother," I said. "Bysshe Adams-Hardy."

"Twidge, why aren't you in school?"

"I *am*," Twidge said. "I'm remoting." She held up her slate. "See? Math."

"I see," she said, turning to glower at me. "It's a serious enough matter to require my great-grandchild's being pulled out of school *and* the hiring of legal assistance, and yet you didn't deem it important enough to notify me. Of course, you *never* tell me anything, Traci."

She swirled herself into the end chair, sending leaves and sweet pea blossoms flying, and decapitating the broccoli centerpiece. "I didn't get Viola's cry for help until yesterday. Viola, you should never leave messages with Hassim. His English is virtually nonexistent. I had to get him to hum me your ring. I recognized your signature, but the phones were out, so I flew home. In the middle of negotiations, I might add."

"How *are* negotiations going, Grandma Karen?" Viola asked.

"They *were* going extremely well. The Israelis have given the Palestinians half of Jerusalem, and they've agreed to time-share the Golan Heights." She turned to glare momentarily at me. "*They* know the importance of communication." She turned back to Viola. "So why are they picking on you, Viola? Don't they like your new livein?"

"I am *not* her livein," Bysshe protested.

I have often wondered how on earth my mother-in-law became a mediator and what she does in all those negotiation sessions with Serbs and Catholics and North and South Koreans and Protestants and Croats. She takes sides, jumps to conclusions, misinterprets everything you say, refuses to listen. And yet she talked South Africa into a Mandelan government and would probably get the Palestinians to observe Yom Kippur. Maybe she just bullies everyone into submission. Or maybe they have to band together to protect themselves against her.

Bysshe was still protesting. "I never even met Viola till today. I've only talked to her on the phone a couple of times."

"You must have done something," Karen said to Viola. "They're obviously out for your blood."

"Not mine," Viola said. "Perdita's. She's joined the Cyclists."

"The Cyclists? I left the West Bank negotiations because you don't approve of Perdita joining a biking club? How am I supposed to explain this to the president of Iraq? She will not understand, and neither do I. A biking club!"

"The Cyclists do not ride bicycles," Mother said.

"They menstruate," Twidge said.

There was a dead silence of at least a minute, and I thought, it's finally happened. My mother-in-law and I are actually going to be on the same side of a family argument.

"All this fuss is over Perdita's having her shunt removed?" Karen said finally. "She's of age, isn't she? And this is obviously a case where personal sovereignty applies. You should know that, Traci. After all, you're a judge."

I should have known it was too good to be true.

"You mean you approve of her setting back the Liberation twenty years?" Mother said.

"I hardly think it's that serious," Karen said. "There are anti-shunt groups in the Middle East, too, you know, but no one takes them seriously. Not even the Iraqis, and they still wear the veil."

"Perdita is taking them seriously."

Karen dismissed Perdita with a wave of her black sleeve. "They're a trend, a fad. Like microskirts. Or those dreadful electronic eyebrows. A few women wear silly fashions like that for a little while, but you don't see women as a whole giving up pants or going back to wearing hats."

"But Perdita. . . ." Viola said.

"If Perdita wants to have her period, I say let her. Women functioned perfectly well without shunts for thousands of years."

Mother brought her fist down on the table. "Women also functioned *perfectly well* with concubinage, cholera, and corsets," she said, emphasizing each word with her fist. "But that is no reason to take them on voluntarily, and I have no intention of allowing Perdita—"

"Speaking of Perdita, where is the poor child?" Karen said.

"She'll be here any minute," Mother said. "I invited her to lunch so we could discuss this with her."

"Ha!" Karen said. "So you could browbeat her into changing her mind, you mean. Well, I have no intention of collaborating with you. I intend to listen to the poor thing's point of view with interest and an open mind. Respect, that's the key word, and one you all seem to have forgotten. Respect and common courtesy."

A barefoot young woman wearing a flowered smock and a red scarf tied around her left arm came up to the table with a sheaf of pink folders.

"It's about time," Karen said, snatching one of the folders

away from her. "Your service here is dreadful. I've been sitting here ten minutes." She snapped the folder open. "I don't suppose you have Scotch."

"My name is Evangeline," the young woman said. "I'm Perdita's docent." She took the folder away from Karen. "She wasn't able to join you for lunch, but she asked me to come in her place and explain the Cyclist philosophy to you."

She sat down in the wicker chair next to me.

"The Cyclists are dedicated to freedom," she said. "Freedom from artificiality, freedom from body-controlling drugs and hormones, freedom from the male patriarchy that attempts to impose them on us. As you probably already know, we do not wear shunts."

She pointed to the red scarf around her arm. "Instead, we wear this as a badge of our freedom and our femaleness. I'm wearing it today to announce that my time of fertility has come."

"We had that, too," Mother said, "only we wore it on the back of our skirts."

I laughed.

The docent glared at me. "Male domination of women's bodies began long before the so-called 'Liberation,' with government regulation of abortion and fetal rights, scientific control of fertility, and finally the development of ammenerol, which eliminated the reproductive cycle altogether. This was all part of a carefully planned takeover of women's bodies, and by extension, their identities, by the male patriarchal regime."

"What an interesting point of view!" Karen said enthusiastically.

It certainly was. In point of fact, ammenerol hadn't been invented to eliminate menstruation at all. It had been developed for shrinking malignant tumors, and its uterine lining-absorbing properties had only been discovered by accident.

"Are you trying to tell us," Mother said, "that men *forced* shunts on women?! We had to *fight* everyone to get it approved by the FDA!"

It was true. What surrogate mothers and anti-abortionists and the fetal rights issue had failed to do in uniting women, the prospect of not having to menstruate did. Women had organized rallies, petitioned, elected senators, passed amendments, been excommunicated, and gone to jail, all in the name of Liberation.

"Men were *against* it," Mother said, getting rather red in the face. "And the religious right and the maxipad manufacturers, and the Catholic Church—"

"They knew they'd have to allow women priests," Viola said.

"Which they did," I said.

"The Liberation hasn't freed you," the docent said loudly. "Except from the natural rhythms of your life, the very wellspring of your femaleness."

She leaned over and picked a daisy that was growing under the table. "We in the Cyclists celebrate the onset of our menses and rejoice in our bodies," she said, holding the daisy up. "Whenever a Cyclist comes into blossom, as we call it, she is honored with flowers and poems and songs. Then we join hands and tell what we like best about our menses."

"Water retention," I said.

"Or lying in bed with a heating pad for three days a month," Mother said.

"*I* think I like the anxiety attacks best," Viola said. "When I went off the ammenerol, so I could have Twidge, I'd have these days where I was convinced the space station was going to fall on me."

A middle-aged woman in overalls and a straw hat had come over while Viola was talking and was standing next to Mother's chair. "I had these mood swings," she said. "One minute I'd feel cheerful and the next like Lizzie Borden."

"Who's Lizzie Borden?" Twidge asked.

"She killed her parents," Bysshe said. "With an ax."

Karen and the docent glared at both of them. "Aren't you supposed to be working on your math, Twidge?" Karen said.

"I've always wondered if Lizzie Borden had PMS," Viola said, "and that was why—"

"No," Mother said. "It was having to live before tampons and ibuprofen. An obvious case of justifiable homicide."

"I hardly think this sort of levity is helpful," Karen said, glowering at everyone.

"Are you our waitress?" I asked the straw-hatted woman hastily.

"Yes," she said, producing a slate from her overalls pocket.

"Do you serve wine?" I asked.

"Yes. Dandelion, cowslip, and primrose."

"We'll take them all," I said.

"A bottle of each?"

"For now. Unless you have them in kegs."

"Our specials today are watermelon salad and *choufleur gratiné*," she said, smiling at everyone. Karen and the docent did not smile back. "You hand-pick your own cauliflower from the patch up front. The floratarian special is sautéed lily buds with marigold butter."

There was a temporary truce while everyone ordered. "I'll have the sweet peas," the docent said, "and a glass of rose water."

Bysshe leaned over to Viola. "I'm sorry I sounded so horrified when your grandmother asked if I was your livein," he said.

"That's okay," Viola said. "Grandma Karen can be pretty scary."

"I just didn't want you to think I didn't like you. I do. Like you, I mean."

"Don't they have soyburgers?" Twidge asked.

As soon as the waitress left, the docent began passing out the pink folders she'd brought with her. "These will explain the working philosophy of the Cyclists," she said, handing me one, "along with practical information on the menstrual cycle." She handed Twidge one.

"It looks just like those books we used to get in junior high," Mother said, looking at hers. " 'A Special Gift,' they were called, and they had all these pictures of girls with pink ribbons in their hair, playing tennis and smiling. Blatant misrepresentation."

She was right. There was even the same drawing of the fallopian tubes I remembered from my middle school movie, a drawing that had always reminded me of *Alien* in the early stages.

"Oh, yuck," Twidge said. "This is disgusting."

"Do your math," Karen said.

Bysshe looked sick. "Did women really do this stuff?"

The wine arrived, and I poured everyone a large glass. The docent pursed her lips disapprovingly and shook her head. "The Cyclists do not use the artificial stimulants or hormones that the male patriarchy has forced on women to render them docile and subservient."

"How long do you menstruate?" Twidge asked.

"Forever," Mother said.

"Four to six days," the docent said. "It's there in the booklet."

"No, I mean, your whole life or what?"

"A woman has her menarche at twelve years old on the average and ceases menstruating at age fifty-five."

"I had my first period at eleven," the waitress said, setting a bouquet down in front of me. "At school."

"I had my last one on the day the FDA approved *ammenerol*," Mother said.

"Three hundred and sixty-five divided by twenty-eight," Twidge said, writing on her slate. "Times forty-three years." She looked up. "That's five hundred and fifty-nine periods."

"That can't be right," Mother said, taking the slate away from her. "It's at least five thousand."

"And they all start on the day you leave on a trip," Viola said.

"Or get married," the waitress said.

Mother began writing on the slate.

I took advantage of the ceasefire to pour everyone some more dandelion wine.

Mother looked up from the slate. "Do you realize with a period of five days, you'd be menstruating for nearly three thousand days? That's over eight solid years."

"And in between there's PMS," the waitress said, delivering flowers.

"What's PMS?" Twidge asked.

"Pre-menstrual syndrome was the name the male medical establishment fabricated for the natural variation in hormonal levels that signal the onset of menstruation," the docent said. "This mild and entirely normal fluctuation was exaggerated by men into a debility." She looked at Karen for confirmation.

"I used to cut my hair," Karen said.

The docent looked uneasy.

"Once I chopped off one whole side," Karen went on. "Bob had to hide the scissors every month. And the car keys. I'd start to cry every time I hit a red light."

"Did you swell up?" Mother asked, pouring Karen another glass of dandelion wine.

"I looked just like Orson Welles."

"Who's Orson Welles?" Twidge asked.

"Your comments reflect the self-loathing thrust on you by the patriarchy," the docent said. "Men have brainwashed women into thinking menstruation is evil and unclean. Women even called their menses 'the curse' because they accepted men's judgment."

"I called it the curse because I thought a witch must have laid a curse on me," Viola said. "Like in 'Sleeping Beauty.'"

Everyone looked at her.

"Well, I did," she said. "It was the only reason I could think of for such an awful thing happening to me." She handed the folder back to the docent. "It still is."

"I think you were awfully brave," Bysshe said to Viola, "going off the ammenerol to have Twidge."

"It was awful," Viola said. "You can't imagine."

Mother sighed. "When I got my period, I asked my mother if Annette had it, too."

"Who's Annette?" Twidge said.

"A Mouseketeer," Mother said and added, at Twidge's uncomprehending look, "On TV."

"High-rez," Viola said.

"The Mickey Mouse Club," Mother said.

"There was a high-rezzer called the Mickey Mouse Club?" Twidge said incredulously.

"They were days of dark oppression in many ways," I said.

Mother glared at me "Annette was every young girl's ideal," she said to Twidge. "Her hair was curly, she had actual breasts, her pleated skirt was always pressed, and I could not imagine that she could have anything so *messy* and undignified. Mr. Disney would never have allowed it. And if Annette didn't have one, I wasn't going to have one either. So I asked my mother—"

"What did she say?" Twidge cut in.

"She said every woman had periods," Mother said. "I asked her, 'Even the Queen of England?' and she said, 'Even the Queen.'"

"Really?" Twidge said. "But she's so *old!*"

"She isn't having it now," the docent said irritatedly. "I told you, menopause occurs at age fifty-five."

"And then you have hot flashes," Karen said, "and osteoporosis and so much hair on your upper lip you look like Mark Twain."

"Who's—" Twidge said.

"You are simply reiterating negative male propaganda," the docent interrupted, looking very red in the face.

"You know what I've always wondered?" Karen said, leaning conspiratorially close to Mother. "If Maggie Thatcher's menopause was responsible for the Falklands War."

"Who's Maggie Thatcher?" Twidge said.

The docent, who was now as red in the face as her scarf, stood up. "It is clear there is no point in trying to talk to you. You've all been completely brainwashed by the male patriarchy." She began grabbing up her folders. "You're blind, all of you! You don't even see that you're victims of a male conspiracy to deprive you of your biological identity, of your very womanhood. The Liberation wasn't a liberation at all. It was only another kind of slavery!"

"Even if that were true," I said, "even if it had been a conspiracy to bring us under male domination, it would have been worth it."

"She's right, you know," Karen said to Mother. "Traci's absolutely right. There are some things worth giving up anything for, even your freedom, and getting rid of your period is definitely one of them."

"Victims!" the docent shouted. "You've been stripped of your femininity, and you don't even care!" She stomped out, destroying several squash and a row of gladiolas in the process.

"You know what I hated most before the Liberation?" Karen said, pouring the last of the dandelion wine into her glass. "Sanitary belts."

"And those cardboard tampon applicators," Mother said.

"I'm never going to join the Cyclists," Twidge said.

"Good," I said.

"Can I have dessert?"

I called the waitress over, and Twidge ordered sugared violets. "Anyone else want dessert?" I asked. "Or more primrose wine?"

"I think it's wonderful the way you're trying to help your sister," Bysshe said, leaning close to Viola.

"And those Modess ads," Mother said. "You remember, with those glamorous women in satin brocade evening dresses and long white gloves, and below the picture was written, 'Modess, because. . . .' I thought Modess was a perfume."

Karen giggled. "I thought it was a brand of *champagne!*"

"I don't think we'd better have any more wine," I said.

The phone started singing the minute I got to my chambers the next morning, the universal ring.

"Karen went back to Iraq, didn't she?" I asked Bysshe.

"Yeah," he said. "Viola said there was some snag over whether to put Disneyland on the West Bank or not."

"When did Viola call?"

Bysshe looked sheepish. "I had breakfast with her and Twidge this morning."

"Oh." I picked up the phone. "It's probably Mother with a plan to kidnap Perdita. Hello?"

"This is Evangeline, Perdita's docent," the voice on the phone said. "I hope you're happy. You've bullied Perdita into surrendering to the enslaving male patriarchy."

"I have?" I said.

"You've obviously employed mind control, and I want you to know we intend to file charges." She hung up. The phone rang again immediately, another universal.

"What is the good of signatures when no one ever uses them?" I said and picked up the phone.

"Hi, Mom," Perdita said. "I thought you'd want to know I've changed my mind about joining the Cyclists."

"Really?" I said, trying not to sound jubilant.

"I found out they wear this red scarf thing on their arm. It covers up Sitting Bull's horse."

"That is a problem," I said.

"Well, that's not all. My docent told me about your lunch.

Did Grandma Karen really tell you you were right?"

"Yes."

"Gosh! I didn't believe that part. Well, anyway, my docent said you wouldn't listen to her about how great menstruating is, that you all kept talking about the negative aspects of it, like bloating and cramps and crabbiness, and I said, 'What are cramps?' and she said, 'Menstrual bleeding frequently causes headaches and discomfort,' and I said, 'Bleeding?!? Nobody ever said anything about bleeding!' Why didn't you tell me there was blood involved, Mother?"

I had, but I felt it wiser to keep silent.

"And you didn't say a word about its being painful. And all the hormone fluctuations! Anybody'd have to be crazy to want to go through that when they didn't have to! How did you stand it before the Liberation?"

"They were days of dark oppression," I said.

"I *guess!* Well, anyway, I quit and now my docent is really mad. But I told her it was a case of personal sovereignty, and she has to respect my decision. I'm still going to become a floratarian, though, and I don't want you to try to talk me out of it."

"I wouldn't dream of it," I said.

"You know, this whole thing is really your fault, Mom! If you'd told me about the pain part in the first place, none of this would have happened. Viola's right! You never tell us *anything!*"

"Did Grandma Karen really tell you you were right?"

"Yes."

"Gosh! I didn't believe that part. Well, anyway, my docent said you wouldn't listen to her about how great menstruating is, that you'd just talking about the negative aspects of it, like bloating and cramps and crabbiness, and I said, 'What are cramps?' and she said, 'Menstrual bleeding frequently causes headaches and discomfort,' and I said, 'Bleeding?! Nobody ever said anything about bleeding! Why didn't you tell me there was blood involved, Mother?'"

"I had, but I felt it wiser to keep silent."

"And you didn't say a word about its being painful. And all the hormone fluctuations! Anybody'd have to be crazy to want to go through that when they didn't have to! How did you stand it before the Liberation?"

"They were days of dark oppression," I said.

"I guess! Well, anyway, I quit and now my docent is really mad. But I told her it was a case of personal sovereignty, and she has to respect my decision. I'm still going to become a flontarian, though, and I don't want you to try to talk me out of it."

"I wouldn't dream of it," I said.

"You know, this whole thing is really your fault, Mom! If you'd told me about the pain part in the first place, none of this would have happened. Viola's right! You never tell us anything!"

Beginning with Uhura's Song, a Star Trek novel judged superior by many, Janet Kagan has risen by dint of her thorough grounding in such subjects as linguistics. This neatly told tale combines her deft sense of humor with a firm grasp of character.

The Nutcracker Coup
by Janet Kagan

Marianne Tedesco had "The Nutcracker Suite" turned up full blast for inspiration, and as she whittled she now and then raised her knife to conduct Tchaikovsky. That was what she was doing when one of the locals poked his delicate snout around the corner of the door to her office. She nudged the sound down to a whisper in the background and beckoned him in.

It was Tatep, of course. After almost a year on Rejoicing (that was the literal translation of the world's name), she still had a bit of trouble recognizing the Rejoicers by snout alone, but the three white quills in Tatep's ruff had made him the first real "individual" to her. Helluva thing for a junior diplomat *not* to be able to tell one local from another but there it was. Marianne was desperately trying to learn the snout shapes that distinguished the Rejoicers to each other.

"Good morning, Tatep. What can I do for you?"

"Share?" said Tatep.

"Of course. Shall I turn the music off?" Marianne knew that *The Nutcracker Suite* was as alien to him as the rattling and scraping of his music was to her. She was beginning to like pieces here and there of the Rejoicer style, but she didn't know if Tatep felt the same way about Tchaikovsky.

"Please, leave it on," he said. "You've played it every day

this week—am I right? And now I find you waving your knife to the beat. Will you share the reason?"

She *had* played it every day this week, she realized. "I'll try to explain. It's a little silly, really, and it shouldn't be taken as characteristic of human. Just as characteristic of Marianne."

"Understood." He climbed the stepstool she'd cobbled together her first month on Rejoicing and settled himself on his haunches comfortably to listen. At rest, the wicked quills adorning his ruff and tail seemed just that: adornments. By local standards, Tatep was a handsome male.

He was also a quadruped, and human chairs weren't the least bit of use to him. The stepstool let him lounge on its broad upper platform or sit upright on the step below that—in either case, it put a Rejoicer eye to eye with Marianne. This had been so successful an innovation in the embassy that they had hired a local artisan to make several for each office. Chornian's stepstools were a more elaborate affair, but Chornian himself had refused to make one to replace "the very first." A fine sense of tradition, these Rejoicers.

That was, of course, the best way to explain the Tchaikovsky. "Have you noticed, Tatep, that the further away from home you go, the more important it becomes to keep traditions?"

"Yes," he said. He drew a small piece of sweetwood from his pouch and seemed to consider it thoughtfully. "Ah! I hadn't thought how very strongly you must need tradition! You're very far from home indeed. Some thirty light years, is it not?" He bit into the wood, shaving a delicate curl from it with one corner of his razor sharp front tooth. The curl he swallowed, then he said, "Please, go on."

The control he had always fascinated Marianne—she would have preferred to watch him carve, but she spoke instead. "My family tradition is to celebrate a holiday called Christmas."

He swallowed another shaving and repeated, "Christmas."

"For some humans Christmas is a religious holiday. For my family, it was more of . . . a turning of the seasons. Now, Esperanza and I couldn't agree on a date—her homeworld's calendar runs differently than mine—but we both agreed on a need to celebrate Christmas once a year. So, since it's a solstice festival, I asked Muhammed what was the shortest day of the year on Rejoicing. He says that's Tamemb Nap Ohd."

Tatep bristled his ruff forward, confirming Muhammed's date.

"So I have decided to celebrate Christmas Eve on Tamemb Nap Ohd and to celebrate Christmas Day on Tememb Nap Chorr."

"Christmas is a revival, then? An awakening?"

"Yes, something like that. A renewal. A promise of spring to come."

"Yes, we have an Awakening on Tememb Nap Chorr as well."

Marianne nodded. "Many peoples do. Anyhow, I mentioned that I wanted to celebrate and a number of other people at the embassy decided it was a good idea. So, we're trying to put together something that resembles a Christmas celebration—mostly from local materials."

She gestured toward the player. "That piece of music is generally associated with Christmas. I've been playing it because it—gives me an anticipation of the Awakening to come."

Tatep was doing fine finishing work now, and Marianne had to stop to watch. The bit of sweetwood was turning into a pair of tommets—the Embassy staff had dubbed them "notrabbits" for their sexual proclivities—engaged in their mating dance. Tatep rattled his spines, amused, and passed the carving into her hands. He waited quietly while she turned it this way and that, admiring the exquisite workmanship.

"You don't get the joke," he said, at last.

"No, Tatep. I'm afraid I don't. Can you share it?"

"Look closely at their teeth."

Marianne did, and got the joke. The creatures were tommets, yes, but the teeth they had were not tommet teeth. They were the same sort of teeth that Tatep had used to carve them. Apparently, "fucking like tommets" was a Rejoicer joke.

"It's a gift for Hapet and Achinto. They had *six* children! We're all pleased and amazed for them."

Four to a brood was the usual, but birthings were few and far between. A couple that had more than two birthings in a lifetime was considered unusually lucky.

"Congratulate them for me, if you think it appropriate," Marianne said. "Would it be proper for the embassy to send a gift?"

"Proper and most welcome. Hapet and Achinto will need help feeding that many."

"Would you help me choose? Something to make children grow healthy and strong, and something as well to delight their senses."

"I'd be glad to. Shall we go to the market or the wood?"

"Let's go chop our own, Tatep. I've been sitting behind this desk too damn long. I could use the exercise."

As Marianne rose, Tatep put his finished carving into his pouch and climbed down. "You will share more about Christmas with me while we work? You can talk and chop at the same time."

Marianne grinned. "I'll do better than that. You can help me choose something that we can use for a Christmas tree, as well. If it's something that is also edible when it has seasoned for a few weeks' time, that would be all the more to the spirit of the festival."

The two of them took a leisurely stroll down the narrow cobbled streets. Marianne shared more of her Christmas customs with Tatep and found her anticipation growing apace as she did.

At Tatep's suggestion they paused at Killim the glassblower's, where Tatep helped Marianne describe and order a dozen ornamental balls for the tree. Unaccustomed to the idea of purely ornamental glass objects, Killim was fascinated. "She says," reported Tatep when Marianne missed a few crucial words of her reply, "she'll make a number of samples and you'll return on Debem Op Chorr to choose the most proper."

Marianne nodded. Before she could thank Killim, however, she heard the door behind her open, heard a muffled squeak of surprise, and turned. Halemtat had ordered yet another of his subjects clipped—Marianne saw that much before the local beat a hasty retreat from the door and vanished.

"Oh, god," she said aloud. "Another one." That, she admitted to herself for the first time, was why she was making such an effort to recognize the individual Rejoicers by facial shape alone. She'd seen no less than fifty clipped in the year she'd been on Rejoicing. There was no doubt in her mind that this was a new one—the blunted tips of its quills had been bright and crisp. "Who is it this time, Tatep?"

Tatep ducked his head in shame. "Chornian," he said.

For once, Marianne couldn't restrain herself. "Why?" she asked, and she heard the unprofessional belligerence in her own voice.

"For saying something I dare not repeat, not even in your language," Tatep said, "unless I wish to have *my* quills clipped."

Marianne took a deep breath. "I apologize for asking, Tatep. It was stupid of me." Best thing to do would be to get the hell out and let Chornian complete his errand without being shamed in front of the two of them. "Though," she said aloud, not caring if it was professional or not, "it's Halemtat who should be shamed, not Chornian."

Tatep's eyes widened, and Marianne knew she'd gone too far. She thanked the glassblower politely in Rejoicer and promised to return on Debem Op Chorr to examine the samples.

As they left Killim's, Marianne heard the scurry behind them—Chornian entering the shop as quickly and as unobtrusively as possible. She set her mouth—her silence raging—and followed Tatep without a backward glance.

At last they reached the communal wood. Trying for some semblance of normalcy, Marianne asked Tatep for the particulars of an unfamiliar tree.

"*Huep*," he said. "Very good for carving, but not very good for eating." He paused a moment, thoughtfully. "I think I've put that wrong. The flavor is *very* good, but it's very low in food value. It grows prodigiously, though, so a lot of people eat too much of it when they shouldn't."

"Junk food," said Marianne, nodding. She explained the term to Tatep and he concurred. "Youngsters are particularly fond of it but it wouldn't be a good gift for Hapet and Achinto."

"Then let's concentrate on good *healthy* food for Hapet and Achinto," said Marianne.

Deeper in the wood, they found a stand of the trees the embassy staff had dubbed gnomewood for its gnarly, stunted appearance. Tatep proclaimed this perfect, and Marianne set about to chop the proper branches. Gathering food was more a matter of pruning than chopping down, she'd learned, and she followed Tatep's careful instructions so she did not damage the tree's productive capabilities in the process.

"Now this one—just here," he said. "See, Marianne? Above the bole, for new growth will spring from the bole soon after your Awakening. If you damage the bole, however, there will be no new growth on this branch again."

Marianne chopped with care. The chopping took

some of the edge off her anger. Then she inspected the gnomewood and found a second possibility. "Here," she said. "Would this be the proper place?"

"Yes," said Tatep, obviously pleased that she'd caught on so quickly. "That's right." He waited until she had lopped off the second branch and properly chosen a third and then he said, "Chornian said Halemtat had the twining tricks of a *talemtat*. One of his children liked the rhyme and repeated it."

"*Talemtat* is the vine that strangles the tree it climbs, am I right?" She kept her voice very low.

Instead of answering aloud, Tatep nodded.

"Did Halemtat—did Halemtat order the child clipped as well?"

Tatep's eyelids shaded his pupils darkly. "The entire family. He ordered the entire family clipped."

So that was why Chornian was running the errands. He would risk his own shame to protect his family from the awful embarrassment—for a Rejoicer—of appearing in public with their quills clipped.

She took out her anger on yet another branch of the gnomewood. When the branch fell—on her foot, as luck would have it—she sat down of a heap, thinking to examine the bruise, then looked Tatep straight in the eye. "How long? How long does it take for the quills to grow out again?" After much of a year, she hadn't yet seen evidence that an adult's quills regenerated at all. "They do regrow?"

"After several Awakenings," he said. "The regrowth can be quickened by eating *welspeth*, but . . ."

But *welspeth* was a hot-house plant in this country. Too expensive for somebody like Chornian.

"I see," she said. "Thank you, Tatep."

"Be careful where you repeat what I've told you. Best you not repeat it at all." He cocked his head at her and added, with a rattle of quills, "I'm not sure where Halemtat would clip a human, or even if you'd feel shamed by a clipping, but I wouldn't like to be responsible for finding out."

Marianne couldn't help but grin. She ran a hand through her pale white hair. "I've had my head shaved—that was long ago and far away—and it was intended to shame me."

"Intended to?"

"I painted my naked scalp bright red and went about my business as usual. I set something of a new fashion and, in the end, it was the shaver who was—quite properly—shamed."

Tatep's eyelids once again shaded his eyes. "I must think about that," he said, at last. "We have enough branches for a proper gift now, Marianne. Shall we consider the question of your Christmas tree?"

"Yes," she said. She rose to her feet and gathered up the branches. "And another thing as well. . . . I'll need some more wood for carving. I'd like to carve some gifts for my friends, as well. That's another tradition of Christmas."

"Carving gifts? Marianne, you make Christmas sound as if it were a Rejoicing holiday!"

Marianne laughed. "It is, Tatep. I'll gladly share my Christmas with you."

Clarence Doggett was Super Plenipotentiary Representing Terra to Rejoicing and today he was dressed to live up to his extravagant title in striped silver tights and a purple silk weskit. No less than four hoops of office jangled from his belt. Marianne had, since meeting him, conceived the theory that the more stylishly outré his dress the more likely he was to say yes to the request of a subordinate. Scratch that theory. . . .

Clarence Doggett straightened his weskit with a tug and said, "We have no reason to write a letter of protest about Emperor Halemtat's treatment of Chornian. He's deprived us of a valuable worker, true, but . . ."

"Whatever happened to human rights?"

"They're not human, Marianne. They're aliens."

At least he hadn't called them "Pincushions" as he usually did, Marianne thought. Clarence Doggett was the unfortunate result of what the media had dubbed "the Grand Opening." One day humans had been alone in the galaxy, and the next they'd found themselves only a tiny fraction of the intelligent species. Setting up five hundred embassies in the space of a few years had strained the diplomatic service to the bursting point. Rejoicing, considered a backwater world, got the scrapings from the bottom of the barrel. Marianne was trying very hard not to be one of those scrapings, despite the example set by Clarence. She clamped her jaw shut very hard.

Clarence brushed at his fashionably large mustache and added, "It's not as if they'll *really* die of shame, after all."

"Sir," Marianne began.

He raised his hands. "The subject is closed. How are the plans coming for the Christmas bash?"

"Fine, sir," she said without enthusiasm. "Killim—she's the local glassblower—would like to arrange a trade for some dyes, by the way. Not just for the Christmas tree ornaments, I gather, but for some project of her own. I'm sending letters with Nick Minski to a number of glassblowers back home to find out what sort of dye is wanted."

"Good work. Any trade item that helps tie the Rejoicers into the galactic economy is a find. You're to be commended."

Marianne wasn't feeling very commended, but she said, "Thank you, sir."

"And keep up the good work—this Christmas idea of yours is turning out to be a big morale booster."

That was the dismissal. Marianne excused herself and, feet dragging, she headed back to her office. " 'They're not human,' " she muttered to herself. " 'They're aliens. It's not as if they'll *really* die of shame. . . .' " She slammed her door closed behind her and snarled aloud, "But Chornian can't keep up work and the kids can't play with their friends and his mate Chaylam can't go to the market. What if they starve?"

"They won't starve," said a firm voice. Marianne jumped.

"It's just me," said Nick Minski. "I'm early." He leaned back in the chair and put his long legs up on her desk. "I've been watching how the neighbors behave. Friends—your friend Tatep included—take their leftovers to Chornian's family. They won't starve. At least, Chornian's family won't. I'm not sure what would happen to someone who is generally unpopular."

Nick was head of the ethnology team studying the Rejoicers. At least he had genuine observations to base his decisions on.

He tipped the chair to a precarious angle. "I can't begin to guess whether or not helping Chornian will land Tatep in the same hot water, so I can't reassure you there. I take it from your muttering that Clarence won't make a formal protest."

Marianne nodded.

He straightened the chair with a bang that made Marianne start. "Shit," he said. "Doggett's such a pissant."

Marianne grinned ruefully. "God, I'm going to miss you, Nick. Diplomats aren't permitted to speak in such matter-of-fact terms."

"I'll be back in a year. I'll bring you fireworks for your next Christmas." He grinned.

"We've been through that, Nick. Fireworks may be part of your family's Christmas tradition, but they're not part of mine. All that banging and flashing of light just wouldn't *feel* right to me, not on Christmas."

"Meanwhile," he went on, undeterred, "you think about my offer. You've learned more about Tatep and his people than half the folks on my staff; academic credentials or no, I can swing putting you on the ethnology team. We're short-handed as it is. I'd rather have skipped the rotation home this year, but . . ."

"You can't get everything you want, either."

He laughed. "I think they're afraid we'll all go native if we don't go home one year in five." He preened and grinned suddenly. "How d'you think I'd look in quills?"

"Sharp," she said and drew a second burst of laughter from him.

There was a knock at the door. Marianne stretched out a toe and tapped the latch. Tatep stood on the threshold, his quills still bristling from the cold. "Hi, Tatep—you're just in time. Come share."

His laughter subsiding to a chuckle, Nick took his feet from the desk and greeted Tatep in high-formal Rejoicer. Tatep returned the favor, then added by way of explanation, "Marianne is sharing her Christmas with me."

Nick cocked his head at Marianne. "But it's not for some time yet. . . ."

"I know," said Marianne. She went to her desk and pulled out a wrapped package. "Tatep, Nick is my very good friend. Ordinarily, we exchange gifts on Christmas Day, but since Nick won't be here for Christmas, I'm going to give him his present now."

She held out the package. "Merry Christmas, Nick. A little too early, but—"

"You've hidden the gift in paper," said Tatep. "Is that also traditional?"

"Traditional but not necessary. Some of the pleasure is the surprise involved," Nick told the Rejoicer. With a sidelong glance and a smile at Marianne, he held the package to his ear and shook it. "And some of the pleasure is in trying to guess what's in the package." He shook it and listened again. "Nope, I haven't the faintest idea."

He laid the package in his lap.

Tatep flicked his tail in surprise. "Why don't you open it?"

"In my family, it's traditional to wait until Christmas Day to open your presents, even if they're wrapped and sitting

under the Christmas tree in plain sight for three weeks
or more."

Tatep clambered onto the stool to give him a stare of
open astonishment from a more effective angle.

"Oh, no!" said Marianne. "Do you really mean it, Nick?
You're *not* going to open it until Christmas Day?"

Nick laughed again. "I'm teasing." To Tatep, he said,
"It's traditional in my family to wait—but it's also traditional
to find some rationalization to open a gift the minute you
lay hands on it. Marianne wants to see my expression; I
think that takes precedence in this case."

His long fingers found a cranny in the paper wrapping
and began to worry it ever so slightly. "Besides, our respective
homeworlds can't agree on a date for Christmas. . . . On
some world *today* must be Christmas, right?"

"Good rationalizing," said Marianne, with a sigh and a
smile of relief. "Right!"

"Right," said Tatep, catching on. He leaned precariously
from his perch to watch as Nick ripped open the wrapping
paper.

"Tchaikovsky made me think of it," Marianne said.
"Although, to be honest, Tchaikovsky's nutcracker wasn't
particularly traditional. This one *is*: take a close look."

He did. He held up the brightly painted figure, took
in its green weskit, its striped silver tights, its flamboyant
mustache. Four metal loops jangled at its carved belt and
Nick laughed aloud.

With a barely suppressed smile, Marianne handed him
a "walnut" of the local variety.

Nick stopped laughing long enough to say, "You mean,
this is a genuine, honest-to-god, *working* nutcracker?"

"Well, of course it is! My family's been making them for
years." She made a motion with her hands to demonstrate.
"Go ahead—crack that nut!"

Nick put the nut between the cracker's prominent jaws
and, after a moment's hesitation, closed his eyes and went

ahead. The nut gave with an audible and very satisfying craaack! and Nick began to laugh all over again.

"Share the joke," said Tatep.

"Gladly," said Marianne. "The Christmas nutcracker, of which that is a prime example, is traditionally carved to resemble an authority figure—particularly one nobody much likes. It's a way of getting back at the fraudulent, the pompous. Through the years they've poked fun at everybody from princes to policemen to"—Marianne waved a gracious hand at her own carved figure—"well, surely you recognize *him*."

"Oh, my," said Tatep, his eyes widening. "Clarence Doggett, is it not?" When Marianne nodded, Tatep said, "Are you about to get your head shaved again?"

Marianne laughed enormously. "If I do, Tatep, this time I'll paint my scalp red and green—traditional Christmas colors—and hang one of Killim's glass ornaments from my ear. Not likely, though," she added, to be fair. "Clarence doesn't go in for head shaving." To Nick, who had clearly taken in Tatep's "again," she said, "I'll tell you about it sometime."

Nick nodded and stuck another nut between Clarence's jaws. This time he watched as the nut gave way with a explosive bang. Still laughing, he handed the nutmeat to Tatep, who ate it and rattled his quills in laughter of his own. Marianne was doubly glad she'd invited Tatep to share the occasion—now she knew exactly what to make *him* for Christmas.

Christmas Eve found Marianne at a loss—something was missing from her holiday and she hadn't been able to put her finger on precisely what that something was.

It wasn't the color of the tree Tatep had helped her choose. The tree was the perfect Christmas tree shape, and if its foliage was a red so deep it approached black, that didn't matter a bit. "Next year we'll have Killim make some green ornaments," Marianne said to Tatep, "for the proper contrast."

Tinsel—silver thread she'd bought from one of the Rejoicer weavers and cut to length—flew in all directions. All seven of the kids who'd come to Rejoicing with their ethnologist parents were showing the Rejoicers the "proper" way to hang tinsel, which meant more tinsel was making it onto the kids and the Rejoicers than onto the tree.

Just as well. She'd have to clean the tinsel off the tree before she passed it on to Hapet and Achinto—well-seasoned and just the thing for growing children.

Nick would really have enjoyed seeing this, Marianne thought. Esperanza was filming the whole party, but that just wasn't the same as being here.

Killim brought the glass ornaments herself. She'd made more than the commissioned dozen. The dozen glass balls she gave to Marianne. Each was a swirl of colors, each unique. Everyone ooohed and aaahed—but the best was yet to come. From her sidepack, Killim produced a second container. "Presents," she said. "A present for your Awakening Tree."

Inside the box was a menagerie of tiny, bright glass animals: notrabbits, fingerfish, wispwings. . . . Each one had a loop of glass at the top to allow them to be hung from the tree. Scarcely trusting herself with such delicate objects of art, Marianne passed them on to George to string and hang.

Later, she took Killim aside and, with Tatep's help, thanked her profusely for the gifts. "Though I'm not sure she should have. Tell her I'll be glad to pay for them, Tatep. If she'd had them in her shop, I'd have snapped them up on the spot. I didn't know how badly our Christmas needed them until I saw her unwrap them."

Tatep spoke for a long time to Killim, who rattled all the while. Finally, Tatep rattled too. "Marianne, three humans have commissioned Killim to make animals for them to send home." Killim said something Marianne didn't catch. "Three humans in the last five minutes. She says, Think of this set as a—as an advertisement."

"No, you may not pay me for them," Killim said, still rattling. "I have gained something to trade for my dyes."

"She says," Tatep began.

"It's okay, Tatep. That I understood."

Marianne hung the wooden ornaments she'd carved and painted in bright colors, then she unsnagged a handful of tinsel from Tatep's ruff, divided it in half, and they both flung it onto the tree. Tatep's handful just barely missed Matsimoto, who was hanging strings of beads he'd bought in the bazaar, but Marianne's got Juliet, who was hanging chains of paper cranes it must have taken her the better part of the month to fold. Juliet laughed and pulled the tinsel from her hair to drape it—length by length and *neatly*—over the deep red branches.

Then Kelleb brought out the star. Made of silver wire delicately filigreed, it shone just the way a Christmas tree star should. He hoisted Juliet to his shoulders and she affixed it to the top of the tree and the entire company burst into cheers and applause.

Marianne sighed and wondered why that made her feel so down. "If Nick had been here," Tatep observed, "I believe he could have reached the top without an assistant."

"I think you're right," said Marianne. "I wish he *were* here. He'd enjoy this." Just for a moment, Marianne let herself realize that what was missing from this Christmas was Nick Minski.

"Next year," said Tatep.

"Next year," said Marianne. The prospect brightened her.

The tree glittered with its finery. For a moment they all stood back and admired it—then there was a scurry and a flurry as folks went to various bags and hiding places and brought out the brightly wrapped presents. Marianne excused herself from Tatep and Killim and brought out hers to heap at the bottom of the tree with the rest.

Again there was a moment's pause of appreciation. Then Clarence Doggett—of all people—raised his glass and said, "A toast! A Christmas toast! Here's to Marianne, for bringing Christmas thirty light years from old Earth!"

Marianne blushed as they raised their glasses to her. When they'd finished, she raised hers and found the right traditional response: "A Merry Christmas—and God bless us, every one!"

"Okay, Marianne. It's your call," said Esperanza. "Do we open the presents now or"—her voice turned to a mock whine—"do we *hafta* wait till tomorrow?"

Marianne glanced at Tatep. "What day is it now?" she asked. She knew enough about local time reckoning to know what answer he'd give. "Why, today is Tememb Nap Chorr."

She grinned at the faces around her. "By Rejoicer reckoning, the day changes when the sun sets—it's been Christmas Day for an hour at least now. But stand back and let the kids find their presents first."

There was a great clamor and rustle of wrapping paper and whoops of delight as the kids dived into the pile of presents.

As Marianne watched with rising joy, Tatep touched her arm. "More guests," he said, and Marianne turned.

It was Chornian, his mate Chaylam, and their four children. Marianne's jaw dropped at the sight of them. She had invited the six with no hope of a response and here they were. "And all dressed up for Christmas!" she said aloud, though she knew Christmas was *not* the occasion. "You're as glittery as the Christmas tree itself," she told Chornian, her eyes gleaming with the reflection of it.

Ruff and tail, each and every one of Chornian's short-clipped quills was tipped by a brilliant red bead. "Glass?" she asked.

"Yes," said Chornian. "Killim made them for us."

"You look magnificent! Oh—how wonderful!" Chaylam's clipped quills had been dipped in gold; when she shifted shyly, her ruff and tail rippled with light. "You sparkle like sun on the water," Marianne told her. The children's ruffs and tails had been tipped in gold and candy pink and vivid yellow and—the last but certainly not the least—in beads every color of the rainbow.

"A kid after my own heart," said Marianne. "I think that would have been my choice too." She gave a closer look. "No two alike, am I right? Come—join the party. I was afraid I'd have to drop your presents by your house tomorrow. Now I get to watch you open them, to see if I chose correctly."

She escorted the four children to the tree and, thanking her lucky stars she'd had Tatep write their names on their packages, she left them to hunt for their presents. Those for their parents she brought back with her.

"It was difficult," Chornian said to Marianne. "It was difficult to walk through the streets with pride but—we did. And the children walked the proudest. They give us courage."

Chaylam said, "If only on their behalf."

"Yes," agreed Chornian. "Tomorrow I shall walk in the sunlight. I shall go to the bazaar. My clipped quills will glitter, and I will not be ashamed that I have spoken the truth about Halemtat."

That was all the Christmas gift Marianne needed, she thought to herself, and handed the wrapped package to Chornian. Tatep gave him a running commentary on the habits and rituals of the human Awakening as he opened the package. Chornian's eyes shaded and Tatep's running commentary ceased abruptly as they peered together into the box.

"Did I get it right?" said Marianne, suddenly afraid she'd committed some awful faux pas. She'd scoured the bazaar for *welspeth* shoots and, finding none, she'd pulled enough strings with the ethnology team to get some imported.

Tatep was the one who spoke. "You got it right," he said. "Chornian thanks you." Chornian spoke rapid-fire Rejoicer for a long time; Marianne couldn't follow the half of it. When he'd finished, Tatep said simply, "He regrets that he has no present to give you."

"It's not necessary. Seeing those kids all in spangles brightened up the party—that's present enough for me!"

"Nevertheless," said Tatep, speaking slowly so she wouldn't miss a word. "Chornian and I make you this present."

Marianne knew the present Tatep drew from his pouch was from Tatep alone, but she was happy enough to play along with the fiction if it made him happy. She hadn't expected a present from Tatep and she could scarcely wait to see what it was he felt appropriate to the occasion.

Still, she gave it the proper treatment—shaking it, very gently, beside her ear. If there was anything to hear, it was drowned out by the robust singing of carols from the other side of the room. "I can't begin to guess, Tatep," she told him happily.

"Then open it."

She did. Inside the paper, she found a carving, the rich wine-red of burgundy-wood, bitter to the taste and therefore rarely carved but treasured because none of the kids would gnaw on it as they tested their teeth. The style of carving was so utterly Rejoicer that it took her a long moment to recognize the subject, but once she did, she knew she'd treasure the gift for a lifetime.

It was unmistakeably Nick—but Nick as seen from Tatep's point of view, hence the unfamiliar perspective. It was Looking Up At Nick.

"Oh, Tatep!" And then she remembered just in time and added, "Oh, Chornian! Thank you both so very much. I can't *wait* to show it to Nick when he gets back. Whatever made you think of doing Nick?"

Tatep said, "He's your best *human* friend. I know you miss him. You have no pictures; I thought you would feel better with a likeness."

She hugged the sculpture to her. "Oh, I do. Thank you, both of you." Then she motioned, eyes shining. "Wait. Wait right here, Tatep. Don't go away."

She darted to the tree and, pushing aside wads of rustling paper, she found the gift she'd made for Tatep. Back she darted to where the Rejoicers were waiting.

"I waited," Tatep said solemnly.

She handed him the package. "I hope this is worth the wait."

Tatep shook the package. "I can't begin to guess," he said.

"Then open it. *I* can't stand the wait!"

He ripped away the paper as flamboyantly as Nick had—to expose the brightly colored nutcracker and a woven bag of nuts.

Marianne held her breath. The problem had been, of course, to adapt the nutcracker to a recognizable Rejoicer version. She'd made the Emperor Halemtat sit back on his haunches, which meant far less adaptation of the cracking mechanism. Overly plump, she'd made him, and spiky. In his right hand, he carried an oversized pair of scissors—of the sort his underlings used for clipping quills. In his left, he carried a sprig of *talemtat*, that unfortunate rhyme for his name.

Chornian's eyes widened. Again, he rattled off a spate of Rejoicer too fast for Marianne to follow . . . except that Chornian seemed anxious.

Only then did Marianne realize what she'd done. "Oh, my God, Tatep! He wouldn't clip your quills for *having* that, would he?"

Tatep's quills rattled and rattled. He put one of the nuts between Halemtat's jaws and cracked with a vengeance. The nutmeat he offered to Marianne, his quills still rattling.

"If he does, Marianne, you'll come to Killim's to help me chose a good color for *my* glass beading!"

He cracked another nut and handed the meat to Chornian. The next thing Marianne knew, the two of them were rattling at each other—Chornian's glass beads adding a splendid tinkling to the merriment.

Much relieved, Marianne laughed with them. A few minutes later, Esperanza dashed out to buy more nuts—so Chornian's children could each take a turn at the cracking.

Marianne looked down at the image of Nick cradled in her arm. "I'm sorry you missed this," she told it, "but I promise I'll write everything down for you before I go to bed tonight. I'll try to remember every last bit of it for you."

"Dear Nick," Marianne wrote in another letter some months later. "You're not going to approve of this. I find I haven't been ethnologically correct—much less diplomatic. I'd only meant to share my Christmas with Tatep and Chornian and, for that matter, whoever wanted to join in the festivities. To hear Clarence tell it, I've sent Rejoicing to hell in a handbasket.

"You see, it does Halemtat no good to clip quills these days. There are some seventy-five Rejoicers walking around town clipped and beaded—as gaudy and as shameless as you please. I even saw one newly male (teenager) with beads on the ends of his unclipped spines!

"Killim says thanks for the dyes, by the way. They're just what she had in mind. She's so busy, she's taken on two apprentices to help her. She makes 'Christmas ornaments' and half the art galleries in the known universe are after her for more and more. The apprentices make glass beads. One of them—one of Chornian's kids, by the way—hit upon the bright idea of making simple sets of beads that can be stuck on the ends of quills cold. Saves time and trouble over the hot glass method.

"What's more—

"Well, yesterday I stopped by to say 'hi' to Killim, when who should turn up but Koppen—you remember him? He's one of Halemtat's advisors? You'll never guess what he wanted: a set of quill tipping beads.

"No, he hadn't had his quills clipped. Nor was he buying them for a friend. He was planning, he told Killim, to tell Halemtat a thing or two—I missed the details because he went too fast—and he expected he'd be clipped for it, so he was planning ahead. Very expensive *blue* beads for him, if you please, Killim!

"I find myself unprofessionally pleased. There's a thing or two Halemtat *ought* to be told. . . .

"Meanwhile, Chornian has gone into the business of making nutcrackers. —All right, so sue me, I showed him how to make the actual cracker work. It was that or risk his taking Tatep's present apart to find out for himself.

"I'm sending holos—including a holo of the one I made—because you've got to see the transformation Chornian's worked on mine. The difference between a human-carved nutcracker and a Rejoicer-carved nutcracker is as unmistakable as the difference between Looking Up At Nick and . . . well, *looking up at Nick*.

"I still miss you, even if you do think fireworks are appropriate at Christmas.

"See you soon—if Clarence doesn't boil me in my own pudding and bury me with a stake of holly through my heart."

Marianne sat with her light pen poised over the screen for a long moment, then she added, "Love, Marianne," and saved it to the next outgoing Dirt-bound mail.

Rejoicing
Midsummer's Eve
(Rejoicer reckoning)

Dear Nick—

This time it's not my fault. This time it's Esperanza's doing. Esperanza decided, for *her* contribution to our round of holidays, to celebrate Martin Luther King Day. (All right—if I'd known about Martin Luther King I'd probably have suggested a celebration myself but I didn't. Look him up; you'll like him.) And she invited a handful of the Rejoicers to attend as well.

Now, the final part of the celebration is that each person in turn "has a dream." This is not like wishes, Nick. This is more on the order of setting yourself a goal, even one that looks to all intents and purposes to be unattainable, but one you will strive to attain. Even Clarence got so into the occasion that he had a dream that he would stop thinking of the Rejoicers as "Pincushions" so he could start thinking of them as Rejoicers. Esperanza said later Clarence didn't quite get the point but for him she supposed that was a step in the right direction.

Well, after that, Tatep asked Esperanza, in his very polite fashion, if it would be proper for him to have a dream as well. There was some consultation over the proper phrasing—Esperanza says her report will tell you all about that—and then Tatep rose and said, "I have a dream . . . I have a dream that someday no one will get his quills clipped for speaking the truth."

(You'll see it on the tape. Everybody agreed that this was a good dream, indeed.)

After which, Esperanza had her dream "for human rights for all." Following which, of course, we all took turns trying to explain the concept of "human rights" to a half-dozen Rejoicers. Esperanza ended up translating five different constitutions for them—*and* an entire book of speeches by Martin Luther King.

Oh, god. I just realized . . . maybe it *is* my fault. I'd forgotten till just now. Oh. You judge, Nick.

About a week later Tatep and I were out gathering wood

for some carving he plans to do—for Christmas, he says, but he wanted to get a good start on it—and he stopped gnawing long enough to ask me, "Marianne, what's 'human'?"

"How do you mean?"

"I think when Clarence says 'human,' he means something different than you do."

"That's entirely possible. Humans use words pretty loosely at the best of times—there, I just did it myself."

"What do you mean when you say 'human'?"

"Sometimes I mean the species *homo sapiens*. When I say, Humans use words pretty loosely, I do. Rejoicers seem to be more particular about their speech, as a general rule."

"And when you say 'human rights,' what do you mean?"

"When I say 'human rights,' I mean *Homo sapiens* and *Rejoicing sapiens*. I mean any *sapiens*, in that context. I wouldn't guarantee that Clarence uses the word the same way in the same context."

"You think I'm human?"

"I *know* you're human. We're friends, aren't we? I couldn't be friends with—oh, a notrabbit—now, could I?"

He made that wonderful rattly sound he does when he's amused. "No, I can't imagine it. Then, if I'm human, I ought to have human rights."

"Yes," I said, "You bloody well ought to."

Maybe it is all my fault. Esperanza will tell you the rest—she's had Rejoicers all over her house for the past two weeks—they're watching every scrap of film she's got on Martin Luther King.

I don't know how this will all end up, but I wish to hell you were here to watch.

Love, Marianne

Marianne watched the Rejoicer child crack nuts with his Halemtat cracker and a cold, cold shiver went up her spine. That was the eleventh she'd seen this week.

Chornian wasn't the only one making them, apparently; somebody else had gone into the nutcracker business as well. This was, however, the first time she'd seen a child cracking nuts with Halemtat's jaw.

"Hello," she said, stooping to meet the child's eyes. "What a pretty toy! Will you show me how it works?"

Rattling all the while, the child showed her, step by step. Then he (or she—it wasn't polite to ask before puberty) said, "Isn't it funny? It makes Mama laugh and laugh and laugh."

"And what's your mama's name?"

"Pilli," said the child. Then it added, "With the green and white beads on her quills."

Pilli—who'd been clipped for saying that Halemtat had been overcutting the imperial reserve so badly that the trees would never grow back properly.

And then she realized that, less than a year ago, no child would have admitted that its mama had been clipped. The very thought of it would have shamed both mother *and* child.

Come to think of it . . . she glanced around the bazaar and saw no less than four clipped Rejoicers shopping for dinner. Two of them she recognized as Chornian and one of his children, the other two were new to her. She tried to identify them by their snouts and failed utterly—she'd have to ask Chornian. She also noted, with utterly unprofessional satisfaction, that she *could* ask Chornian such a thing now. That too would have been unthinkable and shaming less than a year ago.

Less than a year ago. She was thinking in Dirt terms because of Nick. There wasn't any point dropping him a line; mail would cross in deep space at this late a date. He'd be here just in time for "Christmas." She wished like hell he was already here. He'd know what to make of all this, she was certain.

As Marianne thanked the child and got to her feet, three

Rejoicers—all with the painted ruff of quills at their necks that identified them as Halemtat's guards—came waddling officiously up. "Here's one," said the largest. "Yes," said another. "Caught in the very act."

The largest squatted back on his haunches and said, "You will come with us, child, Halemtat decrees it."

Horror shot through Marianne's body.

The child cracked one last nut, rattled happily, and said, "I get my quills clipped?"

"Yes," said the largest Rejoicer. "You will have your quills clipped." Roughly, he separated child from nutcracker and began to tow the child away, each of them in that odd three-legged gait necessitated by the grip.

All Marianne could think to do was call after the child, "I'll tell Pilli what happened and where to find you!"

The child glanced over its shoulder, rattled again, and said, "Ask her could I have silver beads like Hortap!"

Marianne picked up the discarded nutcracker—lest some other child find it and meet the same fate—and ran full speed for Pilli's house.

At the corner, two children looked up from their own play and galloped along beside her until she skidded to a halt by Pilli's bakery. They followed her in, rattling happily to themselves over the race they'd run. Marianne's first thought was to shoo them off before she told Pilli what had happened, but Pilli greeted the two as if they were her own, and Marianne found herself blurting out the news.

Pilli gave a slow inclination of the head. "Yes," she said, pronouncing the words carefully so Marianne wouldn't miss them, "I expected that. Had it not been the nutcracker, it would have been words." She rattled. "That child is the most outspoken of my brood."

"But—" Marianne wanted to say, Aren't you afraid? but the question never surfaced.

Pilli gave a few coins to the other children and said, "Run to Killim's, my dears, and ask her to make a set of silver beads, if she doesn't already have one on hand. Then run tell your father what has happened."

The children were off in the scurry of excitement.

Pilli drew down the awning in front of her shop, then paused. "I think you are afraid for my child."

"Yes," said Marianne. Lying had never been her strong suit; maybe Nick was right—maybe diplomacy wasn't her field.

"You are kind," said Pilli. "But don't be afraid. Even Halemtat wouldn't dare to order a child *hashay*."

"I don't understand the term."

"*Hashay?*" Pilli flipped her tail around in front of her and held out a single quill. "Chippet will be clipped here," she said, drawing a finger across the quill about half-way up its length. "*Hashay* is to clip here." The finger slid inward, to a spot about a quarter of an inch from her skin. "Don't worry, Marianne. Even Halemtat wouldn't dare to *hashay* a child."

I'm supposed to be reassured, thought Marianne. "Good," she said aloud, "I'm relieved to hear that." In truth, she hadn't the slightest idea what Pilli was talking about—and she was considerably less than reassured by the ominous implications of the distinction. She'd never come across the term in any of the ethnologists' reports.

She was still holding the Halemtat nutcracker in her hands. Now she considered it carefully. Only in its broadest outlines did it resemble the one she'd made for Tatep. This nutcracker was purely Rejoicer in style and—she almost dropped it at the sudden realization—peculiarly Tatep's style of carving. Tatep was making them too?

If *she* could recognize Tatep's distinctive style, surely Halemtat could—what then?

Carefully, she tucked the nutcracker under the awning—let Pilli decide what to do with the object; Marianne couldn't make the decision for her—and set off at a quick pace for Tatep's house.

On the way, she passed yet another child with a Halemtat

nutcracker. She paused, found the child's father and passed the news to him that Halemtat's guards were clipping Pilli's child for the "offense." The father thanked her for the information and, with much politeness, took the nutcracker from the child.

This one, Marianne saw, was *not* carved in Tatep's style or in Chornian's. This one was the work of an unfamiliar set of teeth.

Having shooed his child indoors, the Rejoicer squatted back on his haunches. In plain view of the street, he took up the bowl of nuts his child had left uncracked and began to crack them, one by one, with such deliberation that Marianne's jaw dropped.

She'd never seen an insolent Rejoicer but she would have bet money she was seeing one now. He even managed to make the crack of each nut resound like a gunshot. With the sound still ringing in her ears, Marianne quickened her steps toward Tatep's.

She found him at home, carving yet another nutcracker. He swallowed, then held out the nutcracker to her and said, "What do you think, Marianne? Do you approve of my portrayal?"

This one wasn't Halemtat, but his—for want of a better word—grand vizier, Corten. The grand vizier always looked to her as if he smirked. She knew the expression was due to a slightly malformed tooth but, to a human eye, the result was a smirk. Tatep's portrayal had the same smirk, only more so. Marianne couldn't help it . . . she giggled.

"Aha!" said Tatep, rattling up a rainstorm's worth of sound. "For once, you've shared the joke without the need of explanation!" He gave a long grave look at the nutcracker. "The grand vizier has earned his keep this once!"

Marianne laughed, and Tatep rattled. This time the sound of the quills sobered Marianne. "I think your work will get you clipped, Tatep," she said, and she told him about Pilli's child.

He made no response. Instead, he dropped to his feet and went to the chest in the corner, where he kept any number of carvings and other precious objects. From the chest, he drew out a box. Three-legged, he walked back to her. "Shake this! I'll bet you can guess what's inside."

Curious, she shook the box: it rattled. "A set of beads," she said.

"You see? I'm prepared. They rattle like a laugh, don't they?—a laugh at Halemtat. I asked Killim to make the beads red because that was the color you painted your scalp when you were clipped."

"I'm honored. . . ."

"But?"

"But I'm afraid for you. For *all* of you."

"Pilli's child wasn't afraid."

"No. No, Pilli's child wasn't afraid. Pilli said even Halemtat wouldn't dare *hashay* a child." Marianne took a deep breath and said, "But you're not a child." And I don't know what *hashay*ing does to a Rejoicer, she wanted to add.

"I've swallowed a talpseed," Tatep said, as if that said it all.

"I don't understand."

"Ah! I'll share, then. A talpseed can't grow unless it has been through the"—he patted himself—"stomach? digestive system? of a Rejoicer. Sometimes they don't grow even then. To swallow a talpseed means to take a step toward the growth of something important. I swallowed a talpseed called 'human rights.' "

There was nothing Marianne could say to that but: "I understand."

Slowly, thoughtfully, Marianne made her way back to the embassy. Yes, she understood Tatep—hadn't she been screaming at Clarence for just the same reason? But she was terrified for Tatep—for them all.

Without consciously meaning to, she bypassed the

embassy for the little clutch of domes that housed the ethnologists. Esperanza—it was Esperanza she had to see.

She was in luck. Esperanza was at home writing up one of her reports. She looked up and said, "Oh, good. It's time for a break!"

"Not a break, I'm afraid. A question that, I think, is right up your alley. Do you know much about the physiology of the Rejoicers?"

"I'm the expert," Esperanza said, leaning back in her chair. "As far as there is one in the group."

"What happens if you cut a Rejoicer's spine"—she held up her fingers—"*this* close to the skin?"

"Like a cat's claw, sort of. If you cut the tip, nothing happens. If you cut too far down, you hit the blood supply—and maybe the nerve. The quill would bleed most certainly. Might never grow back properly. And it'd hurt like hell, I'm sure—like gouging the base of your thumbnail."

She sat forward suddenly. "Marianne, you're shaking. What is it?"

Marianne took a deep breath but couldn't stop shaking. "What would happen if somebody did that to all of Ta"—she found she couldn't get the name out—"all of a Rejoicer's quills?"

"He'd bleed to death, Marianne." Esperanza took her hand and gave it a firm squeeze. "Now, I'm going to get you a good stiff drink and you are going to tell me all about it."

Fighting nausea, Marianne nodded. "Yes," she said with enormous effort. "Yes."

"Who the *hell* told the Pincushions about 'human rights'?" Clarence roared. Furious, he glowered down at Marianne and waited for her response.

Esperanza drew herself up to her full height and stepped between the two of them. "Martin Luther King told the *Rejoicers* about human rights. You were there when he did it. Though you seem to have forgotten *your* dream, obviously the Rejoicers haven't forgotten theirs."

"There's a goddamned revolution going on out there!" Clarence waved a hand vaguely in the direction of the center of town.

"That is certainly what it looks like," Juliet said mildly. "So why are we here instead of out there observing?"

"You're here because I'm responsible for your safety."

"Bull," said Matsimoto. "Halemtat isn't interested in clipping *us*."

"Besides," said Esperanza. "The supply ship will be landing in about five minutes. Somebody's got to go pick up the supplies—and Nick. Otherwise, he's going to step right into the thick of it. The last mail went out two months ago. Nick's had no warning that the situation has"—she frowned slightly, then brightened as she found the proper phrase—"changed *radically*."

Clarence glared again at Marianne. "As a member of the embassy staff, you are assigned the job. You will pick up the supplies and Nick."

Marianne, who'd been about to volunteer to do just that, suppressed the urge to say, "Thank you!" and said instead, "Yes, sir."

Once out of Clarence's sight, Marianne let herself breathe a sigh of relief. The supply transport was built like a tank. While Marianne wasn't any more afraid of Halemtat's wrath than the ethnologists, she was well aware that innocent *Dirt* bystanders might easily find themselves stuck—all too literally—in a mob of Rejoicers. When the Rejoicers fought, as she understood it, they used teeth and quills. She had no desire to get too close to a lashing tail-full. An unclipped quill was needle-sharp.

Belatedly, she caught the significance of the clipping Halemtat had instituted as punishment. Slapping a snout with a tail full of glass beads was not nearly as effective as slapping a snout with a morning-star made of spines.

She radioed the supply ship to tell them they'd all have to wait for transport before they came out. Captain's gonna love that, I'm sure, she thought, until she got a response from Captain Tertain. By reputation he'd never set foot on a world other than Dirt and certainly didn't intend to do so now. So she simply told Nick to stay put until she came for him.

Nick's cheery voice over the radio said only, "It's going to be a very special Christmas this year."

"Nick," she said, "You don't know the half of it."

She took a slight detour along the way, passing the narrow street that led to Tatep's house. She didn't dare to stop, but she could see from the awning that he wasn't home. In fact, nobody seemed to be home . . . even the bazaar was deserted.

The supply truck rolled on, and Marianne took a second slight detour. What Esperanza had dubbed "the Grande Allez" led directly to Halemtat's imperial residence. The courtyard was filled with Rejoicers. Well-spaced Rejoicers, she saw, for they were—each and every one—bristled to their fullest extent. She wished she dared go for a closer look, but Clarence would be livid if she took much more time than normal reaching the supply ship. And he'd be checking—she knew his habits well enough to know that.

She floored the accelerator and made her way to the improvised landing field in record time. Nick waved to her from the port and stepped out. Just like Nick, she thought. She'd told him to wait in the ship until she arrived; he'd obeyed to the letter. It was all she could do to keep from hugging him as she hit the ground beside him. With a grateful sigh of relief, she said, "We've got to move fast on the transfer, Nick. I'll fill you in as we load."

By the time the two of them had transferred all the supplies from the ship, she'd done just that.

He climbed into the seat beside her, gave her a long thoughtful look, and said, "So Clarence has restricted all of the other ethnologists to the embassy grounds, has he?" He shook his head in mock sadness and clicked his tongue. "I see I haven't trained my team in the proper response to embassy edicts." He grinned at Marianne. "So the embassy advises that I stay off the streets, does it?"

"Yes," said Marianne. She hated being the one to tell him but he'd asked her. "The Super Plenipotentiary Etc. has issued a full and formal Advisory to all non-governmental personnel. . . ."

"Okay," said Nick. "You've done your job: I've been Advised. Now I want to go have a look at this revolution-in-progress." He folded his arms across his chest and waited.

He was right. All Clarence could do was issue an Advisory; he had no power whatsoever to keep the ethnologists off the streets. And Marianne wanted to see the revolution as badly as Nick did.

"All right," she said. "I *am* responsible for your safety, though, so best we go in the transport. I don't want you stuck." She set the supply-transport into motion and headed back toward the Grande Allez.

Nick pressed his nose to the window and watched the streets as they went. He was humming cheerfully under his breath.

"Uh, Nick—if Clarence calls us . . ."

"We'll worry about that when it happens," he said.

Worry is right, thought Marianne, but she smiled. He'd been humming Christmas carols, like some excited child. Inappropriate as all hell, but she liked him all the more for it.

She pulled the supply-transport to a stop at the entrance to the palace courtyard and turned to ask Nick if he had a good enough view. He was already out the door and making his way carefully into the crowd of Rejoicers. "Hey!" she shouted—and she hit the ground running to catch up with him. "Nick!"

He paused long enough for her to catch his arm, then said, "I need to see this, Marianne. It's my *job*."

"It's *my* job to see you don't get hurt—"

He smiled. "Then you lead. I want to be over there where I can see and hear everything Halemtat and his advisors are up to."

Marianne harbored a brief fantasy about dragging him bodily back to the safety of the supply-transport, but he was twice her weight and, from his expression, not about to cooperate. Best she lead, then. Her only consolation was that, when Clarence tried to radio them, there'd be nobody to pick up and receive his orders.

"Hey, Marianne!" said Chornian from the crowd. "Over here! Good view from here!"

And safer too. Grateful for the invitation, Marianne gingerly headed in that direction. Several quilled Rejoicers eased aside to let the two of them safely through. Better to be surrounded by beaded Rejoicers.

"Welcome back, Nick," said Chornian. He and Chaylam stepped apart to create a space of safety for the two humans. "You're just in time."

"So I see. What's going on?"

"Halemtat just had Pilli's Chippet clipped for playing with a Halemtat cracker. Halemtat doesn't *like* the Halemtat crackers."

Beside him, a fully quilled Rejoicer said, "Halemtat doesn't like much of anything. I think a proper prince ought to rattle his spines once or twice a year at least."

Marianne frowned up at Nick, who grinned and said, "Roughly translated: Hapter thinks a proper prince ought to have a sense of humor, however minimal."

"Rattle your spines, Halemtat!" shouted a voice from the crowd. "Let's see if you can do it."

"Yes," came another voice—and Marianne realized it was Chornian's—"Rattle your spines, Great Prince of the Nutcrackers!"

All around them, like rain on a tin roof, came the sound of rattling spines. Marianne looked around—the laughter swept through the crowd, setting every Rejoicer in vibrant motion. Even the grand vizier rattled briefly, then caught himself, his ruff stiff with alarm.

Halemtat didn't rattle.

From his pouch, Chornian took a nutcracker and a nut. Placing the nut in the cracker's smirking mouth, Chornian made the bite cut through the rattling of the crowd like the sound of a shot. From somewhere to her right, a second crack resounded. Then a third. . . . Then the rattling took up a renewed life.

Marianne felt as if she were under water. All around her spines shifted and rattled. Chornian's beaded spines chattered as he cracked a second nut in the smirking face of the nutcracker.

Then one of Halemtat's guards ripped the nutcracker from Chornian's hands. The guard glared at Chornian, who rattled all the harder.

Looking over his shoulder to Halemtat, the guard called, "He's already clipped. What shall I do?"

"Bring me the nutcracker," said Halemtat. The guard glared again at Chornian, who had not stopped laughing, and loped back with the nutcracker in hand. Belatedly, Marianne recognized the smirk on the nutcracker's face.

The guard handed the nutcracker to the grand vizier— Marianne knew beyond a doubt that he recognized the smirk too.

"Whose teeth carved this?" demanded Halemtat.

An unclipped Rejoicer worked his way to the front of the crowd, sat proudly back on his haunches, and said, "Mine." To the grand vizier, he added, with a slight rasp of his quills that was a barely suppressed laugh, "What do you think of my work, Corten? Does it amuse you? You have a strong jaw."

Rattling swept the crowd again.

Halemtat sat up on his haunches. His bristles stood straight out. Marianne had never seen a Rejoicer bristle quite that way before. "Silence!" he bellowed.

Startled, either by the shout or by the electrified bristle of their ruler, the crowd spread itself thinner. The laughter had subsided only because each of the Rejoicers had gone as bristly as Halemtat. Chornian shifted slightly to keep Marianne and Nick near the protected cover of his beaded ruff.

"Marianne," said Nick softly, "That's Tatep."

"I know," she said. Without meaning to, she'd grabbed his arm for reassurance.

Tatep. . . . He sat back on his haunches, as if fully at ease—the only sleeked Rejoicer in the courtyard. He might have been sitting in Marianne's office discussing different grades of wood, for all the excitement he displayed.

Halemtat, rage quivering in every quill, turned to his guards and said, "Clip Tatep. *Hashay.*"

"*No!*" shouted Marianne, starting forward. As she realized she'd spoken Dirtside and opened her mouth to shout it again in Rejoicer, Nick grabbed her and clapped a hand over her mouth.

"*No!*" shouted Chornian, seeming to translate for her, but speaking his own mind.

Marianne fought Nick's grip in vain. Furious, she bit the hand he'd clapped over her mouth. When he yelped and removed it—still not letting her free—she said, "It'll kill him! He'll bleed to death! Let me go." On the last word, she kicked him hard, but he didn't let go.

A guard produced the ritual scissors and handed them to the official in charge of clipping. She held the instrument aloft and made the ritual display, clipping the air three times. With each snap of the scissors, the crowd chanted, "No. No. No."

Taken aback, the official paused. Halemtat clicked at her and she abruptly remembered the rest of the ritual. She turned to make the three ritual clips in the air before Halemtat.

This time the voice of the crowd was stronger. "No. No. No," came the shout with each snap.

Marianne struggled harder as the official stepped toward Tatep. . . .

Then the grand vizier scuttled to intercept. "No," he told the official. Turning to Halemtat, he said, "The image is mine. *I* can laugh at the caricature. Why is it, I wonder, that you can't, Halemtat? Has some disease softened your spines so that they no longer rattle?"

Marianne was so surprised she stopped struggling against Nick's hold—and felt the hold ease. He didn't let go, but held her against him in what was almost an embrace. Marianne held her breath, waiting for Halemtat's reply.

Halemtat snatched the ritual scissors from the official and threw them at Corten's feet. "You," he said. "You will *hashay* Tatep."

"No," said Corten. "I won't. *My* spines are still stiff enough to rattle."

Chornian chose that moment to shout once more, "Rattle your spines, Halemtat! Let us hear you rattle your spines!"

And without so much as a by-your-leave the entire crowd suddenly took up the chant: "Rattle your spines! Rattle your spines!"

Halemtat looked wildly around. He couldn't have rattled if he'd wanted to—his spines were too bristled to touch one to another. He turned his glare on the official, as if willing her to pick up the scissors and proceed.

Instead, she said, in perfect cadence with the crowd, "Rattle your spines!"

Halemtat made an imperious gesture to his guard—and the guard said, "Rattle your spines!"

Halemtat turned and galloped full tilt into his palace. Behind him the chant continued—"Rattle your spines! Rattle your spines!"

Then, quite without warning, Tatep rattled his spines. The next thing Marianne knew, the entire crowd was laughing and laughing and laughing at their vanished ruler.

Marianne went limp against Nick. He gave her a suggestion of a hug, then let her go. Against the rattle of the crowd, he said, "I thought you were going to get yourself killed, you little idiot."

"I couldn't—I couldn't stand by and do *nothing*; they might have killed Tatep."

"I thought doing nothing was a diplomat's job."

"You're right; some diplomat I make. Well, after this little episode, I probably don't have a job anyhow."

"My offer's still open."

"Tell the truth, Nick. If I'd been a member of your team fifteen minutes ago, would you have let me go?"

He threw back his head and laughed. "Of course not," he said. "But at least I understand why you bit the hell out of my hand."

"Oh, god, Nick! I'm so sorry! Did I hurt you?"

"Yes," he said. "But I accept your apology—and next time I won't give you that option."

" 'Next time,' huh?"

Nick, still grinning, nodded.

Well, there was that to be said for Nick: he was realistic.

"Hi, Nick," said Tatep. "Welcome back."

"Hi, Tatep. Some show you folks laid on. What happens next?"

Tatep rattled the length of his body. "Your guess is as good as mine," he said. "I've never done anything like this before. Corten's still rattling. In fact, he asked me to make him a grand vizier nutcracker. I think I'll make him a present of it—for Christmas."

He turned to Marianne. "Share?" he said. "I was too

busy to watch at the time. Were you and Nick mating? If you do it again, may I watch?"

Marianne turned a vivid shade of red, and Nick laughed entirely too much. "You explain it to him," Marianne told Nick firmly. "Mating habits are not within my diplomatic jurisdiction. And I'm still in the diplomatic corps—at least, until we get back to the embassy."

Tatep sat back on his haunches, eagerly awaiting Nick's explanation. Marianne shivered with relief and said hastily, "No, it wasn't mating, Tatep. I was so scared for you I was going to charge in and—well, I don't know what I was going to do after that—but I couldn't just stand by and let Halemtat hurt you." She scowled at Nick and finished, "Nick was afraid I'd get hurt myself and wouldn't let me go."

Tatep's eyes widened in surprise. "Marianne, you would have fought for me?"

"Yes. You're my friend."

"Thank you," he said solemnly. Then to Nick, he said, "You were right to hold her back. Rattling is a better way than fighting." He turned again to Marianne. "You surprise me," he said. "You showed us how to rattle at Halemtat."

He shook from snout to tail-tip, with a sound like a hundred snare drums. "Halemtat turned tail and *ran* from our rattling!"

"And now?" Nick asked him.

"Now I'm going to go home. It's almost dinner time and I'm hungry enough to eat an entire tree all by myself." Still rattling, he added, "Too bad the hardwood I make the nutcrackers from is so bitter—though tonight I could almost make an exception and dine exclusively on bitter wood."

Tatep got down off his haunches and started for home. Most of the crowd had dispersed as well. It seemed oddly anticlimactic, until Marianne heard and saw the rattles of laughter ripple through the departing Rejoicers.

Beside the supply-transport, Tatep paused. "Nick, at

your convenience—I really *would* like you to share about human mating. For friendship's sake, I should know when Marianne is fighting and when she's mating. Then I'd know whether she needs help or—or what kind of help she needs. After all, some trees need help to mate. . . ."

Marianne had turned scarlet again. Nick said, "I'll tell you all about it as soon as I get settled in again."

"Thank you." Tatep headed for home, for all the world as if nothing unusual had happened. In fact, the entire crowd, laughing as it was, might have been a crowd of picnickers off for home as the sun began to set.

A squawk from the radio brought Marianne back to business. No use putting it off. Time to bite the bullet and check in with Clarence—if nothing else, the rest of the staff would be worried about both of them.

Marianne climbed into the cab. Without prompting, Nick climbed in beside her. For a long moment, they listened to the diatribe that came over the radio, but Marianne made no move to reply. Instead, she watched the Rejoicers laughing their way home from the palace courtyard.

"Nick," she said. "Can you really laugh a dictator into submission?"

He cocked a thumb at the radio. "Give it a try," he said. "It's not worth cursing back at Clarence—you haven't his gift for bureaucratic invective."

Marianne also didn't have a job by the time she got back to the embassy. Clarence had tried to clap her onto the returning supply ship, but Nick stepped in to announce that Clarence had no business sending anybody from his ethnology staff home. In the end, Clarence's bureaucratic invective had failed him and the ethnologists simply disobeyed, as Nick had. All Clarence could do, after all, was issue a directive; if they chose to ignore it, the blame no longer fell on Clarence. Since that was all that worried Clarence, that was all right.

In the end, Marianne found that being an ethnologist was considerably more interesting than being a diplomat . . . especially during a revolution.

She and Nick, with Tatep, had taken time off from their mutual studies to choose this year's Christmas tree—from Halemtat's reserve. "Why," said Marianne, bemused at her own reaction, "do I feel like I'm cutting a Christmas tree with Thomas Jefferson?"

"Because you are," Nick said. "Even Thomas Jefferson did ordinary things once in a while. Chances are, he even hung out with his friends. . . ." He waved. "Hi, Tatep. How goes the revolution?"

For answer, Tatep rattled the length of his body.

"Good," said Nick.

"I may have good news to share with you at the Christmas party," added the Rejoicer.

"Then we look forward to the Christmas party even more than usual," said Marianne.

"And I brought a surprise for Marianne all the way from Dirt," Nick added. When Marianne lifted an eyebrow, he said, "No, no hints."

"Share?" said Tatep.

"Christmas Eve," Nick told him. "After you've shared your news, I think."

The tree-trimming party was in full swing. The newly formed Ad Hoc Christmas Chorus was singing Czech carols—a gift from Esperanza to everybody on both staffs. Clarence had gotten so mellow on the Christmas punch that he'd even offered Marianne her job back—if she was willing to be dropped a grade for insubordination. Marianne, equally mellow, said no but said it politely.

Nick had arrived at last, along with Tatep and Chornian and Chaylam and their kids. Surprisingly, Nick stepped in between verses to wave the Ad Hoc Christmas Chorus to silence. "Attention, please," he shouted over the hubbub.

"Attention, *please!* Tatep has an announcement to make."
When he'd finally gotten silence, Nick turned to Tatep and
said, "You have the floor."

Tatep looked down, then looked up again at Nick.

"I mean," Nick said, "go ahead and speak. Marianne's not
the only one who'll want to know your news, believe me."

But it was Marianne Tatep chose to address.

"We've all been to see Haiemtat," he said. "And Halemtat
has agreed: no one will be clipped again unless five people
from the same village agree that the offense warrants that
severe a punishment. *We* will choose the five, not Halemtat.
Furthermore, from this day forward, anyone may say
anything without fear of being clipped. Speaking one's mind
is no longer to be punished."

The crowd broke into applause. Beside Tatep, Nick
beamed.

Tatep took a piece of parchment from his pouch. "You
see, Marianne? Halemtat signed it and put his bite to it."

"How did you get him to agree?"

"We laughed at him—and we cracked our nutcrackers
in the palace courtyard for three days and three nights
straight, until he agreed."

Chornian rattled. "He said he'd sign anything if we'd all
just go away and let him sleep." He hefted the enormous
package he'd brought with him and rattled again. "Look at
all the shelled nuts we've brought for your Christmas party!"

Marianne almost found it in her heart to feel sorry for
Halemtat. Grinning, she accepted the package and
mounded the table with shelled nuts. "Those are almost
too important to eat," she said, stepping back to admire
their handiwork. "Are you sure they oughtn't to go into
a museum?"

"The important thing," Tatep said, "is that I can say
anything I want." He popped one of the nuts into his
mouth and chewed it down. "Halemtat is a *talemtat*," he
said, and rattled for the sheer joy of it.

"Corten looks like he's been eating too much briarwood," said Chornian—catching the spirit of the thing.

Not recognizing the expression, Marianne cast an eye at Nick, who said, "We'd say, 'Been eating a lemon.'"

One of Chornian's brood sat back on his/her haunches and said, "I'll show you Halemtat's guards—"

The child organized its siblings with much pomp and ceremony (except for the littlest who couldn't stop rattling) and marched them back and forth. After the second repetition, Marianne caught the rough import of their chant: "We're Halemtat's guards/We send our regards/We wish you nothing but ill/Clip! we cut off your quill!"

After three passes, one child stepped on another's tail and the whole troop dissolved into squabbling amongst themselves and insulting each other. "You look like Corten!" said one, for full effect. The adults rattled away at them. The littlest one, delighted to find that insults could be funny, turned to Marianne and said, "Marianne! You're spineless!"

Marianne laughed even harder. When she'd caught her breath, she explained to the child what the phrase meant when it was translated literally into Standard. "If you want a good Dirt insult," she said, mischievously, "I give you 'birdbrain.'" All the sounds in that were easy for a Rejoicer mouth to utter—and when Marianne explained why it was an insult, the children all agreed that it was a very good insult indeed.

"Marianne is a birdbrain," said the littlest.

"No," said Tatep. "*Halemtat* is a birdbrain, not Marianne."

"Let the kid alone, Tatep," said Marianne. "The kid can say anything it wants!"

"True," said Tatep. "True!"

They shooed the children off to look for their presents under the tree, and Tatep turned to Nick. "Share, Nick—your surprise for Marianne."

Nick reached under the table. After a moment's searching, he brought out a large bulky parcel and hoisted it onto the table beside the heap of Halemtat nuts. Marianne caught a double-handful before they spilled onto the floor.

Nick laid a protective hand atop the parcel. "Wait," he said. "I'd better explain. Tatep, every family has a slightly different Christmas tradition—the way you folks do for Awakening. This is part of my family's Christmas tradition. It's *not* part of Marianne's Christmas tradition—but, just this once, I'm betting she'll go along with me." He took his hand from the parcel and held it out to Marianne. "Now you can open it," he said.

Dropping the Halemtat nuts back onto their pile, Marianne reached for the parcel and ripped it open with enough verve to satisfy anybody's Christmas unwrapping tradition. Inside was a box, and inside the box a jumble of gaudy cardboard tubes—glittering in stars and stripes and polka dots and even an entire school of metallic green fish. "Fireworks!" said Marianne. "Oh, Nick. . . ."

He put his finger to her lips. "Before you say another word—you chose today to celebrate Christmas because it was the right time of the Rejoicer year. You, furthermore, said that holidays on Dirt and the other human worlds don't converge—"

Marianne nodded.

Nick let that slow smile spread across his face. "But they *do*. This year, back on Dirt, today is the Fourth of July. The dates won't coincide again in our lifetimes but, just this once, they do. So, just this once—fireworks. You do traditionally celebrate Independence Day with fireworks, don't you?"

The pure impudence in his eyes made Marianne duck her head and look away but, in turning, she found herself looking right into Tatep's bright expectant gaze. In fact, all of the Rejoicers were waiting to see what Nick had chosen for her and if he'd chosen right.

"Yes," she said, speaking to Tatep but turning to smile

at Nick. "After all, today's Independence Day right here on Rejoicing, too. Come on, let's go shoot off fireworks!"

And so, for the next twenty minutes, the night sky of Rejoicing was alive with Roman candles, shooting stars, and all the brightness of all the Christmases and all the Independence Days in Marianne's memory. In the streets, humans ooohed and aaahed and Rejoicers rattled. The pops and bangs even woke Halemtat, but all he could do was come out on his balcony and watch.

A day later Tatep reported the rumor that one of the palace guards even claimed to have heard Halemtat rattle. "I don't believe it for a minute," Nick added when he passed the tale on to Marianne.

"Me neither," she said, "but it's a good enough story that I'd *like* to believe it."

"A perfect Christmas tale, then. What would you like to bet that the story of The First Time Halemtat Rattled gets told every Christmas from now on?"

"Sucker bet," said Marianne. Then the wonder struck her. "Nick? Do traditions start that easily—that quickly?"

He laughed. "What kind of fireworks would you like to have *next* year?"

"One of each," she said. "And about five of those with the gold fish-like things that swirl down and then go *bam!* at you when you least expect it."

For a moment, she thought he'd changed the subject, then she realized he'd answered her question. Wherever she went, for the rest of her life, her Christmas tradition would include fireworks—not just any fireworks, but Fourth of July fireworks. She smiled. "Next year, maybe we should play Tchaikovsky's *1812 Overture* as well as *The Nutcracker Suite*."

He shook his head. "No," he said, "*The Nutcracker Suite* has plenty enough fireworks all by itself—at least *your* version of it certainly did!"

Much fiction focuses on place as a primary frame for action, and in science fiction this usually means a fantastic environment. Lucius Shepherd became well known for his sense of locale, with stories set in Central America, employing an authority unusual in any fiction. His places the reader visits by feel. He resembles Joseph Conrad, conjuring from evocative locales fiction that swirls about an imaginative fulcrum. In this long, atypical Shepherd story, the location is off-Earth, quite artificial, yet still steamy and immediate. His protagonist is offset from the usual herd, alienated, already quite far along in his journey to the Heart of Darkness. He is a master of hallucinogenic, dark epiphanies.

Barnacle Bill The Spacer
by Lucius Shepard

The way things happen, not the great movements of time but the ordinary things that make us what we are, the savage accidents of our births, the simple lusts that because of whimsy or a challenge to one's pride become transformed into complex tragedies of love, the heartless operations of change, the wild sweetness of other souls that intersect the orbits of our lives, travel along the same course for a while, then angle off into oblivion, leaving no formal shape for us to consider, no easily comprehensible pattern from which we may derive enlightenment . . . I often wonder why it is when stories are contrived from such materials as these, the storyteller is generally persuaded to perfume the raw stink of life, to replace bloody loss with talk of noble sacrifice, to reduce the grievous to the wistfully sad. Most people, I suppose, want their truth served with a side of sentiment; the perilous uncertainty of the world dismays them, and they wish to avoid being brought hard against it. Yet by this act of avoidance they neglect the profound sadness that can arise from a contemplation of the human spirit *in extremis* and blind themselves to beauty. That beauty, I mean, which is the iron of our existence. The beauty that enters through a wound, that whispers a black word in our ears at funerals, a word that causes us to shrug off our griever's weakness and say, No more, never again. The beauty that inspires anger, not regret, and provokes struggle, not the idle aesthetic of a beholder. That, to my mind, lies at the core of the only stories worth telling. And that is the fundamental purpose of the storyteller's art, to illumine such beauty, to declare its central importance and make it shine forth from the inevitable wreckage of our hopes and the sorry matter of our decline.

This, then, is the most beautiful story I know.

It all happened not so along ago on Solitaire Station, out beyond the orbit of Mars, where the lightships are assembled and launched, vanishing in thousand-mile-long shatterings, and it happened to a man by the name of William Stamey, otherwise known as Barnacle Bill.

Wait now, many of you are saying, I've heard that story. It's been told and retold and told again. What use could there be in repeating it?

But what have you heard, really?

That Bill was a sweet, balmy lad, I would imagine. That he was a carefree sort with a special golden spark of the Creator in his breast and the fey look of the hereafter in his eye, a friend to all who knew him. That he was touched, not retarded, moonstruck and not sick at heart, ill-fated rather than violated, tormented, sinned against.

If that's the case, then you would do well to give a listen, for there were both man and boy in Bill, neither of them in the least carefree, and the things he did and how he did them are ultimately of less consequence than why he was so moved and how this reflects upon the spiritual paucity and desperation of our age.

Of all that, I would suspect, you have heard next to nothing.

Bill was thirty-two years old at the time of my story, a shambling, sour-smelling, unkempt fellow with a receding hairline and a daft, moony face whose features—weak-looking blue eyes and Cupid's bow mouth and snub nose—were much too small for it, leaving the better part of a vast round area unexploited. His hands were always dirty, his station jumpsuit mapped with stains, and he was rarely without a little cloth bag in which he carried, among other items, a trove of candy and pornographic VR crystals. It was his taste for candy and pornography that frequently brought us together—the woman with whom I lived, Arlie Quires, operated the commissary outlet where Bill would go to replenish his supplies, and on occasion, when my duties with Security Section permitted, I would help Arlie out at the counter. Whenever Bill came in, he would prefer to have me wait on him; he was, you understand, intimidated by everyone he encountered, but by pretty women most of all. And Arlie, lithe and brown and clever of feature, was not only pretty but had a sharp mouth that put him off even more.

There was one instance in particular that should both serve to illustrate Bill's basic circumstance and provide a background for all that later transpired. It happened one day about six months before the return of the lightship *Perseverance*. The shift had just changed over on the assembly platforms, and the commissary bar was filled with workers. Arlie had run off somewhere, leaving me in charge, and from my vantage behind the counter, located in an ante-room whose walls were covered by a holographic photomural of a blue sky day in the now-defunct Alaskan wilderness, and furnished with metal tables and chairs, all empty at that juncture, I could see colored lights playing back and forth within the bar, and hear the insistent rhythms of a pulse group. Bill, as was his habit, peeked in from the corridor to make sure none of his enemies were about, then shuffled on in, glancing left and right, ducking his head, hunching his shoulders, the very image of a guilty party. He shoved his moneymaker at me, three green telltales winking on the slim metal cylinder, signifying the amount of credit he was releasing to the commissary, and demanded in that grating, adenoidal voice of his that I give him "new stuff," meaning by this new VR crystals.

"I've nothing new for you," I told him.

"A ship came in." He gave me a look of fierce suspicion. "I saw it. I was outside, and I saw it!"

Arlie and I had been quarreling that morning, a petty difference concerning whose turn it was to use the priority lines to speak with relatives in London that had subsequently built into a major battle; I was in no mood for this sort of exchange. "Don't be an ass," I said. "You know they won't have unloaded the cargo yet."

His suspicious look flickered, but did not fade. "They unloaded already," he said. "Sleds were going back and forth." His eyes went a bit dreamy and his head wobbled, as if he were imagining himself back out on the skin of the station, watching the sleds drifting in and out of the cargo bays; but he was, I realized, fixed upon a section of the holographic mural in which a brown bear had just ambled out of the woods and was sniffing about a pile of branches and sapling trunks at the edge of a stream that might have been a beaver dam. Though he had never seen a real one, the notion of animals fascinated Bill, and when unable to think of anything salient to say, he would recite facts about giraffes and elephants, kangaroos and whales, and beasts even more exotic, all now receded into legend.

"Bloody hell!" I said. "Even if they've unloaded, with processing and inventory, it'll be a week or more before we see anything from it. If you want something, give me a specific order. Don't just stroll in here and say"—I tried to imitate his delivery— " 'Gimme some new stuff.' "

Two men and a woman stepped in from the corridor as I was speaking; they fell into line, keeping a good distance between themselves and Bill, and on hearing me berating him, they established eye contact with me, letting me know by their complicitors' grins that they supported my harsh response. That made me ashamed of having yelled at him.

"Look here," I said, knowing that he would never be able to manage the specific. "Shall I pick you out something? I can probably find one or two you haven't done."

He hung his great head and nodded, bullied into submissiveness. I could tell by his body language that he wanted to turn and see whether the people behind him had witnessed his humiliation, but he could not bring himself to do so. He twitched and quivered as if their stares were pricking him, and his hands gripped the edge of the counter, fingers kneading the slick surface.

By the time I returned from the stockroom several more people had filtered in from the corridor, and half-a-dozen men and women were lounging about the entrance to the bar, laughing and talking, among them Braulio Menzies, perhaps the most dedicated of Bill's tormentors, a big, balding, sallow man with sleek black hair and thick shoulders and immense forearms and a Mephistophelean salt-and-pepper goatee that lent his generous features a thoroughly menacing aspect. He had left seven children, a wife and a mother behind in São Paolo to take a position as foreman in charge of a metalworkers unit, and the better part of his wages were sent directly to his family, leaving him little to spend on entertainment; if he was drinking, and it was apparent he had been, I could think of nothing that would have moved him to this end other than news from home. As he did not look to be in a cheerful mood, chances were the news had not been good.

Hostility was thick as cheap perfume in the room. Bill was still standing with his head hung down, hands gripping the counter, but he was no longer passively maintaining that attitude—he had gone rigid, his neck was corded, his fingers squeezed the plastic, recognizing himself to be the target of every disparaging whisper and snide laugh. He seemed about to explode, he was so tightly held. Braulio stared at him with undisguised loathing, and as I set Bill's goods down on the counter, the skinny blond girl who was clinging to Braulio's arm sang, "He can't get no woman, least not one that's human, he's Barnacle Bill the Spacer." There was a general outburst of laughter, and Bill's face grew flushed; an ugly, broken noise issued from his throat. The girl, her smallish breasts half-spilling out from a skimpy dress of bright blue plastic, began to sing more of her cruel song.

"Oh, that's brilliant, that is!" I said. "The creative mind never ceases to amaze!" But my sarcasm had no effect upon her.

I pushed three VR crystals and a double handful of hard candy, Bill's favorite, across to him. "There you are," I said, doing my best to speak in a kindly tone, yet at the same time hoping to convey the urgency of the situation. "Don't be hanging about, now."

He gave a start. His eyelids fluttered open, and he lifted his gaze to meet mine. Anger crept into his expression, hardening the simple terrain of his face. He needed anger, I suppose, to maintain some fleeting sense of dignity, to hide from the terror growing inside him, and there was no one else whom he dared confront.

"No!" he said, swatting at the candy, scattering much of it onto the floor. "You cheated! I want more!"

"Gon' mek you a pathway, boogman!" said a gangly black man, leaning in over Bill's shoulder. "Den you best travel!" Others echoed him, and one gave Bill a push toward the corridor.

Bill's eyes were locked on mine. "You cheated me, you give me some more! You owe me more!"

"Right!" I said, my temper fraying. "I'm a thoroughly dishonest human being. I live to swindle yits like yourself." I added a few pieces of candy to his pile and made to shoo him away. Braulio came forward, swaying, his eyes none too clear.

"Let the son'beetch stay, man," he said, his voice burred with rage. "I wan' talk to heem."

I came out from behind the counter and took a stand between Braulio and Bill. My actions were not due to any affection for Bill—though I did not wish him ill, neither did I wish him well; I suppose I perceived him as less a person than an unwholesome problem. In part, I was still motivated by the residue of anger from my argument with Arlie, and of course it was my duty as an officer in the Security Section to maintain order. But I think the actual reason I came to his defense was that I was bored. We were all of us bored on Solitaire. Bored and bad-tempered and despairing, afflicted with the sort of feverish malaise that springs from a sense of futility.

"That's it," I said wearily to Braulio. "That's enough from all of you. Bugger off."

"I don't wan' hort you, John," said Braulio, weaving a bit as he tried to focus on me. "Joos' you step aside."

A couple of his co-workers came to stand beside him. Jammers with silver hubs protruding from their crewcut scalps, the tips of receivers that channeled radio waves, solar energy, any type of signal, into their various brain centers, producing a euphoric kinaesthesia. I had a philosophical bias against jamming, no doubt partially the result of some vestigial Christian reflex. The sight of them refined my annoyance.

"You poor sods are tuned to a dark channel," I said. "No saved by the bell. Not today. No happy endings."

The jammers smiled at one another. God only knows what insane jangle was responsible for their sense of well-being. I smiled, too. Then I kicked the nearer one in the head, aiming at but missing his silver stub; I did for his friend with a smartly delivered backfist. They lay motionless, their smiles still in place. Perhaps, I thought, the jamming had turned the beating into a stroll through the park. Braulio faded a step and adopted a defensive posture. The onlookers edged away. The throb of music from the bar seemed to be giving a readout of the tension in the room.

There remained a need in me for violent release, but I was not eager to mix it with Braulio; even drunk, he would be formidable, and in any case, no matter how compelling my urge to do injury, I was required by duty to make a show of restraint.

"Violence," I said, affecting a comical lower class accent, hoping to defuse the situation. "The wine of the fucking underclass. It's like me father used to say, son, 'e'd say, when you're bereft of reason and the wife's sucked up all the cooking sherry, just amble on down to the pub and have a piss in somebody's face. There's nothing so sweetly logical as an elbow to the throat, no argument so poignant as that made by grinding somebody's teeth beneath your heel. The very cracking of bones is in itself a philosophical language. And when you've captioned someone's beezer with a nice scar, it provides them a pleasant 'omily to read each time they look in the mirror. Aristotle, Plato, Einstein. All the great minds got their start brawling in the pubs. Groin punches. Elbows to the throat. These are often a first step toward the expression of the most subtle mathematical concepts. It's a fantastic intellectual experience we're embarking upon 'ere, and I for one, ladies and gents, am exhilarated by the challenge."

Among the onlookers there was a general slackening of expression and a few titters. Braulio, however, remained focused, his eyes pinned on Bill.

"This is ridiculous," I said to him. "Come on, friend. Do me the favor and shut it down." He shook his head, slowly, awkwardly, like a bear bothered by a bee. "What's the point of it all, man?" I nodded at Bill. "He only wants to vanish. Why don't you let him?"

The blond girl shrilled, "Way you huffin' this bombo's shit, you two gotta be flatbackin', man!"

"I didn't catch your name, darling," I said. "Tarantula,

was it? You'd do well to feed her more often, Braulio. Couple of extra flies a day ought to make her more docile."

I ignored her curses, watching Braulio's shoulders; when the right one dropped a fraction, I tried a round kick; but he ducked under it and rolled away, coming up into the fluid, swaying stance of a *capoeirista*. We circled one another, looking for an opening. The crowd cleared a space around us. Then someone—Bill, I think—brushed against me. Braulio started what appeared to be a cartwheel, but as he braced on one hand at the mid-point of the move, his long left leg whipped out and caught me a glancing blow on the temple. Dazed, I reeled backward, took a harder blow on the side of my neck and slammed into the counter. If he had been sober, that would have done for me; but he was slow to follow, and as he moved in, I kicked him in the liver. He doubled over, and I drove a knee into his face, then swept his legs from under him. He fell heavily, and I was on him, no longer using my techniques, but punching in a frenzy like a streetfighter, venting all my ulcerated emotions. Somebody was clawing at my neck, my face. The blond girl. She was screaming, sobbing, saying, "No, no, stop it, you're killin' him." Then somebody else grabbed me from behind, pinned my arms, and I saw what I had wrought. Braulio's cheekbone was crushed, one eye was swollen shut, his upper lip had been smashed into a pulp.

"He's grievin', man!" The blond girl dropped to her knees beside him. "That's all he be doin'! Grievin' his little ones!" Her hands fluttered about his face. Most of the others stood expressionless, mute, as if the sight of violence had mollified their resentments.

I wrenched free of the man holding me.

"Fuckin' Security bitch!" said the blond. "All he's doin's grievin'."

"I don't give a fat damn what he was doing. There's no law says"—I labored for breath—"says he can exorcise it this way. Is there now?"

This last I addressed to those who had been watching, and though some refused to meet my eyes, from many I received nods and a grumbling assent. They cared nothing about my fate or Braulio's; they had been willing to witness whatever end we might have reached. But now I understood that something had happened to Braulio's children, and I understood too why he had chosen Bill to stand in for those who were truly culpable, and I felt sore in my heart for what I had done.

"Take him to the infirmary," I said, and then gestured at the jammers, who were still down, eyes closed, their smiles in place. "Them, too." I put a hand to my neck; a lump had materialized underneath my right ear and was throbbing away nicely.

Bill moved up beside me, clutching his little cloth sack. His smell and his softness and his witling ways, every facet of his being annoyed me. I think he was about to say something, but I had no wish to hear it; I saw in him then what Braulio must have seen: a pudgy monstrosity, a uselessness with two legs.

"Get out of here!" I said, disgusted with myself for having interceded on his behalf. "Go back to your goddamn crawl and stay there."

His shoulders hitched as if he were expecting a blow, and he started pushing his way through the press at the door. Just before he went off along the corridor, he turned back. I believe he may have still wanted to say something, perhaps to offer thanks or—just as likely— to drive home the point that he was dissatisfied with the quantity of his goods. In his face was a mixture of petulant defiance and fear, but that gave me no clue to his intent. It was his usual expression, one that had been thirty-two years in the making, for due to his peculiar history, he had every cause to be defiant and afraid.

❖   ❖   ❖

Bill's mother had been a medical technician assigned to the station by the Seguin Corporation, which owned the development contract for the lightship program, and so, when his pre-natal scan displayed evidence of severe retardation, she was able to use her position to alter computer records in order to disguise his condition; otherwise, by station law—in effect, the law of the corporation—the foetus would have been aborted. Why she did this, and why she then committed suicide seventeen months after Bill's birth, remain a mystery, though it is assumed that her irrational actions revolved around the probability that Bill's father, a colonist aboard the lightship *Perseverance*, would never more be returning.

The discovery that Bill was retarded incited a fierce controversy. A considerable plurality of the station's work force insisted that the infant be executed, claiming that since living space was at a premium, to allow this worthless creature to survive would be an affront to all those who had made great personal sacrifices in order to come to Solitaire. This group consisted in the main of those whose lives had been shaped by or whose duty it was to uphold the quota system: childless women and administrators and—the largest element of the plurality and of the population in general—people who, like Braulio, had won a job aboard the station and thus succeeded in escaping the crushing poverty and pollution of Earth, but who had not been sufficiently important to have their families sent along, and so had been forced to abandon them. In opposition stood a vocal minority comprised of those whose religious or philosophical bias would not permit such a callous act of violence; but this was, I believe, a stance founded almost entirely on principle, and I doubt that many of those involved were enthusiastic about Bill in the specific. Standing apart from the fray was a sizeable group who, for various social and political reasons, maintained neutrality; yet I would guess that at least half of them would, if asked, have expressed their distaste for the prospect of Bill's continued existence. Fistfights and shouting matches soon became the order of the day. Meetings were held; demands made; ultimatums presented. Finally, though, it was not politics or threats of force or calls to reason that settled the issue, but rather a corporate decision.

Among Seguin's enormous holdings was a company that supplied evolved animals to various industries and government agencies, where they were utilized in environments that had been deemed too stressful or physically challenging for human workers. The difficulty with such animals lay in maintaining control over them—the new nanotechnologies were considered untrustworthy and too expensive, and computer implants, though serviceable, inevitably failed. There were a number of ongoing research programs whose aim it was to perfect the implants, and thus Seguin, seeing an opportunity for a rigorous test, not to mention a minor public relations coup that would speak to the deeply humane concerns of the corporation, decided—in a reversal of traditional scientific methodology—to test on Bill a new implant that would eventually be used to govern the behavior of chimpanzees and dogs and the like.

The implant, a disc of black alloy about the size of a soy wafer, contained a personality designed to entertain and jolly and converse with its host; it was embedded just beneath the skin behind the ear, and it monitored emotional levels, stimulating appropriate activity by means of electrical charges capable of bestowing both pleasure and pain. According to Bill, his implant was named Mister C, and it was—also according to Bill—his best friend, this despite the fact that it would hurt him whenever he was slow to obey its commands. I could always tell when Mister C was talking to him. His face would empty, and his eyes dart about as if trying to see the person who was speaking, and his hands would clench and unclench. Not a pleasant thing to watch. Still, I suppose that Mister C was, indeed, the closest thing Bill had to a friend. Certainly it was attentive to him and was never too busy to hold a conversation; more importantly, it enabled him to perform the menial chores that had been set him: janitorial duties, fetch and carry, and, once he had reached the age of fifteen, the job that eventually earned him the name Barnacle Bill. But none of this assuaged the ill feeling toward him that prevailed throughout the station, a sentiment that grew more pronounced following the incident with Braulio. Two of Braulio's sons had been killed by a death squad who had mistaken them for members of a gang, and this tragedy caused people to begin talking about what an injustice it was that Bill should have so privileged an existence while others more worthy should be condemned to hell on Earth. Before long, the question of Bill's status was raised once again, and the issue was seized upon by Menckyn Samuelson, one of Solitaire's leading lights and—to my shame, because he was such a germ—a fellow Londoner. Samuelson had emigrated to the station as a low temperature physicist and since had insinuated himself into a position of importance in the administration. I did not understand what he stood to gain from hounding Bill—he had, I assumed, some hidden political agenda—but he flogged the matter at every opportunity to whomever would listen and succeeded in stirring up a fiercely negative reaction toward Bill. Opinion came to be almost equally divided between the options of executing him, officially or otherwise, and shipping him back to an asylum on Earth, which—as everyone knew— was only a slower and more expensive form of the first option.

There was a second development resulting from my fight with Braulio, one that had a poignant effect on my personal life, this being that Bill and I began spending a good deal of time together.

It seemed the old Chinese proverb had come into play, the one that states if you save somebody's life you become responsible for them. I had not saved his life, perhaps, but I had certainly spared him grievous injury; thus he came to view me as his protector, and I . . . well, initially I had no desire to be either his protector or his apologist, but I was forced to adopt both these roles. Bill was terrified. Everywhere he went he was cursed or cuffed or ill-treated in some fashion, a drastic escalation of the abuse he had always suffered. And then there was the blond girl's song: "Barnacle Bill the Spacer." Scarcely a day passed when I did not hear a new verse or two. Everyone was writing them. Whenever Bill passed in a corridor or entered a room people would start to sing. It harrowed him from place to place, that song. He woke to it and fell asleep to it, and whatever self-esteem he had possessed was soon reduced to ashes.

When he first began hanging about me, dogging me on my rounds, I tried to put him off, but I could not manage it. I held myself partly to blame for the escalation of feeling against him; if I had not been so vicious in my handling of Braulio, I thought, Bill might not have come to this pass. But there was another, more significant reason behind my tolerance. I had, it appeared, developed a conscience. Or at least so I chose to interpret my growing concern for him. I have had cause to wonder if those protective feelings that emerged from some corner of my spirit were not merely a form of perversity, if I were using my relationship with Bill to demonstrate to the rest of the station that I had more power than most, that I could walk a contrary path without fear of retribution; but I remain convinced that the compassion I came to feel toward him was the product of a renewal of the ideals I had learned in the safe harbor of my family's home back in Chelsea, conceptions of personal honor and trust and responsibility that I had long believed to be as extinct as the tiger and the dove.

It may be there was a premonitory force at work in me, for it occurs to me now that the rebirth of my personal hopes was the harbinger of a more general rebirth; and yet because of all that has happened, because of how my hopes were served, I have also had reason to doubt the validity of every hope, every renewal, and to consider whether the rebirth of hope is truly possible for such diffuse, heartless, and unruly creatures as ourselves.

One day, returning from my rounds with Bill shuffling along at my shoulder, I found a black crescent moon with a red star tipping its lower horn painted on the door of Bill's quarters: the symbol used by the Strange Magnificence, the most prominent of the gang religions flourishing back on Earth, to mark their intended victims. I doubt that Bill was aware of its significance. Yet he seemed to know instinctively the symbol was a threat, and no ordinary one at that. He clung to my arm, begging me to stay with him, and when I told him I had to leave, he threw a tantrum, rolling about on the floor, whimpering, leaking tears, wailing that bad things were going to happen. I assured him that I would have no trouble in determining who had painted the symbol; I could not believe that there were more than a handful of people on Solitaire with ties to the Magnificence. But this did nothing to soothe him. Finally, though I realized it might be a mistake, I told him he could spend the night in my quarters.

"Just this once," I said. "And you'd better keep damn quiet, or you'll be out on your bum."

He nodded, beaming at me, shifting his feet, atremble with eagerness. Had he a tail he would have wagged it. But by the time we reached my quarters, his mood had been disrupted by the dozens of stares and curses directed his way. He sat on a cushion, rocking back and forth, making a keening noise, completely unmindful of the decor, which had knocked me back a pace on opening the door. Arlie was apparently in a less than sunny mood herself, for she had slotted in a holographic interior of dark greens and browns, with heavy chairs and a sofa and tables whose wood had been worked into dragons' heads and clawed feet and such; the walls were adorned with brass light fixtures shaped like bestial masks with glowing eyes, and the rear of the room had been transformed into a receding perspective of sequentially smaller, square segments of black delineated by white lines, like a geometric tunnel into nowhere, still leading, I trusted, to something resembling a bedroom. The overall atmosphere was one of derangement, of a cramped magical lair through whose rear wall a hole had been punched into some negative dimension. Given this, I doubted that she would look kindly upon Bill's presence, but when she appeared in the far reaches of the tunnel—her chestnut hair done up, wearing a white Grecian-style robe, walking through an infinite black depth, looking minute at first, then growing larger by half with each successive segment she entered—she favored him with a cursory nod and turned her attention to me.

" 'Ave you eaten?" she asked, and before I could answer she told me she wasn't hungry, there were some sandwiches, or I could do for myself, whatever I wanted, all in the most dispirited of tones. She was, as I have said, a pretty woman, with a feline cast of feature and sleek, muscular limbs; having too many interesting lines in her face, perhaps, to suit the prevailing standards of beauty, but sensual to a fault. Ordinarily, sexual potential surrounded her like an aura. That day, however, her face had settled into a dolorous mask, her shoulders had slumped, and she seemed altogether drab.

"What's the matter?" I asked.

She shook her head. "Nuffin'."

"Nothing?" I said. "Right! You look like the Queen just

died, and the place is fixed up like the death of philosophy. But everything's just bloody marvelous, right?"

"Do you mind?" she snapped. "It's personal!"

"Personal, is it? Well, excuse me. I certainly wouldn't want to be getting *personal* with you. What the hell's the matter? You been struck by the monthlies?"

She pinned me with a venomous stare. "God, you're disgustin'! What is it? You 'aven't broken any 'eads today, so you've decided to bash me around a bit?"

"All right, all right," I said. "I'm sorry."

"Nao," she said. "G'wan with it. Oi fuckin' love it when you're masterful. Really, Oi do!" She turned and started back along the tunnel. "Oi'll just await your pleasure, shall Oi?" she called over her shoulder. "Oi mean, you will let me know what more Oi can do to serve?"

"Christ!" I said, watching her ass twitching beneath the white cloth, thinking that I would have to make a heartfelt act of contrition before I laid hands on it again. I knew, of course, why I had baited her. It was for the same reason that had brought on her depression, that provoked the vast majority of our aberrant behaviors. Frustration, anger, despair, all feelings that—no matter their immediate causes—in some way arose from the fact that Solitaire had proved to be an abject failure. Of the twenty-seven ships assembled and launched, three had thus far returned. Two of the ships had reported no hospitable environments found. The crew of the third ship had been unable to report anything, being every one of them dead, apparently by each others' hands.

We had gotten a late start on the colonization of space, far too late to save the home planet, and it was unclear whether the piddling colonies on Mars and Europa and in the asteroids would allow us to survive. Perhaps it should have been clear, perhaps we should have realized that despite the horror and chaos of Earth, the brush wars, the almost weekly collapse of governments, our flimsy grasp of the new technologies, despite the failure of Solitaire and everything else . . . perhaps it should have been more than clear that our species possessed a root stubbornness capable of withstanding all but the most dire of cataclysms, and that eventually our colonies would thrive. But they would never be able to absorb the desperate population of Earth, and the knowledge that our brothers and sisters and parents were doomed to a life of diminishing expectations, to famines and wars and accidents of industry that would ultimately kill off billions, it caused those of us fortunate enough to have escaped to become dazed and badly weighted in our heads, too heavy with a sense of responsibility to comprehend the true moral requisites of our good fortune. Even if successful, the lightship program would only bleed off a tiny percentage of Earth's population, and most, I assumed, would be personnel attached to the Seguin Corporation and those whom the corporation or else some corrupt government agency deemed worthy; yet we came to perceive ourselves as the common people's last, best hope, and each successive failure struck at our hearts and left us so crucially dismayed, we developed astonishing talents for self-destruction. Like neurotic Prometheans, we gnawed at our own livers and sought to despoil every happy thing that fell to us. And when we grew too enervated to practice active self-destruction, we sank into clinical depression, as Arlie was doing now.

I sat thinking of these things for a long while, watching Bill rock back and forth, now and then popping a piece of hard candy into his mouth, muttering, and I reached no new conclusions, unless an evolution of distaste for the corporation and the world and the universe could be considered new and conclusive. At length, weary of the repetitive circuit of my thoughts, I decided it was time I tried to make my peace with Arlie. I doubted I had the energy for prolonged apology, but I hoped that intensity would do the trick.

"You can sleep on the couch," I said to Bill, getting to my feet. "The bathroom"—I pointed off along the corridor—"is down there somewhere."

He bobbed his head, but as he kept his eyes on the floor, I could not tell if it had been a response or simply a random movement.

"Did you hear me?" I asked.

"I gotta do somethin'," he said.

"Down there." I pointed again. "The bathroom."

"They gonna kill me 'less I do somethin'."

He was not, I realized, referring to his bodily functions.

"What do you mean?"

His eyes flicked up to me, then away. " 'Less I do somethin' good, really good, they gonna kill me."

"Who's going to kill you?"

"The men," he said.

The men, I thought, sweet Jesus! I felt unutterably sad for him.

"I gotta find somethin'," he said with increased emphasis. "Somethin' good, somethin' makes 'em like me."

I had it now—he had seized on the notion that by some good deed or valuable service he could change people's opinion of him.

"You can't do anything, Bill. You just have to keep doing your job, and this will all wash away, I promise you."

"Mmn-mn." He shook his head vehemently like a child in denial. "I gotta find somethin' good to do."

"Look," I said. "Anything you try is very likely to backfire. Do you understand me? If you do something and you bugger it, people are going to be more angry at you than ever."

He tucked his lower lip beneath the upper and narrowed his eyes and maintained a stubborn silence.

"What does Mister C say about this?" I asked.

That was, apparently, a new thought. He blinked; the tightness left his face. "I don't know."

"Well, ask him. That's what he's there for . . . to help you with your problems."

"He doesn't always help. Sometimes he doesn't know stuff."

"Try, will you? Just give it a try."

He did not seem sure of this tactic, but after a moment he pawed at his head, running his palm along the crewcut stubble, then squeezed his eyes shut and began to mumble, long pattering phrases interrupted by pauses for breath, like a child saying his prayers as fast as he can. I guessed that he was outlining the entire situation for Mister C. After a minute his face went blank, the tip of his tongue pushed out between his lips, and I imagined the cartoonish voice—thus I had been told the implant's voice would manifest—speaking to him in rhymes, in silly patter. Then, after another few seconds, his eyes snapped open and he beamed at me.

"Mister C says good deeds are always good," he announced proudly, obviously satisfied that he had been proven right, and popped another piece of candy into his mouth.

I cursed the simplicity of the implant's programming, sat back down, and for the next half-hour or so I attempted to persuade Bill that his best course lay in doing absolutely nothing, in keeping a low profile. If he did, I told him, eventually the dust would settle and things would return to normal. He nodded and said, yes, yes, uh-huh, yet I could not be certain that my words were having an effect. I knew how resistant he could be to logic, and it was quite possible that he was only humoring me. But as I stood to take my leave of him, he did something that went some ways toward convincing me that I had made an impression: he reached out and caught my hand, held it for a second, only a second, but one during which I thought I felt the sorry hits of his life, the dim vibrations of all those sour loveless nights and lonely ejaculations. When he released

my hand he turned away, appearing to be embarrassed.
I was embarrassed myself. Embarrassed and, I must admit,
a bit repelled at having this ungainly lump display affection
toward me. Yet I was also moved, and trapped between
those two poles of feeling, I hovered above him, not sure
what to do or say. There was, however, no need for me
to deliberate the matter. Before I could summon speech
he began mumbling once again, lost in a chat with
Mister C.

"Good night, Bill," I said.

He gave no response, as still as a Buddha on his cushion.

I stood beside him for a while, less observing him than
cataloguing my emotions, then, puzzling more than a little
over their complexity, I left him to his candy and his terror
and his inner voices.

Apology was not so prickly a chore as I had feared. Arlie
knew as well as I the demons that possessed us, and once
I had submitted to a token humiliation, she relented and
we made love. She was demanding in the act, wild and
noisy, her teeth marked my shoulder, my neck; but as we
lay together afterward in the dark, some trivial, gentle
music trickling in from the speakers above us, she was
tender and calm and seemed genuinely interested in the
concerns of my day.

"God 'elp us!" she said. "You don't actually fink the
Magnificence is at work 'ere, do you?"

"Christ, no!" I said. "Some miserable dwight's actin' on
mad impulse, that's all. Probably done it 'cause his nanny
wiped his bum too hard when he's a babe."

"Oi 'ope not," she said. "Oi've seen their work back 'ome
too many toimes to ever want to see it again."

"You never told me you'd had dealings with the
Magnificence."

"Oi never 'ad what you'd call dealin's with 'em, but they
was all over our piece of 'eaven, they were. 'Alf the bloody

houses sported some kind of daft mark. It was a bleedin'
fertile field for 'em, with nobody 'avin' a job and the lads
just 'angin' about on the corners and smokin' gannie.
'Twas a rare day the Bills didn't come 'round to scrape
up some yobbo wearing his guts for a necktie and the
mark of his crime carved into his fore'ead. Nights you'd
hear 'em chantin' down by the stadium. 'Orrid stuff they
was singin'. Wearin' that cheap black satin gear and those
awrful masks. But it 'ad its appeal. All the senile old
'ooligans were diggin' out their jackboots and razors, and
wantin' to go marchin' again. And in the pubs the soaks
would be sayin', yes, yes, they do the odd bad thing, the
Magnificence, but they've got the public good to 'eart.
The odd bad thing! Jesus! Oi've seen messages written
on the pavement in 'uman bones. Colored girls with their
'ips broken and their legs lashed back behind their necks.
Still breathin' and starin' at you with them 'ollow eyes,
loike they were mad to die. You were lucky, John, to be
living up in Chelsea."

"Lucky enough, I suppose," I said stiffly, leery of drawing
such distinctions; the old British class wars, though
somewhat muted on Solitaire, were far from dormant, and
even between lovers, class could be a dicey subject.
"Chelsea's not exactly the Elysian Fields.

"Oi don't mean nuffin' by it, luv. You don't have to tell
me the 'ole damn world's gone rotten long ago. Oi
remember how just a black scrap of a life looked loike a
brilliant career when Oi was livin' there. Now Oi don't
know how Oi stood it."

I pulled her close against me and we lay without
speaking for a long while. Finally Arlie said, "You know,
it's 'alf nice 'avin' 'im 'ere."

"Bill, you mean?"

"Yeah, Bill."

"I hope you'll still feel that way if he can't find the loo,"
I said.

Arlie giggled. "Nao, I'm serious. It's loike 'avin' family again. The feel of somebody snorin' away in the next room. That's the thing we miss 'avin' here. We're all so bloody isolated. Two's a crowd and all that. We're missin' the warmth."

"I suppose you're right."

I touched her breasts, smoothed my hand along the swell of her hip, and soon we were involved again, more gently than before, more giving to the other, as if what Arlie had said about family had created a resonance in our bodies. Afterward I was so fatigued the darkness seemed to be slowly circulating around us, pricked by tiny bursts of actinic light, the way a djinn must circulate within its prison bottle, a murky cloud of genius and magic. I was at peace lying there, yet I felt strangely excited to be so peaceful and my thoughts, too, were strange, soft, almost formless, the kind of thoughts I recalled having had as a child when it had not yet dawned on me that all my dreams would eventually be hammered flat and cut into steely dies so they could withstand the dreadful pressures of a dreamless world.

Arlie snuggled closer to me, her hand sought mine, clasped it tightly. "Ah, Johnny," she said. "Toimes loike this, Oi fink Oi was born to forget it all."

The next day I was able to track down the villain who had painted the menacing symbol on Bill's door. The cameras in the corridor outside his door had malfunctioned, permitting the act of vandalism to go unobserved; but this was hardly surprising—the damned things were always failing, and should they not fail on their own, it was no great feat to knock them out by using an electromagnet. Lacking a video record, I focused my attention on the personnel files. Only nine people on Solitaire proved to have had even minimal ties with the Strange Magnificence; by process of elimination I was able to reduce the number of possible culprits to three.

The first of them I interviewed, Roger Thirwell, a pale, rabbity polymath in his mid-twenties who had emigrated from Manchester just the year before, admitted his guilt before I had scarcely begun his interrogation.

"I was only tryin' to do the wise and righteous," he said, squaring his shoulders and puffing out his meager chest. "Samuelson's been tellin' us we shouldn't sit back and allow things to just happen. We should let our voices be heard. Solitaire's our home. We should be the ones decide how it's run."

"And so, naturally," I said, "when it came time to let your majestic voice resound, the most compelling topic you could find upon which to make a statement was the fate of a halfwit."

"It's not that simple and you know it. His case speaks to a larger issue. Samuelson says. . . ."

"Fuck you," I said. "And fuck Samuelson." I was sick of him, sick of his Midlands accent, sick especially of his references to Samuelson. What possible service, I wondered, could a dwight such as he have provided for the Magnificence? Something to do with logistics, probably. Anticipating police strategies or solving computer defenses. Yet from what I knew of the Magnificence, it was hard to imagine them putting up with this nit for very long. They would find a hard use for him and then let him fall off the edge of the world.

"Why in hell's name did you paint that thing on his door?" I asked. "And don't tell me Samuelson ordered you to do it."

The light of hope came into his face, and I would have sworn he was about to create some fantasy concerning Samuelson and himself in order to shift the guilt to broader shoulders. But all he said was, "I wanted to scare him."

"You could have achieved that with a bloody stick figure," I said.

"Yeah, but no one else would have understood it.

Samuelson says we ought to try to influence as many people as possible whenever we state our cause, no matter how limited our aims. That way we enlist others in our dialogue."

I was starting to have some idea of what Samuelson's agenda might be, but I did not believe Thirwell could further enlighten me on the subject. "All you've succeeded in doing," I told him, "is to frighten other people. Or is it your opinion that there are those here who would welcome a chapter of the Magnificence?"

He ducked his eyes and made no reply.

"If you're homesick for them, I can easily arrange for you to take a trip back to Manchester," I said.

This elicited from Thirwell a babble of pleas and promises. I saw that I would get no more out of him, and I cautioned him that if he were ever to trouble Bill again I would not hesitate to make good on my threat. I then sent him on his way and headed off to pay a call on Menckyn Samuelson.

Samuelson's apartment, like those belonging to most corporate regals, was situated in a large module adjoining the even larger module that housed the station's propulsion controls, and was furnished with antiques and pictures that would have fetched a dear price back on Earth, but here were absolutely priceless, less evidence of wealth than emblems of faith . . . the faith we were all taught to embrace, that one day life would be as once it had been, a vista of endless potential and possibility. The problem with Samuelson's digs, however, was that his taste was abysmally bad; he had assembled a motley collection of items, Guilford chests and blond Finnish chairs, a Jefferson corner cabinet and freeform video sculptures, Victorian sideboard and fiber-optic chandelier, that altogether created the impression one had stumbled into a pawn shop catering to millionaires. It may be that my amusement at this appalling display showed in my face, for though he presented a smile and an outstretched hand, I sensed a certain stiffness in his manner. Nevertheless, the politician in him brought him through that awkward moment. Soon he was nattering away, pouring me a glass of whiskey, ushering me to an easy chair, plopping himself down into another, giving out with an expansive sigh, and saying, "I'm so awfully glad you've come, John. I've been meaning to have you in for a cup of reminiscence, you know. Two old Londoners like ourselves, we can probably find a few choice topics to bang around."

He lifted his chin, beaming blandly, eyes half-lidded, as if expecting something pleasant to be dashed into his face. It was such a thespian pose, such a clichéd take on upper class manners, so redolent of someone trying to put on airs, I had to restrain a laugh. Everything about him struck me as being just the slightest bit off. He was a lean, middle-aged man, dressed in a loose cotton shirt and moleskin trousers, alert in manner, almost handsome, but the nose was a tad sharp, the eyes set a fraction too close together, the cheekbones not sufficiently prominent, the chin a touch insubstantial, too much forehead and not enough hair. He had the essential features of good breeding, yet none of the charming detail, like the runt of a pedigreed litter.

"Yes," I said. "We must do that sometime. However, today I've come on station business."

"I see." He leaned back, crossed his legs, cradled his whiskey in his lap. "Then p'rhaps after we've concluded your business, there'll be time for a chat, eh?"

"Perhaps." I had a swallow of whiskey, savored the smoky flavor. "I'd like to talk with you about William Stamey."

"Ah, yes. Old Barnacle Bill." Samuelson's brow was creased by a single furrow, the sort of line a cartoonist would use to indicate a gently rolling sea. "A bothersome matter."

"It might be considerably less bothersome if you left it alone."

Not a crack in the veneer. He smiled, shook his head. "I should dearly love to, old fellow. But I'm afraid you've rather a short-sighted view of the situation. The question we must settle is not the question of Bill *per se*, but of general policy. We must develop clear guide. . . ."

"Come on! Give it up!" I said. "I'm not one of your damned pint and kidney pie boys who get all narky and start to drool at the thought of their rights being abused. Their rights! Jesus Christ! The poor scuts have been buggered more times than a Sydney whore, and they still think it feels good. You wouldn't waste a second on this if it were merely a question of policy. I want to know what you're really after."

"Oh my God," Samuelson said, bemused. "You're not going to be an easy lay, are you?"

"Not for you, darling. I'm saving myself for the one I love."

"And just who is that, I wonder." He swirled the whiskey in his glass, watched it settle. "What do you think I'm after?"

"Power. What else is it makes your toby stiffen?"

He made a dry noise. "A simplistic answer. Not inaccurate, I'll admit. But simplistic all the same."

"I'm here for an education," I told him, "not to give a lecture."

"And I may enlighten you," Samuelson said. "I very well may. But let me ask you something first. What's your interest in all this?"

"I'm looking after Bill's interests."

He arched an eyebrow. "Surely there's more to it than that."

"That's the sum of it. Aside from the odd deep-seated psychological motive, of course."

"Of course." His smile could have sliced an onion; when

it vanished, his cheeks hollowed. "I should imagine there's an element of noblesse oblige involved."

"Call it what you like. The fact remains, I'm on the case."

"For now," he said. "These things have a way of changing."

"Is that a threat? Don't waste your time. I'm the oldest slut on the station, Samuelson. I know where all the big balls have been dragging, and I've made certain I'm protected. Should anything happen to me or mine, it's your superiors who're going to start squealing. They'll be most perturbed with you."

"You've nothing on me." This said with, I thought, forced confidence.

"True enough," I said. "But I'm working on it, don't you worry."

Samuelson drained his glass, got to his feet, went to the sideboard and poured himself a fresh whiskey. He held up the bottle, gave me an inquiring look.

"Why not?" I let him fill my glass, which I then lifted in a toast. "To England. May the seas wash over her and make her clean."

He gave an amused snort. "England," he said, and drank. He sat back down, adjusted his bottom. "You're an amazing fellow, John. I've been told as much, but now, having had some firsthand experience, I believe my informants may have underestimated you." He pinched the crease of one trouserleg. "Let me put something to you. Not as a threat, but as an item for discussion. You do understand, don't you, that the sort of protection you've developed is not proof against every circumstance?"

"Absolutely. In the end it all comes down to a question of who's got the biggest guns and the will to use them. Naturally I'm prepared along those lines."

"I don't doubt it. But you're not seeking a war, are you?"

I knocked back half my whiskey, rested the glass on my lap. "Look here, I'm quite willing to live as one with you, no matter. Until lately, you've done nothing to interfere with my agenda. But this dust-up over Bill, and now this bit with your man Thirwell and his paint gun, I won't have it. Too many people here, Brits and Yanks alike, have a tendency to soil their nappy when they catch a scent of the Magnificence. I've no quarrel with you making a power play. And that's what you're doing, old boy. You're stirring up the groundlings, throwing a few scraps to the hounds so they'll be eager for the sound of your voice. You're after taking over the administrative end of things, and you've decided to give climbing the ladder of success a pass in favor of scaling the castle walls. A bloodless coup, perhaps. Or maybe a spot of blood thrown in to slake the fiercest appetites. Well, that's fine. I don't give a fuck who's sitting in the big chair, and I don't much care how they get there, so long as we maintain the status quo. But one thing I won't have is you frightening people."

"People are forever being frightened," he said. "Whether there's a cause for fear or not. But that's not my intent."

"Perhaps not. But you've frightened the bejesus out of Bill, and now you've frightened a good many others by bringing the Magnificence into the picture."

"Thirwell's not my responsibility."

"The hell he's not! He's the walking Book of Samuelson. Every other sentence begins, 'Samuelson says. . . .' Give him a pretty smile, and he'll be your leg-humper for life."

"Leg-humper?" Samuelson looked bewildered.

"A little dog," I said impatiently. "You know the kind. Randy all the time. Jumps up on you and goes to having his honeymoon with your calf."

"I've never heard the term. Not British, is it?"

"American, I think. I heard it somewhere. I don't know."

"Marvelous expression. I'll have to remember it."

"Remember this, too," I said, trying to pick up the beat of my tirade. "I'm holding you responsible for any whisper I hear of the Magnificence. Before we had this heart-to-heart I was inclined to believe you had no part in what

Thirwell did. Now I'm not altogether sure. I think you're quite capable of using fear to manipulate the public. I think you may have known something of Thirwell's history and given him a nudge."

"Even if that were true," he said, "I don't understand the depth of your reaction. We're a long way from the Magnificence here. A daub of paint or two can't have much effect."

My jaw dropped a fraction on hearing that. "You're not from London. You couldn't be and still say that."

"Oh, I'm from London all right," he said coldly. "And I'm no virgin where the Magnificence is concerned. They left my brother stretched on King's Road one morning with the Equation of Undying Love scrawled in his own blood on the sidewalk beneath him. They mailed his private parts to his wife in a plastic container. But I've come a very long way from those days and those places. I'd be terrified of the Magnificence if they were here. But they're not here, and I'll be damned if I'll treat them like the bogeyman just because some sad little twit with too much brain and the social skills of a ferret paints the Magelantic Exorcism on somebody's door."

His statement rang true, but nevertheless I made a mental note to check on his brother. "Wonderful," I said. "It's good you've come to terms with all that. But not everyone here has managed to put as much distance between themselves and their old fears as you seem to have done."

"That may be, but I'm . . ." He broke off, clicked his tongue against his teeth. "All right. I see your point." He tapped his fingers on the arm of his chair. "Let's see if we can't reach an accord. It's not in my interests at the moment to break off my campaign against Bill, but"——he held up a hand to stop me from interrupting—"but I will acknowledge that I've no real ax to grind where he's concerned. He's serving a strictly utilitarian purpose. So here's what I'll do. I will not allow him to be shipped back to Earth. At a certain juncture, I'll defuse the campaign. Perhaps I'll even make a public apology. That should help return him to grace. In addition, I'll do what I can to prevent further incidents involving the Magnificence. Frankly I very much doubt there'll be further problems. If there are, it won't be because I'm encouraging them."

"All well and good," I said. "Very magnanimous, I'm sure. But nothing you've promised guarantees Bill's safety during the interim."

"You'll have to be his guarantee. I'll try to maintain the temper of the station at a simmer. The rest is up to you."

"Up to me? No, you're not going to avoid responsibility that way. I'll do my best to keep him from harm, but if he gets hurt, I'll hurt you. That much I can guarantee."

"Then let's hope that nothing happens to him, shall we? For both our sakes." His smile was so thin, such a sideways stretching of the lip muscles, I thought it must be making his gums ache. "Funny. I can't decide whether we've established a working relationship or declared war."

"I don't think it matters," I said.

"No, probably not." He stood, straightened the fall of his trousers, and again gave me that bland, beaming, expectant look. "Well, I won't keep you any longer. Do drop around once the dust has settled. We'll have that chat."

"About London."

"Right." He moved to the door.

"I don't know as I'd have very much to say about London," I told him. "Nothing fit for reminiscence, at any rate."

"Really?" he said, ushering me out into the corridor. "The old girl's petticoats have gotten a trifle bloody, I'll admit. Terrible; the things that go on nowadays. The hunting parties, hive systems, knife dances. And of course, the Magnificence. But here, you know"—he patted his chest—"in her heart, I firmly believe there's still a bit of

all right. Or maybe it's just I'm the sentimental sort. Like
the song says, 'call 'er satan, call 'er a whore, she'll always
be Mother to me.' "

Unlike Samuelson, I no longer thought of London as
mother or home, or in any framework that smacked of the
wholesome. Even "satan" would have been a euphemism.
London for me was a flurry of night visions: a silhouetted
figure standing in the window of a burning building, not
waving its arms, not leaning out, but calm, waiting to be
taken by the flames; men and women in tight black satin,
white silk masks all stamped with the same feral, exultant
expression, running through the streets, singing; moonlight
painting the eddies of the Thames into silk, water lapping
at a stone pier, and floating just beyond the shadow of the
pier, the enormous bulk of a man I had shot only a minute
before, nearly four hundred pounds of strangler, rapist,
cannibal, brought down by a bullet weighing no more than
one of his teeth; the flash of a shotgun from around a dark
corner, like the flash of heat lightning; the charge of
poisonous light flowing along the blade of a bloody macro-
knife just removed from the body of a fellow detective; a
garbage bag resting on a steel table that contained the
neatly butchered remains of seven infants; the façade of
St. Paul's dyed into a grooved chaos of vermilion, green,
and purple by stone-destroying bacteria released by the
artist, Miralda Hate; the wardrobe of clothing sewn of
human skin and embroidered in gilt and glitter with verses
from William Blake that we found in a vacant Brixton flat;
the blind man who begged each evening on St. Martin's
Lane, spiders crawling in the hollow globes of his glass eyes;
the plague of saints, young men and women afflicted by
a drug that bred in them the artificial personalities of
Biblical characters and inspired them to martyr themselves
during certain phases of the moon; the eyes of wild dogs
in Hyde Park gleaming in the beam of my torch like the

flat discs of highway reflectors; those and a thousand equally blighted memories, that was my London. Nightmare, grief, and endless fever.

It was Solitaire that was home and mother to me, and I treated it with the appropriate respect. Though I was an investigative officer, not a section guard, I spent a portion of nearly every day patrolling various areas, searching less for crime than for symptoms of London, incidences of infection that might produce London-like effects. The station was not one place, but many: one hundred and forty-three modules, several of which were larger than any of the Earth orbit stations, connected by corridors encased in pressure shells that could be disengaged by means of the Central Propulsion Control and—as each module was outfitted with engines—moved to a new position in the complex, or even to a new orbit; should the Central Propulsion Control (CPC) be destroyed or severely damaged, disengagement was automatic, and the modules would boost into pre-programmed orbits. I hardly ever bothered to include places such as the labs, tank farms, infirmaries, data management centers, fusion modules, and such on my unofficial rounds; nor did I include the surface of the station, the electronic and solar arrays, radiator panels, communications and tracking equipment; those areas were well maintained and had no need of a watchman. I generally limited myself to entertainment and dwelling modules like East Louie, where Bill's quarters and mine were located, idiosyncratic environments decorated with holographic scenarios so ancient that they had blanked out in patches and you would often see a coded designation or a stretch of metal wall interrupting the pattern of, say, a hieroglyphic mural; and from time to time I also inspected those sections of the station that were rarely visited and were only monitored via recordings several times a day— storage bays and transport hangars and the CPC (the cameras in those areas were supposed to transmit automatic alarms whenever anyone entered, but the alarm system was on the fritz at least half the time, and due to depleted staff and lack of materials, repairs such as that were not a high priority).

The CPC was an immense, white, portless room situated, as I've said, in the module adjoining that which housed Samuelson's digs and the rest of the corporate dwelling units. The room was segmented by plastic panels into work stations, contained banks of terminals and control panels, and was of little interest to me; but Bill, once he learned its function, was fascinated by the notion that his world could separate into dozens of smaller worlds and arrow off into the nothing, and each time we visited it, he would sit at the main panel and ask questions about its operation. There was never anyone else about, and I saw no harm in answering the questions. Bill did not have sufficient mental capacity to understand the concept of launch codes, let alone to program a computer so it would accept them. Solitaire was the only world he would ever know, and he was eager to accumulate as much knowledge about it as possible. Thus I encouraged his curiosity and showed him how to call up pertinent information on his own computer.

Due to Arlie's sympathetic response, Bill took to sleeping in our front room nearly every night, this in addition to tagging along on my rounds, and therefore it was inevitable that we became closer; however, closeness is not a term I happily apply to the relationship. Suffice it to say that he grew less defiant and petulant, somewhat more open and, as a consequence, more demanding of attention. Because his behavior had been modified to some degree, I found his demands more tolerable. He continued to cling to the notion that in order to save himself he would have to perform some valuable service to the community, but he never insisted that I help him in this; he appeared satisfied merely to hang about and do things with me. And to my surprise I found there were some things I actually enjoyed doing with him. I took especial pleasure in going outside with him, in accompanying him on his rounds and watching as he cleared barnacles away from communications equipment and other delicate mechanisms.

Sauter's Barnacle was, of course, not a true barnacle, yet it possessed certain similarities to its namesake, the most observable of which was a supporting structure that consisted of a hard exoskeleton divided into plates so as to allow movement. They bore a passing resemblance to unopened buds, the largest about the size of a man's fist, and they were variously colored, some streaked with metallic shades of red, green, gold, and silver (their coloration depended to a great extent on the nature of the substrate and their nutrient sources), so that when you saw a colony of them from a distance, spreading over the surface of a module—and all the modules were covered by hundreds of thousands of them—they had the look of glittering beds of moss or lichen. I knew almost nothing about them, only that they fed on dust, that they were sensitive to changes in light, that they were not found within the orbit of Mars, and that wherever there was a space station, they were, as my immediate superior, the Chief of Security, Gerald Sessions, put it, "thick as flies on shit." Once it had been learned that they did no harm, that, indeed, their excretions served to strengthen the outer shells of the modules, interest in them had fallen off sharply. There was, I believe, some ongoing research into their physical characteristics, but it was not of high priority.

Except with Bill.

To Bill the barnacles were purpose, a reason for being. They were, apart from Mister C, the most important creatures in the universe, and he was obsessive in his attentiveness toward them. Watching him stump about over the skin of the station, huge and clumsy in his pressure suit, a monstrous figure made to appear even more monstrous by the light spraying up around him from this or that port, hosing offending clumps of barnacles with bursts of oxygen from the tank that floated alongside him, sending them drifting up from their perches, I had the impression not of someone performing a menial task, but of a gardener tending his prize roses or—more aptly—a shepherd his flock. And though according to the best information, the barnacles were mindless things, incapable of any activity more sophisticated than obeying the basic urges of feeding and reproduction, it seemed they responded to him; even after he had chased them away they would wobble about him like strange pets, bumping against his faceplate and sometimes settling on him briefly, vivid against the white material of the pressure suit, making it appear that he was wearing jeweled rosettes on his back and shoulders. (I did not understand at the time that these were females which, unable to effect true mobility, had been stimulated to detach from the station by the oxygen and now were unable to reattach to the colony.)

With Bill's example before me, I was no longer able to take the barnacles for granted, and I began reading about them whenever I had a spare moment. I discovered that the exoskeleton was an organic-inorganic matrix composed of carbon compounds and silicate minerals, primarily olivine pyroxene, and magnetite, substances commonly found in meteorites. Changes in light intensity were registered by iridescent photophores that dotted the plates; even the finest spray of dust passing between the barnacle and a light source would trigger neurological activity and stimulate the opening of aperture plates, permitting the egress of what Jacob Sauter (the barnacles' Linnaeus, an amateur at biology) had called the "tongue," an organ utilized both in feeding and in the transmission of seminal material from the male to the female. I learned that only the males could move about the colony, and that they did so by first attaching to the substrate with their tongues, which were coated with adhesive material, then detaching at one of their upper plate segments, and finally reattaching to the colony with the stubby segmented stalks that depended from their bottom plates. "In effect," Sauter had written, "they are doing cartwheels."

The most profound thing I discovered, however, had nothing to do with the barnacles, or rather had only peripherally to do with them, and was essentially a rediscovery, a rewakening of my wonderment at the bleak majesty surrounding us. The cold diamond chaos of the stars, shining so brightly they might have just been finished that day; the sun, old god grown small and tolerable to the naked eye; the surreal brilliance and solidity that even the most mundane object acquired against the backdrop of that black, unvarying distance; that blackness itself, somehow managing to seem both ominous and serene, absence and presence, metal-hard and soft as illusion, like a fold in God's magisterial robe; the station with its spidery complexes of interconnecting corridors and modules, all coated with the rainbow swirls and streaks of the barnacles' glittering colors, and beams of light spearing out from it at every angle, like some mad, gay, rickety toy, the sight of which made me expect to hear calliope music; the Earth transport vessels, gray and bulky as whales, berthed in the geometric webs of their docks; the remote white islands of the assembly platforms, and still more remote, made visible by setting one's faceplate for maximum visual enhancement, the tiny silver needle we were soon to hurl into the haystack of the unknown. It was glorious, that vista. It made a comprehensible map of our endeavors and led me to understand that we had not botched it completely. Not yet. I had seen it all before, but Bill's devotion to the barnacles had rekindled the embers of my soul, restored my cognizance of the scope of our adventure, and looking out over the station, I would think I could feel the entire

blast and spin of creation inside my head, the flood of
particles from a trillion suns, the crackling conversations
of electric clouds to whom the frozen seas of ammonia
above which they drifted were repositories of nostalgia,
the endless fall of matter through the less-than-nothing
of a pure anomaly, the white face of Christ blurred and
streaming within the frost-colored fire of a comet's head,
the quasars not yet congealed into dragons and their
centuries, the unerring persistence of meteors that travel
for uncounted millennia through the zero dark to scoot
and burn across the skies onto the exposure plates of mild
astronomers and populate the legends of a summer night
and tumble into cinders over the ghosted peaks of the
Karakoram and then are blown onto the back porches of
men who have never turned their faces to the sky and into
the dreams of children. I would have a plunderous sense
of my own destiny, and would imagine myself hurling
through the plenum at the speed of thought, of wish,
accumulating a momentum that was in itself a charge to
go, to witness, to take, and I was so enlivened I would
believe for an instant that, like a hero returning from war,
I could lift my hand and let shine a blessing down upon
everyone around me, enabling them to see and feel all I
had seen and felt, to know as I knew that despite everything
we were closer to heaven than we had ever been before.

It was difficult for me to regain my ordinary take on life
following these excursions, but after the departure of the
lightship *Sojourner,* an event that Bill and I observed
together from a catwalk atop the solar array in East Louie,
it was thrust hard upon me that I had best set a limit on
my woolgathering and concentrate on the matters at hand,
for it was coming more and more to look as if the Strange
Magnificence had gained a foothold on Solitaire. Scraps
of black satin had been found tied to several crates in one
of the storage bays, one of them containing drugs; copies
of *The Book of Inexhaustible Delirium* began turning up;

and while I was on rounds with Bill one day, I discovered a cache of packet charges in the magnetism lab, each about half the size of a flattened soccer ball, any one of which would have been sufficient to destroy a module; Gerald Sessions and I divided them up and stored them in our apartments, not trusting our staff with the knowledge of their existence. Perhaps the most troubling thing of all, the basic question of whether or not the Magnificence had the common good to heart was being debated in every quarter of the station, an argument inspired by fear and fear alone, and leading to bloody fights and an increase in racial tension and perversion of every sort. The power of the Strange Magnificence, you see, lay in the subversive nihilism of their doctrine, which put forward the idea that it was man's duty to express all his urges, no matter how dark or violent, and that from the universal exorcism of these black secrets would ultimately derive a pure consensus, a vast averaging of all possible behaviors that would in turn reveal the true character of God and the manifest destiny of the race. Thus the leaders of the Magnificence saw nothing contradictory in funding a group in York, say, devoted to the expulsion of Pakistanis from Britain by whatever means necessary while simultaneously supporting a Sufi cult. They had no moral or philosophical problem with anything because according to them the ultimate morality was a work-in-progress. Their tracts were utter tripe, quasi-intellectual homily dressed up in the kind of adjective-heavy, gothic prose once used to give weight to stories of ghosts and ancient evil; their anthems were even less artful, but the style suited the product, and the product was an easy sell to the disenfranchised, the desperate, and the mad, categories into one of which almost everyone alive would fit to some extent, and definitely were one or another descriptive of everyone on Solitaire. As I had promised him, once these symptoms started to manifest, I approached Samuelson again, but he gave every evidence of being as concerned about the Magnificence as was I, and though I was not certain I believed his pose, I was too busy with my official duties and my unofficial one—protecting Bill, who had become the target of increased abuse—to devote much time to him. Then came the day of the launch.

It was beautiful, of course. First a tiny stream of fire, like a scratch made on a wall painted black, revealing a white undercoat. This grew smaller and smaller, and eventually disappeared; but mere seconds after its disappearance, what looked to be an iridescent crack began to spread across the blackness, reaching from the place where *Sojourner* had gone superluminal to its point of departure, widening to a finger's breadth, then a hand's, and more, like an all-colored piece of lightning hardened into a great jagged sword that was sundering the void, and as it swung toward us, widening still, I thought I saw in it intimations of faces and forms and things written, as one sees the images of circuitry and patterns such as might be found on the skin of animals when staring at the grain of a varnished board, and the sight of these half-glimpsed faces and the rest, not quite decipherable yet familiar in the way a vast and complex sky with beams of sunlight shafting down through dark clouds appears to express a familiar glory . . . those sights were accompanied by a feeling of instability, a shivery apprehension of my own insubstantiality which, although it shook me to my soul, disabling any attempt to reject it, was also curiously exalting, and I yearned for that sword to swing through me, to bear me away into a thundering genesis where I would achieve completion, and afterward, after it had faded, leaving me bereft and confused, my focus upon it had been so intent, I felt I had witnessed not an exercise of intricate technology but a simple magical act of the sort used to summon demons from the ready rooms of Hell or to wake a white spirit in the depths of an underground lake. I turned to Bill. His faceplate was awash in reflected light, and what I could make out of his face was colored an eerie green by the read-outs inside his helmet. His mouth was opened, his eyes wide. I spoke to him, saying I can't recall what, but wanting him to second my amazement at the wonderful thing we had seen.

"Somethin's wrong," he said.

I realized then that he was gazing in another direction; he might have seen *Sojourner's* departure, but only out of the corner of his eye. His attention was fixed upon one of the modules—the avionics lab, I believe—from which a large number of barnacles had detached and were drifting off into space.

"Why're they doin' that?" he asked. "Why're they leavin'?"

"They're probably sick of it here," I said, disgruntled by his lack of sensitivity. "Like the rest of us."

"No," he said. "No, must be somethin' wrong. They wouldn't leave 'less somethin's wrong."

"Fine," I said. "Something's wrong. Let's go back in."

He followed me reluctantly into the airlock, and once we had shucked off our suits, he talked about the barnacles all the way back to my quarters, insisting that they would not have vacated the station if there had been nothing wrong.

"They like it here," he said. "There's lots of dust, and nobody bothers 'em much. And they. . . ."

"Christ!" I said. "If something's wrong, figure it out and tell me! Don't just blither on!"

"I can't." He ducked his eyes, swung his arms in exaggerated fashion, as if he were getting ready to skip. "I don't know how to figure it out."

"Ask Mister C." We had reached my door, and I punched out the entry code.

"He doesn't care." Bill pushed out his lower lip to cover the upper, and he shook his head back and forth, actually not shaking it so much as swinging it in great slow arcs. "He thinks it's stupid."

"What?" The door cycled open, the front room was pitch-dark.

"The barnacles," Bill said. "He thinks everything I like is stupid. The barnacles and the CPC and. . . ."

Just then I heard Arlie scream, and somebody came hurtling out of the dark, knocking me into a chair and down onto the floor. In the spill of light from the corridor, I saw Arlie getting to her feet, covering her breasts with her arms. Her blouse was hanging in tatters about her waist; her jeans were pushed down past her hips; her mouth was bloody. She tried to speak, but only managed a sob.

Sickened and terrified at the sight of her, I scrambled out into the corridor. A man dressed all in black was sprinting away, just turning off into one of the common rooms. I ran after him. Each step spiked the boil of my emotions with rage, and by the time I entered the common room, done up as the VR version of a pub, with dart boards and dusty, dark wood, and a few fraudulent old red-cheeked men slumped at corner tables, there was murder in my heart. I yelled at people taking their ease to call Security, then raced into the next corridor.

Not a sign of the man in black.

The corridor was ranged by about twenty doors, the panel of light above most showing blue, signalling that no one was within. I was about to try one of the occupied apartments when I noticed that the telltale beside the airlock hatch was winking red. I went over to the hatch, switched on the closed circuit camera. On the screen above the control panel appeared a grainy black-and-white picture of the airlock's interior; the man I had been chasing was pacing back and forth, making an erratic humming noise. A pale, twitchy young man with a malnourished look and bones that seemed as frail as a bird's, the product of some row-house madonna and her pimply king, of not enough veggies and too many cigarettes, of centuries of a type of ignorance as peculiarly British as the hand-rolled lawns of family estates. I recognized him at once. Roger Thirwell. I also recognized his clothes. The tight black satin trousers and shirt of the Strange Magnificence, dotted with badges proclaiming levels of spiritual attainment and attendance at this or that function.

"Hello, Roger," I said into the intercom. "Lovely day for a rape, isn't it, you filthy bastard?"

He glanced around, then up to the monitor. Fear came into his face, then was washed away by hostility, which in turn was replaced by a sort of sneering happiness: "Send me to Manchester, will you?" he said. "Send me down the tube to bloody Manchester! I think not! Perhaps you realize now I'm not the sort to take threats lying down."

"Yeah, you're a fucking hero! Why don't you come out and show me how much of a man you are."

He appeared distracted, as if he had not heard me. I began to suspect that he was drugged, but drugged or not, I hated him.

"Come on out of there!" I said. "I swear to God, I'll be gentle."

"I'll show you," he said. "You want to see the man I am, I'll show you."

But he made no move.

"I had her in the mouth," he said quietly. "She's got a lovely, lovely mouth."

I didn't believe him, but the words afflicted me nevertheless. I pounded on the hatch. "You beady-eyed piece of shit! Come out, damn you!"

Voices talking excitedly behind me, then somebody put an arm on my shoulder and said in a carefully enunciated baritone, "Let me handle this one, John."

It was Gerald Sessions, my superior, a spindly black man with a handsome, open face and freckly light complexion and spidery arms that possessed inordinate strength. He was a quiet, private sort, not given to displays of emotion, understated in all ways, possessed of the glum manner of someone who continually feels themselves put upon; yet because of our years together, he was a man for whom I had developed some affection, and though I trusted no one completely, he was one of the few people whom I was willing to let watch my back. Standing beside him were four guards, among them his bodyguard and lover, Ernesto Carbajal, a little fume of a fellow with thick, oily yet well-tended black hair and a prissy cast to his features; and behind them, at a remove, was a grave-looking Menckyn Samuelson, nattily attired in dinner jacket and white trousers. Apparently he had been called away from a social occasion.

"No, thank you," I told Gerald. "I plan to hurt the son of a bitch. Send someone round to check on Arlie, will you?"

"It's been taken care of." He studied me a moment. "All right. Just don't kill him."

I turned back to the screen just as Thirwell, who had moved to the outer hatch and was gazing at the control panel, burst into song.

> "Night, my brother, gather round me,
> Breed the reign of violence,
> And with temptations of the spi-i-rit
> Blight the curse of innocence.
> Oh, supple daughters of the twilight,
> Will we have all our pleasures spent,
> when God emerges from the shadows,
> blinding in his Strange Magni-fi-i-cence . . ."

He broke off and let out a weak chuckle. I was so astounded by this behavior that my anger was muted and my investigative sensibilities engaged.

"Who're your contacts on Solitaire?" I asked. "Talk to me, and maybe things will go easier for you."

Thirwell continued staring at the panel, seemingly transfixed by it.

"Give it up, Roger," I said. "Tell us about the Magnificence. You help us, and we'll do right by you, I swear."

He lifted his face to the ceiling and, in a shattered tone, verging on tears, said, "Oh, God!"

"I may be wrong," I said, "but I don't believe he's going to answer you. You'd best brace it up in there, get your head clear."

"I don't know," he said.

"Sure you do. You know. It was your brains got you here. Now use them. Think. You have to make the best of this you can." It was hard to make promises of leniency to this little grout who'd had his hands on Arlie, but the rectitude of the job provided me a framework in which I was able to function. "Look here, I can't predict what's going to happen, but I can give you this much. You tell us what you know, chapter and verse, and I'll speak up for you. There could be mitigating circumstances. Drugs. Coercion. Blackmail. That strike a chord, Roger? Hasn't someone been pushing you into this? Yeah, yeah, I thought so. Mitigating circumstances. That being the case, it's likely the corporation will go lightly with you. And one thing I can promise for certain sure. We'll keep you safe from the Magnificence."

Thirwell turned to the monitor. From the working of his mouth and the darting of his eyes, I could see he was close to falling apart.

"That's it, there's the lad. Come along home."

"The Magnificence." He glanced about, as if concerned that someone might be eavesdropping. "They told me . . . uh . . . I . . ." He swallowed hard and peered at the camera as if trying to see through to the other side of the lens. "I'm frightened," he said in a whispery, conspiratorial tone.

"We're all frightened, Roger. It's shit like the Magnificence keeps us frightened. Time to stop being afraid, don't you think? Maybe that's the only way to stop. Just to do it, I mean. Just to say, the hell with this! I'm . . ."

"P'rhaps if I had a word with him," said Samuelson, leaning in over my shoulder. "You said I had some influence with the boy. P'rhaps . . ."

I shoved him against the wall; Gerald caught him on the rebound and slung him along the corridor, holding a finger up to his lips, indicating that Samuelson should keep very quiet. But the damage was done. Thirwell had turned back to the control panel and was punching in the code that would break the seal on the outer hatch.

"Don't be an ass!" I said. "That way's no good for anyone."

He finished punching in the code and stood staring at the stud that would cycle the lock open. The Danger lights above the inner hatch were winking, and a computer voice had begun repeating, Warning, Warning, The outer hatch has been unsealed, the airlock has not been depressurized, Warning, Warning. . . .

"Don't do it, Roger!"

"I have to," he said. "I realize that now. I was confused, but now it's okay. I can do it."

"Nobody wants this to happen, Roger."

"I do, I want it."

"Listen to me!"

Thirwell's hand went falteringly toward the stud. "Lord of the alley mouths," he said, "Lord of the rifles, Lord of the inflamed, Thou who hath committed every vileness . . ."

"For Christ's sake, man!" I said. "Nobody's going to hurt you. Not the Magnificence, not anyone. I'll guarantee your safety."

". . . every sin, every violence, stand with me now, help me shape this dying into an undying love. . . ." His voice dropped in volume, becoming too low to hear.

"Goddamn it, Thirwell! You silly bastard. Will you stop

jabbering that nonsense! Don't give in to it! Don't listen to what they've taught you. It's all utter rot!"

Thirwell looked up at the camera, at me. Terror warped his features for a moment, but then the lines of tension softened and he giggled. "He's right," he said. "The man's dead on right. You'll never understand."

"Who's right? What won't I understand?"

"Watch," said Thirwell gleefully. "Watch my face."

I kept silent, trying to think of the perfect thing to say, something to foil his demented impulse.

"Are you watching?"

"I want to understand," I said. "I want you to help me understand. Will you help me, Roger? Will you tell me about the Magnificence?"

"I can't. I can't explain it." He drew a deep breath, let it out slowly. "But I'll show you."

He smiled blissfully at the camera as he pushed the stud.

Explosive decompression, even when viewed on a black-and-white-monitor, is not a good thing to see. I looked away. Inadvertently, my eyes went to Samuelson. He was standing about fifteen feet away, hands behind his back, expressionless, like a minister composing himself before delivering his sermon; but there was something else evident in that lean, blank face, something happening beneath the surface, some slight engorgement, and I knew, knew, that he was not distressed in the least by the death, that he was pleased by it. No one of his position, I thought, would be so ingenuous as to interrupt a security man trying to talk in a potential suicide. And if what he had done to Thirwell had been intentional, a poorly disguised threat, if he had that much power and menace at his command, then he might well be responsible for what Thirwell had done to Arlie.

I strolled over to him. His eyes tracked my movements. I stopped about four feet away and studied him, searching for signs of guilt, for hints of a black satin past, of torchlight

and blood and group sing-alongs. There was weakness in
his face, but was it a weakness bred by perversion and
brutality, or was it simply a product of fear? I decided that
for Arlie's sake, for Thirwell's, I should assume the worst.
"Guess what I'm going to do next?" I asked him. Before
he could answer I kicked him in the pit of the stomach,
and as he crumpled, I struck him a chopping left to the
jaw that twisted his head a quarter-turn. Two of the guards
started toward me, but I warned them back. Carbajal fixed
me with a look of prim disapproval.

"That was a stupid damn thing to do," said Gerald,
ambling over and gazing down at Samuelson, who was
moaning, stirring.

"He deserves worse," I said. "Thirwell was coming out.
I'm certain of it. And then this bastard opened his mouth."

"Yeah." Gerald leaned against the wall, crossed his legs.
"So how come you figure he did it?"

"Why don't you ask him? Be interesting to see how he
responds."

Gerald let out a sardonic laugh. "Man's an altruist. He
was trying to help." He picked at a rough place on one
of his knuckles. "The real question I got is how deep he's
in it. Whether he's involved with the Magnificence, or if
he's just trying to convince everyone he is, I need to know
so I can make an informed decision."

I did not much care for the edge of coldness in his voice.
"And what decision is that, pray?"

Carbajal, staring at me over his shoulder, flashed me
a knowing smile.

"He already don't like you, John," said Gerald. "Man told
me so. Now he's gonna want your ass on a plaque. And I
have to decide whether or not I should let him have you."

"Oh, really?"

"This is some serious trap, man. I defy Samuelson, we're
gonna have us one helluva situation. Security lined up
against Administration."

Samuelson was trying to sit up; his jaw was swollen and discolored. I hoped it was broken.

"We could be talkin' about a war," Gerald said.

"I think you're exaggerating," I said. "Even so, a civil war wouldn't be the worst thing that could happen, not so long as the right side won. There are a number of assholes on station who would make splendid casualties."

Gerald said, "No comment."

Samuelson had managed to prop himself up on an elbow. "I want you to arrest him," he said to Gerald.

I looked at Gerald. "Might I have a few words with him before you decide?"

He met my eyes for a few beats, then shook his head in dismay. "Aw, fuck it," he said.

"Thanks, friend," I said.

"Fuck you, too," he said; he walked a couple of paces away and stood gazing off along the corridor; Carbajal went with him, whispered in his ear and rubbed his shoulders.

"Did you hear what I told you?" Samuelson heaved himself up into a sitting position, cupping his jaw. "Arrest him. Now!"

"Here, let me help you up." I grabbed a fistful of Samuelson's jacket, hauled him to his feet, and slammed him into the wall. "There. All better, are we?"

Samuelson's eyes darted left to right, hoping for allies. I bashed his head against the wall to get his attention, and he struggled against my hold.

"Such a tragedy," I said in my best upper crust accent. "The death of young Thirwell, what?"

The fight went out of him; his eyes held on mine.

"That was as calculated a bit of murder as I've seen in many a year," I told him.

"I haven't the foggiest notion what you're talking about!"

"Oh, yes you do! I had him walking the tightrope back. Then you popped in and reminded him of the consequences he'd be facing should he betray the

Magnificence. God only knows what he thought you had in store for him."

"I did no such thing! I was . . ."

I dug the fingers of my left hand in behind his windpipe; I would have liked to squeeze until thumb and fingers touched, but I only applied enough force to make him squeak. "Shut your gob! I'm not finished." I adjusted my grip to give him more air. "You're dirty, Samuelson. You're the germ that's causing all the pale looks around here. I don't know how you got past the screens, but that's not important. Sooner or later I'm going to have your balls for breakfast. And when I've cleaned my plate, I'll send what's left of you to the same place you chased Thirwell. Of course you could tell me the names of everyone on Solitaire who's involved with the Magnificence. That might weaken my resolve. But don't be too long about it, because I am fucking lusting for you. I can scarcely wait for you to thwart me. My saliva gets all thick and ropy when I think of the times we could have together." I gave him a shake, listened to him gurgle. "I know what you are, and I know what you want. You've got a dream, don't you? A vast, splendid dream of men in black satin populating the stars. New planets to befoul. Well, it's just not going to happen. If it ever comes to pass that a ship returns with good news, you won't be on it, son. Nor will any of your tribe. You'll be floating out there in the black grip of Jesus, with your blood all frozen in sprays around you and your hearts stuffed in your fucking mouths." I released him, gave him a cheerful wink. "All right. Go ahead. Your innings."

Samuelson scooted away along the wall, holding his throat. "You're mad!" He glanced over at Gerald. "The both of you!"

Gerald shrugged, spread his hands. "It's part of the job description."

"May we take it," I said to Samuelson, "that you're not intending to confess at this time?"

Samuelson noticed, as had I, that a number of people had come out of the common room and were watching the proceedings. "I'll tell you what I intend," he said, pulling himself erect in an attempt to look impressive. "I intend to make a detailed report concerning your disregard for authority and your abuse of position."

"Now, now," Gerald said, walking toward him. "Let's have no threats. Otherwise somebody"—his voice built into a shout—"somebody might lose their temper!" He accompanied the shout by slapping his palm against the wall, and this sent Samuelson staggering back another dozen feet or so.

Several of the gathering laughed.

"Come clean, man," I said to Samuelson. "Do the right thing. I'm told it's better than sex once those horrid secrets start spilling out."

"If it'll make you feel any easier, you can dress up in your black satins first," Gerald said. "Having that smooth stuff next to your skin, that'll put a nice wiggle on things."

"You know, Gerald," I said. "Maybe these fools are onto something. Maybe the Magnificence has a great deal to offer."

"I'm always interested in upgrading my pleasure potential," he said. "Why don't you give us the sales pitch, Samuelson?"

"Yeah," I said. "Let's hear about all the snarky quivers you get from twisting the arms off a virgin."

The laughter swelled in volume, inspired by Samuelson's expression of foolish impotence.

"You don't understand who you're dealing with," he said. "But you will, I promise."

There, I said to myself, there's his confession. Not enough to bring into court, but for a moment it was there in his face, all the sick hauteur and corrupted passion of his tribe.

"I bet you're a real important man with the Magnificence," said Gerald. "Bet you even got a title."

"Minister of Scum and Delirium," I suggested.

"I like it," said Gerald. "How 'bout Secretary of the Inferior?"

"Grand High Salamander," said Carbajal, and tittered. "Master of the Excremental."

"Stop it," said Samuelson, clenching his fists; he looked ready to stamp his foot and cry.

Several other titular suggestions came from the crowd of onlookers, and Gerald offered, "Queen of the Shitlickers."

"I'm warning you," said Samuelson, then he shouted, "I am warning you!" He was flushed, trembling. All the twitchy material of his inner core exposed. It had been fun bashing him about, but now I wanted to put my heel on him, feel him crunch underfoot.

"Go on," Gerald said. "Get along home. You've done all you can here."

Samuelson shot him an unsteady look, as if not sure what Gerald was telling him.

Gerald waved him off. "We'll talk soon."

"Yes," said Samuelson, straightening his jacket, trying to muster a shred of dignity. "Yes, indeed, we most certainly will." He delivered what I suppose he hoped was a withering stare and stalked off along the corridor.

"There goes an asshole on a mission," said Gerald, watching him round the bend.

"Not a doubt in my mind," I said.

"Trouble." Gerald stuffed his heel against the steel floor, glanced down as if expecting to see a mark. "No shit, the man's trouble."

"So are we," I said.

"Yeah, uh-huh." He sounded unconvinced.

We exchanged a quick glance. We had been through a lot together, Gerald and I, and I knew by the tilt of his head, the wry set of his mouth, that he was very worried. I was about to make a stab at boosting his spirits when I remembered something more pressing.

"Oh, Christ!" I said. "Arlie! I've got to get back."

"Forgot about her, huh?" He nodded gloomily, as if my forgetfulness were something he had long decried. "You know you're an asshole, don't you? You know you don't deserve the love of woman or the friendship of man."

"Yeah, yeah," I said. "Can you handle things here?"

He made a gesture of dismissal. Another morose nod. "Just so you know," he said.

There were no seasons on Solitaire, no quick lapses into cold, dark weather, no sudden transformations into flowers and greenery; yet it seemed that in those days after Thirwell's suicide the station passed through an autumnal dimming, one lacking changes in foliage and temperature, but having in their stead a flourishing of black satin ribbons and ugly rumors, a gradual decaying of the spirit of the place into an oppressive atmosphere of sullen wariness, and the slow occlusion of all the visible brightness of our lives, a slump of patronage in the bars, the common rooms standing empty, incidences of decline that reminded me in sum of the stubborn resistance of the English oaks to their inevitable change, their profuse and solemn green surrendering bit by bit to the sparse imperatives of winter, like a strong man's will gradually being eroded by grief.

War did not come immediately, as Gerald had predicted, but the sporadic violences continued, along with the arguments concerning the true intentions and nature of the Strange Magnificence, and few of us doubted that war, or something akin to it, was in the offing. Everyone went about their duties hurriedly, grimly—everyone, that is, except for Bill. He was so absorbed by his own difficulties, I doubt he noticed any of this, and though the focus of hostility had shifted away from him to an extent, becoming more diffuse and general, he grew increasingly agitated and continued to prattle on about having to "do something" and—this a new chord in his simple symphony—that something must be terribly wrong because the barnacles were leaving.

That they were leaving was undeniable. Every hour saw the migration of thousands more, and large areas of the station's surface had been laid bare. Not completely bare, mind you. There remained a layer of the substrate laid down by the females, greenish silver in color, but nonetheless it was a shock to see the station so denuded. I gave no real credence to Bill's contention that we were in danger, but neither did I totally disregard it, and so, partly to calm him, to reassure him that the matter was being investigated, I went back to Jacob Sauter's notes to learn if such migrations were to be expected.

According to the notes, pre-adult barnacles—Sauter called them "larvae"—free-floated in space, each encapsulated in its own segment of a tube whose ends had been annealed so as to form a ring. Like the adult barnacle, the exterior of the ring was dotted with light-sensitive photophores, and when a suitable place for attachment was sensed, the ring colony was able to orient itself by means of excretions sprayed through pores in the skin of the tube, a method not dissimilar to that utilized by orbital vessels when aligning themselves for re-entry. The slightest change in forward momentum induced secretions to occur along the edge of the colony oriented for imminent attachment, and ultimately the colony stuck to its new home, whereupon the females excreted an acidic substrate that bonded with the metal. The barnacles were hermaphroditic, and the initial metamorphitosis always resulted in female barnacles alone. Once the female colony grew dense, some of the females would become male. When the colony reached a certain density it reproduced *en masse*. As the larval tubes were secreted, they sometimes intertwined, and this would result in braided ring colonies, which helped insure variation in the gene pool. And that was all I could find on the subject of migration. If Sauter were to be believed, by giving up their purchase on the station, the barnacles were essentially placing their fate in the hands of God, taking the chance—and given the vastness of space, the absence of ring secretions, it was an extremely slim chance—that they would happen to bump into something and be able to cling long enough to attach themselves. If one were to judge their actions in human terms, it would appear that they must be terrified of something, otherwise they would stay where they were; but it would require an immense logical leap for me to judge them according to those standards and I had no idea what was responsible for their exodus.

Following my examination of Sauter's notes I persuaded Gerald to accompany me on an inspection tour of Solitaire's surface. I thought seeing the migration for himself might affect him more profoundly than had the camera views, and that he might then join me in entertaining the suspicion that—as unlikely a prospect as it was—Bill had stumbled onto something. But Gerald was not moved to agreement.

"Man, I don't know," he said as we stood on the surface of East Louie, looking out toward the CPC and the administration module. There were a few sparse patches of barnacles around us, creatures that for whatever reason—impaired sensitivity, some form of silicate stubbornness—had not abandoned the station. Now and then one or several would drift up toward the glittering clouds of their fellows that shone against the blackness like outcroppings of mica in anthracite. "What do I know about these damn things! They could be doing anything. Could be they ran out of food, and that's why they're moving. Shit! You giving the idiot way too much credit! He's got his own reasons for wanting this to mean something."

I could not argue with him. It would be entirely consistent

with Bill's character for him to view the migration as part
of his personal apocalypse, and his growing agitation might
stem from the fact that he saw his world being whittled
down, his usefulness reduced, and thus his existence
menaced all the more.

"Still," I said, "it seems odd."

" 'Odd' ain't enough. Weird, now, that might carry some
weight. Crazy. Run amok. They qualify for my attention.
But 'odd' I can live with. You want to worry about this, I
can't stop you. Me, I got more important things to do. And
so do you."

"I'm doing my job, don't you worry."

"Okay. Tell me about it."

Through the glaze of reflection on his faceplate, I could
only make out his eyes and his forehead, and these gave
no clue to his mood.

"There's not very much to tell. As far as I can determine
Samuelson's pure through and through. There's a curious
lack of depth to the background material, a few dead ends
in the investigative reports. Deceased informants. Vanished
employers. That sort of thing. It doesn't feel quite right
to me, but it's nothing I could bring to the corporation.
And it does appear that his elder brother was murdered
by the Magnificence, which establishes at least one of his
bona fides."

"If Samuelson's part of the Magnificence, I . . ."

" 'If,' my ass!" I said. "You know damned well he is."

"I was going to say, his brother's murder is just the kind
of tactic they like to use in order to draw suspicion away
from one of their own. Hell, he may have hated his
brother."

"Or he may have loved him and wanted the pain."

Gerald grunted.

"I've isolated fourteen files that have a sketchiness
reminiscent of Samuelson's," I said. "Of course that doesn't
prove anything. Most of them are administration and most

are relatively new on Solitaire. But only a couple are his close associates."

"That makes it more likely they're all dirty. They don't believe in bunching up. I'll check into it." I heard a burst of static over my earphones, which meant that he had let out a heavy sigh. "The damn thing is," he went on, "Samuelson might not be the lead dog. Whoever's running things might be keeping in the shadows for now."

"No, not a chance," I said. "Samuelson's too lovely in the part."

A construction sled, a boxy thing of silver struts powered by a man in a rocket pack, went arcing up from the zero physics lab and boosted toward one of the assembly platforms; all manner of objects were lashed to the struts, some of them—mostly tools, vacuum welders and such— trailing along in its wake, giving the sled a raggedy, gypsy look.

"Those explosives you got stashed," Gerald said, staring after the sled.

"They're safe."

"I hope so. We didn't have 'em, they might have moved on us by now. Done a hostage thing. Or maybe just blown something up. I'm pretty sure nothing else has been brought on station, so you just keep a close watch on that shit. That's our hole card."

"I don't like waiting for them to make the first move."

"I know you don't. Was up to you, we'd be stiffening citizens right and left, and figuring out later if they guilty or not. That's how come you got the teeth, and I'm holding the leash."

Though his face was hidden, I knew he was not smiling.

"Your way's not always the right of it, Gerald," I said. "Sometimes my way's the most effective, the most secure."

"Yeah, maybe. But not this time. This is too bullshit, this mess. Too many upper level people involved. We scratch the wrong number off the page, we be down the tube in a fucking flash. You don't want to be scuffling around back on Earth, do you? I sure as hell don't."

"I'd prefer it to having my lungs sucked out through my mouth like Thirwell."

"Would you, now? Me, I'm not so sure. I want a life that's more than just gnawing bones, John. I ain't up to that kind of hustle no more. And I don't believe you are, either."

We stood without speaking for a minute or so. It was getting near time for a shift change, and everywhere bits of silver were lifting from the blotched surface of the station, flocking together in the brilliant beams of light shooting from the transport bays, their movements as quick and fitful as the play of dust in sunlight.

"You're thinking too much these days, man," Gerald said. "You're not sniffing the air, you're not feeling things here." He made a slow, ungainly patting motion above his gut.

"That's rot!"

"Is it? Listen to this. 'Life has meaning but no theme. There is no truth we can assign to it that does not in some way lessen the bright flash of being that is its essential matter. There is no lesson learned that does not signal a misapprehension of our stars. There is no moral to this darkness.' That's some nice shit. Extremely profound. But the man who wrote that, he's not watching the water for sharks. He's too busy thinking."

"I'm so pleased," I said, "you've been able to access my computer once again. I know the childlike joy it brings you. And I'm quite sure Ernesto is absolutely thrilled at having a peek."

"Practice makes perfect."

"Any further conclusions you've drawn from poking around in my personal files?"

"You got one helluva fantasy life. Or else that Arlie, man, she's about half some kind of beast. How come you write all that sex stuff down?"

"Prurience," I said. "Damn! I don't know why I put up with this shit from you."

"Well, I do. I'm the luckiest Chief of Security in the system, see, 'cause I've got me a big, bad dog who's smart and loyal, and"—he lifted one finger of his gauntleted hand to signify that this was key—"who has no ambition to take my job."

"Don't be too sure."

"No, man, you don't want my job. I mean, you'd accept it if it was handed to you, but you like things the way they are. You always running wild and me trying to cover your ass . . ."

"I hope you're not suggesting that I'm irresponsible.'

"You're responsible, all right. You just wouldn't want the kind of responsibility I've got. It'd interfere with your style. The way you move around the station, talking bullshit to the people, everything's smooth, then all of a sudden you go Bam! Bam!, and take somebody down, then the next second you're talking about Degas or some shit, and then, Bam!, somebody else on the floor, you say, Oops, shit, I guess I messed up, will you please forgive me, did I ever tell you 'bout Paris in the springtime when all the poets turn into cherryblossoms, Bam! It's fucking beautiful, man. You got half the people so scared they crawl under the damn rug when they see you coming, and the other half loves you to death, and most all of 'em would swear you're some kind of Robin Hood, you whip 'em 'cause you love 'em and it's your duty, and you only use your powers for goodness and truth. They don't understand you like I do. They don't see you're just a dangerous, amoral son of a bitch."

"Is this the sort of babble that goes into your personnel reports?"

"Not hardly. I present you as a real citizen. A model of integrity and courage and resourcefulness."

"Thanks for that," I said coldly.

"Just don't ever change, man. Don't ever change."

The sleds that had lifted from the station had all disappeared, but others were materializing from the blackness, tiny points of silver and light coming home from the assembly platforms, looking no more substantial than the clouds of barnacles. Finally Gerald said, "I got things to take care of." He waved at the barnacles. "Leave this shit alone, will you? After everything else gets settled, maybe then we'll look into it. Right now all you doing is wasting my fucking time."

I watched him moving off along the curve of the module toward the airlock, feeling somewhat put off by his brusque reaction and his analysis. I respected him a great deal as a professional, and his clinical assessment of my abilities made me doubt that his respect for me was so unqualified.

There was a faint click against the side of my helmet. I reached up and plucked off a barnacle. Lying in the palm of my gauntlet, its plates closed, its olive surface threaded with gold and crimson, it seemed cryptic, magical, rare, like something one would find after a search lasting half a lifetime, a relic buried with a wizard king, lying in his ribcage in place of a heart. I had shifted my position so that the light from the port behind me cast my shadow over the surface, and, a neurological change having been triggered by the shift in light intensity, some of the barnacles in the shadow were opening their plates and probing the vacuum with stubby gray "tongues," trying to feed. It was an uncanny sight, the way their "tongues" moved, stiffly, jerkily, like bad animation, like creatures in a grotesque garden hallucinated by Hawthorne or Baudelaire, and standing there among them, with the technological hodgepodge of the station stretching away in every direction, I felt as if I were stranded in a pool of primitive time, looking out onto the future. It was, I realized, a feeling akin to that I'd had in London whenever I thought about the space colonies, the outposts strung across the system.

Gnawing bones.

As my old Classics professor would have said, Gerald's metaphor was "a happy choice."

And now I had time to consider, I realized that Gerald was right: after all the years on Solitaire, I would be ill-suited for life in London, my instincts rusty, incapable of readjusting to the city's rabid intensity. But I did not believe he was right to wait for Samuelson to move against us. Once the Magnificence set their sights on a goal, they were not inclined to use half-measures. I was too disciplined to break ranks with Gerald, but there was nothing to prevent me from preparing myself for the day of judgment. Samuelson might bring us down, I told myself, but I would see to it that he would not outlive us. I was not aware, however, that judgment day was almost at hand.

Perhaps it was the trouble of those days that brought Arlie and I closer together, that reawakened us to the sweetness of our bodies and the sharp mesh of our souls, to all those things we had come to take for granted. And perhaps Bill had something to do with it. As dismal an item as he was, it may be his presence served—as Arlie had suggested—to supply us with some missing essential of warmth or heart. But whatever the cause, it was a great good time for us, and I came once again to perceive her not merely as someone who could cure a hurt or make me stop thinking for a while, but as the embodiment of my hopes. After everything I had witnessed, all the shabby, bloody evidence I had been presented of our kind's pettiness and greed that I could feel anything so pure for another human being . . . Christ it astounded me! And if that much could happen, then why not the fulfillment of other, more improbable hopes? For instance, suppose a ship were to return with news of a habitable world . I pictured the two of us boarding, flying away, landing, being washed clean in the struggle of a stern simple life.

Foolishness, I told myself, Wild ignorance. Yet each time I fell into bed with Arlie, though the darkness that covered us always seemed imbued with a touch of black satin, with the sickly patina of the Strange Magnificence, I would sense in the back of my mind that in touching her I was flying away again, and in entering her I was making landfall on some perfect blue-green sphere. There came a night, however, when to entertain such thoughts seemed not mere folly but the height of indulgence.

It was close upon half-eleven, and the three of us, Bill, Arlie, and I, were sitting in the living room, the walls playing a holograph scenario of a white-capped sea and Alps of towering cumulus, with whales breeching and a three-masted schooner coasting on the wind vanishing whenever and it reached a corner, then reappearing on the ajoining wall. Bill and Arlie were on the sofa, and she was telling him stories about Earth, lies about the wonderful animals that lived there, trying to distract him from his obsessive nattering about the barnacles. I had just brought out several of the packet charges that Gerald and I had a hidden away, and I was working at reshaping them into smaller units, a project that had occupied me for several nights. Bill had previously seemed frightened by them and had never mentioned them, that night, however, he pointed at the charges and said, " 'Splosives?"

"Very good," I said. "The ones we found, you and I. The ones I was working with yesterday. Remember?"

"Uh-huh." He watched me re-insert a timer into one of the charges and then asked what I was doing.

"Making some presents," I told him.

"Birthday presents?"

"More like Guy Fawkes Day presents."

He had no clue as to the identity of Guy Fawkes, but he nodded sagely as though he had. "Is one for Gerald?"

"You might say they're all for Gerald."

He watched me a while longer, then said, "Why is it presents? Don't 'splosives hurt?"

" 'E's just havin' a joke," Arlie said.

Bill sat quietly for a minute or so, his eyes tracking my fingers at last he said, "Why won't you talk to Gerald about the barnacles? You should tell him it's important."

"Give it a rest, Billy," Arlie said, patting his arm.

"What do you expect Gerald to do?" I said. "Even if he agreed with you, there's nothing to be done."

"Leave," he said. "Like the barnacles."

"What a marvelous idea! We'll just pick up and abandon the place."

"No, no!" he shrilled. "CPC! CPC!"

"Listen 'ere," said Arlie. "There's not a chance in 'ell the corporation's goin' to authorize usin' the CPC for somethin' loike that. So put it from mind, dear, won't you?"

"Don't need the corporation," Bill said in a whiny tone.

"He's got the CPC on the brain," I said. "Every night I come in here and find him running the file."

Arlie shushed me and asked, "What's that you said, Bill?"

He clamped his lips together, leaned back against the wall, his head making a dark, ominous-looking interruption in the path of the schooner; a wave of bright water appeared to crash over him, sending up a white spray.

"You 'ave somethin' to tell us, dear?"

"Be grateful for the silence," I said.

A few seconds later Bill began to weep, to wail that it wasn't fair, that everyone hated him.

We did our best to soothe him, but to no avail. He scrambled to his feet and went to beating his fists against his thighs, hopping up and down, shrieking at the top of his voice, his face gone as red as a squalling infant's. Then of a sudden he clutched the sides of his head. His legs stiffened, his neck cabled. He fell back on the sofa, twitching, screaming, clawing at the lump behind his ear. Mister C had intervened and was punishing him with electric shocks. It was a hideous thing to see, this enormous, babyish man jolted by internal lightnings, strings of drool braiding his chin, the animation ebbing from his face, his protests growing ever more feeble, until at last he sat staring blankly into nowhere, an ugly, outsized doll in a stained white jumpsuit.

Arlie moved close to him, mopped his face with a tissue. Her mouth thinned; the lines bracketing the corners of her lips deepened. "God, 'e's a disgustin' object," she said. "I don't know what it is about 'im touches me so."

"Perhaps he reminds you of your uncle."

"I realize this is hard toimes for you, luv," she said, continuing to mop Bill's face. "But do you really find it necessary to treat me so sarcastic, loike I was one of your culprits?"

"Sorry," I said.

She gave an almost imperceptible shrug. Something shifted in her face, as if an opaque mask had slid aside, revealing her newly vulnerable. "What you fink's goin' to 'appen to 'im?"

"Same as'll happen to us, probably. It appears our fates have become intertwined." I picked up another charge. "Anyway, what's it matter, the poor droob? His best pal is a little black bean that zaps him whenever he throws a wobbler. He's universally loathed, and his idea of a happy time is to pop a crystal and flog the bishop all night long. As far as I can tell, his fate's already bottomed out."

She clicked her tongue against her teeth. "Maybe it's us Oi see in 'im."

"You and me? That's a laugh."

"Nao, I mean all of us. Don't it seem sometimes we're all 'elpless loike 'im? Just big, loopy animals without a proper sense of things."

"I don't choose to think that way."

Displeasure came into her face, but before she could voice it, a loud buzzer went off in the bedroom—Gerald's private alarm, a device he would only use if unable to communicate with me openly. I jumped to my feet and grabbed a hand laser from a drawer in the table beside the sofa.

"Don't let anyone in," I told Arlie. "Not under any circumstances."

She nodded, gave me a brisk hug. "You 'urry back."

The corridors of East Louie were thronged, hundreds of people milling about the entrances of the common rooms and the commissaries. I smelled hashish, perfume, pheromone sprays. Desperate with worry, I pushed and elbowed my way through the crowds toward Gerald's quarters, which lay at the opposite end of the module. When I reached his door, I found it partway open and the concerned brown face of Ernesto Carbajal, peering out at me. He pulled me into the foyer. The room beyond was dark; a slant of light fell across the carpet from the bedroom door, which was open a foot or so; but I could make out nothing within.

"Where's Gerald?" I asked.

Carbajal's hands made delicate, ineffectual gestures in the air, as if trying to find a safe hold on something with a lot of sharp edges. "I didn't know what to do," he said. "I didn't know . . . I . . ."

I watched him flutter and spew. He was Gerald's man, and Gerald claimed he was trustworthy. For my part, I had never formed an opinion. Now, however, I saw nothing that made me want to turn my back on him. And so, of course, I determined that I would do exactly that as soon as a suitable opportunity presented itself.

"You gave the alarm?" I asked him.

"Yes, I didn't want anyone to hear . . . the intercom. You know, it . . . I . . ."

"Yeah, yeah, I know. Calm down!" I pushed him against the wall, kept my hand flat against his chest. "Where's Gerald?"

His eyes flicked toward the bedroom; for an instant the flesh of his face seemed to sag away from the bone, to lose all its firmness. "There," he said. "Back there. Oh, God!"

It was at that moment I knew Gerald was dead, but I refused to let the knowledge affect me. No matter how terrible the scene in the bedroom, Carbajal's reactions—though nicely done—were too flighty for a professional; even considering his involvement with Gerald, he should have been able to manage a more businesslike façade.

"Let's have a look, shall we?"

"No, I don't want to go back in there!"

"All right, then," I said. "You wait here."

I crossed to the bedroom, keeping an ear out for movement behind me. I swallowed, held my breath. The surface of the door seemed hot to the touch, and when I slid it open, I had the thought that the heat must be real, that all the glare off the slick red surfaces within had permeated the metal. Gerald was lying on the bed, the great crimson hollow of his stomach and chest exposed and empty, unbelievably empty, cave empty, with things like glistening, pulpy red fruit resting by his head, hands and feet; but I did not admit to the sight, I kept a distant focus. I heard a step behind me and turned, throwing up my guard as Carbajal, his face distorted by a grimace, struck at me with a knife. I caught his knife arm, bent the elbow backward against the doorframe; I heard it crack as he screamed and shoved him back into the living room. He staggered off-balance, but did not fall. He righted himself, began to move in a stealthy crouch, keeping his shattered elbow toward me, willing to accept more pain in order to protect his good left hand. Disabled or not, he was still very fast, dangerous with his kicks. But I knew I had him so long as I was careful, and I chose to play him rather than end it with the laser. The more I punished him, I thought, the less resistant he would be to interrogation. I feinted, and when he jumped back, I saw him wince. A chalky wash spread across his skin. Every move he made was going to hurt him.

"You might as well hazard it all on one throw, Ernesto," I told him. "If you don't, you're probably going to fall over before I knock you down."

He continued to circle me, unwilling to waste energy on a response; his eyes looked all dark, brimming with concentrated rage. Passing through the spill of light from the bedroom, he seemed ablaze with fury, a slim little devil with a crooked arm.

"It's not your karate let you down, Ernesto. It's that ridiculous drama queen style of acting. Absolutely vile! I thought you might start beating your breast and crying out to Jesus for succor. Of course that's the weakness all you yobbos in the Magnificence seem to have. You're so damned arrogant, you think you can fool everyone with the most rudimentary tactics. I wonder why that is. Never mind. In a moment I'm going to let you tell me all about it."

I gave him an opening, a good angle of attack. I'm certain he knew it was a trap, but he was in so much pain, so eager to stop the pain, that his body reacted toward the opening before his mind could cancel the order. He swung his right leg in a vicious arc. I stepped inside the kick, executed a hip throw; as he flew into the air and down, I wrenched his good arm out of the socket with a quick twist. He gave a cry, but wriggled out of my reach and bridged to his feet, both arms dangling. I took him back down with a leg sweep and smashed his right kneecap with my heel. Once his screaming had subsided I sat down on the edge of a coffee table and showed him the laser.

"Now we can talk undisturbed," I said brightly. "I hope you feel like talking, because otherwise . . ."

He cursed in Spanish, spat toward me.

"I can see there's no fooling you, Ernesto. You obviously know you're not leaving here alive, not after what you've

done. But you do have one life choice remaining that might
be of some interest. Quickly"—I flourished the laser—
"or slowly. What's your pleasure?"

He lay without moving, his chest heaving, blinking
from time to time, a neutral expression on his face,
perhaps trying to think of something he could tell me
that would raise the stakes. His breath whistled in his
throat; sweat beaded his forehead. My thoughts kept
pulling me back into that red room, and as I sat there
the pull became irresistible. I saw it clearly this time.
The heart lying on the pillow above Gerald's head, the
other organs arranged neatly beside his hands and feet;
the darkly crimson hollow with its pale flaps. Things
written in blood on the wall. It made me weary to see
it, and the most wearisome thing of all was the fact that
I was numb, that I felt almost nothing. I knew I would
have to rouse myself from this spiritual malaise and go
after Samuelson. I could trust no one to help me wage
a campaign—quick retaliation was the best chance I
had. Perhaps the only chance. The Magnificence had
a number of shortcomings. Their arrogance, a crudeness
of tactics, an infrastructure that allowed unstable
personalities to rise to power. To be truthful, the fear
and ignorance of their victims was their greatest
strength. But their most pertinent flaw was that they
tended to give their subordinates too little autonomy.
With Samuelson out of the picture, the rest might very
well scatter. And then I realized there was something
I could do that would leave nothing to chance.

"Ernesto," I said, "now I've considered it, there's really
not a thing you can tell me that I want to know."

"No," he said. "No, I have something. Please!"

I shrugged. "All right. Let's hear it."

"The bosses," he said. "I know where they are."

"The Magnificence, you mean? Those bosses?"

A nod. "Administration. They're all there."

"They're there right this moment?"

Something must have given a twinge, for he winced and said, *"Dios!"* When he recovered he added, "Yes. They're waiting. . . ." Another pain took him away for a moment.

"Waiting for the revolution to be won?" I suggested.

"Yes."

"And just how many bosses are we speaking about?"

"Twenty. Almost twenty, I think."

Christ, I thought, nearly half of the administration gone to black satin and nightmare.

I got to my feet, pocketed the laser.

"Wha . . ."Ernesto said, and swallowed; his pallor had increased, and I realized he was going into shock. His dark eyes searched my face.

"I'm going, Ernesto," I said. "I don't have the time to treat you as you did Gerald. But my fervent hope is that someone else with more time on their hands will find you. Perhaps one of your brothers in the Magnificence. Or one of Gerald's friends. Neither, I suspect, will view your situation in a favorable light. And should no one come upon you in the foreseeable future, I suppose I shall have to be satisfied with knowing you died a lingering death." I bent to him. "Getting cold, isn't it? You've had the sweet bit, Ernesto. There'll be no more pretending you've a pretty pair of charlies and playing sweet angelina to the hard boys. No more gobble offs for you, dearie. It's all fucking over."

I would have loved to hurt him some more, but I did not believe I would have been able to stop once I got started. I blew him a kiss, told him that if the pain got too bad he could always swallow his tongue, and left him to what would almost certainly be the first of his final misgivings.

When I returned to my quarters Arlie threw her arms about me and held me tight while I gave her the news about Gerald. I still felt nothing. Telling her was like hearing my own voice delivering a news summary.

"I've got work to do," I said. "I can't protect you here. They're liable to pay a visit while I'm away. You'll have to come with me."

She nodded, her face buried in my shoulder.

"We have to go outside," I said. "We can use one of the sleds. Just a short hop over to Administration, a few minutes there, and we're done. Can you manage?"

Arlie liked having something solid underfoot; going outside was a dread prospect for her, but she made no objection.

"What are you intendin'?" she asked, watching me gather the packet charges I had left scattered about the floor.

"Nothing nice," I said, peering under the sofa; I was, it appeared, short four charges. "Don't worry about it."

"Don't you get cheeky with me! Oi'm not some low-heel Sharon you've only just met. Oi've a right to know what you're about."

"I'm going to blow up the damned place," I said, moving the sofa away from the wall.

She stared at me, open-mouthed. "You're plannin' to blow up Admin? 'Ave you done your crust? What you finkin' of?"

I told her about the suspicious files and what Ernesto had said, but this did little to soothe her.

"There's twenty other people livin' in there!" she said. "What about them?"

"Maybe they won't be at home." I pushed the sofa back against the wall. "I'm missing four charges here. You seen 'em?"

"It's almost one o'clock. Some of 'em might be out, Oi grant you. But whether it's twenty or fifteen, you're talkin' about the murder of innocent people."

"Look here," I said, continuing my search, heaving chairs about to bleed off my anger. "First of all, they're not people. They're corporation deadlegs. Using the word 'innocent' to describe them makes as much sense as using the word 'dainty' to describe a pig's eating habits. At one time or another they're every one put the drill to some poor Joey's backside and made it bleed. And they'd do it again in a flicker, because that's all they fucking know how to do. Secondly, if they were in my shoes, if they had a chance to rid the station of the Magnificence with only twenty lives lost, they wouldn't hesitate. Thirdly"— I flipped up the cushions on the sofa—"and most importantly, I don't have a bloody choice! Do you understand me? There's no one I can trust to help. I don't have a loyal force with which to lay siege to them. This is the only way I can settle things. I'm not thrilled with the idea of murdering—as you say—twenty people in order to do what's necessary. And I realize it allows you to feel morally superior to think of me as a villain. But if I don't do something soon there'll be hearts and livers strewn about the station like party favors, and twenty dead is going to seem like nothing!" I hurled a cushion into the corner. "Shit! Where are they?"

Arlie was still staring at me, but the outrage had drained from her face. "Oi 'aven't seen 'em."

"Bill," I said, struck by a notion. "Where he'd get to?" "Bill?"

"Yeah, Bill. The fuckwit. Where is he?"

" 'E's away somewhere," she said. " 'E was in the loo for a while, then Oi went in the bedroom, and when Oi come out 'e was gone."

I crossed to the bathroom, hoping to find the charges there. But when the door slid open, I saw only that the floor was spattered with bright, tacky blood; there was more blood in the sink, along with a kitchen knife, matted hair, handfuls of wadded, becrimsoned paper towels. And something else: a thin black disc about the size of a soy wafer. It took me a while to absorb all this, to put it together with Bill's recent obsessions, and even after I had done so, my conclusion was difficult to credit. Yet I could think of no other explanation that would satisfy the conditions.

"Arlie," I called. "You seen this?"

"Nao, what?" she said, coming up behind me; then: "Holy Christ!"

"That's his implant, isn't it?" I said, pointing to the disc.

"Yeah, I s'pose it is. My God! Why'd he do that?" She put a hand to her mouth. "You don't fink 'e took the charges. . . ."

"The CPC," I said. "He knew he couldn't do anything with Mister C along for the ride, so he cut the bastard out. And now he's gone for the CPC. Jesus! That's just what we needed, isn't it! Another fucking maniac on the loose!"

"It must 'ave 'urt 'im somethin' fierce!" Arlie said wonderingly. "I mean, he 'ad to 'ave done it quick and savage, or else Mister C would 'ave 'ad time to stop 'im. And I never heard a peep."

"I wouldn't worry about Bill if I were you. You think twenty dead's a tragedy? Think what'll happen if he blows the CPC. How many do you reckon will be walking between modules when they disengage? How many others will be killed by falling things? By other sorts of accidents?"

I went back into the living room, shouldered my pack; I handed Arlie a laser. "If you see anyone coming after us, use it. Burn them low if that's all you can bear, but burn them. All right?"

She gave a tight, anxious nod and looked down at the weapon in her hand.

"Come on," said. "Once we get to the airlock we'll be fine."

But I was none too confident of our chances. Thanks to the greed of madmen and the single-mindedness of our resident idiot, it seemed that the chances of everyone on Solitaire were growing slimmer by the second.

❖   ❖   ❖

I suppose some of you will say at this juncture that I should have known bad things were going to happen, and further will claim that many of the things that did happen might have been forestalled had I taken a few basic precautions and shown the slightest good sense. What possessed me, you might ask, to run out of my quarters leaving explosives scattered about the floor where Bill could easily appropriate them? And couldn't I have seen that his fascination with the CPC might lead to some perilous circumstance? And why had I not perceived his potential for destructiveness? Well, what had possessed me was concern for a friend, the closest to a friend that I had ever known. And as to Bill, his dangerous potentials, he had never displayed any sign that he was capable of enduring the kind of pain he must have endured, or of employing logic sufficiently well so as to plan even such a simple act as he perpetrated. It was desperation, I'm certain, that fathered the plan, and how was I to factor in desperation with the IQ of a biscuit and come up with the sum of that event? No, I reject guilt and credit both. My part in things was simpler than demanded by that complex twist of fate. I was only there, it seems, to finish things, to stamp out a few last fires and—in the end—to give a name to the demons of that place and time. And yet perhaps there was something in that whole fury of moments that was mine. Perhaps I saw an opportunity to take a step away from the past, albeit a violent step, and moved by a signal of some sort, one too slight to register except in my cells, I took it. I would like to think I had a higher purpose in mind, and was not merely acting out the imperatives of some fierce vanity.

We docked the sled next to an airlock in the administration module, my reasoning being that if we were forced to flee, it would take less time to run back to administration than it would to cycle the CPC airlock, but instead of entering there, we walked along the top of the corridor that connected administration and the CPC, working our way along molded troughs of plastic covered with the greenish silver substrate left by the barnacles, past an electric array, beneath a tree of radiator panels thirty times as tall as a man, and entered the emergency lock at its nether end. There was a sled docked beside it, and realizing that Bill must have used it, I thought how terrified he must have been to cross even that much of the void without Mister C to lend him guidance. Before entering, I set the timer of one of the charges in the pack to a half-second delay and stuck it in the hip pouch of my pressure suit. I would be able to trigger the switch with just the touch of my palm against the pouch. A worst case eventuality.

The cameras inside the CPC were functioning, but since there were no security personnel in evidence, I had to assume that the automatic alarms had failed and that— as usual—no one was bothered to monitor the screens. We had not gone twenty feet into the main room when we saw Bill, dressed in a pressure suit, helmet in hand, emerge from behind a plastic partition, one of many which—as I have said—divided the cavernous white space into a maze of work stations. He looked stunned, lost, and when he noticed us he gave no sign of recognition; the side of his neck was covered with dried blood, and he held his head tipped to that side, as one might when trying to muffle pain by applying pressure to the injured spot. His mouth hung open, his posture was slack, and his eyes were bleary. Under the trays of cold light his complexion was splotchy and dappled with the angry red spots of pimples just coming up.

"The explosives," I said. "Where are they? Where'd you put them?"

His eyes wandered up, grazed my face, twitched toward Arlie, and then lowered to the floor. His breath made an ugly glutinous noise.

He was a pitiable sight, but I could not afford pity; I was enraged at him for having betrayed my trust. "You miserable fucking stain!" I said. "Tell me where they are!" I palmed the back of his head with my left hand; with my right I knuckled the ragged wound behind his ear. He tried to twist away, letting out a wail; he put his hands up to his chest and pushed feebly at me. Tears leaked from his eyes. "Don't!" he bawled. "Don't! It hurts!"

"Tell me where the explosives are," I said, "or I'll hurt you worse. I swear to Christ, I won't ever stop hurting you."

"I don't remember!" he whined.

"I take you into my house," I said. "I protect you, I feed you, I wash your messes up. And what do you do? You steal from me." I slapped him, eliciting a shriek. "Now tell me where they are!"

Arlie was watching me, a hard light in her eyes; but she said nothing.

I nodded toward the labyrinth of partitions. "Have a fucking look round, will you? We don't have much time!"

She went off, and I turned again to Bill.

"Tell me," I said, and began cuffing him about the face, not hard, but hurtful, driving him back with the flurries, setting him to stagger and wail and weep. He fetched up against a partition, eyes popped, that tiny pink mouth pursed in a moue. "Tell me," I repeated, and then said it again, said it every time I hit him, "Tell me, tell me, tell me, tell me . . .", until he dropped to his knees, cowering, shielding his head with his arms, and yelled, "Over there! It's over there!"

"Where?" I said, hauling him to his feet. "Take me to it."

I pushed him ahead of me, keeping hold of the neck ring of his suit, yanking, jerking, not wanting to give him a second to gather himself, to make up a lie. He yelped, grunted, pleaded, saying, "Don't!", "Stop it!", until at last he bumped and spun round a corner, and there, resting atop a computer terminal, was one of the charges, a red light winking on the timer, signaling that it had been activated. I picked it up and punched in the deactivation code. The read-out showed that fifty-eight seconds had remained before detonation.

"Arlie!" I shouted. "Get back here! Now!"

I grabbed Bill by the neck ring, pulled him close. "Did you set all the timers the same?"

He gazed at me, uncomprehending.

"Answer me, damn you! How did you set the timers?"

He opened his mouth, made a scratchy noise in the back of his throat; runners of saliva bridged between his upper and lower teeth.

My interior clock was ticking down, 53, 52, 51. . . . Given the size of the room, there was no hope of locating the other three charges in less than a minute. I would have risked a goodly sum on the proposition that Bill had been inconsistent, but I was not willing to risk my life.

Arlie came trotting up and smiled. "You found one!"

"We've got fifty seconds," I told her. "Or less. Run!"

I cannot be certain how long it took us to negotiate the distance between where we had stood and the hatch of the administration module; it seemed an endless time, and I kept expecting to feel the corridor shake and sway and tear loose from its fittings, and to go whirling out into the vacuum. Having to drag Bill along slowed us considerably, and I spent perhaps ten seconds longer opening the hatch with my pass key; but altogether, I would guess we came very near to the fifty second limit.

And I am certain that as I sealed the hatch behind us, that limit was exceeded. Bill had, indeed, proved inconsistent.

As I stepped in through the inner hatch, I found that Admin had been transformed into a holographic rendering of a beautiful starfield spread across a velvety black depth in which—an oddly charming incongruity—fifteen or twenty doors were visible, a couple of them open, slants of white light spilling out, it seemed, from God's office space behind the walls of space and time. We were walking on gas clouds, nebulae, and constellate beings. Then I noticed the body of a woman lying some thirty feet away, blood pooled wide as a table beneath her. No one else was in sight, but as we proceeded toward the airlock, the outlines of the hatch barely perceptible beneath the astronomical display, three men in black gear stepped out from a doorway farther along the passage. I fired at them, as did Arlie, but our aim was off. Strikes of ruby light smoked the starry expanse beside them as they ducked back into cover. I heard shouts, then shouted answers. The next second, as I fumbled with the hatch, laser fire needled from several doorways, pinning us down. Whoever was firing could have killed us easily, but they satisfied themselves by scoring near misses. Above Bill's frightened cries and the sizzle of burning metal, I could hear laughter. I tossed my laser aside and told Arlie to do the same. I touched the charge in my hip pouch. I believed if necessary I would be able to detonate it, but the thought made me cold.

A group of men and women, some ten or eleven strong, came along the corridor toward us, Samuelson in the lead. Like the rest, he wore black satin trousers and a blouse of the same material adorned with badges. Creatures, it appeared, wrought from the same mystic stuff as the black walls and ceiling and floor. He was smiling broadly and nodding, as if our invasion were a delightful interlude that he had been long awaiting.

"How kind of you to do your dying with us, John," he said as we came to our feet; they gathered in a semi-circle around us, hemming us in against the hatch. "I never expected to have this opportunity. And with your lady, too. We're going to have such fun together."

"Bet she's a real groaner," said a muscular, black-haired man at his shoulder.

"Well, we'll find out soon enough, won't we?" said Samuelson.

"Try it," said Arlie, "and Oi'll squeeze you off at the knackers!"

Samuelson beamed at her, then glanced at Bill. "And how are you today, sir? What brings you along, I wonder, on this merry outing?"

Bill returned a look of bewilderment that after a moment, infected by Samuelson's happy countenance, turned into a perplexed smile.

"Do me a favor," I said to Samuelson, moving my hand so that the palm was almost touching the switch of the charge at my hip. "There's something I've been yearning to know. Does that gear of yours come with matching underwear? I'd imagine it must. Bunch of ginger-looking poofs and lizzies like you got behind you, I suppose wearing black nasties is *de rigueur*."

"For somebody who's 'bout to major in high-pitched screams," said a woman at the edge of the group, a heavyset blonde with a thick American accent and an indecipherable tattoo on her bicep, "you gotta helluva mouth on you, I give ya that."

"That's just John's unfortunate manner," Samuelson said. "He's not very good at defeat, you see. It should be interesting to watch him explore the boundaries of this particular defeat."

My hand had begun to tremble on the switch; I found myself unable to control it.

"What is it with you, Samuelson?" said the blonde woman. "Every time you chop someone, you gotta play Dracula? Let's just do 'em and get on with business."

There was a brief argument concerning the right of the woman to speak her mind, the propriety of mentally preparing the victim, of "tasting the experience," and other assorted drivel. Under different circumstances, I would have laughed to see how ludicrous and inept a bunch were these demons; I might have thought how their ineptitude spoke to the terminal disarray back on Earth, that such a feeble lot could have gained so much power. But I was absorbed by the trembling of my hand, the sweat trickling down my belly, and the jellied weakness of my legs. I imagined I could feel the cold mass of explosives turning, giving a kick, like a dark and fatal child striving to break free of the womb. Before long I would have to reveal the presence of the charge and force a conclusion, one way or another, and I was not sure I was up to it. My hand wanted to slap the switch, pushed against, it seemed, by all the weighty detritus of my violent life.

Finally Samuelson brought an end to the argument. "This is my show, Amy. I'll do as I please. If you want to discuss method during Retreat, I'll be happy to satisfy. Until then, I'd appreciate your full cooperation."

He said all this with the mild ultra-sincerity of a priest settling a squabble among the Ladies Auxiliary concerning a jumble sale; but when he turned to me, all the anger that he must have repressed came spewing forth.

"You naff little scrote!" he shouted. "I'm sick to death of you getting on my tits! When I've done working over your slippery and that great dozy blot beside you, I'm going to paint you red on red."

I did not see what happened at that moment with Arlie. Somebody tried to fondle her, I believe, and there was a commotion beside me, too brief to call a struggle, and then she had a laser in her hand and was firing. A beam of crimson light no thicker than a knitting needle spat from the muzzle and punched its way through the temple of a compact graying man, exiting through the top of his skull, dropping him in a heap. Another beam spitted the shoulder of the blonde woman. All this at close quarters, people shrieking, stumbling, pushing together, nudging me, nearly causing me to set off the charge. Then the laser was knocked from Arlie's hand, and she was thrown to the floor.

Samuelson came to stand astraddle her, his laser aimed at her chest.

"Carve the bitch up!" said the blonde woman, holding her shoulder.

"Splendid idea," Samuelson said, adjusting the setting of his laser. "I'll just do a little writing to begin with. Start with an inspirational saying, don't you think? Or maybe"—he chuckled—"John Loves Arlie."

"No," I said, my nerves steadied by this frontal assault; I pulled out the packet charge. "No, you're not going to do that. Because unless you do the right thing, in about two seconds the best part of you is going to be sliding all greasylike down the walls. I'll give you to three to put down your weapons." I drew a breath and tried to feel Arlie beside me. "One." I stared at Samuelson, coming hard at him with all the fire left in me. "You best tell 'em how mad I am for you." I squared my shoulders; I prayed I had the guts to press the switch on three. "That's two."

"Do it!" he said to his people. "Do it now!" They let their weapons fall.

"Back it off," I said, feeling relief, but also a ghostly momentum as if the count had continued on in some alternate probability and I was now blowing away in fire and ruin. I picked up my pack, grabbed Samuelson by the shirtfront as the rest retreated along the corridor. "Open the hatch," I told Arlie, who had scrambled up from the floor.

I heard her punching out the code, and a moment later, I heard the hatch swing open. I backed around the door, slung Samuelson into the airlock, slamming him up against Bill, who had wandered in on his own. At that precise moment, the CPC exploded.

The sound of the explosion was immense, a great wallop of pressure and noise that sent me reeling into the airlock, reeling and floating up, the artificial gravity systems no longer operative; but what was truly terrifying was the vented hiss that followed the explosion, signaling disengagement from the connecting corridors, and the sickening sway of the floor, and then the roar of ignition as the module's engines transformed what had been a habitat into a ship. I pictured the whole of Solitaire coming apart piece by piece, each one igniting and moving off into the nothing, little glowing bits, like the break-up of an electric reef.

Arlie had snatched up one of the lasers and she was now training it at Samuelson, urging him into his pressure suit—a difficult chore considering the acceleration. But he was managing. I helped Bill on with his helmet and fitted mine in place just as the boost ended and we drifted free. Then I broke the seal on the outer hatch, started the lock cycling.

Once the lock had opened, I told Arlie she would have to drive the sled. I watched as she fitted herself into the harness of the rocket pack, then I lashed Samuelson to one of the metal struts, Bill to another. I set the charge I had been carrying on the surface of the station, took two more out of the pack. I set the timers for ninety seconds. I had no thought in my head as I was doing this; I might have been a technician stripping a wire, a welder joining a seam. Yet as I prepared to activate the charges, I realized that I was not merely ridding the station of the Strange Magnificence, but of the corporation's personnel. I had, of course, known this before, but I had not understood what it meant. Within a month, probably considerably less, the various elements of the station would reunite, and when they did, for the first time in our history, Solitaire would be a free place, without a corporate presence to strike the fear of God and Planet Earth into the hearts and minds of the workers. Oh, it was true, some corporates might have been in other modules when the explosion occurred, but most of them were gone, and the survivors would not be able to wield much power; it would be six months at least before their replacements arrived and a new administration could be installed. A lot could happen in that time. My comprehension of this was much less linear than I am reporting; it came to me as a passion, a hope, and as I activated the timers, I had a wild sense of freedom that, though I did not fathom it then, seems now to have been premonitory and inspired.

I lashed and locked myself on to a strut close to Arlie and told her to get the hell gone, pointing out as a destination the web of a transport dock that we were passing. I did not see the explosion, but I saw the white flare of it in Arlie's faceplace as she turned to watch; I kept my eyes fixed for a time on the bits and pieces of Solitaire passing silently around us, and when I turned to her, as the reflected fire died away and her eyes were revealed, wide and lovely and dark, I saw no hatred in her, no disgust. Perhaps she had already forgiven me for being the man I was. Not kindly, and yet not without kindness. Merely someone who had learned to do the necessary and to live with it. Someone whose past had burned a shadow that stretched across his future.

I told her to reverse the thrusters and stop the sled. There was one thing left to do, though I was not so eager to have done with it as once I had been. Out in the dark, in the nothing, with all those stars pointing their hot eyes at you and trying to spear your mind with their secret colors, out in that absolute desert the questions of villainy and heroism grow remote. The most terrible of sins and the sweetest virtues often become compressed in the midst of all that sunless cold; compared to the terrible inhumanity of space, they both seem warmly human and comprehensible. And thus when I approached the matter of ending Samuelson's life I did so without relish, without the vindictive spirit that I might have expressed had we been back on Solitaire.

I inched my way back to where I had tied him and locked on to a strut; I trained the laser on the plastic rope that lashed him to the sled and burned it through. His legs floated up, and he held on to a strut with his gauntleted hands.

"Please, God! Don't!" he said, the panic in his voice made tinny and comical by my helmet speaker; he stared down through the struts that sectioned off the void into which he was about to travel—silver frames each enclosing a rectangle of unrelieved black, some containing a few scraps of billion-year-old light. "Please!"

"What do you expect from me?" I asked. "What do you expect from life? Mercy? Or the accolade? Here." I pointed at the sweep of stars and poetry, the iron puzzle of the dock beginning to loom, to swell into a massive crosshatching of girders, each strung with white lights, with Mars a phantom crescent below and the sun a yellow coal. "You longed for God, didn't you? Where is He if not here? Here's your strange magnificence." I gestured with the laser. "Push off. Hard. If you don't push hard enough, we'll come after you and give you a nudge. You can open your faceplate whenever you want it to end."

He began to plead, to bargain. "I can make you wealthy," he said. "I can get you back to Earth. Not London. Nova Sibersk. One of the towers."

"Of course you can," I said. "And I would be a wise man, indeed, to trust that promise, now wouldn't I?"

"There are ways," Samuelson said. "Ways to guarantee it. It's not that difficult. Really. I can. . . ."

"Thirwell smiled at me," I reminded him. "He sang. Are your beliefs so shallow you won't even favor us with a tune?"

"Do you want me to sing? Do you want me to be humiliated? If that's what it'll take to get you to listen to me, I'll do it. I'll do anything."

"No," I said. "That's not what I want." His eyes were big with the idea of death. I knew what he was feeling: all his life was suddenly thrilling, precious, new; and he

was almost made innocent by the size and intensity of his
fear, almost cleansed and converted by the knowledge that
all this sensey splendor was about to go on forever and
ever without him. It was a hard moment, and he did not
do well by it.

When he began to weep I burned a hole in his radio
housing to silence him. He put a hand up to shield his face,
fearing I would burn the helmet; I kicked his other hand
loose from the sled, sending him spinning away slowly,
head over heels toward the sun, a bulky white figure
growing toylike and clever against the black ground of his
future, like one of those little mechanical monkeys that
spins round and round on a plastic bar. I knew he would
never open his faceplate—the greater the villain, the
greater their inability to accept fate. He would be a long
time dying.

I checked on Bill—he was sleeping!—and returned to
my place beside Arlie. We boosted again toward the dock.
I thought about Gerald, about the scattered station, about
Bill, but I could not concentrate on them. It was as if what
I saw before me had gone inside my skull, and my mind
was no longer a storm of electric impulse, but an immense
black emptiness lit by tiny stars and populated by four
souls, one of whom was only now beginning to know the
terrible loneliness of his absent god.

We entrusted Bill to the captain of the docked transport,
Steel City, a hideous name for a hideous vessel, pitted and
gray and ungainly in form, like a sad leviathan. There was
no going back to Solitaire for Bill. They had checked the
recordings taken in the CPC, and they knew who had been
responsible for the break-up of the station, for the nearly
one hundred and thirty lives that had been lost, for the
billions in credit blown away. Even under happier
circumstances, without Mister C to guide him, he would
not be able to survive. Nor would he survive on Earth.

But there he would at least have a slight chance. The corporation had no particular interest in punishing him. They were not altogether dissatisfied with the situation, being pleased to learn that their failsafe system worked, and they would, they assured us, see to it that he was given institutional care. I knew what that portended. Shunted off to some vast dark building with a Catholic statue centering a seedy garden out front, and misplaced, lost among the howling damned and terminally feeble, and eventually, for want of any reason to do otherwise, going dark himself, lying down and breathing, perhaps feeding from time to time, for a while, and then, one day, simply giving up, giving out, going away on a rattle of dishes on the dinner cart or a wild cry ghosting up from some nether region or a shiver of winter light on a cracked linoleum floor, some little piece of brightness to which he could attach himself and let go of the rest. It was horrible to contemplate, but we had no choice. Back on the station he would have been torn apart.

The *Steel City* was six hours from launching inbound when Arlie and I last saw Bill. He was in a cell lit by a bilious yellow tray of light set in the ceiling, wearing a gray ship's jumpsuit; his wound had been dressed, and he was clean, and he was terrified. He tried to hold us, he pleaded with us to take him back home, and when we told him that was impossible, he sat cross-legged on the floor, rocking back and forth, humming a tune that I recognized as "Barnacle Bill the Spacer." He had apparently forgotten its context and the cruel words. Arlie kneeled beside him and told stories of the animals he would soon be seeing. There were tigers sleek as fire, she said, and elephants bigger than small towns, and birds faster than rain, and wolves with mysterious lights in their eyes. There were serpents too, she said, green ones with ruby tongues that told the most beautiful stories in the world, and cries so musical had been heard in the Mountains of the Moon that no one dared seek out the creature who had uttered them for fear of being immolated by the sight of such beauty, and the wind, she said, the wind was also an animal, and to those who listened carefully to it, it would whisper its name and give them a ride around the world in a single day. Birds as bright as the moon, great lizards who roared when it thundered as if answering questions, white bears with golden claws and magical destinies. It was a wonderland to which he was traveling, and she expected him to call and tell us all the amazing things that he would do and see.

Watching them, I had a clearer sense of him than ever before. I knew he did not believe Arlie, that he was only playing at belief, and I saw in this his courage, the stubborn, clean drive to live that had been buried under years of abuse and denial. He was not physically courageous, not in the least, but I for one knew how easy that sort of courage was to sustain, requiring only a certain careless view of life and a few tricks to inspire a red madness. And I doubted I could have withstood all he had suffered, the incessant badgering and humiliation, the sharp rejection, the sexual defeats, the monstrous loneliness. Years of it. Decades. God knows, he had committed an abysmal stupidity, but we had driven him to it, we had menaced and tormented him, and in return—an act of selfishness and desperation, I admit, yet selfishness in its most refined form, desperation in its most gentle incarnation—he had tried to save us, to make us love him.

It is little enough to know of a man or a woman, that he or she has courage. Perhaps there might have been more to know about Bill had we allowed him to flourish, had we given his strength levers against which to test itself and thus increase. But at the moment knowing what I knew seemed more than enough, and it opened me to all the feelings I had been repressing, to thoughts of Gerald in particular. I saw that my relationship with him—in fact most of my relationships—were similar to the one I'd had with Bill; I had shied away from real knowledge, real intimacy. I felt like weeping, but the pity of it was, I would only be weeping for myself.

Finally it was time for us to leave. Bill pawed us, gave us clumsy hugs, clung to us, but not so desperately as he might have; he realized, I am fairly certain, that there would be no reprieve. And, too, he may not have thought he deserved one. He was ashamed, he believed he had done wrong, and so it was with a shameful attitude, not at all demanding, that he asked me if they would give him another implant, if I would help him get one.

"Yeah, sure, Bill," I said. "I'll do my best."

He sat back down on the floor, touched the wound on his neck. "I wish he was here," he said.

"Mister C?" said Arlie, who had been talking to a young officer; he had just come along to lead us back to our sled. "Is that who you're talkin' about, dear?"

He nodded, eyes on the floor.

"Don't you fret, luv. You'll get another friend back 'ome. A better one than Mister C. One what won't 'urt you."

"I don't mind he hurts me," Bill said. "Sometimes I do things wrong."

"We all of us do wrong, luv. But it ain't always necessary for us to be 'urt for it."

He stared up at her as if she were off her nut, as if he could not imagine a circumstance in which wrong was not followed by hurt.

"That's the gospel," said the officer. "And I promise, we'll be takin' good care of you, Bill." He had been eyefucking Arlie, the officer had, and he was only saying this to impress her with his humanity. Chances were, as soon as we were out of sight, he would go to kicking and yelling at Bill. Arlie was not fooled by him.

"Goodbye, Bill," she said, taking his hand, but he did not return her pressure, and his hand slipped out of her grasp, flopped onto his knee; he was already retreating from us, receding into his private misery, no longer able to manufacture a brave front. And as the door closed on him, that first of many doors, leaving him alone in that sickly yellow space, he put his hands to the sides of his head as if his skull could not contain some terrible pain, and began rocking back and forth, and saying, almost chanting the words, like a bitter monk his hopeless litany, "Oh, no . . . oh, no . . . oh, no. . . ."

Some seventy-nine hours after the destruction of the CPC and the dispersal of Solitaire, the lightship *Perseverance* came home . . . came home with such uncanny accuracy, that had the station been situated where it should have been, the energies released by the ship's re-entry from the supraluminal would have annihilated the entire facility and all on board. The barnacles, perhaps sensing some vast overload of light through their photophores . . . the barnacles and an idiot man had proved wiser than the rest of us. And this was no ordinary homecoming in yet another way, for it turned out that the voyage of the *Perseverance* had been successful. There was a new world waiting on the other side of the nothing, unspoiled, a garden of possibility, a challenge to our hearts and a beacon to our souls.

I contacted the corporation. They, of course, had heard the news, and they also recognized that had Bill not acted the *Perseverance* and all aboard her would have been destroyed along with Solitaire. He was, they were delighted to attest, a hero, and they would treat him as such. How's that, I asked. Promotions, news specials, celebrations, parades, was their answer. What he really wants, I told them, is to come back to Solitaire. Well, of course, they said, we'll see what we can do. When it's time, they said. We'll do right by him, don't you worry. How about another implant, I asked. Absolutely, no problem, anything he needs. By the time I broke contact, I understood that Bill's fate would be little different now he was a hero than it would have been when he was a mere fool and a villain. They would use him, milk his story for all the good it could do them, and then he would be discarded, misplaced, lost, dropped down to circulate among the swirling masses of the useless, the doomed, and the forgotten.

Though I had already—in concert with others—formed a plan of action, it was this duplicity on the corporation's part that hardened me against them, and thereafter I threw myself into the implementation of the plan. A few weeks from now, the *Perseverance* and three other starships soon to be completed will launch for the new world. Aboard will be the population of Solitaire, minus a few unsympathetic personnel who have been rendered lifeless, and the populations of other, smaller stations in the asteroid belt and orbiting Mars. Solitaire itself, and the other stations, will be destroyed. It will take the corporation decades, perhaps a century, to rebuild what has been lost, and by the time they are able to reach us, we hope to have grown strong, to have fabricated a society free of corporations and Strange Magnificences, composed of those who have learned to survive without the quotas and the dread consolations of the Earth. It is an old dream, this desire to say, No more, Never again, to build a society cleansed of the old compulsions and corruptions, the ancient, vicious ways, and perhaps it is a futile one, perhaps the fact that men like myself, violent men, men who will do the necessary, who will protect against all enemies with no thought for moral fall-out, must be included on the roster, perhaps this preordains that it will fail. Nevertheless, it needs to be dreamed every so often, and we are prepared to be the dreamers.

So that is the story of Barnacle Bill. My story, and Arlie's as well, yet his most of all, though his real part in it, the stuff of his thoughts and hopes, the pain he suffered and the fear he overcame, those things can never be told. Perhaps you have seen him recently on the HV, or even in person, riding in an open car at the end of a parade with men in suits, eating an ice and smiling, but in truth he is already gone into history, already part of the past, already half-forgotten, and when the final door has closed on him, it may be that his role in all this will be reduced to a mere footnote or simply a mention of his name, the slightest token of a life. But I will remember him, not in memorial grace, not as a hero, but as he was, in all his graceless ways and pitiable form. It is of absolute importance to remember him thus, because that, I have come to realize, the raw and the deformed, the ugly, the miserable miracles of our days, the unalloyed baseness of existence, that is what we must learn to love, to accept, to embrace, if we are to cease the denials that weaken us, if we are ever to admit our dismal frailty and to confront the natural terror and heartbreak weather of our lives and live like a strong light across the sky instead of retreating into darkness.

The barnacles have returned to Solitaire. Or rather, new colonies of barnacles have attached to the newly reunited station, not covering it completely, but dressing it up in patches. I have taken to walking among them, weeding them as Bill once did; I have become interested in them, curious as to how they perceived a ship coming from light years away, and I intend to carry some along with us on the voyage and make an attempt at a study. Yet what compels me to take these walks is less scientific curiosity than a kind of furious nostalgia, a desire to remember and hold the center of those moments that have so changed the direction of our lives, to think about Bill and how it must have been for him, a frightened lump of a man with a clever voice in his ear, alone in all that daunting immensity, fixing his eyes on the bright clots of life at his feet. Just today Arlie joined me on such a walk, and it seemed we were passing along the rim of an infinite dark eye flecked with a trillion bits of color, and that everything of our souls and of every other soul could be seen in that eye, that I could look down to Earth through the haze and scum of the ocean air and see Bill where he stood looking up and trying to find us in that mottled sky, and I felt all the eerie connections a man feels when he needs to believe in something more than what he knows is real, and I tried to tell myself he was all right, walking in his garden in Nova Siberia, taking the air with an idiot woman so beautiful it nearly made him wise. But I could not sustain the fantasy. I could only mourn, and I had no right to mourn, having never loved him—or if I did, even in the puniest of ways, it was never his person I loved, but what I had from him, the things awakened in me by what had happened. Just the thought that I could have loved him, maybe that was all I owned of right.

We were heading back toward the East Louie airlock, when Arlie stooped and plucked up a male barnacle. Dark green as an emerald it was, except for its stubby appendage. Glowing like magic, alive with threads of color like a potter's glaze.

"That's a rare one," I said. "Never saw one that color before."

"Bill would 'ave fancied it," she said.

"Fancied, hell. He would have hung the damned thing about his neck."

She set it back down, and we watched as it began working its way across the surface of the barnacle patch, doing its slow, ungainly cartwheels, wobbling off-true, lurching in flight, nearly missing its landing, but somehow making it, somehow getting there. It landed in the shadow of some communications gear, stuck out its tongue and tried to feed. We watched it for a long, long while, with no more words spoken, but somehow there was a little truth hanging in the space between us, in the silence, a poor thing not worth naming, and maybe not even having a name, it was such an infinitesimal slice of what was, and we let it nourish us as much as it could, we took its luster and added it to our own. We sucked it dry, we had its every flavor, and then we went back inside arm in arm, to rejoin the lie of the world.

1994
52nd Convention
Winnipeg

Death on the Nile
by Connie Willis

Georgia on My Mind
by Charles Sheffield

Down in the Bottomlands
by Harry Turtledove

It is becoming impossible to have a Hugo volume without Connie Willis looming over the landscape. For good reason, too—she is the preeminent crowd-pleaser of the genre, charming audiences with a quick wit, and with artful insight into the way the future will intersect our lives. Many a writer, hoping for an award, has been left grinding his/ her teeth as Connie strides to the podium, there to pick up yet another Nebula block of crystal or rocket-shaped Hugo.

This story carries off its assumptions with an airy ease which is the envy of writers like me. The really terrible news for her fellow authors is that Connie is equally good at novel length. Something must be done about this woman!

It is becoming impossible to have a Hugo ceremony without Connie Willis looming over the landscape. For good reason too—she is the preeminent award-pleaser of the genre, charming audiences with a quick wit, and with artful insight into the way the future will intersect our lives. Many a writer, hoping for an award, has been left grinding his/her teeth as Connie strides to the podium, there to pick up yet another Nebula block of crystal or rocket ship of Hugo.

This story carries off its assumptions with an easy relish that is the envy of writers like me. The really terrible curse for her fellow authors is that Connie is equally good at great length. Something must be done about this terminal...

Death on the Nile
by Connie Willis

Chapter 1: Preparing for Your Trip—What To Take

" 'To the ancient Egyptians,' " Zoe reads, " 'Death was a separate country to the west—' " The plane lurches. " '—the west to which the deceased person journeyed.' "

We are on the plane to Egypt. The flight is so rough the flight attendants have strapped themselves into the nearest empty seats, looking scared, and the rest of us have subsided into a nervous window-watching silence. Except Zoe, across the aisle, who is reading aloud from a travel guide.

This one is Somebody or Other's *Egypt Made Easy*. In the seat pocket in front of her are Fodor's *Cairo* and Cooke's *Touring Guide to Egypt's Antiquities*, and there are half a dozen others in her luggage. Not to mention Frommer's *Greece on $35 a Day* and the Savvy Traveler's *Guide to Austria* and the three or four hundred other guidebooks she's already read out loud to us on this trip. I toy briefly with the idea that it's their combined weight that's causing the plane to yaw and career and will shortly send us plummeting to our deaths.

" 'Food, furniture, and weapons were placed in the tomb,' " Zoe reads, " 'as provi—' " The plane pitches sideways. " '—sions for the journey.' "

The plane lurches again, so violently Zoe nearly drops the book, but she doesn't miss a beat. " 'When King Tutankhamun's tomb was opened,' " she reads, " 'it contained trunks full of clothing, jars of wine, a golden boat, and a pair of sandals for walking in the sands of the afterworld.' "

My husband Neil leans over me to look out the window, but there is nothing to see. The sky is clear and cloudless, and below us there aren't even any waves on the water.

" 'In the afterworld the deceased was judged by Anubis, a god with the head of a jackal,' " Zoe reads, " 'and his soul was weighed on a pair of golden scales.' "

I am the only one listening to her. Lissa, on the aisle, is whispering to Neil, her hand almost touching his on the armrest. Across the aisle, next to Zoe and *Egypt Made Easy*, Zoe's husband is asleep and Lissa's husband is staring out the other window and trying to keep his drink from spilling.

"Are you doing all right?" Neil asks Lissa solicitously.

"It'll be exciting going with two other couples," Neil said when he came up with the idea of our all going to Europe together. "Lissa and her husband are lots of fun, and Zoe knows everything. It'll be like having our own tour guide."

It is. Zoe herds us from country to country, reciting historical facts and exchange rates. In the Louvre, a French tourist asked her where the Mona Lisa was. She was thrilled. "He thought we were a tour group!" she said. "Imagine that!"

Imagine that.

" 'Before being judged, the deceased recited his confession,' " Zoe reads, " 'a list of sins he had not committed, such as, I have not snared the birds of the gods, I have not told lies, I have not committed adultery.' "

Neil pats Lissa's hand and leans over to me. "Can you trade places with Lissa?" Neil whispers to me.

I already have, I think. "We're not supposed to," I say,

pointing at the lights above the seats. "The seat belt sign is on."

He looks at her anxiously. "She's feeling nauseated."

So am I, I want to say, but I am afraid that's what this trip is all about, to get me to say something. "Okay," I say, and unbuckle my seat belt and change places with her. While she is crawling over Neil, the plane pitches again, and she half-falls into his arms. He steadies her. Their eyes lock.

" 'I have not taken another's belongings,' " Zoe reads. " 'I have not murdered another.' "

I can't take any more of this. I reach for my bag, which is still under the window seat, and pull out my paperback of Agatha Christie's *Death On the Nile*. I bought it in Athens.

"About like death anywhere," Zoe's husband said when I got back to our hotel in Athens with it.

"What?" I said.

"Your book," he said, pointing at the paperback and smiling as if he'd made a joke. "The title. I'd imagine death on the Nile is the same as death anywhere."

"Which is what?" I asked.

"The Egyptians believed death was very similar to life," Zoe cut in. She had bought *Egypt Made Easy* at the same bookstore. "To the ancient Egyptians the afterworld was a place much like the world they inhabited. It was presided over by Anubis, who judged the deceased and determined their fates. Our concepts of heaven and hell and of the Day of Judgment are nothing more than modern refinements of Egyptian ideas," she said, and began reading out loud from *Egypt Made Easy*, which pretty much put an end to our conversation, and I still don't know what Zoe's husband thought death would be like, on the Nile or elsewhere.

I open *Death on the Nile* and try to read, thinking maybe Hercule Poirot knows, but the flight is too bumpy. I feel

almost immediately queasy, and after half a page and three
more lurches I put it in the seat pocket, close my eyes and
toy with the idea of murdering another. It's a perfect
Agatha Christie setting. She always has a few people in
a country house or on an island. In *Death on the Nile* they
were on a Nile steamer, but the plane is even better. The
only other people on it are the flight attendants and a
Japanese tour group who apparently do not speak English
or they would be clustered around Zoe, asking directions
to the Sphinx.

The turbulence lessens a little, and I open my eyes and
reach for my book again. Lissa has it.

She's holding it open, but she isn't reading it. She is
watching me, waiting for me to notice, waiting for me to
say something. Neil looks nervous.

"You were done with this, weren't you?" she says,
smiling. "You weren't reading it."

Everyone has a motive for murder in an Agatha Christie.
And Lissa's husband has been drinking steadily since Paris,
and Zoe's husband never gets to finish a sentence. The
police might think he had snapped suddenly. Or that it
was Zoe he had tried to kill and shot Lissa by mistake. And
there is no Hercule Poirot on board to tell them who really
committed the murder, to solve the mystery and explain
all the strange happenings.

The plane pitches suddenly, so hard Zoe drops her
guidebook, and we plunge a good five thousand feet before
it recovers. The guidebook has slid forward several rows,
and Zoe tries to reach for it with her foot, fails, and looks
up at the seat belt sign as if she expects it to go off so she
can get out of her seat to retrieve it.

Not after that drop, I think, but the seat belt sign pings
almost immediately and goes off.

Lissa's husband instantly calls for the flight attendant
and demands another drink, but they have already gone
scurrying back to the rear of the plane, still looking pale

and scared, as if they expected the turbulence to start up again before they make it. Zoe's husband wakes up at the noise and then goes back to sleep. Zoe retrieves *Egypt Made Easy* from the floor, reads a few more riveting facts from it, then puts it facedown on the seat and goes back to the rear of the plane.

I lean across Neil and look out the window, wondering what's happened, but I can't see anything. We are flying through a flat whiteness.

Lissa is rubbing her head. "I cracked my head on the window," she says to Neil. "Is it bleeding?"

He leans over her solicitously to see.

I unsnap my seat belt and start to the back of the plane, but both bathrooms are occupied, and Zoe is perched on the arm of an aisle seat, enlightening the Japanese tour group. "The currency is in Egyptian pounds," she says. "There are one hundred piasters in a pound." I sit back down.

Neil is gently massaging Lissa's temple. "Is that better?" he asks.

I reach across the aisle for Zoe's guidebook. "Must-See Attractions," the chapter is headed, and the first one on the list is the Pyramids.

"Giza, Pyramids of. West bank of Nile, 9 mi. (15 km.) SW of Cairo. Accessible by taxi, bus, rental car. Admission L.E.3. Comments: You can't skip the Pyramids, but be prepared to be disappointed. They don't look at all like you expect, the traffic's terrible, and the view's completely ruined by the hordes of tourists, refreshment stands, and souvenir vendors. Open daily."

I wonder how Zoe stands this stuff. I turn the page to Attraction Number Two. It's King Tut's tomb, and whoever wrote the guidebook wasn't thrilled with it either. "Tutankhamun, Tomb of. Valley of the Kings, Luxor, 400 mi. (668 km.) south of Cairo. Three unimpressive rooms. Inferior wall paintings."

There is a map, showing a long, straight corridor (labeled Corridor) and the three unimpressive rooms opening one onto the other in a row—Anteroom, Burial Chamber, Hall of Judgment.

I close the book and put it back on Zoe's seat. Zoe's husband is still asleep. Lissa's is peering back over his seat. "Where'd the flight attendants go?" he asks. "I want another drink."

"Are you sure it's not bleeding? I can feel a bump," Lissa says to Neil, rubbing her head. "Do you think I have a concussion?"

"No," Neil says, turning her face toward his. "Your pupils aren't dilated." He gazes deeply into her eyes.

"Stewardess!" Lissa's husband shouts. "What do you have to do to get a drink around here?"

Zoe comes back, elated. "They thought I was a professional guide," she says, sitting down and fastening her seatbelt. "They asked if they could join our tour." She opens the guidebook. " 'The afterworld was full of monsters and demigods in the form of crocodiles and baboons and snakes. These monsters could destroy the deceased before he reached the Hall of Judgment.' "

Neil touches my hand. "Do you have any aspirin?" he asks. "Lissa's head hurts."

I fish in my bag for it, and Neil gets up and goes back to get her a glass of water.

"Neil's so thoughtful," Lissa says, watching me, her eyes bright.

" 'To protect against these monsters and demigods, the deceased was given *The Book of the Dead*,' " Zoe reads. " 'More properly translated as *The Book of What is in the Afterworld*, *The Book of the Dead* was a collection of directions for the journey and magic spells to protect the deceased.' "

I think about how I am going to get through the rest of the trip without magic spells to protect me. Six days in Egypt and then three in Israel, and there is still the trip home on a plane like this and nothing to do for fifteen hours but watch Lissa and Neil and listen to Zoe.

I consider cheerier possibilities. "What if we're not going to Cairo?" I say. "What if we're dead?"

Zoe looks up from her guidebook, irritated.

"There've been a lot of terrorist bombings lately, and this is the Middle East," I go on. "What if that last air pocket was really a bomb? What if it blew us apart, and right now we're drifting down over the Aegean Sea in little pieces?"

"Mediterranean," Zoe says. "We've already flown over Crete."

"How do you know that?" I ask. "Look out the window." I point out Lissa's window at the white flatness beyond. "You can't see the water. We could be anywhere. Or nowhere."

Neil comes back with the water. He hands it and my aspirin to Lissa.

"They check the planes for bombs, don't they?" Lissa asks him. "Don't they use metal detectors and things?"

"I saw this movie once," I say, "where the people were all dead, only they didn't know it. They were on a ship, and they thought they were going to America. There was so much fog they couldn't see the water."

Lissa looks anxiously out the window.

"It looked just like a real ship, but little by little they began to notice little things that weren't quite right. There were hardly any people on board, and no crew at all."

"Stewardess!" Lissa's husband calls, leaning over Zoe into the aisle. "I need another ouzo."

His shouting wakes Zoe's husband up. He blinks at Zoe, confused that she is not reading from her guidebook. "What's going on?" he asks.

"We're all dead," I say. "We were killed by Arab terrorists. We think we're going to Cairo but we're really going to heaven. Or hell."

Lissa, looking out the window, says, "There's so much fog I can't see the wing." She looks frightenedly at Neil. "What if something's happened to the wing?"

"We're just going through a cloud," Neil says. "We're probably beginning our descent into Cairo."

"The sky was perfectly clear," I say, "and then all of a sudden we were in the fog. The people on the ship noticed the fog, too. They noticed there weren't any running lights. And they couldn't find the crew." I smile at Lissa. "Have you noticed how the turbulence stopped all of a sudden? Right after we hit that air pocket. And why—"

A flight attendant comes out of the cockpit and down the aisle to us, carrying a drink. Everyone looks relieved, and Zoe opens her guidebook and begins thumbing through it, looking for fascinating facts.

"Did someone here want an ouzo?" the flight attendant asks.

"Here," Lissa's husband says, reaching for it.

"How long before we get to Cairo?" I say.

She starts toward the back of the plane without answering. I unbuckle my seat belt and follow her. "When will we get to Cairo?" I ask her.

She turns, smiling, but she is still pale and scared-looking. "Did you want another drink, ma'am? Ouzo? Coffee?"

"Why did the turbulence stop?" I say. "How long till we get to Cairo?"

"You need to take your seat," she says, pointing to the seat belt sign. "We're beginning our descent. We'll be at our destination in another twenty minutes." She bends over the Japanese tour group and tells them to bring their seat backs to an upright position.

"What destination? Our descent to where? We aren't beginning any descent. The seat belt sign is still off," I say, and it bings on.

I go back to my seat. Zoe's husband is already asleep

again. Zoe is reading out loud from *Egypt Made Easy*. "The visitor should take precautions before traveling in Egypt. A map is essential, and a flashlight is needed for many of the sites."

Lissa has gotten her bag out from under the seat. She puts my *Death on the Nile* in it and gets out her sunglasses. I look past her and out the window at the white flatness where the wing should be. We should be able to see the lights on the wing even in the fog. That's what they're there for, so you can see the plane in the fog. The people on the ship didn't realize they were dead at first. It was only when they started noticing little things that weren't quite right that they began to wonder.

"A guide is recommended," Zoe reads.

I have meant to frighten Lissa, but I have only managed to frighten myself. We are beginning our descent, that's all, I tell myself, and flying through a cloud. And that must be right.

Because here we are in Cairo.

Chapter Two: Arriving at the Airport

"So this is Cairo?" Zoe's husband says, looking around. The plane has stopped at the end of the runway and deplaned us onto the asphalt by means of a metal stairway.

The terminal is off to the east, a low building with palm trees around it, and the Japanese tour group sets off toward it immediately, shouldering their carry-on bags and camera cases.

We do not have any carry-ons. Since we always have to wait at the baggage claim for Zoe's guidebooks anyway, we check our carry-ons, too. Every time we do it, I am convinced they will go to Tokyo or disappear altogether, but now I'm glad we don't have to lug them all the way to the terminal. It looks like it is miles away, and the Japanese are already slowing.

Zoe is reading the guidebook. The rest of us stand around her, looking impatient. Lissa has caught the heel of her sandal in one of the metal steps coming down and is leaning against Neil.

"Did you twist it?" Neil asks anxiously.

The flight attendants clatter down the steps with their navy-blue overnight cases. They still look nervous. At the bottom of the stairs they unfold wheeled metal carriers and strap the overnight cases to them and set off for the terminal. After a few steps they stop, and one of them takes off her jacket and drapes it over the wheeled carrier, and they start off again, walking rapidly in their high heels.

It is not as hot as I expected, even though the distant terminal shimmers in the heated air rising from the asphalt. There is no sign of the clouds we flew through, just a thin white haze which disperses the sun's light into an even glare. We are all squinting. Lissa lets go of Neil's arm for a second to get her sunglasses out of her bag.

"What do they drink around here?" Lissa's husband asks, squinting over Zoe's shoulder at the guidebook. "I want a drink."

"The local drink is zibib," Zoe says. "It's like ouzo." She looks up from the guidebook. "I think we should go see the Pyramids."

The professional tour guide strikes again. "Don't you think we'd better take care of first things first?" I say. "Like customs? And picking up our luggage?"

"And finding a drink of . . . what did you call it? Zibab?" Lissa's husband says.

"No," Zoe says. "I think we should do the Pyramids first. It'll take an hour to do the baggage claim and customs, and we can't take our luggage with us to the Pyramids. We'll have to go to the hotel, and by that time everyone will be out there. I think we should go right now." She gestures at the terminal. "We can run out and see them and be back before the Japanese tour group's even through customs."

She turns and starts walking in the opposite direction from the terminal, and the others straggle obediently after her.

I look back at the terminal. The flight attendants have passed the Japanese tour group and are nearly to the palm trees.

"You're going the wrong way," I say to Zoe. "We've got to go to the terminal to get a taxi."

Zoe stops. "A taxi?" she says. "What for? They aren't far. We can walk it in fifteen minutes."

"Fifteen minutes?" I say. "Giza's nine miles west of Cairo. You have to cross the Nile to get there."

"Don't be silly," she says, "they're right there," and points in the direction she was walking, and there, beyond the asphalt in an expanse of sand, so close they do not shimmer at all, are the Pyramids.

Chapter Three: Getting Around

It takes us longer than fifteen minutes. The Pyramids are farther away than they look, and the sand is deep and hard to walk in. We have to stop every few feet so Lissa can empty out her sandals, leaning against Neil.

"We should have taken a taxi," Zoe's husband says, but there are no roads, and no sign of the refreshment stands and souvenir vendors the guidebook complained about, only the unbroken expanse of deep sand and the white, even sky, and in the distance the three yellow pyramids, standing in a row.

" The tallest of the three is the Pyramid of Cheops, built

in 2690 B.C.,' " Zoe says, reading as she walks. " 'It took thirty years to complete.' "

"You have to take a taxi to get to the Pyramids," I say. "There's a lot of traffic."

"It was built on the west bank of the Nile, which the ancient Egyptians believed was the land of the dead."

There is a flicker of movement ahead, between the pyramids, and I stop and shade my eyes against the glare to look at it, hoping it is a souvenir vendor, but I can't see anything.

We start walking again.

It flickers again, and this time I catch sight of it running, hunched over, its hands nearly touching the ground. It disappears behind the middle pyramid.

"I saw something," I say, catching up to Zoe. "Some kind of animal. It looked like a baboon."

Zoe leafs through the guidebook and then says, "Monkeys. They're found frequently near Giza. They beg for food from the tourists."

"There aren't any tourists," I say.

"I know," Zoe says happily. "I told you we'd avoid the rush."

"You have to go through customs, even in Egypt," I say. "You can't just leave the airport."

" 'The pyramid on the left is Kheophren,' " Zoe says, "built in 2650 B.C.' "

"In the movie, they wouldn't believe they were dead even when somebody told them," I say. "Giza is *nine* miles from Cairo."

"What are you talking about?" Neil says. Lissa has stopped again and is leaning against him, standing on one foot and shaking her sandal out. "That mystery of Lissa's, *Death on the Nile*?"

"This was a movie," I say. "They were on this ship, and they were all dead."

"We saw that movie, didn't we, Zoe?" Zoe's husband says.

"Mia Farrow was in it, and Bette Davis. And the detective guy, what was his name—"

"Hercule Poirot," Zoe says. "Played by Peter Ustinov. The Pyramids are open daily from 8 A.M. to 5 P.M. Evenings there is a *Son et Lumière* show with colored floodlights and a narration in English and Japanese.' "

"There were all sorts of clues," I say, "but they just ignored them."

"I don't like Agatha Christie," Lissa says. "Murder and trying to find out who killed who. I'm never able to figure out what's going on. All those people on the train together."

"You're thinking of *Murder on the Orient Express*," Neil says. "I saw that."

"Is that the one where they got killed off one by one?" Lissa's husband says.

"I saw that one," Zoe's husband says. "They got what they deserved, as far as I'm concerned, going off on their own like that when they knew they should keep together."

"Giza is nine miles west of Cairo," I say. "You have to take a taxi to get there. There is all this traffic."

"Peter Ustinov was in that one, too, wasn't he?" Neil says. "The one with the train?"

"No," Zoe's husband says. "It was the other one. What's his name—"

"Albert Finney," Zoe says.

Chapter Four: Places of Interest

The Pyramids are closed. Fifty yards (45.7 m.) from the base of Cheops there is a chain barring our way. A metal sign hangs from it that says "Closed" in English and Japanese.

"Prepare to be disappointed," I say.

"I thought you said they were open daily," Lissa says, knocking sand out of her sandals.

"It must be a holiday," Zoe says, leafing through her guidebook. "Here it is. 'Egyptian holidays.'" She begins reading. "'Antiquities sites are closed during Ramadan, the Muslim month of fasting in March. On Fridays the sites are closed from eleven to one P.M.'"

It is not March, or Friday, and even if it were, it is after one P.M. The shadow of Cheops stretches well past where we stand. I look up, trying to see the sun where it must be behind the pyramid, and catch a flicker of movement, high up. It is too large to be a monkey.

"Well, what do we do now?" Zoe's husband says.

"We could go see the Sphinx," Zoe muses, looking through the guidebook. "Or we could wait for the *Son et Lumière* show."

"No," I say, thinking of being out here in the dark.

"How do you know that won't be closed, too?" Lissa asks.

Zoe consults the book. "There are two shows daily, seven-thirty and nine P.M."

"That's what you said about the Pyramids," Lissa says. "*I* think we should go back to the airport and get our luggage. I want to get my other shoes."

"*I* think we should go back to the hotel," Lissa's husband says, "and have a long, cool drink."

"We'll go to Tutankhamun's tomb," Zoe says. "'It's open every day, including holidays.'" She looks up expectantly.

"King Tut's tomb?" I say. "In the Valley of the Kings?"

"Yes," she says, and starts to read. "'It was found intact in 1922 by Howard Carter. It contained—'"

All the belongings necessary for the deceased's journey to the afterworld, I think. Sandals and clothes and *Egypt Made Easy*.

"I'd rather have a drink," Lissa's husband says.

"And a nap," Zoe's husband says. "You go on, and we'll meet you at the hotel."

"I don't think you should go off on your own," I say. "I think we should keep together."

"It will be crowded if we wait," Zoe says. "I'm going now. Are you coming, Lissa?"

Lissa looks appealingly up at Neil. "I don't think I'd better walk that far. My ankle's starting to hurt again."

Neil looks helplessly at Zoe. "I guess we'd better pass."

"What about you?" Zoe's husband says to me. "Are you going with Zoe or do you want to come with us?"

"In Athens, you said death was the same everywhere," I say to him, "and I said, 'Which is what?' and then Zoe interrupted us and you never did answer me. What were you going to say?"

"I've forgotten," he says, looking at Zoe as if he hopes she will interrupt us again, but she is intent on the guidebook.

"You said, 'Death is the same everywhere,'" I persist, "and I said, 'Which is what?' What did you think death would be like?"

"I don't know . . . unexpected, I guess. And probably pretty damn unpleasant." He laughs nervously. "If we're going to the hotel, we'd better get started. Who else is coming?"

I toy with the idea of going with them, of sitting safely in the hotel bar with ceiling fans and palms, drinking zibib while we wait. That's what the people on the ship did. And in spite of Lissa, I want to stay with Neil.

I look at the expanse of sand back toward the east. There is no sign of Cairo from here, or of the terminal, and far off there is a flicker of movement, like something running.

I shake my head. "I want to see King Tut's tomb." I go over to Neil. "I think we should go with Zoe," I say, and put my hand on his arm. "After all, she's our guide."

Neil looks helplessly at Lissa and then back at me. "I don't know. . . ."

"The three of you can go back to the hotel," I say to Lissa, gesturing to include the other men, "and Zoe and

Neil and I can meet you there after we've been to the tomb."

Neil moves away from Lissa. "Why can't you and Zoe just go?" he whispers at me.

"I think we should keep together," I say. "It would be so easy to get separated."

"How come you're so stuck on going with Zoe anyway?" Neil says. "I thought you said you hated being led around by the nose all the time."

I want to say, Because she has the book, but Lissa has come over and is watching us, her eyes bright behind her sunglasses. "I've always wanted to see the inside of a tomb," I say.

"King Tut?" Lissa says. "Is that the one with the treasure, the necklaces and the gold coffin and stuff?" She puts her hand on Neil's arm. "I've always wanted to see that."

"Okay," Neil says, relieved. "I guess we'll go with you, Zoe."

Zoe looks expectantly at her husband.

"Not me," he says. "We'll meet you in the bar."

"We'll order drinks for you," Lissa's husband says. He waves goodbye, and they set off as if they know where they are going, even though Zoe hasn't told them the name of the hotel.

" 'The Valley of the Kings is located in the hills west of Luxor,' " Zoe says and starts off across the sand the way she did at the airport. We follow her.

I wait until Lissa gets a shoeful of sand and she and Neil fall behind while she empties it.

"Zoe," I say quietly. "There's something wrong."

"Umm," she says, looking up something in the guidebook's index.

"The Valley of the Kings is four hundred miles south of Cairo," I say. "You can't walk there from the Pyramids."

She finds the page. "Of course not. We have to take a boat."

She points, and I see we have reached a stand of reeds, and beyond it is the Nile.

Nosing out from the rushes is a boat, and I am afraid it will be made of gold, but it is only one of the Nile cruisers. And I am so relieved that the Valley of the Kings is not within walking distance that I do not recognize the boat until we have climbed on board and are standing on the canopied deck next to the wooden paddlewheel. It is the steamer from *Death on the Nile*.

Chapter 5: Cruises, Day Trips, and Guided Tours

Lissa is sick on the boat. Neil offers to take her below, and I expect her to say yes, but she shakes her head. "My ankle hurts," she says, and sinks down in one of the deck chairs. Neil kneels by her feet and examines a bruise no bigger than a piaster.

"Is it swollen?" she asks anxiously. There is no sign of swelling, but Neil eases her sandal off and takes her foot tenderly, caressingly, in both hands. Lissa closes her eyes and leans back against the deck chair, sighing.

I toy with the idea that Lissa's husband couldn't take any more of this either, and that he murdered us all and then killed himself.

"Here we are on a ship," I say, "like the dead people in that movie."

"It's not a ship, it's a steamboat," Zoe says. " 'The Nile steamer is the most pleasant way to travel in Egypt and one of the least expensive. Costs range from $180 to $360 per person for a four-day cruise.' "

Or maybe it was Zoe's husband, finally determined to shut Zoe up so he could finish a conversation, and then he had to murder the rest of us one after the other to keep from being caught.

"We're all alone on the ship," I say, "just like they were."

"How far is it to the Valley of the Kings?" Lissa asks.

" 'Three-and-a-half miles (5 km.) west of Luxor,' " Zoe says, reading. " 'Luxor is four hundred miles south of Cairo.' "

"If it's that far, I might as well read my book," Lissa says, pushing her sunglasses up on top of her head. "Neil, hand me my bag."

He fishes *Death on the Nile* out of her bag, and hands it to her, and she flips through it for a moment, like Zoe looking for exchange rates, and then begins to read.

"The wife did it," I say. "She found out her husband was being unfaithful."

Lissa glares at me. "I already knew that," she says carelessly. "I saw the movie," but after another half-page she lays the open book face-down on the empty deck chair next to her.

"I can't read," she says to Neil. "The sun's too bright." She squints up at the sky, which is still hidden by its gauzelike haze.

" 'The Valley of the Kings is the site of the tombs of sixty-four pharoahs,' " Zoe says. " 'Of these, the most famous is Tutankhamun's.' "

I go over to the railing and watch the Pyramids recede, slipping slowly out of sight behind the rushes that line the shore. They look flat, like yellow triangles stuck up in the sand, and I remember how in Paris Zoe's husband wouldn't believe the *Mona Lisa* was the real thing. "It's a fake," he insisted before Zoe interrupted. "The real one's much larger."

And the guidebook said, Prepare to be disappointed, and the Valley of the Kings is four hundred miles from the Pyramids like it's supposed to be, and Middle Eastern airports are notorious for their lack of security. That's how all those bombs get on planes in the first place, because they don't make people go through customs. I shouldn't watch so many movies.

" 'Among its treasures, Tutankhamun's tomb contained a golden boat, by which the soul would travel to the world of the dead,' " Zoe says.

I lean over the railing and look into the water. It is not muddy, like I thought it would be, but a clear waveless blue, and in its depths the sun is shining brightly.

" 'The boat was carved with passages from the *Book of the Dead*,' " Zoe reads, " 'to protect the deceased from monsters and demigods who might try to destroy him before he reached the Hall of Judgment.' "

There is something in the water. Not a ripple, not even enough of a movement to shudder the image of the sun, but I know there is something there.

" 'Spells were also written on papyruses buried with the body,' " Zoe says.

It is long and dark, like a crocodile. I lean over farther, gripping the rail, trying to see into the transparent water, and catch a glint of scales. It is swimming straight toward the boat.

" 'These spells took the form of commands,' " Zoe reads. " 'Get back, you evil one! Stay away! I adjure you in the name of Anubis and Osiris.' " The water glitters, hesitating.

" 'Do not come against me,' " Zoe says. " 'My spells protect me. I know the way.' "

The thing in the water turns and swims away. The boat follows it, nosing slowly in toward the shore.

"There it is," Zoe says, pointing past the reeds at a distant row of cliffs. "The Valley of the Kings."

"I suppose this'll be closed, too," Lissa says, letting Neil help her off the boat.

"Tombs are never closed," I say, and look north, across the sand, at the distant Pyramids.

Chapter 6: Accommodations

The Valley of the Kings is not closed. The tombs stretch along a sandstone cliff, black openings in the yellow rock, and there are no chains across the stone steps that lead down to them. At the south end of the valley a Japanese tour group is going into the last one.

"Why aren't the tombs marked?" Lissa asks. "Which one is King Tut's?" and Zoe leads us to the north end of the valley, where the cliff dwindles into a low wall. Beyond it, across the sand, I can see the Pyramids, sharp against the sky.

Zoe stops at the very edge of a slanting hole dug into the base of the rocks. There are steps leading down into it. "Tutankhamun's tomb was found when a workman accidentally uncovered the top step," she says.

Lissa looks down into the stairwell. All but the top two steps are in shadow, and it is too dark to see the bottom. "Are there snakes?" she asks.

"No," Zoe, who knows everything, says. "Tutankhamun's tomb is the smallest of the pharaohs' tombs in the Valley." She fumbles in her bag for her flashlight. "The tomb consists of three rooms—an antechamber, the burial chamber containing Tutankhamun's coffin, and the Hall of Judgment."

There is a slither of movement in the darkness below us, like a slow uncoiling, and Lissa steps back from the edge. "Which room is the stuff in?"

"Stuff?" Zoe says uncertainly, still fumbling for her flashlight. She opens her guidebook. "Stuff?" she says again, and flips to the back of it, as if she is going to look "stuff" up in the index.

"Stuff," Lissa says, and there is an edge of fear in her voice. "All the furniture and vases and stuff they take with them. You said the Egyptians buried their belongings with them."

"King Tut's treasure," Neil says helpfully.

"Oh, the treasure," Zoe says, relieved. "The belongings buried with Tutankhamun for his journey into the afterworld. They're not here. They're in Cairo in the museum."

"In Cairo?" Lissa says. "They're in Cairo? Then what are we doing here?"

"We're dead," I say. "Arab terrorists blew up our plane and killed us all."

"I came all the way out here because I wanted to see the treasure," Lissa says.

"The coffin is here," Zoe says placatingly, "and there are wall paintings in the antechamber," but Lissa has already led Neil away from the steps, talking earnestly to him.

"The wall paintings depict the stages in the judgment of the soul, the weighing of the soul, the recital of the deceased's confession," Zoe says.

The deceased's confession. I have not taken that which belongs to another. I have not caused any pain. I have not committed adultery.

Lissa and Neil come back, Lissa leaning heavily on Neil's arm. "I think we'll pass on this tomb thing," Neil says apologetically. "We want to get to the museum before it closes. Lissa had her heart set on seeing the treasure."

" 'The Egyptian Museum is open from 9 A.M. to 4 P.M. daily, 9 to 11:15 A.M. and 1:30 to 4 P.M. Fridays,' " Zoe says, reading from the guidebook. " 'Admission is three Egyptian pounds.' "

"It's already four o'clock," I say, looking at my watch. "It will be closed before you get there." I look up.

Neil and Lissa have already started back, not toward the boat but across the sand in the direction of the Pyramids. The light behind the Pyramids is beginning to fade, the sky going from white to gray-blue.

"Wait," I say, and run across the sand to catch up with

them. "Why don't you wait and we'll all go back together? It won't take us very long to see the tomb. You heard Zoe, there's nothing inside."

They both look at me.

"I think we should stay together," I finish lamely.

Lissa looks up alertly, and I realize she thinks I am talking about divorce, that I have finally said what she has been waiting for.

"I think we should all keep together," I say hastily. "This is Egypt. There are all sorts of dangers, crocodiles and snakes and . . . it won't take us very long to see the tomb. You heard Zoe, there's nothing inside."

"We'd better not," Neil says, looking at me. "Lissa's ankle is starting to swell. I'd better get some ice on it."

I look down at her ankle. Where the bruise was there are two little puncture marks, close together, like a snake bite, and around them the ankle is starting to swell.

"I don't think Lissa's up to the Hall of Judgment," he says, still looking at me.

"You could wait at, the top of the steps," I say. "You wouldn't have to go in."

Lissa takes hold of his arm, as if anxious to go, but he hesitates. "Those people on the ship," he says to me. "What happened to them?"

"I was just trying to frighten you," I say. "I'm sure there's a logical explanation. It's too bad Hercule Poirot isn't here—he'd be able to explain everything. The Pyramids were probably closed for some Muslim holiday Zoe didn't know about, and that's why we didn't have to go through customs either, because it was a holiday."

"What happened to the people on the ship?" Neil says again.

"They got judged," I say, "but it wasn't nearly as bad as they'd thought. They were all afraid of what was going to happen, even the clergyman, who hadn't committed any sins, but the judge turned out to be somebody he knew.

A bishop. He wore a white suit, and he was very kind, and most of them came out fine."

"Most of them," Neil says.

"Let's *go*," Lissa says, pulling on his arm.

"The people on the ship," Neil says, ignoring her. "Had any of them committed some horrible sin?"

"My ankle hurts," Lissa says. "Come *on*."

"I have to go," Neil says, almost reluctantly. "Why don't you come with us?"

I glance at Lissa, expecting her to be looking daggers at Neil, but she is watching me with bright, lidless eyes.

"Yes. Come with us," she says, and waits for my answer.

I lied to Lissa about the ending of *Death on the Nile*. It was the wife they killed. I toy with the idea that they have committed some horrible sin, that I am lying in my hotel room in Athens, my temple black with blood and powder burns. I would be the only one here then, and Lissa and Neil would be demigods disguised to look like them. Or monsters.

"I'd better not," I say, and back away from them.

"Let's go then," Lissa says to Neil, and they start off across the sand. Lissa is limping badly, and before they have gone very far, Neil stops and takes off his shoes.

The sky behind the Pyramids is purple-blue, and the Pyramids stand out flat and black against it.

"Come on," Zoe calls from the top of the steps. She is holding the flashlight and looking at the guidebook. "I want to see the Weighing of the Soul."

Chapter 7: Off the Beaten Track

Zoe is already halfway down the steps when I get back, shining her flashlight on the door below her. "When the tomb was discovered, the door was plastered over and stamped with the seals bearing the cartouche of Tutankhamun," she says.

"It'll be dark soon," I call down to her. "Maybe we should go back to the hotel with Lissa and Neil." I look back across the desert, but they are already out of sight.

Zoe is gone, too. When I look back down the steps, there is nothing but darkness. "Zoe!" I shout and run down the sand-drifted steps after her. "Wait!"

The door to the tomb is open, and I can see the light from her flashlight bobbing on rock walls and ceiling far down a narrow corridor.

"Zoe!" I shout, and start after her. The floor is uneven, and I trip and put my hand on the wall to steady myself. "Come back! You have the book!"

The light flashes on a section of carved-out wall, far ahead, and then vanishes, as if she has turned a corner.

"Wait for me!" I shout and stop because I cannot see my hand in front of my face.

There is no answering light, no answering voice, no sound at all. I stand very still, one hand still on the wall, listening for footsteps, for quiet padding, for the sound of slithering, but I can't hear anything, not even my own heart beating.

"Zoe," I call out, "I'm going to wait for you outside," and turn around, holding onto the wall so I don't get disoriented in the dark, and go back the way I came.

The corridor seems longer than it did coming in, and I toy with the idea that it will go on forever in the dark, or that the door will be locked, the opening plastered over and the ancient seals affixed, but there is a line of light under the door, and it opens easily when I push on it.

I am at the top of a stone staircase leading down into a long wide hall. On either side the hall is lined with stone pillars, and between the pillars I can see that the walls are painted with scenes in sienna and yellow and bright blue.

It must be the anteroom because Zoe said its walls were

painted with scenes from the soul's journey into death, and
there is Anubis weighing the soul, and, beyond it, a baboon
devouring something, and, opposite where I am standing
on the stairs, a painting of a boat crossing the blue Nile.
It is made of gold, and in it four souls squat in a line, their
kohl-outlined eyes looking ahead at the shore. Beside
them, in the transparent water, Sebek, the crocodile
demigod, swims.

I start down the steps. There is a doorway at the far end
of the hall, and if this is the anteroom, then the door must
lead to the burial chamber.

Zoe said the tomb consists of only three rooms, and I
saw the map myself on the plane, the steps and straight
corridor and then the unimpressive rooms leading one into
another, anteroom and burial chamber and Hall of
Judgment, one after another.

So this is the anteroom, even if it is larger than it was
on the map, and Zoe has obviously gone ahead to the burial
chamber and is standing by Tutankhamun's coffin, reading
aloud from the travel guide. When I come in, she will look
up and say, " 'The quartzite sarcophagus is carved with
passages from *The Book of the Dead*.'"

I have come halfway down the stairs, and from here
I can see the painting of the weighing of the soul. Anubis,
with his jackal's head, standing on one side of the yellow
scales, and the deceased on the other, reading his
confession from a papyrus.

I go down two more steps, till I am even with the scales,
and sit down. Surely Zoe won't be long—there's nothing
in the burial chamber except the coffin—and even if she
has gone on ahead to the Hall of Judgment, she'll have
to come back this way. There's only one entrance to the
tomb. And she can't get turned around because she has
a flashlight. And the book. I clasp my hands around my
knees and wait.

I think about the people on the ship, waiting for

judgment. "It wasn't as bad as they thought," I'd told Neil, but now, sitting here on the steps, I remember that the bishop, smiling kindly in his white suit, gave them sentences appropriate to their sins. One of the women was sentenced to being alone forever.

The deceased in the painting looks frightened, standing by the scale, and I wonder what sentence Anubis will give him, what sins he has committed.

Maybe he has not committed any sins at all, like the clergyman, and is worried over nothing, or maybe he is merely frightened at finding himself in this strange place, alone. Was death what he expected?

"Death is the same everywhere," Zoe's husband said. "Unexpected." And nothing is the way you thought it would be. Look at the *Mona Lisa*. And Neil. The people on the ship had planned on something else altogether, pearly gates and angels and clouds, all the modern refinements. Prepare to be disappointed.

And what about the Egyptians, packing their clothes and wine and sandals for their trip. Was death, even on the Nile, what they expected? Or was it not the way it had been described in the travel guide at all? Did they keep thinking they were alive, in spite of all the clues?

The deceased clutches his papyrus and I wonder if he has committed some horrible sin. Adultery. Or murder. I wonder how he died.

The people on the ship were killed by a bomb, like we were. I try to remember the moment it went off—Zoe reading out loud and then the sudden shock of light and decompression, the travel guide blown out of Zoe's hands and Lissa falling through the blue air, but I can't. Maybe it didn't happen on the plane. Maybe the terrorists blew us up in the airport in Athens, while we were checking our luggage.

I toy with the idea that it wasn't a bomb at all, that I murdered Lissa, and then killed myself, like in *Death on the Nile.* Maybe I reached into my bag, not for my paperback but for the gun I bought in Athens, and shot Lissa while she was looking out the window. And Neil bent over her, solicitous, concerned, and I raised the gun again, and Zoe's husband tried to wrestle it out of my hand, and the shot went wide and hit the gas tank on the wing.

I am still frightening myself. If I'd murdered Lissa, I would remember it, and even Athens, notorious for its lack of security, wouldn't have let me on board a plane with a gun. And you could hardly commit some horrible crime without remembering it, could you?

The people on the ship didn't remember dying, even when someone told them, but that was because the ship was so much like a real one, the railings and the water and the deck. And because of the bomb. People never remember being blown up. It's the concussion or something, it knocks the memory out of you. But I would surely have remembered murdering someone. Or being murdered.

I sit on the steps a long time, watching for the splash of Zoe's flashlight in the doorway. Outside it will be dark, time for the *Son et Lumière* show at the pyramids.

It seems darker in here, too. I have to squint to see Anubis and the yellow scales and the deceased, awaiting judgment. The papyrus he is holding is covered with long, bordered columns of hieroglyphics and I hope they are magic spells to protect him and not a list of all the sins he has committed.

I have not murdered another, I think. I have not committed adultery. But there are other sins.

It will be dark soon, and I do not have a flashlight. I stand up. "Zoe!" I call, and go down the stairs and between the pillars. They are carved with animals—cobras and baboons and crocodiles.

"It's getting dark," I call, and my voice echoes hollowly

among the pillars. "They'll be wondering what happened to us."

The last pair of pillars is carved with a bird, its sandstone wings outstretched. A bird of the gods. Or a plane.

"Zoe?" I say, and stoop to go through the low door. "Are you in here?"

Chapter Eight: Special Events

Zoe isn't in the burial chamber. It is much smaller than the anteroom, and there are no paintings on the rough walls or above the door that leads to the Hall of Judgment. The ceiling is scarcely higher than the door, and I have to hunch down to keep from scraping my head against it.

It is darker in here than in the anteroom, but even in the dimness I can see that Zoe isn't here. Neither is Tutankhamun's sarcophagus, carved with *The Book of the Dead*. There is nothing in the room at all, except for a pile of suitcases in the corner by the door to the Hall of Judgment.

It is our luggage. I recognize my battered Samsonite and the carry-on bags of the Japanese tour group. The flight attendants' navy-blue overnight cases are in front of the pile, strapped like victims to their wheeled carriers.

On top of my suitcase is a book, and I think, "It's the travel guide," even though I know Zoe would never have left it behind, and I hurry over to pick it up.

It is not *Egypt Made Easy*. It is my *Death on the Nile*, lying open and face-down the way Lissa left it on the boat, but I pick it up anyway and open it to the last pages; searching for the place where Hercule Poirot explains all the strange things that have been happening, where he solves the mystery.

I cannot find it. I thumb back through the book, looking

for a map. There is always a map in Agatha Christie, showing who had what stateroom on the ship, showing the stairways and the doors and the unimpressive rooms leading one into another, but I cannot find that either. The pages are covered with long unreadable columns of hieroglyphics.

I close the book. "There's no point in waiting for Zoe," I say, looking past the luggage at the door to the next room. It is lower than the one I came through, and dark beyond. "She's obviously gone on to the Hall of Judgment."

I walk over to the door, holding the book against my chest. There are stone steps leading down. I can see the top one in the dim light from the burial chamber. It is steep and very narrow.

I toy briefly with the idea-that it will not be so bad after all, that I am dreading it like the clergyman, and it will turn out to be not judgment but someone I know, a smiling bishop in a white suit, and mercy is not a modern refinement after all.

"I have not murdered another," I say, and my voice does not echo. "I have not committed adultery."

I take hold of the doorjamb with one hand so I won't fall on the stairs. With the other I hold the book against me. "Get back, you evil ones," I say. "Stay away. I adjure you in the name of Osiris and Poirot. My spells protect me. I know the way."

I begin my descent.

Among hard sf writers, Charles Sheffield is as rigorous as any, and more so than most. His Cambridge education stands by him, informing his prose in subtle turns of phrase. When we first met, he accused me of pick-pocketing much of his personal past, since I had used Cambridge and its academic class nuances to form the background of my novel, Timescape. "I can't use my own life!" he said in mock outrage. I would have offered him my own doctoral turf, La Jolla in the 1960s, except that I had gobbled up that terrain in the same novel (that old injunction, write about what you know, is still chewing up a lot of my own history; I just finished a novel set in my own physics department, at University of California, Irvine, running up to the present, so I am fresh out of easily lifted setting). So I ended up offering Charles Alabama in the 1940s and 50s, the only ground from my growing up that I hadn't already trod.

"Georgia on My Mind" draws on several of Charles's experiences, blending them in artful contrast, and spiraling to a striking conclusion. He is a master of the apparently innocuous fact, which then undermines your sense of equilibrium, a classic sf technique. What's more, you may count on his information being solidly grounded, well researched and deftly set forth.

Georgia On My Mind
by Charles Sheffield

I first tangled with digital computers late in 1958. That may sound like the dark ages, but we considered ourselves infinitely more advanced than our predecessors of a decade earlier, when programming was done mostly by sticking plugs into plug-boards and a card-sequenced programmable calculator was held to be the height of sophistication.

Even so, 1958 was still early enough that the argument between analog and digital computers had not yet been settled, decisively, in favor of the digital. And the first computer that I programmed was, by anyone's standards, a brute.

It was called DEUCE, which stood for Digital Electronic Universal Computing Engine, and it was, reasonably enough to card players, the next thing after the ACE (for Automatic Computing Engine), developed by the National Physical Laboratory at Teddington. Unlike ACE, DEUCE was a commercial machine; and some idea of its possible shortcomings is provided by one of the designers' comments about ACE itself: "If we had known that it was going to be developed commercially, we would have finished it."

DEUCE was big enough to walk inside. The engineers would do that, tapping at suspect vacuum tubes with a screwdriver when the whole beast was proving balky.

Which was often. Machine errors were as common a cause of trouble as programming errors; and programming errors were dreadfully frequent, because we were working at a level so close to basic machine logic that it is hard to imagine it today.

I was about to say that the computer had no compilers or assemblers, but that is not strictly true. There was a floating-point compiler known as ALPHA-CODE, but it ran a thousand times slower than a machine code program and no one with any self-respect ever used it. We programmed in absolute, to make the best possible use of the machine's 402 words of high-speed (mercury delay line) memory, and its 8,192 words of back-up (rotating drum) memory. Anything needing more than that had to use punched cards as intermediate storage, with the programmer standing by to shovel them from the output hopper back into the input hopper.

When I add that binary-to-decimal conversion routines were usually avoided because they wasted space, that all instructions were defined in binary, that programmers therefore had to be very familiar with the binary representation of numbers, that we did our own card punching with hand (not electric) punches, and that the machine itself, for some reason that still remains obscure to me, worked with binary numbers whose most significant digit was on the right, rather than on the left—so that 13, for example, became 1011, rather than the usual 1101—well, by this time the general flavor of DEUCE programming ought to be coming through.

Now, I mention these things not because they are interesting (to the few) or because they are dull (to the many) but to make the point that anyone programming DEUCE in those far-off days was an individual not to be taken lightly. We at least thought so, though I suspect that to high management we were all hare-brained children who did incomprehensible things, many of them in the middle of the night (when de-bug time was more easily to be had).

A few years later more computers became available, the diaspora inevitably took place, and we all went off to other interesting places. Some found their way to university professorships, some into commerce, and many to foreign parts. But we did tend to keep in touch, because those early days had generated a special feeling.

One of the most interesting characters was Bill Rigley. He was a tall, dashing, wavy-haired fellow who wore English tweeds and spoke with the open "a" sound that to most Americans indicates a Boston origin. But Bill was a New Zealander, who had seen at firsthand things, like the Great Barrier Reef, that the rest of us had barely heard of. He didn't talk much about his home and family, but he must have pined for them, because after a few years in Europe and America he went back to take a faculty position in the Department of Mathematics (and later the computer science department, when one was finally created) at the University of Auckland.

Auckland is on the north island, a bit less remote than the bleaker south island, but a long way from the east coast of the United States, where I had put down my own roots. Even so, Bill and I kept in close contact, because our scientific interests were very similar. We saw each other every few years in Stanford, or London, or wherever else our paths intersected, and we knew each other at the deep level where few people touch. It was Bill who helped me to mourn when my wife, Eileen, died, and I in turn knew (but never talked about) the dark secret that had scarred Bill's own life. No matter how long we had been separated our conversations, when we met, picked up as though they had never left off.

Bill's interests were encyclopedic, and he had a special fondness for scientific history. So it was no surprise that when he went back to New Zealand he would wander around there, examining its contribution to world science. What was a surprise to me was a letter from him a few months ago, stating that in a farmhouse near Dunedin, towards the south end of the south island, he had come across some bits and pieces of Charles Babbage's Analytical Engine.

Even back in the late 1950s, we had known all about Babbage. There was at the time only one decent book about digital computers, Bowden's *Faster Than Thought*, but its first chapter talked all about that eccentric but formidable Englishman, with his hatred of street musicians and his low opinion of the Royal Society (existing only to hold dinners, he said, at which they gave each other medals). Despite these odd views, Babbage was still our patron saint. For starting in 1834 and continuing for the rest of his life, he tried—unsuccessfully—to build the world's first programmable digital computer. He understood the principles perfectly well, but he was thwarted because he had to work with mechanical parts. Can you imagine a computer built of cogs and toothed cylinders and gears and springs and levers?

Babbage could. And he might have triumphed even over the inadequacy of the available technology, but for one fatal problem: he kept thinking of improvements. As soon as a design was half assembled, he would want to tear it apart and start using the bits to build something better. At the time of Babbage's death in 1871, his wonderful Analytical Engine was still a dream. The bits and pieces were carted off to London's Kensington Science Museum, where they remain today.

Given our early exposure to Babbage, my reaction to Bill Rigley's letter was pure skepticism. It was understandable that Bill would want to find evidence of parts of the Analytical Engine somewhere on his home stamping-ground; but his claim to have done so was surely self-delusion.

I wrote back, suggesting this in as tactful a way as I could;

and received in prompt reply not recantation, but the most extraordinary package of documents I had ever seen in my life (I should say, to that point, there were stranger to come).

The first was a letter from Bill, explaining in his usual blunt way that the machinery he had found had survived on the south island of New Zealand because "we don't chuck good stuff away, the way you lot do." He also pointed out, through dozens of examples, that in the nineteenth century there was much more contact between Britain and its antipodes than I had ever dreamed. A visit to Australia and New Zealand was common among educated persons, a kind of expanded version of the European Grand Tour. Charles Darwin was of course a visitor, on the *Beagle*, but so also were scores of less well-known scientists, world travelers, and gentlemen of the leisured class. Two of Charles Babbage's own sons were there in the 1850s.

The second item in the package was a batch of photographs of the machinery that Bill had found. It looked to me like what it was, a bunch of toothed cylinders and gears and wheels. They certainly resembled parts of the Analytical Engine, or the earlier Difference Machine, although I could not see how they might fit together.

Neither the letter nor the photographs was persuasive. Rather the opposite. I started to write in my mind the letter that said as much, but I hesitated for one reason: many historians of science know a lot more history than science, and few are trained computer specialists. But Bill was the other way round, the computer expert who happened to be fascinated by scientific history. It would be awfully hard to fool him—unless he chose to fool himself.

So I had another difficult letter to write. But I was spared the trouble, for what I could not dismiss or misunderstand was the third item in the package. It was a copy of a programming manual, hand-written, for the Babbage Analytical Engine. It was dated July 7, 1854. Bill said that he had the original in his possession. He also told me that I was the only person who knew of his discovery, and he asked me to keep it to myself.

And here, to explain my astonishment, I have to dip again into computer history. Not merely to the late 1950s, where we started, but all the way to 1840. In that year an Italian mathematician, Luigi Federico Menabrea, heard Babbage talk in Turin about the new machine that he was building. After more explanations by letter from Babbage, Menabrea wrote a paper on the Analytical Engine, in French, which was published in 1842. And later that year Ada Lovelace (Lord Byron's daughter; Lady Augusta Ada Byron Lovelace, to give her complete name) translated Menabrea's memoir, and added her own lengthy notes. Those notes formed the world's first software manual; Ada Lovelace described how to program the Analytical Engine, including the tricky techniques of recursion, looping, and branching.

So, twelve years before 1854, a programming manual for the Analytical Engine existed; and one could argue that what Bill had found in New Zealand was no more than a copy of the one written in 1842 by Ada Lovelace.

But there were problems. The document that Bill sent me went far beyond the 1842 notes. It tackled the difficult topics of indirect addressing, relocatable programs and subroutines, and it offered a new language for programming the Analytical Engine—what amounted to a primitive assembler.

Ada Lovelace just might have entertained such advanced ideas, and written such a manual. It is possible that she had the talent, although all signs of her own mathematical notebooks have been lost. But she died in 1852, and there was no evidence in any of her surviving works that she ever blazed the astonishing trail defined in the document that I received from Bill. Furthermore, the manual bore on its first page the author's initials, L.D. Ada Lovelace for her published work had used her own initials, A.A.L.

I read the manual, over and over, particularly the final section. It contained a sample program, for the computation of the volume of an irregular solid by numerical integration—and it included a page of *output*, the printed results of the program.

At that point I recognized only three possibilities. First, that someone in the past few years had carefully planted a deliberate forgery down near Dunedin, and led Bill Rigley to "discover" it. Second, that Bill himself was involved in attempting an elaborate hoax, for reasons I could not fathom.

I had problems with both these explanations. Bill was perhaps the most cautious, thorough, and conservative researcher that I had ever met. He was painstaking to a fault, and he did not fool easily. He was also the last man in the world to think that devising a hoax could be in any way amusing.

Which left the third possibility. Someone in New Zealand had built a version of the Analytical Engine, made it work, and taken it well beyond the place where Charles Babbage had left off.

I call that the third possibility, but it seemed at the time much more like the third *impossibility*. No wonder that Bill had asked for secrecy. He didn't want to become the laughing-stock of the computer historians.

Nor did I. I took a step that was unusual in my relationship with Bill: I picked up the phone and called him in New Zealand.

"Well, what do you think?" he said, as soon as he recognized my voice on the line.

"I'm afraid to think at all. How much checking have you done?"

"I sent paper samples to five places, one in Japan, two in Europe and two in the United States. The dates they assign to the paper and the ink range from 1840 to 1875, with 1850 as the average. The machinery that I found had been protected by wrapping in sacking soaked in linseed oil. Dates for that ranged from 1830 to 1880." There was a pause at the other end of the line. "There's more. Things I didn't have until two weeks ago."

"Tell me."

"I'd rather not. Not like this." There was another, longer silence. "You are coming out, aren't you?"

"Why do you think I'm on the telephone? Where should I fly to?"

"Christchurch. South Island. We'll be going farther south, past Dunedin. Bring warm clothes. It's winter here."

"I know. I'll call as soon as I have my arrival time."

And that was the beginning.

The wavy mop of fair hair had turned to grey, and Bill Rigley now favored a pepper-and-salt beard which with his weather-beaten face turned him into an approximation of the Ancient Mariner. But nothing else had changed, except perhaps for the strange tension in his eyes.

We didn't shake hands when he met me at Christchurch airport, or exchange one word of conventional greeting. Bill just said, as soon as we were within speaking range, "If this wasn't happening to me, I'd insist it couldn't happen to anybody," and led me to his car.

Bill was South Island born, so the long drive from Christchurch to Dunedin was home territory to him. I, in that odd but pleasant daze that comes after long air travel—after you deplane, and before the jet lag hits you—stared out at the scenery from what I thought of as the driver's seat (they still drive on the left, like the British).

We were crossing the flat Canterbury Plains, on a straight road across a level and empty expanse of muddy fields. It was almost three months after harvest—wheat or barley, from the look of the stubble—and there was nothing much to see until at Timaru when we came to the coast road, with dull grey sea to the left and empty brown coastal plain on the right. I had visited South Island once before, but that had been a lightning trip, little more than a tour of Christchurch. Now for the first time I began to appreciate Bill's grumbling about "overcrowded" Auckland on the north island. We saw cars and people, but in terms of what I was used to it was a thin sprinkle of both. It was late afternoon, and as we drove farther south it became colder and began to rain. The sea faded from view behind a curtain of fog and drizzle.

We had been chatting about nothing from the time we climbed into the car. It was talk designed to avoid talking, and we both knew it. But at last Bill, after a few seconds in which the only sounds were the engine and the *whump-whump-whump* of windshield wipers, said: "I'm glad to have you here. There's been times in the past few weeks when I've seriously wondered if I was going off my head. What I want to do is this. Tomorrow morning, after you've had a good sleep, I'm going to show you *everything*, just as I found it. Most of it just *where* I found it. And then I want you to tell me what you think is going on."

I nodded. "What's the population of New Zealand?"

Without turning my head, I saw Bill's quick glance. "Total? Four million, tops."

"And what was it in 1850?"

"That's a hell of a good question. I don't know if anyone can really tell you. I'd say, a couple of hundred thousand. But the vast majority of those were native Maori. I know where you're going, and I agree totally. There's no way that anyone could have built a version of the Analytical Engine in New Zealand in the middle of the last century. The manufacturing industry just didn't exist here. The final assembly could be done, but the sub-units would have to be built and shipped in big chunks from Europe."

"From Babbage?"

"Absolutely not. He was still alive in 1854. He didn't

die until 1871, and if he had learned that a version of the
Analytical Engine was being built *anywhere*, he'd have
talked about it nonstop all over Europe."

"But if it wasn't Babbage—"

"Then who was it? I know. Be patient for a few more
hours. Don't try to think it through until you've rested,
and had a chance to see the whole thing for yourself."

He was right. I had been traveling nonstop around the
clock, and my brain was going on strike. I pulled my
overcoat collar up around my ears, and sagged lower in
my seat. In the past few days I had absorbed as much
information about Babbage and the Analytical Engine as
my head could handle. Now I needed to let it sort itself
out, along with what Bill was going to show me.

Then we would see if I could come up with a more
plausible explanation for what he had found.

As I drifted into half-consciousness, I flashed on to the
biggest puzzle of all. Until that moment I had been telling
myself, subconsciously, that Bill was just plain wrong. It
was my way of avoiding the logical consequences of his
being *right*. But suppose he *were* right. Then the biggest
puzzle was not the appearance of an Analytical Engine,
with its advanced programming tools, in New Zealand. It
was the *disappearance* of those things, from the face of
the Earth.

Where the devil had they gone?

Our destination was a farmhouse about fifteen miles
south of Dunedin. I didn't see much of it when we arrived,
because it was raining and pitch-black and I was three-
quarters asleep. If I had any thoughts at all as I was shown
to a small, narrow room and collapsed into bed, it was that
in the morning, bright and early, Bill would show me
everything and my perplexity would end.

It didn't work out that way. For one thing, I overslept
and felt terrible when I got up. I had forgotten what a long,

sleepless journey can do to your system. For the past five years I had done less and less traveling, and I was getting soft. For another thing, the rain had changed to sleet during the night and was driving down in freezing gusts. The wind was blowing briskly from the east, in off the sea. Bill and I sat at the battered wooden table in the farm kitchen, while Mrs. Trevelyan pushed bacon, eggs, homemade sausage, bread and hot sweet tea into me until I showed signs of life. She was a spry, red-cheeked lady in her middle sixties, and if she was surprised that Bill had finally brought someone else with him to explore Little House, she hid it well.

"Well, then," she said, when I was stuffed. "If you're stepping up the hill you'll be needing a mac. Jim put the one on when he went out, but we have plenty of spares."

Jim Trevelyan was apparently off somewhere tending the farm animals, and had been since dawn. Bill grinned sadistically at the look on my face. "You don't want a little rain to stop work, do you?"

I wanted to go back to bed. But I hadn't come ten thousand miles to lie around. The "step up the hill" to Little House turned out to be about half a mile, through squelching mud covered with a thin layer of sour turf.

"How did you ever find this place'?" I asked Bill.

"By asking and looking. I've been into a thousand like this before, and found nothing."

We were approaching a solidly-built square house made out of mortared limestone blocks. It had a weathered look, but the slate roof and chimney were intact. To me it did not seem much smaller than the main farmhouse.

"It's not called 'Little House' because it's small," Bill explained. "It's Little House because that's where the little ones are supposed to live when they first marry. You're seeing a twentieth-century tragedy here. Jim and Annie Trevelyan are fourth-generation farmers. They have five children. Everyone went off to college, and not a one has come back to live in Little House and wait their turn to run the farm. Jim and Annie hang on at Big House, waiting and hoping."

As we went inside, the heavy wooden door was snug-fitting and moved easily on oiled hinges.

"Jim Trevelyan keeps the place up, and I think they're glad to have me here to give it a lived-in feel," said Bill. "I suspect that they both think I'm mad as a hatter, but they never say a word. Hold tight to this, while I get myself organized."

He had been carrying a square box lantern. When he passed it to me I was astonished by the weight—and he had carried it for half a mile.

"Batteries, mostly," Bill explained. "Little House has oil lamps, but of course there's no electricity. After a year or two wandering around out-of-the-way places I decided there was no point in driving two hundred miles to look at something if you can't see it when you get there. I can recharge this from the car if we have to."

As Bill closed the door the sound of the wind dropped to nothing. We went through a washhouse to a kitchen furnished with solid wooden chairs, table, and dresser. The room was freezing cold, and I looked longingly at the scuttle of coal and the dry kindling standing by the fireplace.

"Go ahead," said Bill, "while I sort us out here. Keep your coat on, though—you can sit and toast yourself later."

He lit two big oil lamps that stood on the table, while I placed layers of rolled paper, sticks, and small pieces of coal in the grate. It was thirty years since I had built a coal fire, but it's not much of an art. In a couple of minutes I could stand up, keep one eye on the fire to make sure it was catching properly, and take a much better look at the room. There were no rugs, but over by the door leading through to the bedrooms was a long strip of coconut matting. Bill rolled it back, to reveal a square wooden trapdoor. He slipped his belt through the iron ring and lifted, grunting with effort until the trap finally came free and turned upward on brass hinges.

"Storage space," he said. "Now we'll need the lantern. Turn it on, and pass it down to me."

He lowered himself into the darkness, but not far. His chest and head still showed when he was standing on the lower surface. I switched on the electric lantern and handed it down to Bill.

"Just a second," I said. I went across to the fireplace, added half a dozen larger lumps of coal, then hurried back to the trapdoor. Bill had already disappeared when I lowered myself into the opening.

The storage space was no more than waist high, with a hard dirt floor. I followed the lantern light, to where a wooden section at the far end was raised a few inches off the ground on thick beams. On that raised floor stood three big tea chests. The lantern threw a steady, powerful light on them.

"I told you you'd see just what I saw," said Bill. "These have all been out and examined, of course, but everything is very much the way it was when I found it. All right, hardware first."

He carefully lifted the lid off the right-hand tea chest. It was half full of old sacks. Bill lifted one, unfolded it, and handed me the contents. I was holding a solid metal cylinder, lightly oiled and apparently made of brass. The digits from 0 through 9 ran around its upper part, and at the lower end was a cog wheel of slightly greater size.

I examined it carefully, taking my time. "It could be," I said. "it's certainly the way the pictures look."

I didn't need to tell him which pictures. He knew that I had thought of little but Charles Babbage and his Analytical Engines for the past few weeks, just as he had.

"I don't think it was made in England," said Bill. "I've been all over it with a lens, and I can't see a manufacturer's mark. My guess is that it was made in France."

"Any particular reason?"

"The numerals. Same style as some of the best French clock-makers—see, I've been working, too." He took the cylinder and wrapped it again, with infinite care, in the oiled sacking. I stared all around us, from the dirt floor to the dusty rafters. "This isn't the best place for valuable property."

"It's done all right for 140 years. I don't think you can say as much of most other places." There was something else that Bill did not need to say. This was a perfect place for valuable property—so long as no one thought that it had any value.

"There's nowhere near enough pieces here to make an Analytical Engine, of course," he went on. "These must have just been spares. I've taken a few of them to Auckland. I don't have the original of the programming manual here, either. That's back in Auckland, too, locked up in a safe at the university.

"I brought a copy, if we need it."

"So did I." We grinned at each other. Underneath my calm I was almost too excited to speak, and I could tell that he felt the same. "Any clue as to who 'L.D.' might be, on the title page?"

"Not a glimmer." The lid was back on the first tea chest and Bill was removing the cover of the second. "But I've got another L.D. mystery for you. That's next."

He was wearing thin gloves and opening, very carefully, a folder of stained cardboard, tied with a ribbon like a legal brief. When it was untied he laid it on the lid of the third chest.

"I'd rather you didn't touch this at all," he said. "It may be pretty fragile. Let me know whenever you want to see the next sheet. And here's a lens."

They were drawings. One to a sheet, Indian ink on fine white paper, and done with a fine-nibbed pen. And they had nothing whatsoever to do with Charles Babbage, programming manuals, or Analytical Engines. What they did have, so small that first I had to peer, then use the lens, was a tiny, neat 'L.D.' at the upper right-hand corner of each sheet.

They were drawings of animals, the sort of multi-legged, random animals that you find scuttling around in tidal pools, or hidden away in rotting tree bark. Or rather, as I realized when I examined them more closely, the sheets in the folder were drawings of one animal, seen from top, bottom, and all sides.

"Well?" said Bill expectantly.

But I was back to my examination of the tiny artist's mark. "It's not the same, is it. That's a different 'L.D.' from the software manual."

"You're a lot sharper than I am," said Bill. "I had to look fifty times before I saw that. But I agree completely, the 'L' is different, and so is the 'D'. What about the animal?"

"I've never seen anything like it. Beautiful drawings, but I'm no zoologist. You ought to photograph these, and take them to your biology department."

"I did. You don't know Ray Weddle, but he's a top man. He says they have to be just drawings, made up things, because there's nothing like them, and there never has been." He was carefully retying the folder, and placing it back in the chest. "I've got photographs of these with me, too, but I wanted you to see the originals, exactly as I first saw them. We'll come back to these, but meanwhile: next exhibit."

He was into the third tea chest, removing more wrapped pieces of machinery, then a thick layer of straw, and now his hands were trembling. I hated to think how Bill must have sweated and agonized over this, before telling anyone. The urge to publish such a discovery had to be overwhelming; but the fear of being derided as part of the scientific lunatic fringe had to be just as strong.

If what he had produced so far was complex and mystifying, what came next was almost laughably simple—if it were genuine. Bill was lifting, with a good deal of effort, a bar, about six inches by two inches by three. It gleamed hypnotically in the light of the lantern.

"It is, you know," he said, in answer to my shocked expression. "Twenty-four carat gold, solid. There are thirteen more of them."

"But the Trevelyans, and the people who farmed here before that—"

"Never bothered to look. These were stowed at the bottom of a chest, underneath bits of the Analytical Engine and old sacks. I guess nobody ever got past the top layer until I came along." He smiled at me. "Tempted? If I were twenty years younger, I'd take the money and run."

"How much?"

"What's gold worth these days. US currency?"

"God knows. Maybe three hundred and fifty dollars an ounce?"

"You're the calculating boy wonder, not me. So you do the arithmetic. Fourteen bars, each one weighs twenty-five pounds—I'm using avoirdupois, not troy, even though it's gold."

"One point nine six million. Say two million dollars, in round numbers. How long has it been here?"

"Who knows? But since it was *under* the parts of the Analytical Engine, I'd say it's been there as long as the rest."

"And who owns it?"

"If you asked the government, I bet they'd say that they do. If you ask me, it's whoever found it. Me. And now maybe me and thee." He grinned, diabolical in the lantern light. "Ready for the next exhibit?"

I wasn't. "For somebody to bring a fortune in gold here, and just *leave* it. . . ."

Underneath his raincoat, Bill was wearing an old sports jacket and jeans. He owned, to my knowledge, three suits, none less than ten years old. His vices were beer, travel to museums, and about four cigars a year. I could not see him as the Two Million Dollar Man, and I didn't believe he could see himself that way. His next words confirmed it.

"So far as I'm concerned," he said, "this all belongs to the Trevelyans. But I'll have to explain to them that gold may be the least valuable thing here." He was back into the second tea chest, the one that held the drawings, and his hands were trembling again.

"These are what I *really* wanted you to see," he went on, in a husky voice. "I've not had the chance to have them dated yet, but my bet is that they're all genuine. You can touch them, but be gentle."

He was holding three slim volumes, as large as accounting ledgers. Each one was about twenty inches by ten, and bound in a shiny black material like thin sandpapery leather. I took the top one when he held it out, and opened it.

I saw neat tables of numbers, column after column of them. They were definitely not the product of any Analytical Engine, because they were hand-written and had occasional crossings-out and corrections.

I flipped on through the pages. Numbers. Nothing else, no notes, no signature. Dates on each page. They were all in October, 1855. The handwriting was that of the programming manual.

The second book had no dates at all. It was a series of exquisitely detailed machine drawings, with elaborately interlocking cogs and gears. There was writing, in the form of terse explanatory notes and dimensions, but it was in an unfamiliar hand.

"I'll save you the effort," said Bill as I reached for the lens. "These are definitely not by L.D. They are exact copies of some of Babbage's own plans for his calculating engines. I'll show you other reproductions if you like, back in Auckland, but you'll notice that these aren't *photographs*. I don't know what copying process was used. My bet is that all these things were placed here at the same time—whenever that was."

I wouldn't take Bill's word for it. After all, I had come to New Zealand to provide an independent check on his ideas. But five minutes were enough to make me agree, for the moment, with what he was saying.

"I'd like to take this and the other books up to the kitchen," I said, as I handed the second ledger back to him. "I want to have a really good look at them."

"Of course." Bill nodded. "That's exactly what I expected. I told the Trevelyans that we might be here in Little House for up to a week. We can cook for ourselves, or Annie says she'd be more than happy to expect us at mealtimes. I think she likes the company."

I wasn't sure of that. I'm not an elitist, but my own guess was that the conversation between Bill and me in the next few days was likely to be incomprehensible to Annie Trevelyan or almost anyone else.

I held out my hand for the third book. This was all handwritten, without a single drawing. It appeared to be a series of letters, running on one after the other, with the ledger turned sideways to provide a writing area ten inches across and twenty deep. There were no paragraphs within the letters. The writing was beautiful and uniform, by a different hand than had penned the numerical tables of the first book, and an exact half inch space separated the end of one letter from the beginning of the next.

The first was dated 12th October, 1850. It began:

My dear J.G., The native people continue to be as friendly and as kind in nature as one could wish, though they, alas, cling to their paganism. As our ability to understand them increases, we learn that their dispersion is far wider than we at first suspected. I formerly mentioned

*the northern islands, ranging from Taheete to Raratonga.
However, it appears that there has been a southern spread
of the Maori people also, to lands far from here. I wonder
if they may extend their settlements all the way to the great
Southern Continent, explored by James Cook and more
recently by Captain Ross. I am myself contemplating a
journey to a more southerly island, with native assistance.
Truly, a whole life's work is awaiting us. We both feel that,
despite the absence of well-loved friends such as yourself,
Europe and finance is "a world well lost." Louisa has
recovered completely from the ailment that so worried me
two years ago, and I must believe that the main reason
for that improvement is a strengthening of spirit. She has
begun her scientific work again, more productively, I
believe, than ever before. My own efforts in the biological
sciences prove ever more fascinating. When you write again
tell us, I beg you, not of the transitory social or political
events of London, but of the progress of science. It is in
this area that L. and I are most starved of new knowledge.
With affection, and with the assurance that we think of
you and talk of you constantly, L.D.*

The next letter was dated 14 December, 1850. Two
months after the first. Was that time enough for a letter
to reach England, and a reply to return? The initials at
the end were again L.D.

I turned to the back of the volume. The final twenty
pages or so were blank, and in the last few entries the
beautiful regular handwriting had degenerated to a more
hasty scribble. The latest date that I saw was October, 1855.

Bill was watching me intently. "Just the one book of
letters?" I said.

He nodded. "But it doesn't mean they stopped. Only
that we don't have them."

"If they didn't stop, why leave the last pages blank? Let's
go back upstairs. With the books."

I wanted to read every letter, and examine every page.

But if I tried to do it in the chilly crawl space beneath the kitchen, I would have pneumonia before I finished. Already I was beginning to shiver.

"First impressions?" asked Bill, as he set the three ledgers carefully on the table and went back to close the trap-door and replace the coconut matting. "I know you haven't had a chance to read, but I can't wait to hear what you're thinking."

I pulled a couple of the chairs over close to the fireplace. The coal fire was blazing, and the chill was already off the air in the room.

"There are two L.D.'s," I said. "Husband and wife?"

"Agreed. Or maybe brother and sister."

"One of them—the woman—wrote the programming manual for the Analytical Engine. The other one, the man—if it is a man, and we can't be sure of that—did the animal drawings, and he wrote letters. He kept fair copies of what he sent off to Europe, in that third ledger. No sign of the replies, I suppose?"

"You've now seen everything that I've seen." Bill leaned forward and held chilled hands out to the fire. "I knew there were two, from the letters. But I didn't make the division of labor right away, the way you did. I bet you're right, though. Anything else?"

"Give me a chance. I need to read." I took the third book, the one of letters, from the table and returned with it to the fireside. "But they sound like missionaries."

"Missionaries and scientists. The old nineteenth-century mixture." Bill watched me reading for two minutes, then his urge to be up and doing something—or interrupt me with more questions—took over. His desire to talk was burning him up, while at the same time he didn't want to stop me from working.

"I'm going back to Big House," he said abruptly. "Shall I tell Annie we'll be there for a late lunch?"

I thought of the old farmhouse, generation after

generation of life and children. Now there were just the two old folks, and the empty future. I nodded. "If I try to talk about this to them, make me stop."

"I will. If I can. And if I don't start doing it myself." He buttoned his raincoat, and paused in the doorway. "About the gold. I considered telling Jim and Annie when I first found it, because I'm sure that legally they have the best claim to it. But I'd hate their kids to come hurrying home for all the wrong reasons. I'd appreciate your advice on timing. I hate to play God."

"So you want me to. Tell me one thing. What reason could there be for somebody to come down here to South Island in the 1850s, *in secret*, and never tell a soul what they were doing? That's what we are assuming."

"I'm tempted to say, maybe they found pieces of an Analytical Engine, one that had been left untouched here for a century and a half. But that gets a shade too recursive for my taste. And they did say what they were doing. Read the letters."

And then he was gone, and I was sitting in front of the warm fire. I stewed comfortably in wet pants and shoes, and read. Soon the words and the heat carried me away 140 years into the past, working my way systematically through the book's entries.

Most of the letters concerned religious or business matters, and went to friends in England, France, and Ireland. Each person was identified only by initials. It became obvious that the female L.D. had kept her own active correspondence, not recorded in this ledger, and casual references to the spending of large sums of money made Bill's discovery of the gold bars much less surprising. The L.D.'s, whoever they were, had great wealth in Europe. They had not traveled to New Zealand because of financial problems back home.

But not all the correspondence was of mundane matters back in England. Scattered in among the normal chat to friends were the surprises, as sudden and as unpredictable as lightning from a clear sky. The first of them was a short note, dated January, 1851:

Dear J.G., L. has heard via A.v.H. that C.B. despairs of completing his grand design. In his own words, "There is no chance of the machine ever being executed during my own life and I am even doubtful of how to dispose of the drawings after its termination." This is a great tragedy, and L. is beside herself at the possible loss. Can we do anything about this? If it should happen to be no more than a matter of money. . . .

And then, more than two years later, in April, 1853:

Dear J.G., Many thanks for the shipped materials, but apparently there was rough weather on the journey, and inadequate packing, and three of the cylinders arrived with one or more broken teeth. I am enclosing identification for these items. It is possible that repair can be done here, although our few skilled workmen are a far cry from the machinists of Bologna or Paris. However, you would do me a great favor if you could determine whether this shipment was in fact insured, as we requested. Yours etc. L.D.

Cylinders, with toothed gear wheels. It was the first hint of the Analytical Engine, but certainly not the last. I could deduce, from other letters to J.G., that three or four earlier shipments had been made to New Zealand in 1852, although apparently these had all survived the journey in good condition.

In the interests of brevity, L.D. in copying the letters had made numerous abbreviations: w. did service for both "which" and "with," "for" was shortened to f. and so on. Most of the time it did not hinder comprehension at all, and reconstruction of the original was easy, but I cursed when people were reduced to initials. It was impossible to expand those back to discover their identity. A.v.H. was probably the great world traveler and writer, Alexander von Humboldt, whose fingerprint appears all across the natural science of Europe in the first half of the last century; and C.B. ought surely to be Charles Babbage. But who the devil was J.G.? Was it a man, or could it be a woman?

About a third of the way through the book, I learned that this was not just copies of letters sent to Europe. It probably began that way, but at some point L.D. started to use it also as a private diary. So by February, 1854, after a gap of almost four months, I came across this entry:

22 February. Home at last, and thanks be to God that L. did not accompany me, for the seas to the south are more fierce than I ever dreamed, although the natives on the crew make nothing of them. They laugh in the teeth of the gale, and leap from ship to dingy with impunity, in the highest sea. However, the prospect of a similar voyage during the winter months would deter the boldest soul, and defies my own imagination.

L. has made the most remarkable progress in her researches since my departure. She now believes that the design of the great engine is susceptible to considerable improvement, and that it could become capable of much more variation and power than ever A.L. suspected. The latter, dear lady, struggles to escape the grasp of her tyrannical mother, but scarce seems destined to succeed. At her request, L. keeps her silence, and allows no word of her own efforts to be fed back to England. Were this work to become known, however, I feel sure that many throughout Europe would be astounded by such an effort—so ambitious, so noble, and carried through, in its entirety, by a woman!

So the news of Ada Lovelace's tragic death, in 1852, had apparently not been received in New Zealand. I wondered, and read on:

Meanwhile, what of the success of my own efforts? It has been modest at best. We sailed to the island, named

Rormaurma by the natives, which my charts show as Macwherry or Macquarie. It is a great spear of land, fifteen miles long but very narrow, and abundantly supplied with penguins and other seabirds. However, of the "cold-loving people" that the natives had described to me, if I have interpreted their language correctly, there was no sign, nor did we find any of the artifacts, which the natives insist these people are able to make for speech and for motion across the water. It is important that the reason for their veneration of these supposedly "superior men" be understood fully by me, before the way of our Lord can be explained to and accepted by the natives.

On my first time through the book I skimmed the second half of the letter. I was more interested in the "remarkable progress" that L.D. was reporting. It was only later that I went back and pondered that last paragraph for a long time.

The letters offered an irregular and infuriating series of snapshots of the work that Louisa was performing. Apparently she was busy with other things, too, and could only squeeze in research when conscience permitted. But by early 1855, L.D. was able to write, in a letter to the same unknown correspondent:

Dear J.G., It is finished, and it is working and truth to tell, no one is more surprised than I. I imagine you now, shaking your head when you read those words, and I cannot deny what you told me, long ago, that our clever dear is the brains of the family—a thesis I will never again attempt to dispute.

It is finished, and it is working! I was reading that first sentence again, with a shiver in my spine, when the door opened. I looked up in annoyance. Then I realized that the room was chilly, the fire was almost out, and when I glanced at my watch it was almost three o'clock.

It was Bill. "Done reading?" he asked, with an urgency that made me sure he would not like my answer.

"I've got about ten pages to go on the letters. But I haven't even glanced at the tables and the drawings." I stood up, stiffly, and used the tongs to add half a dozen pieces of coal to the fire. "If you want to talk now, I'm game."

The internal struggle was obvious on his face, but after a few seconds he shook his head. "No. It might point you down the same mental path that I took, without either of us trying to do that. We both know how natural it is for us to prompt one another. I'll wait. Let's go on down to Big House. Annie told me to come and get you, and by the time we get there she'll have tea on the table."

My stomach growled at the thought. "What about these?"

"Leave them just where they are. You can pick up where you left off, and everything's safe enough here." But I noticed that after Bill said that, he carefully pulled the fire-guard around the fender, so there was no possibility of stray sparks.

The weather outside had cleared, and the walk down the hill was just what I needed. We were at latitude 46 degrees south, it was close to the middle of winter, and already the Sun was sloping down to the hills in the west. The wind still blew, hard and cold. If I took a beeline south, there was no land between me and the "great Southern Continent" that L.D. had written about. Head east or west, and I would find only open water until I came to Chile and Argentina. No wonder the winds blew so strongly. They had an unbroken run around half the world to pick up speed.

Mrs. Trevelyan's "tea" was a farmer's tea, the main cooked meal of the day. Jim Trevelyan was already sitting, knife and fork in hand, when we arrived. He was a man in his early seventies, but thin, wiry, and alert. His only real sign of age was his deafness, which he handled by leaning forward with his hand cupped around his right ear, while he stared with an intense expression at any speaker.

The main course was squab pie, a thick crusted delicacy made with mutton, onions, apples and cloves. I found it absolutely delicious, and delighted Annie Trevelyan by eating three helpings. Jim Trevelyan served us a homemade dark beer. He said little, but nodded his approval when Bill and I did as well with the drink as with the food.

After the third tankard I was drifting off into a pleasant dream state. I didn't feel like talking, and fortunately I didn't need to. I did my part by imitating Jim Trevelyan, listening to Annie as she told us about Big House and about her family, and nodding at the right places.

When the plates were cleared away she dragged out an old suitcase, full of photographs. She knew every person, and how each was related to each, across four generations. About halfway through the pile she stopped and glanced up self-consciously at me and Bill. "I must be boring you."

"Not a bit," I said. She wasn't, because her enthusiasm for the past was so great. In her own way she was as much a historian as Bill or me.

"Go on, please," added Bill. "It's really very interesting."

"All right." She blushed. "I get carried away, you know. But it's so good to have *youngsters* in the house again."

Bill caught my eye. Youngsters? Us? His grizzled beard, and my receding hairline. But Annie was moving on, backwards into the past. We went all the way to the time of the first Trevelyan, and the building of Big House itself. At the very bottom of the case sat two framed pictures.

"And now you've got me," Annie said, laughing. "I don't know a thing about these two, though they're probably the oldest thing here."

She passed them across the table for our inspection, giving one to each of us. Mine was a painting, not a photograph. It was of a plump man with a full beard and clear grey eyes. He held a church warden pipe in one hand,

and he patted the head of a dog with the other. There was no hint as to who he might be.

Bill had taken the other, and was still staring at it. I held out my hand. Finally, after a long pause, he passed it across.

It was another painting. The man was in half-profile, as though torn between looking at the painter and the woman. He was dark-haired, and wore a long, drooping moustache. She stood by his side, a bouquet of flowers in her hands and her chin slightly lifted in what could have been an expression of resolution or defiance. Her eyes gazed straight out of the picture, into me and through my heart. Across the bottom, just above the frame, were four words in black ink: "Luke and Louisa Derwent."

I could not speak. It was Bill who broke the silence. "How do you come to have these two, if they're not family?"

His voice was gruff and wavering, but Annie did not seem to notice.

"Didn't I ever tell you? The first Trevelyan built Big House, but there were others here before that. They lived in Little House—it was built first, years and years back, I'm not sure when. These pictures have to be from that family, near as I can tell."

Bill turned to glance at me. His mouth was hanging half-open, but at last he managed to close it and say, "Did you— I mean, are there *other* things? Things here, I mean, things that used to be in Little House."

Annie shook her head. "There used to be, but Grandad, Jim's dad, one day not long after we were married he did a big clear out. He didn't bother with the things you've been finding, because none of us ever used the crawl space under the kitchen. And I saved those two because I like pictures. But everything else went."

She must have seen Bill and me subside in our chairs, because she shook her head and said, "Now then, I've been talking my fool head off, and never given you any afters. It's apple pie and cheese."

As she rose from her place and went to the pantry, and Jim Trevelyan followed her out of the kitchen, Bill turned to me. "Can you believe it, I never thought to *ask*? I mean, I did ask Jim Trevelyan about things that used to be in Little House, and he said his father threw everything out but what's there now. But I left it at that. I never asked Annie."

"No harm done. We know now, don't we? Luke Derwent, he's the artist, and Louisa, she's the mathematician and engineer."

"And the programmer—a century before computer programming was supposed to exist." Bill stopped. We were not supposed to be discussing this until I had examined the rest of the materials. But we were saved from more talk by the return of Jim Trevelyan. He was holding a huge book, the size of a small suitcase, with a black embossed cover and brass-bound corners.

"I told you Dad chucked everything," he said. "And he did, near enough, threw it out or burned it. But he were a religious man, and he knew better than to destroy a Bible." He dropped it on the table, with a thump that shook the solid wood. "This comes from Little House. If you want to take a look at it, even take it on back there with you, you're very welcome."

I pulled the book across to me and unhooked the thick metal clasp that held it shut. I knew, from the way that some of the pages did not lie fully closed at their edges, that there must be inserts. The room went silent, as I nervously leafed through to find them.

The disappointment that followed left me as hollow as though I had eaten nothing all day. There were inserts, sure enough: dried wildflowers, gathered long, long ago, and pressed between the pages of the Bible. I examined every one, and riffled through the rest of the book to make sure nothing else lay between the pages. At last I took a deep breath and pushed the Bible away from me.

Bill reached out and pulled it in front of him. "There's one other possibility," he said. "If their family happened to be anything like mine. . . ."

He turned to the very last page of the Bible. The flyleaf was of thick, yellowed paper. On it, in faded multi-colored inks, a careful hand had traced the Derwent family tree.

Apple pie and cheese were forgotten, while Bill and I, with the willing assistance of Jim and Annie Trevelyan, examined every name of the generations shown, and made a more readable copy as we went.

At the time it finally seemed like more disappointment. Not one of us recognized a single name, except for those of Luke and Louisa Derwent, and those we already knew. The one fact added by the family tree was they were half-brother and sister, with a common father. There were no dates, and Luke and Louisa were the last generation shown.

Bill and I admitted that we were at a dead end. Annie served a belated dessert, and after it the two of us wrapped the two pictures in waterproof covers (though it was not raining) and headed back up the hill to Little House, promising Annie that we would certainly be back for breakfast.

We were walking in silence, until halfway up the hill Bill said suddenly, "I'm sorry. I saw it, too, the resemblance to Eileen. I knew it would hit you. But I couldn't do anything about it."

"It was the expression, more than anything," I said. "That tilt to the chin, and the look in her eyes. But it was just coincidence, they're not really alike. That sort of thing is bound to happen."

"Hard on you, though."

"I'm fine."

"Great." Bill's voice showed his relief. "I wasn't going to say anything, but I had to be sure you were all right."

"I'm fine."

Fine, except that no more than a month ago a well-meaning friend of many years had asked me, "Do you think of Eileen as the love of your life?"

And my heart had dropped through a hole in the middle of my chest, and lodged like a cold rock in the pit of my belly.

When we reached Little House I pleaded residual travel fatigue and went straight to bed. With so much of Jim Trevelyan's powerful home-brew inside me, my sleep should have been deep and dreamless. But the dead, once roused, do not lie still so easy.

Images of Eileen and the happy past rose before me, to mingle and merge with the Derwent picture. Even in sleep, I felt a terrible sadness. And the old impotence came back, telling me that I had been unable to change in any way the only event in my life that really mattered.

With my head still half a world away in a different time zone, I woke long before dawn. The fire, well damped by Bill before he went to bed, was still glowing under the ash, and a handful of firewood and more coal was all it needed to bring it back to full life.

Bill was still asleep when I turned on the two oil lamps, pulled the three books within easy reach, and settled down to read. I was determined to be in a position to talk to him by the time we went down to Big House for breakfast, but it was harder than I expected. Yesterday I had been overtired, now I had to go back and reread some of the letters before I was ready to press on.

I had been in the spring of 1855, with some sort of Analytical Engine finished and working. But now, when I was desperate to hear more details, Luke Derwent frustrated me. He vanished for four months from the ledger, and returned at last not to report on Louisa's doings, but brimming over with wonder at his own.

21 September, 1855. Glory to Almighty God, and let me

pray that I never again have doubts. L. and I have wondered, so many times, about our decision to come here. We have never regretted it, but we have asked if it was done for selfish reasons. Now, at last, it is clear that we are fulfilling a higher purpose.

Yesterday I returned from my latest journey to Macquarie Island. They were there! The "cold-loving people," just as my native friends assured me. In truth, they find the weather of the island too warm in all but the southern winter months of May to August, and were almost ready to depart again when our ship made landfall. For they are migrant visitors, and spend the bulk of the year in a more remote location.

The natives term them "people," and I must do the same, for although they do not hold the remotest outward aspect of humans, they are without doubt intelligent. They are able to speak to the natives, with the aid of a box that they carry from place to place. They possess amazing tools, able to fabricate the necessities of life with great speed. According to my native translators, although they have their more permanent base elsewhere in this hemisphere, they come originally from "far, far off." This to the Maori natives means from far across the seas, although I am less sure of this conclusion.

And they have wonderful powers in medical matters. The Maori natives swear that one of their own number, so close to death from gangrenous wounds that death was no more than a day away, was brought to full recovery within hours. Another woman was held, frozen but alive, for a whole winter, until she could be treated and restored to health by the wonderful medical treatment brought from their permanent home by the "cold-loving people" (for whom in truth it is now incumbent upon me to find a better name). I should add that they are friendly, and readily humored me in my desire to make detailed drawings of their form. They asked me through my Maori interpreter *to speak English, and assured me that upon my next visit they would be able to talk to me in my own language.*

All this is fascinating. But it pales to nothing beside the one central question: Do these beings possess immortal souls? We are in no position to make a final decision on such a matter, but L. and I agree that in our actions we must assume that the answer is yes. For if we are in a position to bring to Christ even one of these beings who would otherwise have died unblessed, then it is our clear duty to do so.

It was a digression from the whole subject of the Analytical Engine, one so odd that I sat and stared at the page for a long time. And the next entry, with its great outburst of emotion, seemed to take me even farther afield.

Dear J.G., I have the worst news in the world. How can I tell you this—L.'s old disease is returned, and, alas, much worse than before. She said nothing to me, but yesterday I discovered bright blood on her handkerchief, and such evidence she could not deny. At my insistence she has visited a physician, and the prognosis is desperate indeed. She is amazingly calm about the future, but I cannot remain so sanguine. Pray for her, my dear friend, as I pray constantly.

The letter was dated 25 September, just a few days after his return from his travels. Immediately following, as though Luke could not contain his thoughts, the diary ran on:

Louisa insists what I cannot believe: that her disease is no more than God's just punishment, paid for the sin of both of us. Her calm and courage are beyond belief. She is delighted that I remain well, and she seems resigned to the prospect of her death, as I can never be resigned. But what can I do? What? I cannot sit idly, and watch her slowly decline. Except that it will not be slow. Six months, no more.

His travels among the colony of the "cold-loving people"

were forgotten. The Analytical Engine was of no interest to him. But that brief diary entry told me a great deal. I pulled out the picture of Luke and Louisa Derwent, and was staring at it when Bill emerged rumple-haired from the bedroom.

This time, I was the one desperate to talk. "I know! I know why they came all the way to New Zealand."

He stared, at me and at the picture I was holding. "How can you?"

"We ought to have seen it last night. Remember the family tree in the Bible? It showed they're half-brother and half sister. And *this*." I held the painting out towards him.

He rubbed his eyes, and peered at it. "I saw. What about it?"

"Bill, it's a *wedding picture*. See the bouquet, and the ring on her finger? They couldn't possibly have married back in England, the scandal would have been too great. But here, where nobody knew them, they could make a fresh start and live as man and wife."

He was glancing across to the open ledger, and nodding. "Damn it, you're right. It explains everything. Their sin," he said. You got to that?"

"I was just there."

"Then you're almost at the end. Read the last few pages, then let's head down to Big House for breakfast. We can talk on the way."

He turned and disappeared back into the bedroom. I riffled through the ledger. As he said, I was close to the place where the entries gave way to blank pages.

There was just one more letter, to the same far-off friend. It was dated 6 October, 1855, and it was calm, even clinical.

Dear J.G., L. and I will in a few days be embarking upon a long journey to a distant island, where dwell a certain pagan native people; these are the Heteromorphs (to employ L.'s preferred term for them, since they are very different in appearance from other men, although apparently sharing our rational powers). To these beings we greatly wish to carry the blessings of Our Lord, Jesus Christ. It will be a dangerous voyage. Therefore, if you hear nothing from us within four years, please dispose of our estate according to my earlier instructions. I hope that this is not my last letter to you; however, should that prove to be the case, be assured that we talk of you constantly, and you are always in our thoughts. In the shared love of our savior, L.D.

It was followed by the scribbled personal notes.

I may be able to deceive Louisa, and the world, but I do not deceive myself. God forgive me, when I confess that the conversion of the Heteromorphs is not my main goal. For while the message of Christ might wait until they return to their winter base on Macquarie Island, other matters cannot wait. My poor Louisa. Six months, at most. Already she is weakening, and the hectic blush sits on her cheek. Next May would be too late. I must take Louisa now, and pray that the Maori report of powerful Heteromorph medical skills is not mere fable.

We will carry with us the word of Christ. Louisa is filled with confidence that this is enough for every purpose, while I, rank apostate, am possessed by doubts. Suppose that they remain, rejecting divine truth, a nation of traders? I know exactly what I want from them. But what do I have to offer in return?

Perhaps this is truly a miracle of God's bounty. For I can provide what no man has ever seen before, a marvel for this and every age: Louisa's great Engine, which, in insensate mechanic operation, appears to mimic the thought of rational, breathing beings. This, surely, must be of inestimable value and interest, to any beings, no matter how advanced.

Then came a final entry, the writing of a man in frantic haste.

Louisa has at last completed the transformations of the information that I received from the Heteromorphs. We finally have the precise destination, and leave tomorrow on the morning tide. We are amply provisioned, and our native crew is ready and far more confident than I. Like Rabelais, "Je m'en vais chercher un grand peut-être." God grant that I find it.

I go to seek a "great perhaps." I shivered, stood up and went through to the bedroom, where Bill was pulling on a sweater.

"The Analytical Engine. They took it with them when they left."

"I agree." His expression was a strange blend of satisfaction and frustration. "But now tell me this. *Where did they go?*"

"I can't answer that."

"We have to. Take a look at this." Bill headed past me to the kitchen, his arms still halfway into the sleeves. He picked up the folder of drawings that we had brought from the crawl space. "You've hardly glanced at these, but I've spent as much time on them as on the letters. Here."

He passed me a pen-and-ink drawing that showed one of the creatures seen from the front. There was an abundance of spindly legs—I counted fourteen, plus four thin, whiskery antennae—and what I took to be two pairs of eyes and delicate protruding eyestalks.

Those were the obvious features. What took the closer second look were the little pouches on each side of the body, not part of the animal and apparently strapped in position. Held in four of the legs was a straight object with numbers marked along its length.

"That's a scale bar," said Bill, when I touched a finger to it. "If it's accurate, and I've no reason to think Luke went would have drawn it wrong, his 'Heteromorphs' were about three feet tall."

"And those side pouches are for tools."

"Tools, food, communications equipment—they could be anything. See, now, why I told you I thought for the past couple of weeks I was going mad? To have this hanging in front of me, and have no idea how to handle it."

"That place he mentioned. Macquarie Island?"

"Real enough. About seven hundred miles south and west of here. But I can promise you, there's nothing there relating to this. It's too small, it's been visited too often. Anything like the Heteromorphs would have been reported, over and over. And it's not where Derwent said he was going. He was heading somewhere else, to their more permanent base. Wherever that was." Bill's eyes were gleaming, and his mouth was quivering. He had been living with this for too long, and now he was walking the edge. "What are we going to *do*?"

"We're heading down to Big House, so Annie can feed us. And we're going to talk this through." I took his arm. "Come on."

The cold morning air cut into us as soon as we stepped outside the door. As I had hoped, it braced Bill and brought him down.

"Maybe we've gone as far as we can go," he said, in a quieter voice. "Maybe we ought to go public with everything, and just tell the world what we've found."

"We could. But it wouldn't work."

"Why not?"

"Because when you get right down to it, we haven't found anything. Bill, if it hadn't been you who sent me that letter and package of stuff, do you know what I would have said?"

"Yeah. Here's another damned kook."

"Or a fraud. I realized something else when I was reading those letters. If Jim and Annie Trevelyan had found everything in the crawl space, and shipped it to Christchurch, it would have been plausible. You can tell in a minute they know nothing about Babbage, or computers, or programming. But if you wanted two people who could have engineered a big fat hoax, you'd have to go a long way to find someone better qualified than the two of us. People would say, ah, they're computer nuts, and they're science history nuts, and they planned a fake to fool everybody."

"But we didn't!"

"Who knows that, Bill, other than me and you? We have nothing to *show*. What do we do, stand up and say, oh, yes, there really was an Analytical Engine, but it was taken away to show to these aliens? And unfortunately we don't know where they are, either."

Bill sighed. "Right on. We'd be better off saying it was stolen by fairies."

We had reached Big House. When we went inside, Annie Trevelyan took one look at our faces and said, "Ay, you've had bad news then." And as we sat down at the table and she began to serve hot cakes and sausage. "Well, no matter what it is, remember this: you are both young, and you've got your health. Whatever it is, it's not the end of the world."

It only seemed like it. But I think we realized that Annie Trevelyan was smarter than both of us.

"I'll say it again," said Bill, after a moment or two. "What do we do now?"

"We have breakfast, and then we go back to Little House, and we go over *everything*, together. Maybe we're missing something."

"Yeah. So far, it's a month of my life." But Bill was starting to dig in to a pile of beef sausage, and that was a good sign. He and I are both normally what Annie called "good eaters," and others, less kind, would call gluttons.

She fed us until we refused another morsel of food, then ushered us out. "Go and get on with it," she said cheerfully. "You'll sort it out. I know you will."

It was good to have the confidence of at least one person in the world. Stuffed with food, we trudged back up the hill. I felt good, and optimistic. But I think that was because the materials were so new to me. Bill must have stared at them already until his eyes popped out.

Up at Little House once more, the real work started. We went over the letters and diary again, page by page, date by date, phrase by phrase. Nothing new there, although now that we had seen it once, we could see the evidence again and again of the brother-sister/husband-wife ambivalence.

The drawings came next. The Heteromorphs were so alien in appearance that we were often guessing as to the function of organs or the small objects that on close inspection appeared to be slung around their bodies or held in one of the numerous claws, but at the end of our analysis we had seen nothing to change our opinions, or add to our knowledge.

We were left with one more item: the ledger of tables of numbers, written in the hand of Louisa Derwent. Bill opened it at random and we stared at the page in silence.

"It's dated October, 1855, like all the others," I said at last, "That's when they left."

"Right. And Luke wrote 'Louisa has completed the necessary calculations.' " Bill was scowling down at a list of numbers, accusing it of failing to reveal to us its secrets. "Necessary for what?"

I leaned over his shoulder. There were twenty-odd entries in the table, each a two or three digit number. "Nothing obvious. But it's reasonable to assume that this has something to do with the journey, because of the date. What else would Louisa have been working on in the last few weeks?"

"It doesn't look anything like a navigation guide. But it could be intermediate results. Worksheets." Bill went back to the first page of the ledger, and the first table.

"These could be distances to places they would reach on the way."

"They could. Or they could be times, or weights, or angles, or a hundred other things. Even if they are distances, we have no idea what units they are in. They could be miles, or nautical miles, or kilometers, or anything."

It sounds as though I was offering destructive criticism, but Bill knew better. Each of us had to play devil's advocate, cross-checking the other every step of the way, if we were to avoid sloppy thinking and unwarranted assumptions.

"I'll accept all that," he said calmly. "We may have to try and abandon a dozen hypotheses before we're done. But let's start making them, and see where they lead. There's one main assumption, though, that we'll *have* to make: these tables were somehow used by Luke and Louisa Derwent, to decide how to reach the Heteromorphs. Let's take it from there, and let's not lose sight of the only goal we have: We want to find the location of the Heteromorph base."

He didn't need to spell out to me the implications. If we could find the base, maybe the Analytical Engine would still be there. And I didn't need to spell out to him the other, overwhelming probability: chances were, the Derwents had perished on the journey, and their long-dead bodies lay somewhere on the ocean floor.

We began to work on the tables, proposing and rejecting interpretations for each one. The work was tedious, time-consuming, and full of blind alleys, but we did not consider giving up. From our point of view, progress of sorts was being made as long as we could think of and test new working assumptions. Real failure came only if we ran out of ideas.

We stopped for just two things: sleep, and meals at Big House. I think it was the walk up and down the hill, and the hours spent with Jim and Annie Trevelyan, that kept us relatively sane and balanced.

Five days fled by. We did not have a solution; the

information in the ledger was not enough for that. But we finally, about noon on the sixth day, had a problem.

A *mathematical* problem. We had managed, with a frighteningly long list of assumptions and a great deal of work, to reduce our thoughts and calculations to a very unpleasant-looking nonlinear optimization. If it possessed a global maximum, and could be solved for that maximum, it might yield, at least in principle, the location on Earth whose probability of being a destination for the Derwents was maximized.

Lots of "ifs." But worse than that, having come this far neither Bill nor I could see a systematic approach to finding a solution. Trial-and-error, even with the fastest computer, would take the rest of our lives. We had been hoping that modern computing skills and vastly increased raw computational power could somehow compensate for all the extra information that Louisa Derwent had available to her and we were lacking. So far, the contest wasn't even close.

We finally admitted that, and sat in the kitchen staring at each other.

"Where's the nearest phone?" I asked.

"Dunedin, probably. Why?"

"We've gone as far as we can alone. Now we need expert help."

"I hate to agree with you." Bill stood up. "But I have to. We're out of our depth. We need the best numerical analyst we can find."

"That's who I'm going to call."

"But what will you tell him? What do we tell *anyone*?"

"Bits and pieces. As little as I can get away with." I was pulling on my coat, and picking up the results of our labors. "For the moment, they'll have to trust us."

"They'll have to be as crazy as we are," he said.

The good news was that the people we needed tended to be just that. Bill followed me out.

❖ ❖ ❖

We didn't stop at Dunedin. We went all the way to Christchurch, where Bill could hitch a free ride on the university phone system.

We found a quiet room, and I called Stanford's computer science department. I had an old extension, but I reached the man I wanted after a couple of hops—I was a little surprised at that, because as a peripatetic and sociable bachelor he was as often as not in some other continent.

"Where are you?" Gene said, as soon as he knew who was on the line.

That may sound like an odd opening for a conversation with someone you have not spoken to for a year, but usually when one of us called the other, it meant that we were within dinner-eating distance. Then we would have a meal together, discuss life, death, and mathematics, and go our separate ways oddly comforted.

"I'm in Christchurch. Christchurch, New Zealand."

"Right." There was a barely perceptible pause at the other end of the line, then he said, "Well, you've got my attention. Are you all right?"

"I'm fine. But I need an algorithm." I sketched out the nature of the problem, and after I was finished he said, "It sounds a bit like an under-determined version of the Traveling Salesman problem, where you have incomplete information about the nodes."

"That's pretty much what we decided. We know a number of distances, and we know that some of the locations and the endpoint have to be on land. Also, the land boundaries place other constraints on the paths that can be taken. Trouble is, we've no idea how to solve the whole thing."

"This is really great," Gene said—and meant it. I could almost hear him rubbing his hands at the prospect of a neat new problem. "The way you describe it, it's definitely non-polynomial unless you can provide more information. I don't know how to solve it, either, but I do have ideas. You have to give me *all* the details."

"I was planning to. This was just to get you started thinking. I'll be on a midnight flight out of here, and I'll land at San Francisco about eight in the morning. I can be at your place by eleven-thirty. I'll have the written details."

"That urgent?"

"It feels that way. Maybe you can talk me out of it over dinner."

After I rang off, Bill Rigley gave me a worried shake of his head. "Are you sure you know what you're doing? You'll have to tell him quite a bit."

"Less than you think. Gene will help, I promise." I had just realized what I was doing. I was cashing intellectual chips that I had been collecting for a quarter of a century.

"Come on," I said. "Let's go over everything one more time. Then I have to get out of here."

The final division of labor had been an easy one to perform. Bill had to go back to Little House, and make absolutely sure that we had not missed one scrap of information that might help us. I must head for the United States, and try to crack our computational problem. Bill's preliminary estimate, of 2,000 hours on a Cray-YMP, was not encouraging.

I arrived in San Francisco one hour behind schedule, jet lagged to the gills. But I made up for lost time on the way to Palo Alto, and was sitting in the living room of Gene's house on Constanza by midday.

True to form, he had not waited for my arrival. He had already been in touch with half a dozen people scattered around the United States and Canada, to see if there was anything new and exciting in the problem area we were working. I gave him a restricted version of the story of Louisa Derwent and the vanished Analytical Engine, omitting all suggestion of aliens, and then showed him my copy of our analyses and the raw data from which we had drawn it. While he started work on that, I borrowed his telephone and wearily tackled the next phase.

Gene would give us an algorithm, I was sure of that, and it would be the best that today's numerical analysis could provide. But even with that best, I was convinced that we would face a most formidable computational problem.

I did not wait to learn just how formidable. Assuming that Bill and I were right, there would be other certainties. We would need a digital data base of the whole world, or at least the southern hemisphere, with the land/sea boundaries defined. This time my phone call gave a less satisfactory answer. The Defense Mapping Agency might have what I needed, but it was almost certainly not generally available. My friend (with a guarantee of anonymity) promised to do some digging, and either finagle me a loaner data set or point me to the best commercial sources.

I had one more call to make, to Marvin Minsky at the MIT Media Lab. I looked at the clock as I dialed. One forty-five. On the East Coast it was approaching quitting time for the day. Personally, I felt long past quitting time.

I was lucky again. He came to the phone sounding slightly surprised. We knew each other, but not all that well—not the way that I knew Bill, or Gene.

"Do you still have a good working relationship with Thinking Machines Corporation?" I asked.

"Yes." If a declarative word can also be a question, that was it.

"And Danny Hillis is still chief scientist, right?"

"He is."

"Good. Do you remember in Pasadena a few years ago you introduced us?"

"At the Voyager Neptune flyby. I remember it very well." Now his voice sounded more and more puzzled. No wonder. I was tired beyond belief, and struggling to stop my thoughts spinning off into non-sequiturs.

"I think I'm going to need a couple of hundred hours of time," I said, "on the fastest Connection Machine there is."

"You're talking to the wrong person."

"I may need some high priority access." I continued as though I had not heard him. "Do you have a few minutes while I tell you why I need it?"

"It's your nickel." Now the voice sounded a little bit skeptical, but I could tell he was intrigued.

"This has to be done in person. Maybe tomorrow morning?"

"Friday? Hold on a moment."

"Anywhere you like," I said, while a muttered conversation took place at the other end of the line. "It won't take long. Did you say tomorrow is *Friday*?"

I seemed to have lost a day somewhere. But that didn't matter. By tomorrow afternoon I would be ready and able to sleep for the whole weekend.

Everything had been rushing along, faster and faster, towards an inevitable conclusion. And at that point, just where Bill and I wanted the speed to be at a maximum, events slowed to a crawl.

In retrospect, the change of pace was only in our minds. By any normal standards, progress was spectacularly fast.

For example, Gene produced an algorithm in less than a week. He still wanted to do final polishing, especially to make it optimal for parallel processing, but there was no point in waiting before programming began. Bill had by this time flown in from New Zealand, and we were both up in Massachusetts. In ten days we had a working program and the geographic data base was on-line.

Our first Connection Machine run was performed that same evening. It was a success, if by "success" you mean that it did not bomb. But it failed to produce a well-defined maximum of any kind.

So then the tedious time began. The input parameters that we judged to be uncertain had to be run over their full permitted ranges, in every possible variation. Naturally, we had set up the program to perform that parametric variation automatically, and to proceed to the next case whenever the form of solution was not satisfactory. And just as naturally, we could hardly bear to leave the computer. We wanted to see the results of each run, to be there when—or if—the result we wanted finally popped out.

For four whole days, nothing emerged that was even encouraging. Any computed maxima were hopelessly broad and unacceptably poorly-defined.

We went on haunting the machine room, disappearing only for naps and hurried meals. It resembled the time of our youth, when hands-on program debugging was the only sort known. In the late night hours I felt a strange confluence of computer generations. Here we were, working as we had worked many years ago, but now we were employing today's most advanced machine in a strange quest for its own earliest ancestor.

We must have been a terrible nuisance to the operators, as we brooded over input and fretted over output, but no one said an unkind word. They must have sensed, from vague rumors, or from the more direct evidence of our behavior, that something very important to us was involved in these computations. They encouraged us to eat and rest; and it seemed almost inevitable that when at last the result that Bill and I had been waiting for so long emerged from the electronic blizzard of activity within the Connection Machine, neither of us would be there to see it.

The call came at eight-thirty in the morning. We had left an hour earlier, and were eating a weary breakfast in the Royal Sonesta motel, not far from the installation.

"I have something I think you should see," said the

hesitant voice of the shift operator. He had watched us sit dejected over a thousand outputs, and he was reluctant now to raise our hopes. "One of the runs shows a sharp peak. Really narrow and tight."

They had deduced what we were looking for. "We're on our way," said Bill. Breakfast was left half-eaten—a rare event for either of us—and in the car neither of us could think of anything to say.

The run results were everything that the operator had suggested. The two-dimensional probability density function was a set of beautiful concentric ellipses, surrounding a single land location. We could have checked coordinates with the geographic data base, but we were in too much of a hurry. Bill had lugged a Times atlas with him all the way from Auckland, and parked it in the computer room. Now he riffled through it, seeking the latitude and longitude defined by the run output.

"My God!" he said after a few seconds. "It's South Georgia."

After my first bizarre reaction—South Georgia! How could the Derwents have undertaken a journey to so preposterous a destination, in the southeastern United States?—I saw where Bill's finger lay.

South Georgia *Island*. I had hardly heard of it, but it was a lonely smear of land in the far south of the Atlantic Ocean.

Bill, of course, knew a good deal about the place. I have noticed this odd fact before, people who live south of the equator seem to know far more about the geography of their hemisphere than we do about ours. Bill's explanation, that there is a lot less southern land to know about, is true but not completely convincing.

It did not matter, however, because within forty-eight hours I too knew almost all there was to know about South Georgia. It was not very much. The Holy Grail that Bill and I had been seeking so hard was a desolate island, about a hundred miles long and twenty miles wide. The highest mountains were substantial, rising almost to ten thousand feet, and their fall to the sea was a dreadful chaos of rocks and glaciers. It would not be fair to say that the interior held nothing of interest, because no one had ever bothered to explore it.

South Georgia had enjoyed its brief moment of glory at the end of the last century, when it had been a base for Antarctic whalers, and even then only the coastal area had been inhabited. In 1916, Shackleton and a handful of his men made a desperate and successful crossing of the island's mountains, to obtain help for the rest of his stranded trans-Antarctic expedition. The next interior crossing was not until 1955, by a British survey team.

That is the end of South Georgia history. Whaling was the only industry. With its decline, the towns of Husvik and Grytviken dwindled and died. The island returned to its former role, as an outpost beyond civilization.

None of these facts was the reason, though, for Bill Rigley's shocked "My God!" when his finger came to rest on South Georgia. He was amazed by the location. The island lies in the Atlantic ocean, at 54 degrees south. It is six thousand miles away from New Zealand, or from the Heteromorph winter outpost on Macquarie Island.

And those are no ordinary six thousand miles, of mild winds and easy trade routes.

"Look at the choice Derwent had to make," said Bill. "Either he went *west*, south of Africa and the Cape of Good Hope. That's the long way, nine or ten thousand miles, and all the way against the prevailing winds. Or he could sail *east*. That way would be shorter, maybe six thousand miles, and mostly with the winds. But he would have to go across the South Pacific, and then through the Drake Passage between Cape Horn and the Antarctic Peninsula."

His words meant more to me after I had done some reading. The southern seas of the Roaring Forties cause no shivers today, but a hundred years ago they were a legend to all sailing men, a region of cruel storms, monstrous waves, and deadly winds. They were worst of all in the Drake Passage, but that wild easterly route had been Luke Derwent's choice. It was quicker, and he was a man for whom time was running out.

While I did my reading, Bill was making travel plans. Were we going to South Georgia? Of course we were, although any rational process in my brain told me, more strongly than ever, that we would find nothing there. Luke and Louisa Derwent never reached the island. They had died, as so many others had died, in attempting that terrible southern passage below Cape Horn.

There was surely nothing to be found. We knew that. But still we drained our savings, and Bill completed our travel plans. We would fly to Buenos Aires, then on to the Falkland Islands. After that came the final eight hundred miles to South Georgia, by boat, carrying the tiny two-person survey aircraft whose final assembly must be done on the island itself.

Already we knew the terrain of South Georgia as well as anyone had ever known it. I had ordered a couple of SPOT satellite images of the island, good cloud-free pictures with ten-meter resolution. I went over them again and again, marking anomalies that we wanted to investigate.

Bill did the same. But at that point, oddly enough, our individual agendas diverged. His objective was the Analytical Engine, which had dominated his life for the past few months. He had written out, in full, the sequence of events that led to his discoveries in New Zealand, and to our activities afterwards. He described the location and nature of all the materials at Little House. He sent copies of everything, dated, signed, and sealed, to the library of his own university, to the British Museum, to the Library of Congress, and to the Reed Collection of rare books and manuscripts in the Dunedin Public Library. The discovery of the Analytical Engine—or of any part of it—somewhere on South Georgia Island would validate and render undeniable everything in the written record.

And I? I wanted to find evidence of Louisa Derwent's Analytical Engine, and even more so of the Heteromorphs. But beyond that, my thoughts turned again and again to Luke Derwent, in his search for the "great perhaps."

He had told Louisa that their journey was undertaken to bring Christianity to the cold-loving people; but I knew better. Deep in his heart he had another, more selfish motive. He cared less about the conversion of the Heteromorphs than about access to their great medical powers. Why else would he carry with him, for trading purposes, Louisa's wondrous construct, the "marvel for this and every age"—a clanking mechanical computer, to beings who possessed machines small and powerful enough to serve as portable language translators.

I understood Luke Derwent completely, in those final days before he sailed east. The love of his life was dying, and he was desperate. Would he, for a chance to save her, have risked death on the wild southern ocean? Would he have sacrificed himself, his whole crew, and his own immortal soul, for the one-in-a-thousand chance of restoring her to health? Would anyone take such a risk?

I can answer that. Anyone would take the risk, and count himself blessed by the gods to be given the opportunity.

I want to find the Analytical Engine on South Georgia, and I want to find the Heteromorphs. But more than either of those, I want to find evidence that Luke Derwent succeeded, in his final, reckless gamble. I want him to have beaten the odds. I want to find Louisa Derwent, frozen but alive in the still glaciers of the island, awaiting her resurrection and restoration to health.

I have a chance to test the kindness of reality. For in just two days, Bill and I fly south and seek our evidence, our own "great perhaps." Then I will know.

But now, at the last moment, when we are all prepared, events have taken a more complex turn. And I am not sure if what is happening will help us, or hinder us.

Back in Christchurch, Bill had worried about what I would tell people when we looked for help in the States. I told him that I would say as little as we could get away with, and I kept my word. No one was given more than a small part of the whole story, and the main groups involved were separated by the width of the continent.

But we were dealing with some of the world's smartest people. And today, physical distance means nothing. People talk constantly across the computer nets. Somewhere, in the swirling depths of GEnie, or across the invisible web of an Ethernet, a critical connection was made. And then the inevitable crosstalk began.

Bill learned of this almost by accident, discussing with a travel agent the flights to Buenos Aires. Since then I have followed it systematically.

We are not the only people heading for South Georgia Island. I know of at least three other groups, and I will bet that there are more.

Half the MIT Artificial Intelligence lab seems to be flying south. So is a substantial fraction of the Stanford Computer Science Department, with additions from Lawrence Berkeley and Lawrence Livermore. And from southern California, predictably, comes an active group centered on Los Angeles. Niven, Pournelle, Forward, Benford and Brin cannot be reached. A number of JPL staff members are mysteriously missing. Certain other scientists and writers from all over the country do not return telephone calls.

What are they all doing? It is not difficult to guess. We are talking about individuals with endless curiosity, and lots of disposable income. Knowing their style, I would not be surprised if the *Queen Mary* were refurbished in her home at Long Beach, and headed south.

Except that they, like everyone else, will be in a hurry,

and go by air. No one wants to miss the party. These are the people, remember, who did not hesitate to fly to Pasadena for the *Voyager* close flybys of the outer planets, or to Hawaii and Mexico to see a total solar eclipse. Can you imagine them missing a chance to be in on the discovery of the century, of any century? Not only to *observe* it, but maybe to become part the discovery process itself. They will converge on South Georgia in their dozens—their scores—their hundreds, with their powerful laptop computers and GPS terminals and their private planes and advanced sensing equipment.

Logic must tell them, as it tells me, that we will find absolutely nothing. Luke and Louisa Derwent are a century dead, deep beneath the icy waters of the Drake Passage. With them, if the machine ever existed, lie the rusting remnants of Louisa's Analytical Engine. The Heteromorphs, if they were ever on South Georgia Island, are long gone.

I know all that. So does Bill. But win or lose, Bill and I are going. So are all the others.

And win or lose, I know one other thing. After we, and our converging, energetic, curious, ingenious, sympathetic horde, are finished, South Georgia will never be the same.

This is for Garry Tee—who is a professor of Computer Science at the University of Auckland;

—who is a mathematician, computer specialist, and historian of science;

—who discovered parts of Babbage's Difference Machine in Dunedin, New Zealand;

—who programmed the DEUCE computer in the late 1950s, and has been a colleague and friend since that time;

—who is no more Bill Rigley than I am the narrator of this story.

Charles Sheffield
December 31, 1991

Few historians have ever written speculative fiction. There seems a natural contradiction between the precise inspection of the past and the colorful, evocative envisioning of the future.

There are notable exceptions, of course: the entire subgenre of alternate history, which flows forward from the early nineteenth century. This method of inspecting the currents of history has produced such masterworks as L. Sprague DeCamp's Lest Darkness Fall *and Ward Moore's* Bring the Jubilee. *To tinker with history and test one's ideas is enticing; I edited a series of books of alternate history, including four volumes of* What Might Have Been *and* Hitler Victorious; *the subject is endlessly attractive.*

But we were earnest amateurs; Harry Turtledove is the real thing, with a Ph.D. in Byzantine history; indeed, I believe him to be the first historian to become a professional practitioner of the organized imagination known as speculative fiction. After years of slaving in the bowels of the Los Angeles city government (a labyrinth powerfully recalling ancient Byzantium), Harry had the pure courage to set off on a career as a free-lance writer, something I have simply never been brave enough to try.

His story here shows off his best facets: meticulous research, incisive imagination and storytelling drive.

Down In The Bottomlands
by Harry Turtledove

A double handful of tourists climbed down from the omnibus, chattering with excitement. From under the long brim of his cap, Radnal vez Krobir looked them over, comparing them with previous groups he'd led through Trench Park. About average, he decided: an old man spending money before he died; younger folks searching for adventure in an over-civilized world; a few who didn't fit into all obvious category and might be artists, writers, researchers, or anything else under the sun.

He looked over the women in the tour group with a different sort of curiosity. He was in the process of buying a bride from her father, but he hadn't done it; legally and morally, he remained a free agent. Some of the women were worth looking over, too: a couple of tall, slim, dark Highheads from the eastern lands who stuck by each other, and another of Radnal's own Strongbrow race —shorter, stockier, fairer, with deep-set light eyes under heavy brow ridges.

One of the Highhead girls gave him a dazzling smile. He smiled back as he walked toward the group, his wool robes flapping around him. "Hello, friends," he called. "Do you all understand Tarteshan? Ah, good."

Cameras clicked as he spoke. He was used to that; people from every tour group wasted pictures on him,

419

though he wasn't what they'd come to see. He went into his usual welcoming speech: "On behalf of the Hereditary Tyranny of Tartesh and the staff of Trench Park, I'm pleased to welcome you here today. If you haven't read my button, or if you just speak Tarteshan but don't know our syllabary, my name is Radnal vez Krobir. I'm a field biologist with the park, doing a two-year stretch of guide duty."

"Stretch?" said the woman who'd smiled at him. "You make it sound like a sentence in the mines."

"I don't mean it like that—quite." He grinned his most disarming grin. Most of the tourists grinned back. A few stayed sober-faced, likely the ones who suspected the gibe was real and the grin put on. There was some truth in that. He knew it, but the tourists weren't supposed to.

He went on, "In a bit, I'll take you over to the donkeys for the trip down into the Trench itself. As you know, we try to keep our mechanical civilization out of the park so we can show you what all the Bottomlands were like not so long ago. You needn't worry. The donkeys are very surefooted. We haven't lost one—or even a tourist—in years."

This time, some of the chuckles that came back were nervous. Probably only a couple of this lot had ever done anything so archaic as getting on the back of an animal. Too bad for the ones just thinking about that now. The rules were clearly stated. The pretty Highhead girls looked particularly upset. The placid donkeys worried them more than the wild beasts of the Trench.

"Let's put off the evil moment as long as we can," Radnal said. "Come under the colonnade for half a daytenth or so and we'll talk about what makes Trench Park unique."

The tour group followed him into the shade. Several people sighed in relief. Radnal had to work to keep his face straight. The Tarteshan sun was warm, but if they had trouble here, they'd cook down in the Trench. That was their lookout. If they got heat-stroke, he'd set them right again. He'd done it before.

He pointed to the first illuminated map. "Twenty million years ago, as you'll see, the Bottomlands didn't exist. A long stretch of sea separated what's now the southwest section of the Great Continent from the rest. Notice that what were then two lands masses first joined in the east, and a land bridge rose here." He pointed again, this time more precisely. "This sea, now a long arm of the Western Ocean, remained."

He walked over to the next map, drawing the tourists with him. "Things stayed like that until about six and a half million years ago. Then, as that southwest section of the Great Continent kept drifting northward, a new range gradually pushed up here, at the western outlet of that inland sea. When it was cut off from the Western Ocean, it began to dry up: it lost more water by evaporation than flowed into it from its rivers. Now if you'll come along. . . ."

The third map had several overlays, in different shades of blue. "The sea took about a thousand years to turn into the Bottomlands. It refilled from the Western Ocean several times, too, as tectonic forces lowered the Barrier Mountains. But for about the last five and a half million years, the Bottomlands have had about the form we know today."

The last map showed the picture familiar to any child studying geography: the trench of the Bottomlands furrowing across the Great Continent like a surgical scar, requiring colors needed nowhere else on the globe to show relief.

Radnal led the tourists out to the donkey corral. The shaggy animals were already bridled and saddled. Radnal explained how to mount, demonstrated, and waited for the tourists to mess it up. Sure enough, both Highhead girls put the wrong foot in the stirrup.

"No, like this," he said, demonstrating again. "Use your left foot, then swing over."

The girl who had smiled at him succeeded on the second try. The other balked. "Help me," she said. Breathing out through his beaky nose in lieu of sighing, Radnal put his hands on her waist and all but lifted her into the saddle as she mounted. She giggled. "You're so strong. He's so strong, Evillia." The other Highhead girl—presumably Evillia—giggled too.

Radnal breathed out again, harder. Tarteshans and other folk of Strongbrow race who lived north of the Bottomlands, and down in them, *were* stronger than most Highheads, but generally weren't as agile. So what, either way?

He went back to work: "Now that we've learned to mount our donkeys, we're going to learn to dismount." The tourists groaned, but Radnal was inexorable. "You still have to carry your supplies from the omnibus and stow them in the saddlebags. I'm your guide, not your servant." The Tarteshan words carried overtones of *I'm your equal, not your slave*.

Most of the tourists dismounted, but Evillia stayed up on her donkey. Radnal strode over to her; even his patience was fraying. "This way." He guided her through the necessary motions.

"Thank you, freeman vez Krobir," she said in surprisingly fluent Tarteshan. She turned to her friend. "You're right, Lofosa; he *is* strong."

Radnal felt his ears grow hot under their coat of down. A brown-skinned Highhead from south of the Bottomlands rocked his hips back and forth and said, "I'm jealous of you." Several tourists laughed.

"Let's get on with it," Radnal said. "The sooner we get the donkeys loaded, the sooner we can begin and the more we'll see." That line never failed; you didn't become a tourist unless you wanted to see as much as you could. As if on cue, the driver brought the omnibus around to the corral. The baggage doors opened with a hiss of compressed air. The driver started chucking luggage out of the bins.

"You shouldn't have any problems," Radnal said. Everyone's gear had been weighed and measured beforehand, to make sure the donkeys wouldn't have to bear anything too bulky or heavy. Most people easily shifted their belongings to the saddlebags. The two Highhead girls, though, had a night demon of a time making everything fit. He thought about helping them, but decided not to. If they had to pay a penalty for making the supply donkeys carry some of their stuff, it was their own fault.

They did get everything in, though their saddlebags bulged like a snake that had just swallowed a half-grown humpless camel. A couple of other people stood around helplessly, with full bags and gear left over. Smiling a smile he hoped was not too predatory, Radnal took them to the scales and collected a tenth of a unit of silver for every unit of excess weight.

"This is an outrage," the dark brown Highhead man said. "Do you know who I am? I am Moblay Sopsirk's son, aide to the Prince of Lissonland." He drew himself up to his full height, almost a Tarteshan cubit more than Radnal's.

"Then you can afford the four and three-tenths," Radnal answered. "I don't keep the silver. It all goes to upkeep for the park."

Grumbling still, Moblay paid. Then he stomped off and swung aboard his animal with more grace than Radnal had noticed him possessing. Down in Lissonland, the guide remembered, important people sometimes rode stripehorses for show. He didn't understand that. He had no interest in getting onto a donkey when he wasn't going down into Trench Park. As long as there were better ways of doing things, why not use them?

Also guilty of overweight baggage were a middle-aged Tarteshan couple. They were overweight themselves, too, but Radnal couldn't do anything about that. Eltsac vez

Martois protested, "The scale at home said we were all right."

"If you read it right," Nocso zev Martois said to her husband. "You probably didn't."

"Whose side are you on?" he snarled. She screeched at him. Radnal waited till they ran down, then collected the silver due the park.

When the tourists had remounted their donkeys, the guide walked over to the gate on the far side of the corral, swung it open, and replaced the key in a pouch he wore belted round his waist under his robe. As he went back to his own animal, he said, "When you ride through there, you enter the park itself, and the waivers you signed come into play. Under Tarteshan law, park guides have the authority of military officers within the park. I don't intend to exercise it any more than I have to; we should get along just fine with simple common sense. But I am required to remind you the authority is there." He also kept a repeating handcannon in one of his donkey's saddlebags, but didn't mention that.

"Please stay behind me and try to stay on the trail," he said. "It won't be too steep today; we'll camp tonight at what was the edge of the continental shelf. Tomorrow we'll descend to the bottom of the ancient sea, as far below mean sea level as a medium-sized mountain is above it. That will be more rugged terrain."

The Strongbrow woman said, "It will be hot, too, much hotter than it is now. I visited the park three or four years ago, and it felt like a furnace. Be warned, everyone."

"You're right, freelady, ah—" Radnal said.

"I'm Toglo zev Pamdal." She added hastily, "Only a distant collateral relation, I assure you."

"As you say, freelady." Radnal had trouble keeping his voice steady. The Hereditary Tyrant of Tartesh was Bortav vez Pamdal. Even his distant collateral relations needed to be treated with sandskink gloves. Radnal was glad Toglo had had the courtesy to warn him who she was—or rather, who her distant collateral relation was. At least she didn't seem the sort who would snoop around and take bad reports on people back to the friends she undoubtedly had in high places.

Although the country through which the donkeys ambled was below sea level, it wasn't very far below. It didn't seem much different from the land over which the tourists' omnibus had traveled to reach the edge of Trench Park: dry and scrubby, with thorn bushes and palm trees like long-handled feather dusters.

Radnal let the terrain speak for itself, though he did remark, "Dig a couple of hundred cubits under the soil hereabouts and you'll find a layer of salt, same as you would anywhere in the Bottomlands. It's not too thick here on the shelf, because this area dried up quickly, but it's here. That's one of the first clues geologists had that the Bottomlands used to be a sea, and one of the ways they map the boundaries of the ancient water."

Moblay Sopsirk's son wiped his sweaty face with a forearm. Where Radnal, like any Tarteshan, covered up against the heat, Moblay wore only a hat, shoes, and a pocketed belt to carry silver, perhaps a small knife or toothpick, and whatever else he thought he couldn't do without. He was dark enough that he didn't need to worry about skin cancer, but he didn't look very comfortable, either.

He said, "Were some of that water back in the Bottomlands, Radnal, Tartesh would have a better climate."

"You're right," Radnal said; he was resigned to foreigners using his familial name with uncouth familiarity. "We'd be several hundredths cooler in summer and warmer in winter. But if the Barrier Mountains fell again, we'd lose the great area that the Bottomlands encompass and the mineral wealth we derive from them: salt, other chemicals left by evaporation, and the petroleum reserves that wouldn't be accessible through deep water. Tarteshans have grown used to heat over the centuries. We don't mind it."

"I wouldn't go that far," Toglo said. "I don't think it's an accident that Tarteshan air coolers are sold all over the world."

Radnal found himself nodding "You have a point, freelady. What we get from the Bottomlands, though, outweighs fuss over the weather."

As he'd hoped, they got to the campsite with the sun still in the sky, and watched it sink behind the mountains to the west. The tourists gratefully descended from their donkeys and stumped about, complaining of how sore their thighs were. Radnal set them to carrying lumber from the metal racks that lined one side of the site.

He lit the cook fires with squirts from a squeeze bottle of starter fuel and a flint-and-steel lighter. "The lazy man's way," he admitted cheerfully. As with his skill on a donkey, that he could start a fire at all impressed the tourists. He went back to the donkeys, and dug out ration packs which he tossed into the flames. When their tops popped and began to vent steam, he fished them out with a long-handled fork.

"Here we are," he said. "Peel off the foil and you have Tarteshan food—not a banquet fit for the gods, perhaps, but plenty to keep you from starving and meeting them before your time."

Evillia read the inscription on the side of her pack. "These are military rations," she said suspiciously. Several people groaned.

Like any other Tarteshan freeman, Radnal had done his required two years in the Hereditary Tyrant's Volunteer Guard. He came to the ration packs' defense: "Like I said, they'll keep you from starving."

The packs—mutton and barley stew, with carrots, onions, and a heavy dose of ground pepper and garlic—weren't too bad. The two Martoisi inhaled theirs and asked for more.

"I'm sorry," Radnal said. "The donkeys carry only so many. If I give you another pack each, someone will go hungry before we reach the lodge."

"We're hungry now," Nocso zev Martois said.

"That's right," Eltsac echoed. They stared at each other, perhaps surprised at agreeing.

"I'm sorry," Radnal said again. He'd never had anyone ask for seconds before. Thinking that, he glanced over to see how Toglo zev Pamdal was faring with such basic fare. As his eyes flicked her way, she crumpled her empty pack and got up to throw it in a refuse bin.

She had a lithe walk, though he could tell little of the shape of her body because of her robes. As young—or even not so young—men will, he wandered into fantasy. Suppose he were dickering with *her* father over bride price instead of with Markaf vez Putun, who acted as if his daughter Wello shat silver and pissed petrol . . . .

He had enough sense to recognize when he was being foolish, which is more than the gods grant most. Toglo's father undoubtedly could make a thousand better matches for her than a none-too-special biologist. Confrontation with brute fact didn't stop him from musing, but did keep him from taking himself too seriously.

He smiled as he pulled sleepsacks out of one of the pack donkeys' panniers. The tourists took turns with a foot pump to inflate them. With the weather so warm, a good many tourists chose to lie on top of the sleepsacks rather than crawl into them. Some kept on the clothes they'd been wearing, some had special sleep clothes, and some didn't bother with clothes. Tartesh had a moderately strong nudity taboo; not enough to give Radnal the horrors at naked flesh, but plenty to make him eye Evillia and Lofosa as they carelessly shed shirts and trousers. They were young, attractive, and even well-muscled for Highheads. They seemed more naked to him because their bodies were less hairy than those of Strongbrows.

He was relieved his robe hid his full response to them.

Speaking to the group, he said, "Get as much sleep as you can tonight. Don't stay up gabbing. We'll be in the saddle most of the day tomorrow, on worse terrain than we saw today. You'll do better if you're rested."

"Yes, clanfather," Moblay Sopsirk's son said, as a youngster might to the leader of his kith grouping—but any youngster who sounded as sassy as Moblay would get the back of his clanfather's hand across his mouth to remind him not to sound that way again.

But, since Radnal had spoken good sense, most of the tourists did try to go to sleep. They did not know the wilds but, with the possible exception of the Martoisi, they were not fools: few fools accumulated enough silver for an excursion to Trench Park. As he usually did the first night with a new group, Radnal disregarded his own advice. He was good at going without sleep and, being familiar with what lay ahead, would waste no energy on the trip down to the Trench itself.

An owl hooted from a hole in a palm trunk. The air smelled faintly spicy. Sage and lavender, oleander, laurel, thyme—many local plants had leaves that secreted aromatic oils. Their coatings reduced water loss—always of vital importance here—and made the leaves unpalatable to insects and animals.

The fading campfires drew moths. Every so often, their glow would briefly light up other, larger shapes: bats and nightjars swooping down to take advantage of the feast set out before them. The tourists took no notice of insects or predators. Their snores rang louder than the owl's cries. After a few trips as tour guide, Radnal was convinced practically everyone snored. He supposed he did, too, though he'd never heard himself do it.

He yawned, lay back on his own sleepsack with hands clasped behind his head, and looked up at the stars, displayed as if on black velvet. There were so many more of them here than in the lights of the big city: yet another reason to work in Trench Park. He watched them slowly whirl overhead; he'd never found a better way to empty his mind and drift toward sleep.

His eyelids were getting heavy when someone rose from his—no, her—sleepsack: Evillia, on her way to the privy shed behind some bushes. His eyes opened wider; in the dim firelight, she looked like a moving statue of polished bronze. As soon as her back was to him, he ran his tongue over his lips.

But instead of getting back into her sack when she returned, Evillia squatted by Lofosa's. Both Highhead girls laughed softly. A moment later, they both climbed to their feet and headed Radnal's way. Lust turned to alarm—what were they doing?

They knelt down, one on either side of him. Lofosa whispered, "We think you're a fine chunk of man."

Evillia set a hand on the tie of his robe, and began to undo it.

"*Both* of you?" he blurted. Lust returned, impossible to disguise since he lay on his back. Incredulity came with it. Tarteshan women—even Tarteshan tarts—weren't so brazen (he thought how Evillia had reminded him of smoothly moving bronze); nor were Tarteshan men. Not that Tarteshan men didn't enjoy lewd imaginings, but they usually kept quiet about them.

The Highhead girls shook with more quiet laughter, as if his reserve were the funniest thing imaginable. "Why not?" Evillia said. "Three can do lots of interesting things two can't."

"But—" Radnal waved to the rest of the tour group. "What if they wake up?"

The girls laughed harder; their flesh shifted more alluringly. Lofosa answered, "They'll learn something."

Radnal learned quite a few things. One was that, being on the far side of thirty, his nights of keeping more than

one woman happy were behind him, though he enjoyed
trying. Another was that, what with sensual distractions,
trying to make two women happy at once was harder
than patting his head with one hand and rubbing his
stomach with the other. Still another was that neither
Lofosa nor Evillia carried an inhibition anywhere about
her person.

He felt himself flagging, knew he'd be limp in more ways
than one come morning. "Shall we have mercy on him?"
Evillia asked—in Tarteshan, so he could understand her
teasing.

"I suppose so," Lofosa said. "This time." She twisted
like a snake, brushed her lips against Radnal's. "Sleep well,
freeman." She and Evillia went back to their sleepsacks,
leaving him to wonder if he'd dreamed they were with him
but too worn to believe it.

This time, his drift toward sleep was more like a dive.
But before he yielded, he saw Toglo zev Pamdal come back
from the privy. For a moment, that meant nothing But
if she was coming back now, she must have gone before,
when he was too occupied to notice . . . which meant she
must have seen him so occupied.

He hissed like an ocellated lizard, though green wasn't
the color he was turning. Toglo got back into her sleepsack
without looking either at him or the two Highhead girls.
Whatever fantasies he'd had about her shriveled. The best
he could hope for come morning was the cool politeness
someone of prominence gives an underling of imperfect
manners. The worst . . .

What if she starts screaming to the group? he wondered.
He supposed he could grit his teeth and carry on. *But what
if she complains about me to the Hereditary Tyrant?* He
didn't like the answers he came up with; *I'll lose my job*
was the first that sprang to mind, and they went downhill
from there.

He wondered why Moblay Sopsirk's son couldn't have

got up to empty his bladder. Moblay would have been envious and admiring, not disgusted as Toglo surely was.

Radnal hissed again. Since he couldn't do anything about what he'd already done, he tried telling himself he would have to muddle along and deal with whatever sprang from it. He repeated that to himself several times. It didn't keep him from staying awake most of the night, no matter how tired he was.

The sun woke the tour guide. He heard some of the group already up and stirring. Though still sandy-eyed and clumsy with sleep, he made himself scramble out of his sack. He'd intended to get moving first, as he usually did, but the previous night's exertion and worry overcame the best of intentions.

To cover what he saw as a failing, he tried to move twice as fast as usual, which meant he kept making small, annoying mistakes: tripping over a stone and almost falling, calling the privy the campfire and the campfire the privy, going to a donkey that carried only fodder when he wanted breakfast packs.

He finally found the smoked sausages and hard bread. Evillia and Lofosa grinned when they took out the sausages, which flustered him worse. Eltsac vez Martois stole a roll from his wife, who cursed him with a dockwalloper's fluency and more than a dockwalloper's volume.

Then Radnal had to give breakfast to Toglo zev Pamdal. "Thank you, freeman," she said, more at ease than he'd dared hope. Then her gray eyes met his. "I trust you slept well?"

It was a conventional Tarteshan morning greeting, or would have been, if she hadn't sounded—no, Radnal decided, she couldn't have sounded amused. "Er—yes," he managed, and fled.

He knew only relief at handing the next breakfast to a

Strongbrow who put away a sketch pad and charcoal to take it. "Thank you," the fellow said. Though he seemed polite enough, his guttural accent and the striped tunic and trousers he wore proclaimed him a native of Morgaf, the island kingdom off the northern coast of Tartesh— and the Tyranny's frequent foe. Their current twenty-year bout of peace was as long as they'd enjoyed in centuries.

Normally, Radnal would have been cautious around a Morgaffo. But now he found him easier to confront than Toglo. Glancing at the sketch pad, he said, "That's a fine drawing, freeman, ah—"

The Morgaffo held out both hands in front of him in his people's greeting. "I am Dokhnor of Kellef, freeman vez Krobir," he said. "Thank you for your interest."

He made it sound like *stop spying on me*. Radnal hadn't meant it that way. With a few deft strokes of his charcoal stick, Dokhnor had picked out the features of the campsite: the fire pits, the oleanders in front of the privy, the tethered donkeys. As a biologist who did field work, Radnal was a fair hand with a piece of charcoal. He wasn't in Dokhnor's class, though. A military engineer couldn't have done better.

That thought triggered his suspicions. He looked at the Morgaffo more closely. The fellow carried himself as a soldier would, which proved nothing. Lots of Morgaffos were soldiers. Although far smaller than Tartesh, the island kingdom had always held its own in their struggles. Radnal laughed at himself. If Dokhnor was an agent, why was he in Trench Park instead of, say, at a naval base along the Western Ocean?

The Morgaffo glowered. "If you have finished examining my work, freeman, perhaps you will give someone else a breakfast."

"Certainly," Radnal answered in a voice as icy as he could make it. Dokhnor certainly had the proverbial Morgaffo arrogance. Maybe that proved he wasn't a spy—a real spy would have been smoother. Or maybe a real spy would think no one would expect him to act like a spy, and act like one as a disguise. Radnal realized he could extend the chain to as many links as his imagination could forge. He gave up.

When all the breakfast packs were eaten, all the sleepsacks deflated and stowed, the group headed over to remount their donkeys for the trip into Trench Park itself. As he had the night before, Radnal warned, "The trail will be much steeper today. As long as we take it slow and careful, we'll be fine."

No sooner were the words out of his mouth than the ground quivered beneath his feet. Everyone stood stock-still; a couple of people exclaimed in dismay. The birds, on the other hand, all fell silent. Radnal had lived in earthquake country his whole life. He waited for the shaking to stop, and after a few heartbeats it did.

"Nothing to get alarmed at," he said when the quake was over. "This part of Tartesh is seismically active, probably because of the inland sea that dried up so long ago. The crust of the Earth is still adjusting to the weight of so much water being gone. There are a lot of fault lines in the area, some quite close to the surface."

Dokhnor of Kellef stuck up a hand. "What if an earth-quake should—how do you say it?—make the Barrier Mountains fall?"

"Then the Bottomlands would flood." Radnal laughed. "Freeman, if it hasn't happened in the last five and a half million years, I won't lose sleep worrying that it'll happen tomorrow, or any time I'm down in Trench Park."

The Morgaffo nodded curtly. "That is a worthy answer. Carry on, freeman."

Radnal had an impulse to salute him—he spoke with the same automatic assumption of authority that Tarteshan officers employed. The tour guide mounted his own donkey, waited until his charges were in ragged line behind him. He waved. "Let's go."

The trail down into Trench Park was hacked and blasted from rock that had been on the bottom of the sea. It was only six or eight cubits wide, and frequently switched back and forth. A motor with power to all wheels might have negotiated it, but Radnal wouldn't have wanted to be at the tiller of one that tried.

His donkey pulled up a gladiolus and munched it. That made him think of something about which he'd forgotten to warn his group. He said, "When we get lower into the park, you'll want to keep your animals from browsing. The soil down there has large amounts of things like selenium and tellurium along with the more usual minerals—they were concentrated there as the sea evaporated. That doesn't bother a lot of the Bottomlands plants, but it will bother—and maybe kill—your donkeys if they eat the wrong ones."

"How will we know which ones are which?" Eltsac vez Martois called.

He fought the urge to throw Eltsac off the trail and let him tumble down into Trench Park. The idiot tourist would probably land on his head, which by all evidence was too hard to be damaged by a fall of a mere few thousand cubits. And Radnal's job was riding herd on idiot tourists. He answered, "Don't let your donkey forage at all. The pack donkeys carry fodder, and there'll be more at the lodge."

The tour group rode on in silence for a while. Then Toglo zev Pamdal said, "This trail reminds me of the one down into the big canyon through the western desert in the Empire of Stekia, over on the Double Continent."

Radnal was both glad Toglo would speak to him and jealous of the wealth that let her travel—just a collateral relation of the Hereditary Tyrant's, eh? "I've only seen pictures," he said wistfully. "I suppose there is some similarity of looks, but the canyon was formed differently from the Bottomlands: by erosion, not evaporation."

"Of course," she said. "I've also only seen pictures myself."

"Oh." Maybe she was a distant relative, then. He went on, "Much more like the big canyon are the gorges our rivers cut before they tumble into what was deep sea bottom to form the Bitter Lakes in the deepest parts of the Bottomlands. There's a small one in Trench Park, though it often dries up—the Dalorz River doesn't send down enough water to maintain it very well."

A little later, when the trail twisted west around a big limestone boulder, several tourists exclaimed over the misty plume of water plunging toward the floor of the park. Lofosa asked, "Is that the Dalorz?"

"That's it," Radnal said. "Its flow is too erratic to make it worth Tartesh's while to build a power station where it falls off the ancient continental shelf, though we've done that with several other bigger rivers. They supply more than three-fourths of our electricity: another benefit of the Bottomlands."

A few small spun-sugar clouds drifted across the sky from west to east. Otherwise, nothing blocked the sun from beating down on the tourists with greater force every cubit they descended. The donkeys kicked up dust at every footfall.

"Does it ever rain here?" Evillia asked.

"Not very often," Radnal admitted. "The Bottomlands desert is one of the driest places on earth. The Barrier Mountains pick off most of the moisture that blows from the Western Ocean, and the other mountain ranges that stretch into the Bottomlands from the north catch most of what's left. But every two or three years Trench Park does get a downpour. It's the most dangerous time to be there—a torrent can tear through a wash and drown you before you know it's coming."

"But it's also the most beautiful time," Toglo zev Pamdal said. "Pictures of Trench Park after a rain first made me want to come here, and I was lucky enough to see it myself on my last visit."

"May I be so fortunate," Dokhnor of Kellef said. "I brought colorsticks as well as charcoal, on the off chance I might be able to draw post-rain foliage."

"The odds are against you, though the freelady was lucky before," Radnal said. Dokhnor spread his hands to show his agreement; like everything he did, the gesture was tight, restrained, perfectly controlled. Radnal had trouble imagining him going into transports of artistic rapture over desert flowers, no matter how rare or brilliant.

He said, "The flowers are beautiful, but they're only the tip of the iceberg, if you'll let me use a wildly inappropriate comparison. All life in Trench Park depends on water, the same as everywhere else. It's adapted to get along with very little, but not none. As soon as any moisture comes, plants and animals try to pack a generation's worth of growth and breeding into the little while it takes to dry up."

About a quarter of a daytenth later, a sign set by the side of the trail announced that the tourists were farther below sea level than they could go anywhere outside the Bottomlands. Radnal read it aloud and pointed out, rather smugly, that the salt lake which was the next most submerged spot on dry land lay close to the Bottomlands, and might almost be considered an extension of them.

Moblay Sopsirk's son said, "I didn't imagine anyone would be so proud of this wasteland as to want to include more of the Great Continent in it." His brown skin kept him from roasting under the desert sun, but sweat sheened his bare arms and torso.

A little more than halfway down the trail, a wide flat rest area was carved out of the rock. Radnal let the tourists halt for a while, stretch their legs and ease their weary hindquarters, and use the odorous privy. He passed out ration packs, ignored his charges' grumbles. He noticed Dokhnor of Kellef ate his meal without complaint.

He tossed his own pack into the bin by the privy, then, a couple of cubits from the edge of the trail, peered down on to the floor of the Bottomlands. After one of the rare rains, the park was spectacular from here. Now it just baked: white salt pans, gray-brown or yellow-brown dirt, a scattering of faded green vegetation. Not even the area around the lodge was watered artificially; the Tyrant's charter ordained that Trench Park be kept pristine.

As they came off the trail and started along the ancient sea bottom toward the lodge, Evillia said, "I thought it would be as if we were in the bottom of a bowl, with mountains all around us. It doesn't really seem that way. I can see the ones we just came down, and the Barrier Mountains to the west, but there's nothing to the east and hardly anything to the south—just a blur on the horizon."

"I expected it would look like a bowl, too, the first time I came here," Radnal said. "We *are* in the bottom of a bowl. But it doesn't look that way because the Bottomlands are broad compared to their depth—it's a big, shallow bowl. What makes it interesting is that its top is at the same level as the bottom of most other geological bowls, and its bottom deeper than any of them."

"What are those cracks?" Toglo zev Pamdal asked, pointing down to breaks in the soil that ran across the tour group's path. Some were no wider than a barleycorn; others, like open, lidless mouths, had gaps of a couple of digits between their sides.

"In arid terrain like this you'll see all kinds of cracks in the ground from mud drying unevenly after a rain," Radnal said. "But the ones you've noticed do mark a fault line. The earthquake we felt earlier was probably triggered along this fault: it marks where two plates in the Earth's crust are colliding."

Nocso zev Martois let out a frightened squeak. "Do you mean that if we have another earthquake, those cracks will open and swallow us down?" She twitched her donkey's reins, as if to speed it up and get as far away from the fault line as she could.

Radnal didn't laugh; the Tyranny paid him for not laughing at tourists. He answered gravely, "If you worry about something that unlikely, you might as well worry about getting hit by a skystone, too. The one has about as much chance of happening as the other."

"Are you *sure*?" Lofosa sounded anxious, too.

"I'm sure." He tried to figure out where she and Evillia were from: probably the Krepalgan Unity, by their accent. Krepalga was the northwesternmost Highhead nation; its western border lay at the eastern edge of the Bottomlands. More to the point, it was earthquake country too. If this was all Lofosa knew about quakes, it didn't say much for her brains.

And if Lofosa didn't have a lot of brains, what did that say about her and Evillia picking Radnal to amuse themselves with? No one cares to think of a sexual partner's judgment as faulty, for that reflects upon him.

Radnal did what any sensible man might have done: he changed the subject. "We'll be at the lodge soon, so you'll want to think about getting your things out of your bags and into your sleep cubicles."

"What I want to think about is getting clean," Moblay Sopsirk's son contradicted.

"You'll each be issued a small bucket of water every day for personal purposes," he said, and overrode a chorus of groans: "Don't complain—our brochures are specific about this. Almost all the fresh water in Trench Park comes down the trail we rode, on the backs of these donkeys. Think how much you'll relish a hot soak when we come out of the park."

"Think how much we'll need a hot soak when we come out of the park," said the elderly Strongbrow man Radnal had tagged as someone spending the silver he'd made in his earlier years (to his embarrassment, he'd forgotten the fellow's name). "It's not so bad for these Highheads here, since their bodies are mostly bare, but all my hair will be a greasy mess by the time this excursion is done." He glared at Radnal as if it were his fault.

Toglo zev Pamdal said, "Don't fret, freeman vez Maprab." Benter vez Maprab, that's who he was, Radnal thought, shooting Toglo a grateful glance. She was still talking to the old Strongbrow: "I have a jar of waterless hair cleaner you can just comb out. It's more than I'd need; I'll share some with you."

"Well, that's kind of you," Benter vez Maprab said, mollified. "Maybe I should have brought some myself."

You certainly should, you old fool, instead of complaining, Radnal thought. He also noted that Toglo had figured out what she'd need before she started her trip. He approved; he would have done the same had he been tourist rather than guide. Of course, if he'd arranged to forget his own waterless hair cleaner, he could have borrowed some from her. He exhaled through his nose. Maybe he'd been too practical for his own good.

Something small and dun-colored darted under his donkey's hooves, then bounced away toward a patch of oleander. "What was that?" several people asked as it vanished among the fallen leaves under the plants.

"It's one of the species of jerboa that live down here," Radnal answered. "Without more than two heartbeats' look, I couldn't tell you which. There are many varieties, all through the Bottomlands. They lived in arid country while the inland sea still existed, and evolved to get the moisture they need from their food. That preadapted them to succeed here, where free water is so scarce."

"Are they dangerous?" Nocso zev Martois asked.

"Only if you're a shrub," Radnal said. "No, actually, that's not quite true. Some eat insects, and one species, the bladetooth, hunts and kills its smaller relatives. It filled the small predator niche before carnivores properly established themselves in the Bottomlands. It's scarce today, especially outside Trench Park, but it is still around, often in the hottest, driest places where no other meat-eaters can thrive."

A little later, the tour guide pointed to a small, nondescript plant with thin, greenish-brown leaves. "Can anyone tell me what that is?"

He asked that question whenever he took a group along the trail, and had only got a right answer once, just after a rain. But now Benter vez Maprab said confidently: "It's a Bottomlands orchid, freeman vez Krobir, and a common type at that. If you'd shown us a red-veined one, that would have been worth fussing over."

"You're right, freeman, it *is* an orchid. It doesn't look much like the ones you see in more hospitable climates, though, does it?" Radnal said, smiling at the elderly Strongbrow—if he was an orchid fancier, that probably explained why he'd come to Trench Park.

Benter only grunted and scowled in reply—evidently he'd had his heart set on seeing a rare red-veined orchid his first day at the park. Radnal resolved to search his bags at the end of the tour: carrying specimens out of the park was against the law.

A jerboa hopped up, started nibbling on an orchid leaf. Quick as a flash, something darted out from behind the plant, seized the rodent, and ran away. The tourists bombarded Radnal with questions: "Did you see that?" "What was it?" "Where'd it go?"

"That was a koprit bird," he answered. "Fast, wasn't it? It's of the butcherbird family, but mostly adapted to life on the ground. It can fly, but it usually runs. Because birds excrete urea in more or less solid form, not in urine like mammals, they've done well in the Bottomlands." He pointed to the lodge, which was only a few hundred cubits ahead now. "See? There's another koprit bird on the roof, looking around to see what it can catch."

A couple of park attendants came out of the lodge. They waved to Radnal, sized up the tourists, then helped them stable their donkeys. "Take only what you'll need tonight into the lodge," said one, Fer vez Canthal. "Leave the rest in your saddle bags for the trip out tomorrow. The less packing and unpacking, the better."

Some tourists, veteran travelers, nodded at the good advice. Evillia and Lofosa exclaimed as if they'd never heard it before. Frowning at their naïveté, Radnal wanted to look away from them, but they were too pretty.

Moblay Sopsirk's son thought so, too. As the group started from the stable to the lodge, he came up behind Evillia and slipped an arm around her waist. At the same moment, he must have tripped, for his startled cry made Radnal whirl toward them.

Moblay sprawled on the dirt floor of the stable. Evillia staggered, flailed her arms wildly, and fell down on top of him, hard. He shouted again, a shout which lost all its breath as she somehow hit him in the pit of the stomach with an elbow while getting back to her feet.

She looked down at him, the picture of concern. "I'm so sorry," she said. "You startled me."

Moblay needed a while before he could sit, let alone stand. At last, he wheezed; "See if I ever touch you again," in a tone that implied it would be her loss.

She stuck her nose in the air. Radnal said, "We should remember we come from different countries and have different customs. Being slow and careful will keep us from embarrassing one another."

"Why, freeman, were you embarrassed last night?" Lofosa asked. Instead of answering, Radnal started to cough. Lofosa and Evillia laughed. Despite what Fer vez Canthal had said, both of them were just toting their saddle bags into the lodge. Maybe they hadn't a lot of brains. But their bodies, those smooth, oh so naked bodies, were something else again.

❖   ❖   ❖

The lodge was not luxurious, but boasted mesh screens to keep out the Bottomlands bugs, electric lights, and fans which stirred the desert air even if they did not cool it. It also had a refrigerator. "No ration packs tonight," Radnal said. The tourists cheered.

The cooking pit was outdoors: the lodge was warm enough without a fire inside. Fer vez Canthal and the other attendant, Zosel vez Glesir, filled it with chunks of charcoal, splashed light oil over them, and fired them. Then they put a disjointed lamb carcass on a grill and hung it over the pit. Every so often, one of them basted it with a sauce full of pepper and garlic. The sauce and melting fat dripped onto the coals. They sputtered and hissed and sent up little clouds of fragrant smoke. Spit streamed in Radnal's mouth.

The refrigerator also held mead, date wine, grape wine, and ale. Some of the tourists drank boisterously. Dokhnor of Kellef surprised Radnal by taking only chilled water. "I am sworn to the Goddess," he explained.

"Not my affair," Radnal answered, but his sleeping suspicions woke. The Goddess was the deity the Morgaffo military aristocracy most commonly followed. Maybe a traveling artist was among her worshipers, but Radnal did not find it likely.

He did not get much time to dwell on the problem Dokhnor presented. Zosel vez Glesir called him over to do the honors on the lamb. He used a big pair of eating sticks to pick up each piece of meat and transfer it to a paper plate.

The Martoisi ate like starving cave cats. Radnal felt guilty; maybe ordinary rations weren't enough for them. Then he looked at how abundant flesh stretched the fabric of their robes. Guilt evaporated. They weren't wasting away.

Evillia and Lofosa had poured down several mugs of date wine. That soon caused them difficulties. Krepalgans usually ate with knife and skewer; they had trouble manipulating their disposable pairs of wooden eating sticks. After cutting her meat into bite-sized chunks, Lofosa chased them around her plate but couldn't pick them up. Evillia managed that, but dropped them on the way to her mouth.

They both seemed cheerful drunks, and laughed at their mishaps. Even stiff-necked Dokhnor unbent far enough to try to show them how to use sticks. His lesson did not do much good, though both Highhead girls moved close enough to him to make Radnal jealous. Evillia said, "You're so deft. Morgaffos must use them every day."

Dokhnor tossed his head in his people's negative. "Our usual tool has prongs, bowl, and a sharp edge, all in one. The Tarteshans say we are a quiet folk because we risk cutting our tongues whenever we open our mouths. But I have traveled in Tartesh, and learned what to do with sticks."

"Let me try again," Evillia said. This time, she dropped the piece of lamb on Dokhnor's thigh. She picked it up with her fingers. After her land lingered on the Morgaffo's leg long enough to give Radnal another pang, she popped the gobbet into her mouth.

Moblay Sopsirk's son began singing in his own language. Radnal did not understand most of the words, but the tune was wild and free and easy to follow. Soon the whole tour group was clapping time. More songs followed. Fer vez Canthal had a ringing baritone. Everyone in the group spoke Tarteshan, but not everyone knew Tartesh's songs well enough to join in. As they had for Moblay, those who could not sing clapped.

When darkness fell, gnats emerged in stinging clouds. Radnal and the group retreated to the lodge, whose screens held the biters away. "Now I know why you wear so many clothes," Moblay said. "They're armor against insects." The dark brown Highhead looked as if he didn't know where to scratch first.

"Of course," Radnal said, surprised Moblay had taken so long to see the obvious. "If you'll hold still for a couple of heartbeats, we have a spray to take away the itch."

Moblay sighed as Radnal sprayed painkiller onto him. "Anyone want another song?" he called.

This time, he got little response. Being under a roof inhibited some people. It reminded others of their long day; Toglo zev Pamdal was not the only tourist to wander off to a sleeping cubicle. Dokhnor of Kellef and old Benter vez Maprab had discovered a war board and were deep in a game. Moblay went over to watch. So did Radnal, who fancied himself a war player.

Dokhnor, who had the blue pieces, advanced a foot-soldier over the blank central band that separated his side of the board from his opponent's. "Across the river," Moblay said.

"Is that what Lissonese name the gap?" Radnal said. "With us, it's the trench."

"And in Morgaf, it's the Sleeve, after the channel that separates our islands from Tartesh," Dokhnor said. "No matter what we call it, though, the game's the same all over the world."

"It's a game that calls for thought and quiet," Benter said pointedly. After some thought, he moved a counselor (that was the name of the piece on the red side of board; its blue equivalent was an elephant) two squares diagonally.

The old Tarteshan's pauses for concentration grew more frequent as the game went on. Dokhnor's attack had the red governor scurrying along the vertical and horizontal lines of his fortress, and his guards along the diagonals, to evade or block the blue pieces. Finally Dokhnor brought one of his cannons in line with the other and said, "That's the end."

Benter glumly nodded. The cannon (the red piece of identical value was called a catapult) was hard to play well: it moved vertically and horizontally, but had to jump over one other piece every time. Thus the rear cannon, not the front, threatened the red governor. But if Benter interposed a guard or one of his chariots, that turned the forward cannon into the threat.

"Nicely played," Benter said. He got up from the war table, headed for a cubicle.

"Care for a game, either of you?" Dokhnor asked the spectators.

Moblay Sopsirk's son shook his head. Radnal said, "I did, till I saw you play. I don't mind facing someone better than I am if I have some chance. Even when I lose, I learn something. But you'd just trounce me, and a little of that goes a long way."

"As you will." Dokhnor folded the war board, poured the disks into their bag. He replaced bag and board on their shelf. "I'm for bed, then." He marched off to the cubicle he'd chosen.

Radnal and Moblay glanced at each other, then toward the war set. By unspoken consent, they seemed to decide that if neither of them wanted a go at Dokhnor of Kellef, playing each other would be rude. "Another night," Radnal said.

"Fair enough." Moblay yawned, displaying teeth that gleamed all the whiter against his brown skin. He said, "I'm about done over—no, it's 'done in' in Tarteshan, isn't it?—anyhow. See you in the morning, Radnal."

Again the tour guide controlled his annoyance at Moblay's failure to use the polite particle *vez*. At first when foreigners forgot that trick of Tarteshan grammar, he'd imagined himself deliberately insulted. Now he knew better, though he still noticed the omission.

A small light came on in Dokhnor's cubicle: a battery-powered reading lamp. The Morgaffo wasn't reading, though. He sat with his behind on the sleeping mat and his back against the wall. His sketch pad lay on his bent knees. Radnal heard the faint *skritch-skritch* of charcoal on paper.

"What's he doing?" Fer vez Canthal whispered. A generation's peace was not enough time to teach most Tarteshans to trust their island neighbors.

"He's drawing," Radnal answered, as quietly. Neither of them wanted to draw Dokhnor's notice. The reply could have come out sounding innocent. It didn't. Radnal went on, "His travel documents say he's an artist." Again, tone spoke volumes.

Zosel vez Glesir said, "If he really were a spy, Radnal vez, he'd carry a camera; not a sketch pad. Everyone carries a camera into Trench Park—he wouldn't even get noticed."

"True," Radnal said. "But he doesn't act like an artist. He acts like a member of the Morgaffo officer caste. You heard him—he's sworn to their Goddess."

Fer vez Canthal said something lewd about the Morgaffo Goddess. But he lowered his voice even further before he did. An officer from Morgaf who heard his deity offended might make formal challenge. Then again, in Tartesh, where dueling was illegal, he might simply commit murder. The only thing certain was that he wouldn't ignore the insult.

"We can't do anything to him—or even about him— unless we find out he is spying," Zosel vez Glesir said.

"Yes," Radnal said. "The last thing Tartesh wants is to hand Morgaf an incident." He thought about what would happen to someone who fouled up so gloriously. Nothing good, that was sure. Then something else occurred to him. "Speaking of the Tyrant, do you know who's in this group? Freelady Toglo zev Pamdal, that's who."

Zosel and Fer whistled softly. "Good thing you warned us," Zosel said. "We'll stay round her like cotton round cut glass."

"I don't think she cares for that sort of thing," Radnal said. "Treat her well, yes, but don't fall all over yourselves."

Zosel nodded. Fer still had Dokhnor of Kellef on his mind. "If he is a spy, what's he doing in Trench Park instead of somewhere important?"

"l thought of that myself," Radnal said. "Cover, maybe. And who knows where he's going after he leaves?"

"I know where I'm going," Zosel said, yawning: "To bed. If you want to stay up all night fretting about spies, go ahead."

"No, thanks," Fer answered. "A spy would have to be crazy or on holiday to come to Trench Park. If he's crazy, we don't have to worry about him, and if he's on holiday, we don't have to worry about him then, either. So I'm going to bed, too."

"If you think I'll stay talking to myself, you're both crazy," Radnal said. All three Tarteshans got up. Dokhnor of Kellef's reading lamp went out, plunging his cubicle into blackness. Radnal dimmed the lights in the common room.

He flopped down onto his sleeping mat with a long sigh. He would sooner have been out in the field, curled up in a sleepsack under gnat netting. This was the price he paid for doing what he wanted most of the time. He knew his own snores would soon join the tourists'.

Then two female shapes appeared in the entrance to his cubicle. *By the gods, not again*, he thought as his eyes opened wide, which showed how tired he was. He said, "Don't you believe in sleep?"

Evillia laughed softly, or maybe Lofosa. "Not when there are better things to do," Lofosa said. "We have some new ideas, too. But we can always see who else is awake."

Radnal almost told her to go ahead, and take Evillia with her. But he heard himself say, "No," instead. The night before had been educational beyond his dreams, the stuff people imagined when they talked about the fringe benefits of a tour guide's job. Until last night, he'd reckoned those stories imaginary: in his two years as a guide, he'd never cavorted with a tourist before. Now . . . he grinned as he felt himself rising to the occasion.

The Highhead girls came in. As they'd promised, the threesome tried some new things. He wondered how long their inventiveness could last, and if he could last as long. He was sure he'd enjoy trying.

His stamina and the girls' ingenuity flagged together. He remembered them getting up from the mat. He thought he remembered them going out into the common room. He was sure he didn't remember anything after that. He slept like a log from a petrified forest.

When the scream jarred him awake, his first muzzy thought was that only a few heartbeats had passed. But a glance at his pocket clock as he closed his robe told him sunrise was near. He dashed out into the common room.

Several tourists were already out there, some dressed, some not. More emerged every moment, as did the other two Trench Park staffers. Everyone kept saying, "What's going on?"

Though no one directly answered the question, no one needed to. As naked as when she'd frolicked with Radnal, Evillia stood by the table where Benter vez Maprab and Dokhnor of Kellef had played war. Dokhnor was there, too, but not standing. He lay sprawled on the floor, head twisted at an unnatural angle.

Evillia had jammed a fist in her mouth to stifle another scream. She took it out, quavered, "Is—is he dead?"

Radnal strode over to Dokhnor, grabbed his wrist, felt for a pulse. He found none, nor was the Morgaffo breathing. "He's dead, all right," Radnal said grimly.

Evillia moaned. Her knees buckled. She toppled onto Radnal's bent back.

When Evillia fainted, Lofosa screamed and ran forward to try to help. Nocso zev Martois screamed, too, even louder. Moblay Sopsirk's son hurried toward Radnal with Evillia. So did Fer vez Canthal and Zosel vez Glesir. So did Toglo zev Pamdal. So did another tourist, a Highhead who'd spoken very little on the way down to the lodge.

Everyone got in everyone else's way. Then the quiet

Highhead stopped being quiet and shouted, "I am a physician, the six million gods curse you! Let me through!"

"Let the physician through," Radnal echoed, sliding Evillia off him and to the ground as gently as he could. "Check her first, freeman Golobol," he added, pleased he'd hung onto the doctor's name. "I'm afraid you're too late to help Dokhnor now."

Golobol was almost as dark as Moblay, but spoke Tarteshan with a different accent. As he turned to Evillia, she moaned and stirred. "She will be all right, oh yes, I am sure," he said. "But this poor fellow—" As Radnal had, he felt for Dokhnor's pulse. As Radnal had, he failed to find it. "You are correct, sir. This man is dead. He has been dead for some time."

"How do you know?" Radnal asked.

"You felt of him, not?" the physician said. "Surely you noticed his flesh has begun to cool. It has, oh yes."

Thinking back, Radnal had noticed, but he'd paid no special attention. He'd always prided himself on how well he'd learned first aid training. But he wasn't a physician, and didn't automatically take everything into account as a physician would. His fit of chagrin was interrupted when Evillia let out a shriek a hunting cave cat would have been proud of.

Lofosa bent by her, spoke to her in her own language. The shriek cut off. Radnal started thinking about what to do next. Golobol said, "Sir, look here, if you would."

Golobol was pointing to a spot on the back of Dokhnor's neck, right above where it bent gruesomely. Radnal had to say, "I don't see anything."

"You Strongbrows are a hairy, folk, that is why," Golobol said. "Here, though—see this, ah, discoloration, is that the word in your language? It is? Good. Yes. This discoloration is the sort of mark to be expected from a blow by the side of the hand, a killing blow."

Despite Bottomlands's heat, ice formed in the pit of

Radnal's stomach. "You're telling me this was murder."

The word cut through the babble filling the common room like a scalpel. There was chaos one heartbeat, silence the next. Into that abrupt, intense silence, Golobol said, "Yes."

"Oh, by the gods, what a mess," Fer vez Canthal said.

Figuring out what to do next became a lot more urgent for Radnal. Why had the gods (though he didn't believe in six million of them) let someone from his tour group get murdered? And why, by all the gods he did believe in, did it have to be the Morgaffo? Morgaf would be suspicious—if not hostile—if any of its people met foul play in Tartesh. And if Dokhnor of Kellef really was a spy, Morgaf would be more than suspicious. Morgaf would be furious.

Radnal walked over to the radiophone. "Whom will you call?" Fer asked.

"First, the park militia. They'd have to be notified in any case. And then—" Radnal took a deep breath. "Then I think I'd best call the Hereditary Tyrant's Eyes and Ears in Tarteshem. Murder of a Morgaffo sworn to the Goddess is a deeper matter than the militia can handle alone. Besides, I'd sooner have an Eye and Ear notify the Morgaffo plenipo than try doing it myself."

"Yes, I can see that," Fer said. "Wouldn't want Morgaffo gunboats running across the Sleeve to raid our coasts because you said something wrong Or—" The lodge attendant shook his head. "No, not even the island king would be crazy enough to start tossing starbombs over something this small." Fer's voice turned anxious. "Would he?"

"I don't think so." But Radnal sounded anxious, too. Politics hadn't been the same since starbombs came along fifty years before. Neither Tartesh nor Morgaf had used them, even in war against each other, but both countries kept building them. So did eight or ten other nations, scattered across the globe. If another big war started, it could easily become The Big War, the one everybody was afraid of.

Radnal punched buttons on the radiophone. After a couple of static bursts, a voice answered: "Trench Park militia, Subleader vez Steries speaking."

"Gods bless you, Liem vez," Radnal said; this was a man he knew and liked. "Vez Krobir here, over at the tourist lodge. I'm sorry to have to tell you we've had a death. I'm even sorrier to have to tell you it looks like murder." Radnal explained what had happened to Dokhnor of Kellef.

Liem vez Steries said, "Why couldn't it have been anyone else but the Morgaffo? Now you'll have to drag in the Eyes and Ears, and the gods only know how much hoorah will erupt."

"My next call was to Tarteshem," Radnal agreed.

"It probably should have been your first one, but never mind," Liem vez Steries said. "I'll be over there with a circumstances man as fast as I can get a helo in the air. Farewell."

"Farewell." Radnal's next call had to go through a human relayer. After a couple of hundred heartbeats, he found himself talking with an Eye and Ear named Peggol vez Menk. Unlike the park militiaman, Peggol kept interrupting with questions, so the conversation took twice as long as the other one had.

When Radnal was through, the Eye and Ear said, "You did right to involve us, freeman vez Krobir. We'll handle the diplomatic aspects, and we'll fly a team down there to help with the investigation. Don't let anyone leave the— lodge, did you call it? Farewell."

The radiophone had a speaking diaphragm in the console, not the more common—and more private—ear-and-mouth handset. Everyone heard what Peggol vez Menk said. Nobody liked it. Evillia said, "Did he mean we're going to have to stay cooped up here—with a murderer?" She started trembling. Lofosa put an arm around her.

Benter vez Maprab had a different objection: "See here, freeman, I put down good silver for a tour of Trench Park, and I intend to have that tour. If not, I shall take legal measures."

Radnal stifled a groan. Tarteshan law, which relied heavily on the principle of trust, came down hard on those who violated contracts in any way. If the old Strongbrow went to court, he'd likely collect enormous damages from Trench Park—and from Radnal, as the individual who failed to deliver the service contracted for.

Worse, the Martoisi joined the outcry. A reasonably upright and upstanding man, Radnal had never had to hire a pleader in his life. He wondered if he had enough silver to pay for a good one. Then he wondered if he'd ever have any silver again, once the tourists, the courts, and the pleader were through with him.

Toglo zev Pamdal cut through the hubbub: "Let's wait a few heartbeats. A man is dead. That's more important than everything else. If the start of our tour is delayed, perhaps Trench Park will regain equity by delaying its end to give us the full touring time we've paid for."

"That's an excellent suggestion, freelady zev Pamdal," Radnal said gratefully. Fer and Zosel nodded.

A distant thunder in the sky grew to a roar. The militia helo kicked up a small dust storm as it set down between the stables and the lodge. Flying pebbles clicked off walls and windows. The motor shut down. As the blades slowed, dust subsided.

Radnal felt as if a good god had frightened a night demon from his shoulders. "I don't think we'll need to extend your time here by more than a day," he said happily.

"How will you manage that, if we're confined here in this gods-forsaken wilderness?" Eltsac vez Martois growled.

"That's just it," Radnal said. "We *are* in a wilderness. Suppose we go out and see what there is to see in Trench Park—where will the culprit flee on donkeyback? If he tries to get away, we'll know who he is because he'll be the only one missing, and we'll track him down with the helo." The tour guide beamed. The tourists beamed back—including, Radnal reminded himself, the killer among them.

Liem vez Steries and two other park militiamen walked into the lodge. They wore soldierly versions of Radnal's costume: their robes, instead of being white, were splotched in shades of tan and light green, as were their long-brimmed caps. Their rank badges were dull; even the metal buckles of their sandals were painted to avoid reflections.

Liem set a recorder on the table Dokhnor and Benter vez Maprab had used for war the night before. The circumstances man started taking pictures with as much abandon as if he'd been a tourist. He asked, "Has the body been moved?"

"Only as much as we needed to make sure the man was dead," Radnal answered.

"We?" the circumstances man asked. Radnal introduced Golobol. Liem got everybody's statement on the wire: first Evillia, who gulped and blinked back tears as she spoke, then Radnal, then the physician, and then the other tourists and lodge attendants. Most of them echoed one another: they'd heard a scream, run out, and seen Evillia standing over Dokhnor's corpse.

Golobol added, "The woman cannot be responsible for his death. He had been deceased some while, between one and two daytenths, possibly. She, unfortunate one, merely discovered the body."

"I understand, freeman," Liem vez Steries assured him. "But because she did, her account of what happened is important."

✦   ✦   ✦

The militiaman had just finished recording the last statement when another helo landed outside the lodge. The instant its dust storm subsided, four men came in. The Hereditary Tyrant's Eyes and Ears looked more like prosperous merchants than soldiers: their caps had patent-leather brims, they closed their robes with silver chains, and they sported rings on each index finger.

"I am Peggol vez Menk," one of them announced. He was short and, by Tarteshan standards, slim; he wore his cap at a dapper angle. His eyes were extraordinarily shrewd, as if he were waiting for someone around him to make a mistake. He spotted Liem vez Steries at once, and asked, "What's been done thus far, Subleader?"

"What you'd expect," the militiaman answered: "Statements from all present, and our circumstances man, Senior Trooper vez Sofana there, has taken some pictures. We didn't disturb the body."

"Fair enough," the Eye and Ear said. One of his men was flashing more photos. Another set a recorder beside the one already on the table. "We'll get a copy of your wire, and we'll make one for ourselves—maybe we'll find questions you missed. You haven't searched belongings yet?"

"No, freeman." Liem vez Steries's voice went wooden. Radnal wouldn't have wanted someone to steal and duplicate his work, either. Eyes and Ears, though, did as they pleased. Why not? They watched Tartesh, but who watched them?

"We'll take care of it." Peggol vez Menk sat down at the table. The photographer stuck in a fresh clip of film, then followed the two remaining Eyes and Ears into the sleeping cubicle nearest the entrance.

It was Golobol's. "Be careful, oh please I beg you," the physician exclaimed. "Some of my equipment is delicate."

Peggol said, "I'll hear the tale of the woman who discovered the body." He pulled out a notepad, glanced at it. "Evillia." A little calmer now, Evillia retold her story using, so far as Radnal could tell, the same words she had before. If Peggol found any new questions, he didn't ask them.

After about a tenth of a daytenth, it was Radnal's turn. Peggol did remember his name without needing to remind himself. Again, his questions were like the ones Liem vez Steries had used. When he asked the last one, Radnal had a question of his own: "Freeman, while the investigation continues, may I take my group out into the Bottomlands?" He explained how Benter vez Maprab had threatened to sue, and why he thought even a guilty tourist unlikely to escape.

The Eye and Ear pulled at his lower lip. He let the hair beneath it grow out in a tuft, which made him seem to have a protruding chin like a Highhead's. When he released the lip, it went back with a liquid plop. Under his tilted cap, he looked wise and cynical. Radnal's hopes plunged. He waited for Peggol to laugh at him for raising the matter.

Peggol said, "Freeman, I know you technically enjoy military rank, but suppose you discover who the killer is, or he strikes again. Do you reckon yourself up to catching him and bringing him back for trial and decapitation?"

"I—" Radnal stopped before he went any further. The ironic question reminded him this wasn't a game. Dokhnor of Kellef might have been a spy, he was dead now, and whoever had killed him might kill again—*might kill me, if I find out who he is*, he thought. He said, "I don't know. I'd like to think so, but I've never had to do that sort of thing."

Something like approval came into Peggol vez Menk's eyes. "You're honest with yourself. Not everyone can say that. Hmm—it wouldn't be just your silver involved in a suit, would it? No, of course not; it would be Trench Park's, too, which means the Hereditary Tyrant's."

"Just what I was thinking," Radnal said, with luck

patriotically. His own silver came first with him. He was
honest enough with himself to be sure of that—but he
didn't have to tell it to Peggol.

"I'm sure you were," the Eye and Ear said, his tone
dry. "The Tyrant's silver really does come first with me.
How's this, then? Suppose you take the tourists out, as
you've contracted to do. But suppose I come with you
to investigate while my comrades keep working here?
Does that seem reasonable?"

"Yes, freeman; thank you," Radnal exclaimed.

"Good," Peggol said. "My concubine has been nagging
me to bring her here. Now I'll see if I want to do that."
He grinned knowingly. "You see, I also keep my own
interests in mind."

The other Eyes and Ears had methodically gone from
one sleeping cubicle to the next, examining the tourists'
belongings. One of them brought a codex out of Lofosa's
cubicle, dropped it on the table in front of Peggol vez
Menk. The cover was a color photo of two good-looking
Highheads fornicating. Peggol flipped through it.
Variations on the same theme filled every page.

"Amusing," he said, "even if it should have been seized
when its owner entered our domains."

"I like that!" Lofosa sounded indignant. "You sancti-
monious Strongbrows, pretending you don't do the same
things—and enjoy them, too. I ought to know."

Radnal hoped Peggol would not ask how she knew. He
was certain she would tell him, in detail; she and Evillia
might have been many things, but not shy. But Peggol said,
"We did not come here to search for filth. She might have
worn out Dokhnor with that volume, but she didn't kill
him with it. Let her keep it, if she enjoys telling the world
what should be kept private."

"Oh, rubbish!" Lofosa scooped up the codex and carried
it back to her cubicle, rolling her hips at every step as if
to contradict Peggol without another word.

The Eyes and Ears brought out nothing more from her sleep cubicle or Evillia's for their chief to inspect. That surprised Radnal; the two women had carried in everything but the donkey they'd ridden. He shrugged—they'd probably filled their saddlebags with feminine fripperies and junk that could have stayed behind in their Tarteshan hostel if not in Krepalga.

Then he stopped thinking about them—the Eye and Ear who'd gone into Dokhnor's cubicle whistled. Peggol vez Menk dashed in there. He came out with his fist tightly closed around something. He opened it. Radnal saw two six-pointed gold stars: Morgaffo rank badges.

"So he was a spy," Fer vez Canthal exclaimed.

"He may have been," Peggol said. But when he got on the radio to Tarteshem, he found Dokhnor of Kellef had declared his battalion leader's rank when he entered the Tyranny. The Eye and Ear scowled. "A soldier, yes, but not a spy after all, it would appear."

Benter vez Maprab broke in "I wish you'd finish your pawing and let us get on with our tour. I haven't many days left, so I hate to squander one."

"Peace, freeman," Peggol said. "A man is dead."

"Which means he'll not complain if I see the much talked about wonders of Trench Park." Benter glared as if he were the Hereditary Tyrant dressing down some churlish underling.

Radnal, seeing how Benter reacted when thwarted, wondered if he'd broken Dokhnor's neck for no better reason than losing a game of war. Benter might be old, but he wasn't feeble. And he was sure to be a veteran of the last war with Morgaf, or the one before that against Morgaf and the Krepalgan Unity both. He would know how to kill.

Radnal shook his head. If things kept on like this, he'd start suspecting Fer and Zosel next, or his own shadow. He wished he hadn't lost the tour guides' draw. He would sooner have been studying the metabolism of the fat sand rat than trying to figure out which of his charges had just committed murder.

Peggol vez Menk said, "We shall have to search the outbuildings before we begin. Freeman vez Krobir already told you we'd go out tomorrow. My professional opinion is that no court would sustain a suit over one day's delay when compensational time is guaranteed."

"Bah!" Benter stomped off. Radnal caught Toglo zev Pamdal's eye. She raised one eyebrow slightly, shook her head. He shifted his shoulders in a tiny shrug. They both smiled. In every group, someone turned out to be a pain in the backside. Radnal let his smile expand, glad Toglo wasn't holding his sport with Lofosa and Evillia against him.

"Speaking of outbuildings, freeman vez Krobir," Peggol said, "there's just the stables, am I right?"

"That and the privy, yes," Radnal said.

"Oh, yes, the privy." The Eye and Ear wrinkled his nose. It was even more prominent than Radnal's. Most Strongbrows had big noses, as if to counterbalance their long skulls. Lissonese, whose noses were usually flattish, sometimes called Tarteshans Snouts on account of that. The name would start a brawl in any port on the Western Ocean.

Fer vez Canthal accompanied one of Peggol's men to the stables; the Eye and Ear obviously needed support against the ferocious, blood-crazed donkeys inside—that was what his body language said, anyhow. When Peggol ordered him out, he'd flinched as if told to invade Morgaf and bring back the king's ears.

"You Eyes and Ears don't often deal with matters outside the big cities, do you?" Radnal asked.

"You noticed that?" Peggol vez Menk raised a wry eyebrow. "You're right; we're urbanites to the core. Threats to the realm usually come among crowds of masking people. Most that don't are a matter for the army, not us."

Moblay Sopsirk's son went over to the shelf where the war board was stored. "If we can't go out today, Radnal, care for the game we didn't have last night?"

"Maybe another time, freeman vez Sopsirk," the tour guide said, turning Moblay's name into its nearest Tarteshan equivalent. Maybe the brown man would take the hint and speak a bit more formally to him. But Moblay didn't seem good at catching hints, as witness his advances toward Evillia and this even more poorly timed suggestion of a game.

The Eye and Ear returned from the stable without the solution to Dokhnor's death. By his low-voiced comments to his friends, he was glad he'd escaped the den of vicious beasts with his life. The Trench Park staffers tried to hide their sniggers. Even a few of the tourists, only two days better acquainted with donkeys than the Eye and Ear, chuckled at his alarm.

Something on the roof said *hig-hig-hig!* in a loud, strident voice. The Eye and Ear who'd braved the stables started nervously. Peggol vez Menk raised his eyebrow again. "What's that, freeman vez Krobir?"

"A koprit bird," Radnal said. "They hardly ever impale people on thorn bushes."

"No, eh? That's good to hear." Peggol's dry cough served him for a laugh.

The midday meal was ration packs. Radnal sent Liem vez Steries a worried look: the extra mouths at the lodge would make supplies run out faster than he'd planned for. Understanding the look, Liem said, "We'll fly in more from the militia outpost if we have to."

"Good."

Between them, Peggol vez Menk and Liem vez Steries spent most of the afternoon on the radiophone. Radnal worried about power, but not as much. Even if the generator ran out of fuel, solar cells would take up most of the slack. Trench Park had plenty of sunshine.

After supper, the militiamen and Eyes and Ears scattered sleepsacks on the common room floor. Peggol set up a watch schedule that gave each of his and Liem's men about half a daytenth each. Radnal volunteered to stand a watch himself.

"No," Peggol answered. "While I do not doubt your innocence, freeman vez Krobir, you and your colleagues formally remain under suspicion here. The Morgaffo plenipo could protest were you given a post which might let you somehow take advantage of us."

Though that made some sense, it miffed Radnal. He retired to his sleeping cubicle in medium dudgeon, lay down, and discovered he could not sleep. The last two nights, he'd been on the edge of dropping off when Evillia and Lofosa called. Now he was awake, and they stayed away.

He wondered why. They'd already shown they didn't care who watched them when they made love. Maybe they thought he was too shy to do anything with militiamen and Eyes and Ears outside the entrance. A few days before, they would have been right. Now he wondered. They took fornication so much for granted that they made any other view of it seem foolish.

Whatever their reasons, they stayed away. Radnal tossed and turned on his sleepsack. He thought about going out to chat with the fellow on watch, but decided not to: Peggol vez Menk would suspect he was up to something nefarious if he tried. That annoyed him all over again, and drove sleep further away than ever. So did the Martoisi's furious row over how one of them—Eltsac said Nocso, Nocso said Eltsac—had managed to lose their only currycomb.

The tour guide eventually dozed off, for he woke with a start when the men in the common room turned up the lights just before sunrise. For a heartbeat or two, he wondered why they were there. Then he remembered.

Yawning, he grabbed his cap, tied the belt on his robe, and headed out of the cubicle. Zosel vez Glesir and a couple of tourists were already in the common room, talking with the militiamen and the Eyes and Ears. Conversation flagged when Lofosa emerged from her sleeping cubicle without dressing first.

"A tough job, this tour guide business must be," Peggol vez Menk said, sounding like everyone else who thought a guide did nothing but roll on the sleepsack with his tourists.

Radnal grunted. This tour, he hadn't done much with Lofosa or Evillia but roll on the sleepsack. *It's not usually like that*, he wanted to say. He didn't think Peggol would believe him, so he kept his mouth shut. If an Eye and Ear didn't believe something, he'd start digging. If he started to dig, he'd keep digging till he found what he was looking for, regardless of whether it was really there.

The tour guide and Zosel dug out breakfast packs. By the time they came back, everyone was up, and Evillia had succeeded in distracting some of the males from Lofosa. "Here you are, freelady," Radnal said to Toglo zev Pamdal when he got to her.

No one paid her any particular attention; she was just a Tarteshan woman in a concealing Tarteshan robe, not a foreign doxy wearing nothing much. Radnal wondered if that irked her. Women, in his experience, did not like being ignored.

If she was irked, she didn't show it. "I trust you slept well, freeman vez Krobir?" she said. She did not even glance toward Evillia and Lofosa. If she meant anything more by her greeting than its words, she also gave no sign of that—which suited Radnal perfectly.

"Yes. I trust you did likewise," he answered.

"Well enough," she said, "though not as well as I did before the Morgaffo was killed. A pity he'll not be able to make his sketches—he had talent. May his Goddess grant him wind and land and water in the world to come. That's what the islanders pray for, not so?"

"I believe so, yes," Radnal said, though he knew little of Morgaffo religious forms.

"I'm glad you've arranged for the tour to continue despite the misfortune that befell him, Radnal vez," she said. "It can do him no harm, and the Bottomlands are fascinating."

"So they are, fr—" Radnal began. Then he stopped, stared, and blinked. Toglo hadn't used formal address, but the middle grade of Tarteshan politesse, which implied she felt she knew him somewhat and didn't disapprove of him. Considering what she'd witnessed at the first night's campsite, that was a minor miracle. He grinned and took a like privilege: "So do I, Toglo zev."

About a tenth of a daytenth later, as he and Fer carried empty ration packs to the disposal bin, the other Trench Park staffer elbowed him in the ribs and said, "You have *all* the women after you eh, Radnal vez?"

Radnal elbowed back, harder. "Go jump in the Bitter Lake, Fer vez. This group's nothing but trouble. Besides, Nocso zev Martois thinks I'm part of the furniture."

"You wouldn't want her," Fer replied, chuckling. "I was just jealous."

"That's what Moblay said," Radnal answered. Having anyone jealous of him for being sexually attractive was a new notion, one he didn't care for. By Tarteshan standards, drawing such notice was faintly disreputable, as if he'd got rich by skirting the law. It didn't bother Evillia and Lofosa—they reveled in it. *Well*, he asked himself, *do you really want to be like Evillia and Lofosa, no matter how ripe their bodies are?* He snorted through his nose. "Let's go back inside, so I can get my crew moving."

After two days of practice, the tourists thought they were seasoned riders. They bounded onto their donkeys, and had little trouble guiding them out of their stalls. Peggol vez Menk looked almost as apprehensive as his henchman who'd gone to search the stable. He drew in his white robe all around him, as if fearing to have it soiled. "You expect me to ride one of these creatures?" he said.

"You were the one who wanted to come along," Radnal answered. "You don't have to ride; you could always hike along beside us."

Peggol glared. "Thank you, no, freeman vez Krobir." He pointedly did *not* say *Radnal vez*. "Will you be good enough to show me how to ascend one of these perambulating peaks?"

"Certainly, freeman vez Menk." Radnal mounted a donkey, dismounted, got on again. The donkey gave him a jaundiced stare, as if asking him to make up his mind. He dismounted once more, and took the snort that followed as the asinine equivalent of a resigned shrug. To Peggol, he said, "Now you try, freeman."

Unlike Evillia or Lofosa, the Eye and Ear managed to imitate Radnal's movements without requiring the tour guide to take him by the waist (just as well, Radnal thought—Peggol wasn't smooth and supple like the Highhead girls). He said, "When back in Tarteshem, freeman vez Krobir, I shall stick exclusively to motors."

"When I'm in Tarteshem, freeman vez Menk, I do the same," Radnal answered.

The party set out a daytenth after sunrise: not as early as Radnal would have liked but, given the previous day's distractions, the best he could expect. He led them south, toward the lowlands at the core of Trench Park. Under his straw hat, Moblay Sopsirk's son was already sweating hard.

Something skittered into hiding under the fleshy leaves of a desert spurge. "What did we just nearly see there, freeman?" Golobol asked.

Radnal smiled at the physician's phrasing. "That was a fat sand rat. It's a member of the gerbil family, one specially adapted to feed off succulent plants that concentrate salt in their foliage. Fat sand rats are common throughout the Bottomlands. They're pests in areas where there's enough water for irrigated agriculture."

Moblay said, "You sound like you know a lot about them, Radnal."

"Not as much as I'd like to, freeman vez Sopsirk," Radnal answered, still trying to persuade the Lissonese to stop being so uncouthly familiar. "I study them when I'm not being a tour guide."

"I hate all kinds of rats," Nocso zev Martois said flatly.

"Oh, I don't know," Eltsac said. "Some rats are kind of cute." The two Martoisi began to argue. Everyone else ignored them.

Moblay said, "Hmp. Fancy spending all your time studying rats."

"And how do you make *your* livelihood, freeman?" Radnal snapped.

"Me?" Flat-nosed, dark, and smooth, Moblay's face was different from Radnal's in every way. But the tour guide recognized the blank mask that appeared on it for a heartbeat: the expression of a man with something to hide. Moblay said, "As I told you, I am aide to my prince, may his years be many." He had said that, Radnal remembered. It might even be true, but he was suddenly convinced it wasn't the whole truth.

Benter vez Maprab couldn't have cared less about the fat sand rat. The spiny spurge under which it hid, however, interested him. He said, "Freeman vez Krobir, perhaps you will explain the relationship between the plants here and the cactuses in the deserts of the Double Continent."

"There is no relationship to speak of." Radnal gave the old Strongbrow an unfriendly look. *Try to make me look bad in front of everyone, will you?* he thought. He went on, "The resemblances come from adapting to similar environments. That's called convergent evolution. As soon as you cut them open, you'll see they're unrelated: spurges have a thick white milky sap, while that of cactuses is clear and watery. Whales and fish look very much alike, too, but that's because they both live in the sea, not because they're kin."

Benter hunched low over his donkey's back. Radnal felt like preening, as if he'd overcome a squadron of Morgaffo marine commandos rather than one querulous old Tarteshan.

Some of the spines of the desert spurge held a jerboa, a couple of grasshoppers, a shoveler skink, and other small, dead creatures. "Who hung them out to dry?" Peggol vez Menk asked.

"A koprit bird," Radnal answered. "Most butcherbirds make a larder of things they've caught but haven't got round to eating yet."

"Oh." Peggol sounded disappointed. Maybe he'd hoped someone in Trench Park enjoyed tormenting animals, so he could hunt down the miscreant.

Toglo zev Pamdal pointed to the impaled lizard, which looked to have spent a while in the sun. "Do they eat things as dried up as that, Radnal vez?"

"No, probably not," Radnal said. "At least, I wouldn't want to." After he got his small laugh, he continued, "A koprit bird's larder isn't just things it intends to eat. It's also a display to other koprit birds. That's especially true in breeding season—it's as if the male says to prospective mates, 'Look what a hunter I am.' Koprits don't display only live things they've caught, either. I've seen hoards with bright bits of yarn, wires, pieces of sparkling plastic, and once even a set of old false teeth, all hung on spines."

"False teeth?" Evillia looked sidelong at Benter vez Maprab. "Some of us have more to worry about than others." Stifled snorts of laughter went up from several tourists. Even Eltsac chuckled. Benter glared at the Highhead girl. She ignored him.

High in the sky, almost too small to see, were a couple of moving black specks. As Radnal pointed them out to the group, a third joined them. "Another feathered optimist," he said. "This is wonderful country for vultures. Thermals from the Bottomlands's floor make soaring effortless. They're waiting for a donkey—or one of us—to keel over and die. Then they'll feast."

"What do they eat when they can't find tourists?" Toglo zev Pamdal asked.

"Humpless camels, or boar, or anything else dead they spy," Radnal said. "The only reason there aren't more of them is that the terrain is too barren to support many large-bodied herbivores."

"I've seen country that isn't," Moblay Sopsirk's son said. "In Duvai, east of Lissonland, the herds range the grasslands almost as they did in the days before mankind. The past hundred years, though, hunting has thinned them out. So the Duvains say, at any rate; I wasn't there then."

"I've heard the same," Radnal agreed. "It isn't like that here."

He waved to show what he meant. The Bottomlands were too hot and dry to enjoy a covering of grass. Scattered over the plain were assorted varieties of succulent spurges, some spiny, some glossy with wax to hold down water loss. Sharing the landscape with them were desiccated-looking bushes—thorny burnets, oleander, tiny Bottomlands olive plants (they were too small to be trees).

Smaller plants huddled in shadows round the base of the bigger ones. Radnal knew seeds were scattered everywhere, waiting for the infrequent rains. But most of the ground was as barren as if the sea had disappeared yesterday, not five and a half million years before.

"I want all of you to drink plenty of water," Radnal said. "In weather like this you sweat more than you think. We've packed plenty aboard the donkeys, and we'll replenish their carrying bladders tonight back at the lodge. Don't be shy—heatstroke can kill you if you aren't careful."

"Warm water isn't very satisfying to drink," Lofosa grumbled.

"I am sorry, freelady, but Trench Park hasn't the resources to haul a refrigerator around for anyone's convenience," Radnal said.

Despite Lofosa's complaint, she and Evillia both drank regularly. Radnal scratched his head, wondering how the Krepalgan girls could seem so fuzz-brained but still muddle along without getting into real trouble.

Evillia had even brought along some flavoring packets, so while everyone else poured down blood-temperature water, she had blood-temperature fruit punch instead. The crystals also turned the water the color of blood. Radnal decided he could do without them.

They got to the Bitter Lake a little before noon. It was more a salt marsh than a lake; the Dalorz River did not drop enough water off the ancient continental shelf to keep a lake bed full against the tremendous evaporation in the eternally hot, eternally dry Bottomlands. Salt pans gleamed white around pools and patches of mud.

"Don't let the donkeys eat anything here," Radnal warned. "The water brings everything from the underground salt layer to the surface. Even Bottomlands' plants have trouble adapting."

That was emphatically true. Despite the water absent everywhere else in Trench Park, the landscape round the Bitter Lake was barren even by Bottomlands standards. Most of the few plants that did struggle to grow were tiny and stunted.

Benter vez Maprab, whose sole interest seemed to be horticulture, pointed to one of the exceptions. "What's that, the ghost of a plant abandoned by the gods?"

"It looks like it," Radnal said; the shrub had skinny, almost skeletal branches and leaves. Rather than being green, it was white with sparkles that shifted as the breeze shook it. "It's a saltbush, and it's found only around the Bitter Lake. It deposits the salts it picks up from ground water as crystals on all its above-ground parts. That does two things: it gets rid of the salt, and having the reflective coating lowers the plant's effective temperature."

"It also probably keeps the saltbush from getting eaten very often," Toglo zev Pamdal said.

"Yes, but with a couple of exceptions," Radnal said. "One is the humpless camel, which has its own ways of getting rid of excess salt. The other is my little friend the fat sand rat, although it prefers desert spurges, which are juicier."

The Strongbrow woman looked around. "One of the things I expected to see when I came down here, both the first time and now, was lots of lizards and snakes and tortoises. I haven't, and it puzzles me. I'd have thought the Bottomlands would be a perfect place for cold-blooded creatures to live."

"If you look at dawn or dusk, Toglo zev, you'll see plenty. But not in the heat of the day. Cold-blooded isn't a good term for reptiles; they have a variable body temperature, not a constant one like birds or mammals. They warm themselves by basking, and cool down by staying out of the midday sun. If they didn't, they'd cook."

"I know just how they feel." Evillia ran a hand through her thick dark hair. "You can stick eating tongs in me now, because I'm done all the way through."

"It's not so bad as that," Radnal said. "I'm sure it's under fifty hundredths, and it can get above fifty even here. And Trench Park doesn't have any of the deepest parts of the Bottomlands. Down another couple of thousand cubits, the extreme temperatures go above sixty."

The non-Tarteshans groaned. So did Toglo zev Pamdal and Peggol vez Menk. Tarteshem had a relatively mild climate; temperatures there went past forty hundredths only from late spring to early fall.

With morbid curiosity, Moblay Sopsirk's son said, "What is the highest temperature ever recorded in the Bottomlands?"

"Just over sixty-six," Radnal said. The tourists groaned again, louder.

Radnal led the line of donkeys around the Bitter Lake. He was careful not to get too close to the little water actually in the lake at this time of year. Sometimes a salt crust formed over mud; a donkey's hoof could poke right through, trapping the animal and slicing its leg against the hard, sharp edge of the crust.

After a while, the tour guide asked, "Do you have all the pictures you want?" When no one denied it, he said, "Then we'll head back toward the lodge."

"Hold on." Eltsac vez Martois pointed across the Bitter Lake. "What are those things over there?"

"I don't see anything, Eltsac," his wife said. "You must be looking at a what-do-you-call-it, a mirage." Then, grudgingly, a heartbeat later, "Oh."

"It's a herd of humpless camels," Radnal said quietly. "Try not to spook them."

The herd was a little one, a couple of long-necked males with a double handful of smaller females, and a few young ones that seemed all leg and awkwardness. Unlike the donkeys, they ambled over the crust around the Bitter Lake. Their hooves were wide and soft, spreading under their weight to keep them from falling through.

A male stood guard as the rest of the herd drank at a scummy pool of water. Golobol looked distressed. "That horrid liquid, surely it will poison them," he said. "I would not drink it to save my life." His round brown face screwed up in disgust.

"If you drank it, it would end your days all the sooner. But humpless camels have evolved along with the

Bottomlands; their kidneys are wonderfully efficient at extracting large amounts of salt."

"Why don't they have humps?" Lofosa asked. "Krepalgan camels have humps." By her tone, what she was used to was right.

"I know Krepalgan camels have humps," Radnal said. "But the camels in the southern half of the Double Continent don't, and neither do these. With the Bottomlands beasts, I think the answer is that any lump of fat—which is what a hump is—is a liability in getting rid of heat."

"In the days before motors, we used to ride our Krepalgan camels," Evillia said. "Has anyone ever tamed your humpless ones?"

"That's a good question," Radnal said, beaming to hide his surprise at her coming up with a good question. He went on, "It has been tried many times, in fact. So far, it's never worked. They're too stubborn to do what a human being wants. If we had domesticated them, you'd be riding them now instead of these donkeys; they're better suited to the terrain here."

Toglo zev Pamdal scratched her mount's ears. "They're also uglier than donkeys."

"Freelady—uh, Toglo zev—I can't argue with you," Radnal said. "They're uglier than anything I can think of, with dispositions to match."

As if insulted by words they couldn't have heard, the humpless camels raised their heads and trotted away from the Bitter Lake. Their backs went up and down, up and down, in time to their rocking gait. Evillia said, "In Krepalga, we sometimes call camels desert barques. Now I see why; riding on one looks like it would make me seasick."

The tourists laughed. So did Radnal. Making a joke in a language that wasn't Evillia's took some brains. Then why, Radnal wondered, did she act so empty-headed? But he shrugged; he'd seen a lot of people *with* brains do impressively stupid things.

"Why don't the camels eat all the forage in Trench Park?" Benter vez Maprab asked. He sounded as if his concern was for the plants, not the humpless camels.

"When the herds get too large for the park's resources, we cull them," Radnal answered. "This ecosystem is fragile. If we let it get out of balance, it would be a long time repairing itself."

"Are any herds of wild humpless camels left outside Trench Park, Radnal vez?" Toglo asked.

"A few small ones, in areas of the Bottomlands too barren for people," the tour guide said. "Not many, though. We occasionally introduce new males into this herd to increase genetic diversity, but they come from zoological parks, not the wild." The herd receded rapidly, shielded from clear view by the dust it kicked up. "I'm glad we had a chance to see them, if at a distance. That's why the gods made long lenses for cameras. But now we should head back to the lodge."

The return journey north struck Radnal as curiously unreal. Though Peggol vez Menk rode among the tourists, they seemed to be pretending as hard as they could that Dokhnor of Kellef had not died, that this was just an ordinary holiday. The alternative was always looking over a shoulder, remembering the person next to you might be a murderer.

The person next to someone was a murderer. Whoever it was, he seemed no different from anyone else. That worried Radnal more than anything.

It even tainted his pleasure from talking with Toglo zev Pamdal. He had trouble imagining her as a killer, but he had trouble imagining anyone in the tour group a killer— save Dokhnor of Kellef, who was dead, and the Martoisi, who might want to kill each other.

He got to the point where he could say "Toglo zev" without prefacing it with "uh." He really wanted to ask her (but lacked the nerve) how she put up with him after watching him at play with the two Highhead girls. Tarteshans seldom thought well of those who made free with their bodies.

He also wondered what he'd do if Evillia and Lofosa came into his cubicle tonight. He'd throw them out, he decided. Edifying a tour group was one thing, edifying the Park Militia and the Eyes and Ears another. But what they did was so edifying. . . . Maybe he wouldn't throw them out. He banged a fist onto his knee, irritated at his own fleshly weakness.

The lodge was only a couple of thousand cubits away when his donkey snorted and stiffened its legs against the ground. "Earthquake!" The word went up in Tarteshan and other languages. Radnal felt the ground jerk beneath him. He watched, and marveled at, the Martoisi clinging to each other atop their mounts.

After what seemed a daytenth but had to be an interval measured in heartbeats, the shaking ceased. Just in time, too; Peggol vez Menk's donkey, panicked by the tremor, was about to buck the Eye and Ear into a thornbush. Radnal caught the beast's reins, calmed it.

"Thank you, freeman vez Krobir," Peggol said. "That was bad."

"You didn't make it any better by letting go of the reins," Radnal told him. "If you were in a motor, wouldn't you hang on to the tiller?"

"I hope so," Peggol said. "But if I were in a motor, it wouldn't try to run away by itself."

Moblay Sopsirk's son looked west, toward the Barrier Mountains. "That was worse than the one yesterday. I feared I'd see the Western Ocean pouring in with a wave as high as the Lion God's mane."

"As I've said before, that's not something you're likely to have to worry about," Radnal said. "A quake would have to be very strong and at exactly the wrong place to disturb the mountains."

"So it would." Moblay did not sound comforted.

Radnal dismissed his concern with the mild scorn you feel for someone who overreacts to a danger you're used to. Over in the Double Continent, they had vast and deadly windstorms. Radnal was sure one of those would frighten him out of his wits.

But the Stekians probably took them in stride, as he lost no sleep over earthquakes.

The sun sank toward the spikes of the Barrier Mountains. As if bloodied by their pricking, its rays grew redder as Bottomlands shadows lengthened. More red sparkled from the glass and metal and plastic of the helos between the lodge and the stables. Noticing them made Radnal return to the here and now. He wondered how the militiamen and Eyes and Ears had done in their search for clues.

They came out as the tour group approached. In their tan, speckled robes, the militiamen were almost invisible against the desert. The Eyes and Ears, with their white and gold and patent leather, might have been spotted from ten thousand cubits away, or from the mountains of the moon.

Liem vez Steries waved to Radnal. "Any luck? Do you have the killer tied up in pink string?"

"Do you see any pink string?" Radnal turned back to face the group, raised his voice: "Let's get the donkeys settled. They can't do it for themselves. When they're fed and watered, we can worry about ourselves." *And about everything that's been going on*, he added to himself.

The tourists were quieter than they'd been the day before; they were growing hardened to riding. Poor Peggol vez Menk assumed a bowlegged gait most often seen in rickets victims. "I was thinking of taking yesterday off," he said lugubriously. "I wish I had—someone else would have taken your call."

"You might have drawn a worse assignment," Radnal

said, helping him unsaddle the donkey. The way Peggol rolled his eyes denied that was possible.

Fer vez Canthal and Zosel vez Glesir came over to help see to the tour group's donkeys. Under the brims of their caps, their eyes sparked with excitement. "Well, Radnal vez, we have a good deal to tell *you*," Fer began.

Peggol had a sore fundament, but his wits still worked. He made a sharp chopping gesture. "Freeman, save your news for a more private time." A smoother motion, this time with upturned palm, pointed out the chattering crowd still inside the stables. "Someone may hear something he should not."

Fer looked abashed. "Your pardon, freeman; no doubt you are right."

"No doubt," Peggol's tone argued that he couldn't be anything but. From under the shiny brim of his cap, his gaze flicked here and there, measuring everyone in turn with the calipers of his suspicion. It came to Radnal, and showed no softening.

Resentment flared in the tour guide, then dimmed. He knew he hadn't killed anyone, but the Eye and Ear didn't.

"I'll get the fire pit started," Fer said.

"Good idea," Eltsac vez Martois said as he walked by. "I'm hungry enough to eat one of those humpless camels, raw and without salt."

"We can do better than that," Radnal said. He noted the I-told-you-so look Peggol sent Fer vez Canthal: if a tourist could overhear one bit of casual conversation, why not another?

Liem vez Steries greeted Peggol with a formal military salute he didn't use five times a year—his body went tetanus-rigid, while he brought his right hand up so the tip of his middle finger brushed the brim of his cap. "Freeman, my compliments. We've all heard of the abilities of the Hereditary Tyrant's Eyes and Ears, but until now I've never seen them in action. Your team is superb, and what they found—" Unlike Fer vez Canthal, Liem had enough sense to close his mouth right there.

Radnal felt like dragging him into the desert to pry loose what he knew. But years of slow research had left him a patient man. He ate supper, sang songs, chatted about the earthquake and what he'd seen on the journey to and from the Bitter Lake. One by one, the tourists sought their sleepsacks.

Moblay Sopsirk's son, however, sought him out for a game of war. For politeness' sake, Radnal agreed to play, though he had so much on his mind that he was sure the brown man from Lissonland would trounce him. Either Moblay had things on his mind, too, or he wasn't the player he thought he was. The game was a comedy of errors which had the spectators biting their lips to keep from blurting out better moves. Radnal eventually won, in inartistic style.

Benter vez Maprab had been an onlooker. When the game ended, he delivered a two-sentence verdict which was also an obituary: "A wasted murder. Had the Morgaffo seen that, he'd've died of embarrassment." He stuck his nose in the air and stalked off to his sleeping cubicle.

"We'll have to try again another time, when we're thinking straighter," Radnal told Moblay, who nodded ruefully.

Radnal put away the war board and pieces. By then, Moblay was the only tourist left in the common room. Radnal sat down next to Liem vez Steries, not across the gaming table from the Lissonese. Moblay refused to take the hint.

Finally Radnal grabbed the rhinoceros by the horn: "Forgive me, freeman, but we have a lot to discuss among ourselves."

"Don't mind me," Moblay said cheerfully. "I'm not in your way, I hope. And I'd be interested to hear how you Tarteshans investigate. Maybe I can bring something useful back to my prince."

Radnal exhaled through his nose. Biting off words one by one, he said, "Freeman vez Sopsirk, you are a subject of this investigation. To be blunt, we have matters to discuss which you shouldn't hear."

"We also have other, weightier, things to discuss," Peggol vez Menk put in. "Remember, freeman, this is not your principality."

"It never occurred to me that you might fear I was guilty," Moblay said. "I know I'm not, so I assumed you did, too. Maybe I'll try and screw the Krepalgan girls, since it doesn't sound like Radnal will be using them tonight."

Peggol raised an eyebrow. "Them?" He packed a world of question into one word.

Under their coat of down, Radnal's ears went hot. Fortunately, he managed to answer a question with a question: "What could be weightier than learning who killed Dokhnor of Kellef?"

Peggol glanced from one sleeping cubicle to the next, as if wondering who was feigning slumber. "Why don't you walk with me in the cool night air? Subleader vez Steries can come with us; he was here all day, and can tell you what he saw himself—things I heard when I took my own evening walk, and which I might garble in reporting them to you."

"Let's walk, then," Radnal said, though he wondered where Peggol vez Menk would find cool night air in Trench Park. Deserts above sea level cooled rapidly when the sun set, but that wasn't true in the Bottomlands.

Getting out in the quiet dark made it seem cooler. Radnal, Peggol, and Liem walked without saying much for a couple of hundred cubits. Only when they were out of earshot of the lodge did the park militiaman announce, "Freeman vez Menk's colleagues discovered a microprint reader among the Morgaffo's effect."

"Did they, by the gods?" Radnal said. "Where, Liem vez? What was it disguised as?"

"A stick of artist's charcoal." The militiaman shook his head. "I thought I knew every trick in the codex, but that's a new one. Now we can rub the plenipo's nose in it if he fusses about losing a Morgaffo citizen in Tartesh. But even that's a small thing, next to what the reader held."

Radnal stared. "Heading off a war with Morgaf is small?"

"It is, freeman vez Krobir," Peggol vez Menk said. "You remember today's earthquake—"

"Yes, and there was another one yesterday, a smaller one," Radnal interrupted. "They happen all the time down here. No one except a tourist like Moblay Sopsirk's son worries about them. You reinforce your buildings so they won't fall down except in the worst shocks, then go on about your business."

"Sensible," Peggol said. "Sensible under most circumstances, anyway. Not here, not now."

"Why not?" Radnal demanded.

"Because, if what was on Dokhnor of Kellef's microprint reader is true—always a question when we're dealing with Morgaffos—someone is trying to engineer a special earthquake."

Radnal's frown drew his heavy eyebrows together above his nose. "I still don't know what you're talking about."

Liem vez Steries inclined his head to Peggol vez Menk. "By your leave, freeman—?" When Peggol nodded, Liem went on, "Radnal vez, over the years somebody—has smuggled the parts for a starbomb into Trench Park."

The tour guide gaped at his friend. "That's insane. If somebody smuggled a starbomb into Tartesh, he'd put it by the Hereditary Tyrant's palace, not here. What does he want, blow up the last big herd of humpless camels in the world?"

"He has more in mind than that," Liem answered. "You see, the bomb is underground, on one of the fault lines nearest the Barrier Mountains." The militiaman's head swiveled to look west toward the sawbacked young mountain range . . .

. . . the mountain range that held back the Western Ocean. The night was warm and dry, but cold sweat prickled on Radnal's back and under his arms. "They want to try to knock the mountains down. I'm no geologist—can they?"

"The gods may know," Liem answered. "I'm no geologist either, so I don't. This I'll tell you: the Morgaffos seem to think it would work."

Peggol vez Menk cleared his throat. "The Hereditary Tyrant discourages research in this area, lest any positive answers fall into the wrong hands. Thus our studies have been limited. I gather, however, that such a result might be obtained."

"The freeman's colleagues radiophoned a geologist known to be reliable," Liem amplified. "They put to him some of what was on the microprint reader, as a theoretical exercise. When they were through, he sounded ready to wet his robes."

"I don't blame him." Radnal looked toward the Barrier Mountains, too. What had Moblay said?—*a wave as high as the Lion God's mane*. If the mountains fell at once, the wave might reach Krepalga before it halted. The deaths, the devastation, would be incalculable. His voice shook as he asked, "What do we do about it?"

"Good question," Peggol said, astringent as usual. "We don't know whether it's really there, who planted it if it is, where it is, or if it's ready. Other than that, we're fine."

Liem's voice turned savage: "I wish all the tourists were Tarteshans. Then we could question them as thoroughly as we needed, until we got truth from them."

Thoroughly, Radnal knew, was a euphemism for *harshly*. Tarteshan justice was more pragmatic than merciful, so much so that applying it to foreigners would strain diplomatic relations and might provoke war. The tour guide said, "We couldn't even be properly thorough with our own people, not when one of them is Toglo zev Pamdal."

"I'd forgotten." Liem made a face. "But you can't suspect her. Why would the Hereditary Tyrant's relative want to destroy the country he's Hereditary Tyrant of? It makes no sense."

"I don't suspect her," Radnal said. "I meant we'll have to use our heads here; we can't rely on brute force."

"I suspect everyone," Peggol vez Menk said, matter-of-factly as if he'd said, *It's hot tonight.* "For that matter, I also suspect the information we found among Dokhnor's effects. It might have been planted there to provoke us to question several foreign tourists thoroughly and embroil us with their governments. Morgaffo duplicity knows no bounds."

"As may be, freeman, but dare we take the chance that this is duplicity, not real danger?" Liem said.

"If you mean, dare we ignore the danger?—of course not," Peggol said. "But it might be duplicity."

"Would the Morgaffos kill one of their own agents to mislead us?" Radnal asked. "If Dokhnor were alive, we'd have no idea this plot was afoot."

"They might, precisely because they'd expect us to doubt they were so coldhearted," Peggol answered. Radnal thought the Eye and Ear would suspect someone of stealing the sun if a morning dawned cloudy. That was what Eyes and Ears were for, but it made Peggol an uncomfortable companion.

"Since we can't question the tourists thoroughly, what shall we do tomorrow?" Radnal said.

"Go on as we have been," Peggol replied unhappily. "If any of them makes the slightest slip, that will justify our using appropriate persuasive measures." Not even a man who sometimes used torture in his work was easy saying the word out loud.

"I can see one problem coming soon, freeman vez Menk—" Radnal said.

"Call me Peggol vez," the Eye and Ear interrupted. "We're in this mess together; we might as well treat each other as friends. I'm sorry—go ahead."

"Sooner or later, Peggol vez, the tour group will want to go west, toward the Barrier Mountains—and toward the fault line where this starbomb may be. If it requires some finishing touches, that will give whoever is supposed to handle them his best chance. If it is someone in the tour group, of course."

"When were you thinking of doing this?" If he'd sounded unhappy before, he was lugubrious now.

Radnal didn't cheer him up: "The western swing was on the itinerary for tomorrow. I could change it, but—"

"But that would warn the culprit—if there is a culprit— we know what's going on. Yes." Peggol fingered the tuft of hair under his lip. "I think you'd better make the change anyhow, Radnal vez." Having heard Radnal use his name with the polite particle, he could do likewise. "Better to alert the enemy than offer him a free opportunity."

Liem vez Steries began, "Freeman vez Menk—"

The Eye and Ear broke in again: "What I told Radnal also holds for you."

"Fair enough, Peggol vez," Liem said. "How could Morgaf have got wind of this plot against Tartesh without our having heard of it, too? I mean no disrespect, I assure you, but this matter concerns me." He waved toward the Barrier Mountains, which suddenly seemed a much less solid bulwark than they had before.

"The question is legitimate, and I take no offense. I see two possible answers," Peggol said (Radnal had a feeling the Eye and Ear saw at least two answers to every question). "One is that Morgaf may be doing this deceitfully to incite us against our other neighbors, as I said before. The other is that the plot is real, and whoever dreamed it up approached the Morgaffos so they could fall on us after the catastrophe."

Each possibility was logical; Radnal wished he could choose between them. Since he couldn't, he said, "There's nothing we can do about it now, so we might as well sleep. In the morning, I'll tell the tourists we're going east, not west. That's an interesting excursion, too. It—"

Peggol raised a hand. "Since I'll see it tomorrow, why not keep me in suspense?" He twisted this way and that. "You can't die of an impacted fundament, can you?"

"I've never heard of it happening, anyhow." Radnal hid a smile.

"Maybe I'll be a medical first, and get written up in all the physicians' codices." Peggol rubbed the afflicted parts. "And I'll have to go riding again tomorrow, eh? How unfortunate."

"If we don't get some sleep soon, we'll both be dozing in the saddle," Radnal said, yawning. "It must be a couple of daytenths past sunset by now. I thought Moblay would never head for his cubicle."

"Maybe he was just fond of you, Radnal." Liem vez Steries put a croon in the guide's name that burlesqued the way the Lissonese kept leaving off the polite particle.

Radnal snapped, "Night demons carry you off, Liem vez, the ideas you come up with." He waited for the militiaman to taunt him about Evillia and Lofosa, but Liem left that alone. He wondered what ideas the two girls from the Krepalgan Unity had come up with, and whether they'd use them with him tonight. He hoped not—as he'd told Peggol, he did need sleep. Then he wondered if putting sleep ahead of fornication meant he was getting old.

If it did, too bad, he decided. Along with Peggol and Liem, he walked back to the lodge. The other militiamen and Eyes and Ears reported in whispers—all quiet.

Radnal turned a curious ear toward Evillia's sleep cubicle, then Lofosa's, and then Moblay Sopsirk's son's.

He didn't hear moans or thumpings from any of them. He wondered whether Moblay hadn't propositioned the Krepalgan girls, or whether they'd turned him down. Or maybe they'd frolicked and gone back to sleep. No, that last wasn't likely; the Eyes and Ears would have been smirking about the eye- and earful they'd got.

Yawning again, Radnal went into his own sleep cubicle, took off his sandals, undid his belt, and lay down. The air-filled sleepsack sighed beneath him like a lover. He angrily shook his head. Two nights with Lofosa and Evillia had filled his mind with lewd notions.

He hoped they would leave him alone again. He knew their dalliance with him was already an entry in Peggol vez Menk's dossier; having the Eye and Ear watch him at play—or listen to him quarreling with them when he sent them away—would not improve the entry.

Those two nights, he'd just been falling asleep when Evillia and Lofosa joined him. Tonight, nervous about whether they'd come, and about everything he'd heard from Peggol and Liem, he lay awake a long time. The girls stayed in their own cubicles.

He dozed off without knowing he'd done so. His eyes flew open when a koprit bird on the roof announced the dawn with a raucous *hig-hig-hig!* He needed a couple of heartbeats to wake fully, realize he'd been asleep, and remember what he'd have to do this morning. He put on his sandals, fastened his belt, and walked into the common room. Most of the militiamen and Eyes and Ears were already awake. Peggol wasn't; Radnal wondered how much knowing he snored would be worth as blackmail. Liem vez Steries said quietly, "No one murdered last night."

"I'm glad to hear it," Radnal said, sarcastic and truthful at the same time.

Lofosa came out of her cubicle. She still wore what Radnal assumed to be Krepalgan sleeping attire, namely skin. Not a hair on her head was mussed, and she'd done something to her eyes to make them look bigger and brighter than they really were. All the men stared at her, some more openly, some less.

She smiled at Radnal and said in a voice like silver bells, "I hope you didn't miss us last night, freeman vez Krobir. It would have been as much fun as the other two, but we were too tired." Before he could answer (he would have needed a while to find an answer), she went outside to the privy.

The tour guide looked down at his sandals, not daring to meet anyone's eyes. He listened to the small coughs that meant the others didn't know what to say to him, either. Finally Liem remarked, "Sounds as though she knows you well enough to call you Radnal vez."

"I suppose so," Radnal muttered. In physical terms, she'd been intimate enough with him to leave off the *vez*. Her Tarteshan was good enough that she ought to know it, too. She'd managed to embarrass him even more by combining the formal address with such a familiar message. She couldn't have made him look more foolish if she'd tried for six moons.

Evillia emerged from her cubicle, dressed, or undressed, like Lofosa. She didn't banter with Radnal, but headed straight for the privy. She and Lofosa met each other behind the helos. They talked for a few heartbeats before each continued on her way.

Toglo zev Pamdal walked into the common room as Lofosa returned from outside. Lofosa stared at the Strongbrow woman, as if daring Toglo to remark on her nakedness. A lot of Tarteshans, especially female Tarteshans, would have remarked on it in detail.

Toglo said only, "I trust you slept well, freelady?" From her casual tone, she might have been talking to a neighbor she didn't know well but with whom she was on good terms.

"Yes, thank you." Lofosa dropped her eyes when she

concluded she couldn't use her abundantly displayed charms to bait Toglo.

"I'm glad to hear it," Toglo said, still sweetly. "I wouldn't want you to catch cold on holiday."

Lofosa took half a step, then jerked as if poked by a pin. Toglo had already turned to greet the others in the common room. For a heartbeat, maybe two, Lofosa's teeth showed in a snarl like a cave cat's. Then she went back into her cubicle to finish getting ready for the day.

"I hope I didn't offend her—too much," Toglo said to Radnal.

"I think you handled yourself like a diplomat," he answered.

"Hmm," she said. "Given the state of the world, I wonder whether that's a compliment." Radnal didn't answer. Given what he'd heard the night before, the state of the world might be worse than Toglo imagined.

His own diplomatic skills got a workout after breakfast, when he explained to the group that they'd be going east rather than west. Golobol said, "I find the change from the itinerary most distressing, yes." His round brown face bore a doleful expression.

Benter vez Maprab found any change distressing. "This is an outrage," he blustered. "The herbaceous cover approaching the Barrier Mountains is far richer than that to the east."

"I'm sorry," Radnal said, an interesting mixture of truth and lie; he didn't mind annoying Benter, but would sooner not have had such a compelling reason.

"I don't mind going east rather than west today," Toglo zev Pamdal said. "As far as I'm concerned, there are plenty of interesting things to see either way. But I would like to know why the schedule has been changed."

"So would I," Moblay Sopsirk's son said. "Toglo is right— what are you trying to hide, anyhow?"

All the tourists started talking—the Martoisi started

shouting—at once. Radnal's own reaction to the Lissonese man was a wish that a trench in Trench Park went down a lot deeper, say, to the red-hot center of the Earth. He would have shoved Moblay into it. Not only was he a boor, to use a woman's name without the polite particle (using it uninvited, even with the particle, would have been an undue liberty), he was a snoop and a rabble-rouser.

Peggol vez Menk slammed his open hand down on the table beside which Dokhnor of Kellef had died. The boom cut through the chatter. Into sudden silence, Peggol said, "Freeman vez Krobir changed your itinerary at my suggestion. Aspects of the murder case suggest that course would be in the best interests of Tartesh."

"This tells us nothing, not a thing." Now Golobol sounded really angry, not just upset at breaking routine. "You say these fine-sounding words, but where is the meaning behind them?"

"If I told you everything you wished to know, freeman, I would also be telling those who should not hear," Peggol said.

"Pfui!" Golobol stuck out his tongue.

Eltsac vez Martois said, "I think you Eyes and Ears think you're little tin demigods."

But Peggol's pronouncement quieted most of the tourists. Ever since starbombs came along, nations had grown more anxious about keeping secrets from one another. That struck Radnal as worrying about the cave cat after he'd carried off the goat, but who could tell? There might be worse things than starbombs.

He said, "As soon as I can, I promise I will tell all of you everything I can about what's going on." Peggol vez Menk gave him a hard look; Peggol wouldn't have told anyone his own name if he could help it.

"What *is* going on?" Toglo echoed. Since Radnal was none too certain himself, he met that comment with dignified silence. He did say, "The longer we quarrel here, the less we'll have the chance to see, no matter which direction we end up choosing."

"That makes sense, freeman vez Krobir," Evillia said. Neither she nor Lofosa had argued about going east as opposed to west.

Radnal looked around the group, saw more resignation than outrage. He said, "Come now, freemen, freeladies, let's head for the stables. There are many fascinating things to see east of the lodge—and to hear, also. There's the Night Demons' Retreat, for instance."

"Oh, good!" Toglo clapped her hands. "As I've said, it rained the last time I was here. The guide was too worried about flash floods to take us out there. I've wanted to see that ever since I read Hicag zev Ginfer's frightener codex."

"You mean *Stones of Doom*?" Radnal's opinion of Toglo's taste fell. Trying to stay polite, he said, "It wasn't as accurate as it might have been."

"I thought it was trash," Toglo said. "But I went to school with Hicag zev and we've been friends ever since, so I had to read it. And she certainly makes the Night Demons' retreat sound exotic, whether there's a breeze of truth in what she writes or not."

"Maybe a breeze—a mild breeze," Radnal said.

"I read it, too. I thought it was very exciting," Nocso zev Martois said.

"The tour guide thinks it's garbage," her husband told her.

"I didn't say *that*," Radnal said. Neither Martois listened to him; they enjoyed yelling at each other more.

"Enough of your own breeze. If we must do this, let's do it, at least," Benter vez Maprab said.

"As you say, freeman." Radnal wished the Night Demons' Retreat really held night demons. With any luck, they'd drag Benter into the stones and no one in the tour group would ever see—or have to listen to—him again. But such convenient things happened only in codices.

❖   ❖   ❖

The tourists were getting better with the donkeys. Even Peggol seemed less obviously out of place on donkeyback than he had yesterday. As the group rode away from the lodge, Radnal looked back and saw park militiamen and Eyes and Ears advancing on the stables to go over them again.

He made himself forget the murder investigation and remember that he was a tour guide. "Because we're off earlier this morning, we're more likely to see small reptiles and mammals that shelter against the worst heat," he said. "Many of them—"

A sudden little *flip* of sandy dirt a few cubits ahead made him stop. "By the gods, there's one now." He dismounted. "I think that's a shoveler skink."

"A what?" By now, Radnal was used to the chorus that followed whenever he pointed out one of the more unusual denizens of the Bottomlands.

"A shoveler skink," he repeated. He crouched down. Yes, sure enough, there was the lure. He knew he had an even-money chance. If he grabbed the tail end, the lizard would shed the appendage and flee. But if he got it by the neck—

He did. The skink twisted like a piece of demented rubber, trying to wriggle free. It also voided. Lofosa made a disgusted noise. Radnal took such things in stride.

After thirty or forty heartbeats, the skink gave up and lay still. Radnal had been waiting for that. He carried the palm-sized lizard into the midst of the tourists. "Skinks are common all over the world, but the shoveler is the most curious variety. It's a terrestrial equivalent of the anglerfish. Look—"

He tapped the orange fleshy lump that grew on the end of the spine about two digits long. "The skink buries itself under sand, with just this lure and the tip of its nose sticking out. See how its ribs extend to either side, so it looks more like a gliding animal than one that lives underground? It has specialized musculature, to make those long rib ends bend in what we'd think of as the wrong way. When an insect comes along, the lizard tosses dirt on it, then twists around and snaps it up. It's a beautiful creature."

"It's the ugliest thing I ever saw," Moblay Sopsirk's son declared.

The lizard didn't care one way or the other. It peered at him through little beady black eyes. If the variety survived another few million years—if the Bottomlands survived another couple of moons, Radnal thought nervously—future specimens might lose their sight altogether, as had already happened with other subterranean skinks.

Radnal walked out of the path, and put the lizard back on the ground. It scurried away, surprisingly fast on its short legs. After six or eight cubits, it seemed to melt into the ground. Within moments, only the bright orange lure betrayed its presence.

Evillia asked, "Do any bigger creatures go around looking for lures to catch the skinks?"

"As a matter of fact, yes," Radnal said. "Koprit birds can see color; you'll often see shoveler skinks impaled in their hoards. Big-eared nightfoxes eat them, too, but they track by scent, not sight."

"I hope no koprit birds come after me," Evillia said, laughing. She and Lofosa wore matching red-orange tunics—almost the same shade as the shoveler skin's lure—with two rows of big gold buttons, and red plastic necklaces with gold clasps.

Radnal smiled. "I think you're safe enough. And now that the lizard is safe, for the time being, shall we go—? No, wait, where's freeman vez Maprab?"

The old Strongbrow emerged from behind a big, wide-spreading thorn bush a few heartbeats later, still refastening the belt to his robe. "Sorry for the delay, but I thought I'd answer nature's call while we paused here."

"I just didn't want to lose you, freeman." Radnal stared

at Benter as he got back onto his donkey. This was the first apology he'd heard from him. He wondered if the tourist was well.

The group rode slowly eastward. Before long, people began to complain. "Every piece of Trench Park looks like every other piece," Lofosa said.

"Yes, when will we see something different?" Moblay Sopsirk's son agreed. Radnal suspected he would have agreed if Lofosa said the sky were pink; he slavered after her. He went on. "It's all hot and flat and dry; even the thorn bushes are boring."

"Freeman, if you wanted to climb mountains and roll in snow, you should have gone someplace else," Radnal said. "That's not what the Bottomlands have to offer. But there are mountains and snow all over the world; there's nothing like Trench Park anywhere. And if you tell me this terrain is like what we saw yesterday around the Bitter Lake, freeman, freelady"—he glanced over at Lofosa— "I think you're both mistaken."

"They certainly are," Benter vez Maprab chimed in. "This area has very different flora from the other one. Note the broader-leafed spurges, the oleanders—"

"They're just plants," Lofosa said. Benter clapped a hand to his head in shock and dismay. Radnal waited for him to have another bad-tempered fit, but he just muttered to himself and subsided.

About a quarter of a daytenth later, Radnal pointed toward a gray smudge on the eastern horizon. "There's the Night Demons' Retreat. I promise it's like nothing you've yet seen in Trench Park."

"I hope it shall be interesting, oh yes," Golobol said.

"I loved the scene where the demons came out at sunset, claws dripping blood," Nocso zev Martois said. Her voice rose in shivery excitement.

Radnal sighed. "*Stones of Doom* is only a frightener, freelady. No demons live inside the Retreat, or come out at sunset or any other time. I've passed the night in a sleepsack not fifty cubits from the stonepile, and I'm still here, with my blood inside me where it belongs."

Nocso made a face. No doubt she preferred melodrama to reality. Since she was married to Eltsac, reality couldn't seem too attractive to her.

The Night Demons' Retreat was a pile of gray granite, about a hundred cubits high, looming over the flat floor of the Bottomlands. Holes of all sizes pitted the granite. Under the merciless sun, the black openings reminded Radnal of skulls' eyes looking at him.

"Some holes look big enough for a person to crawl into," Peggol vez Menk remarked. "Has anybody ever explored them?"

"Yes, many people," Radnal answered. "We discourage it, though, because although no one's ever found a night demon, they're a prime denning place for vipers and scorpions. They also often hold bats' nests. Seeing the bats fly out at dusk to hunt bugs doubtless helped start the legend about the place."

"Bats live all over," Nocso said. "There's only one Night Demons' Retreat, because—"

The breeze, which had been quiet, suddenly picked up. Dust swirled over the ground. Radnal grabbed for his cap. And from the many mineral throats of the Night Demons' Retreat came a hollow moaning and wailing that made the hair on his body want to stand on end.

Nocso looked ecstatic. "There!" she exclaimed. "The cry of the deathless demons, seeking to be free to work horror on the world!"

Radnal remembered the starbomb that might be buried by the Barrier Mountains, and thought of horrors worse than any demons could produce. He said, "Freelady, as I'm sure you know, it's just wind playing some badly tuned flutes. The softer rock around the Retreat weathered away, and the Retreat itself has taken a lot of sandblasting. Whatever bits that weren't as hard as the rest are gone, which explains how and why the openings formed. And now, when the wind blows across them, they make the weird sounds we just heard."

"Hmp!" Nocso said. "If there are gods, how can there not be demons?"

"Freelady, speak to a priest about that, not to me." Radnal swore by the gods of Tartesh but, like most educated folk of his generation, had little other use for them.

Peggol vez Menk said, "Freelady, the question of whether night demons exist does not necessarily have anything to do with the question of whether they haunt the Night Demons' Retreat—except that if there be no demons, they are unlikely to be at the Retreat."

Nocso's plump face filled with rage. But she thought twice about telling off an Eye and Ear. She turned her head and shouted at Eltsac instead. He shouted back.

The breeze swirled around, blowing bits of grit into the tour guide's face. More unmusical notes emanated from the Night Demons' Retreat. Cameras clicked. "I wish I'd brought along a recorder," Toglo zev Pamdal said. "What's interesting here isn't how this place looks, but how it sounds."

"You can buy a wire of the Night Demons' Retreat during a windstorm at the gift shop near the entrance to Trench Park."

"Thank you, Radnal vez; I may do that on my way out. It would be even better, though, if I could have recorded what I heard with my own ears." Toglo's glance slipped to Eltsac and Nocso, who were still barking at each other. "Well, some of what I heard."

Evillia said, "This Night Demons' Retreat was on the sea floor?"

"That's right. As the dried muck and salt that surrounded it eroded, it was left alone here. Think of it as a miniature version of the mountain plains that stick up from the Bottomlands. In ancient days, they were islands. The Retreat, of course, was below the surface back then."

And may be again, he thought. He imagined fish peering into the holes in the ancient granite, crabs scuttling in to scavenge the remains of snakes and sand rats. The picture came to vivid life in his mind. That bothered him; it meant he took this menace seriously.

He was so deep in his own concerns that he needed a couple of heartbeats to realize the group had fallen silent. When he did notice, he looked up in a hurry, wondering what was wrong. From a third of the way up the Night Demons' Retreat, a cave cat looked back.

The cave cat must have been asleep inside a crevice until the tourists' racket woke it. It yawned, showing yellow fangs and pink tongue. Then, with steady amber gaze, it peered at the tourists once more, as if wondering what sauce would go well with them.

"Let's move away from the Retreat," Radnal said quietly. "We don't want it to think we're threatening it." That would have been a good trick, he thought. If the cave cat did decide to attack, his handcannon would hurt it (assuming he was lucky enough to hit), but it wouldn't kill. He opened the flap to his saddlebag just the same. For once, all the tourists did exactly as they were told. Seeing the great predator raised fears that went back to the days of man-apes just learning to walk erect.

Moblay Sopsirk's son asked, "Will more of them be around? In Lissonland, lions hunt in prides."

"No, cave cats are solitary except during mating season," Radnal answered. "They and lions have a common ancestor, but their habits differ. The Bottomlands don't have big herds that make pride hunting a successful survival strategy."

Just when Radnal wondered if the cave cat was going back to sleep, it exploded into motion. Long gray-brown mane flying, it bounded down the steep slope of the Night Demons' Retreat. Radnal yanked out his handcannon. He saw that Peggol vez Menk also had one.

But when the cave cat hit the floor of the Bottomlands, it streaked away from the tour group. Its grayish fur made it almost invisible against the desert. Cameras clicked incessantly. Then the beast was gone.

"How beautiful," Toglo zev Pamdal breathed. After a moment, she turned more practical: "Where does he find water?"

"He doesn't need much, Toglo zev," he answered. "Like other Bottomlands creatures, he makes the most of what he gets from the bodies of his prey. Also"—he pointed north—"there are a few tiny springs in the hills. Back when it was legal to hunt cave cats, a favorite way was to find a spring and lay in wait until the animal came to drink."

"It seems criminal," Toglo said.

"To us, certainly," Radnal half-agreed. "But to a man who's just had his flocks raided or a child carried off, it was natural enough. We go wrong when we judge the past by our standards."

"The biggest difference between past and present is that we moderns are able to sin on a much larger scale," Peggol said. Maybe he was thinking of the buried starbomb. But recent history held enough other atrocities to make Radnal have trouble disagreeing.

Eltsac vez Martois said, "Well, freeman vez Krobir, I have to admit that was worth the price of admission."

Radnal beamed; of all the people from whom he expected praise, Eltsac was the last. Then Nocso chimed in: "But it would have been even more exciting if the cave cat had come toward us and he'd had to shoot at it."

"I'll say," Eltsac agreed. "I'd love to have that on film."

Why, Radnal wondered, did the Martoisi see eye to eye only when they were both wrong? He said, "With respect, I'm delighted the animal went the other way. I'd hate to fire at so rare a creature, and I'd hate even more to miss and have anyone come to harm."

"Miss?" Nocso said the word as if it hadn't occurred to her. It probably hadn't; people in adventure stories shot straight whenever they needed to.

Eltsac said, "Shooting well isn't easy. When I was drafted into the Voluntary Guards, I needed three tries before I qualified with a rifle."

"Oh, but that's you, not a tour guide," Nocso said scornfully. "He has to shoot well."

Through Eltsac's outraged bellow, Radnal said, "I will have you know, I have never fired a handcannon in all my time at Trench Park." He didn't add that, given a choice between shooting at a cave cat and at Nocso, he'd sooner have fired on her.

The wind picked up again. The Night Demons' Retreat made more frightful noises. Radnal imagined how he would have felt if he were an illiterate hunter, say, hearing those ghostly wails for the first time. He was sure he'd've fouled his robes from fear.

But even so, something else also remained true: judging by the standards of the past was even more foolish when the present offered better information. If Nocso believed in night demons for no better reason than that she'd read an exciting frightener about them, that only argued she didn't have the sense the gods gave a shoveler skink. Radnal smiled. As far as he could tell, she *didn't* have the sense the gods gave a shoveler skink.

"We'll go in the direction opposite the one the cave cat took," Radnal said at last. "We'll also stay in a tight group. If you ask me, anyone who goes wandering off deserves to be eaten."

The tourists rode almost in one another's laps. As far as Radnal could tell, the eastern side of the Night Demons' Retreat wasn't much different from the western. But he'd been here tens of times already. Tourists could hardly be blamed for wanting to see as much as they could.

"No demons over here, either, Nocso," Eltsac vez Martois said. His wife stuck her nose in the air. Radnal wondered why they stayed married—for that matter, he wondered why they'd got married—when they sniped at each other so. Pressure from their kith groupings, probably. It didn't seem a good enough reason.

So why was he haggling over bride price with Wello zev Putun's father? The Putuni were a solid family in the lower aristocracy, a good connection for an up-and-coming man. He couldn't think of anything wrong with Wello, but she didn't much stir him, either. Would she have read *Stones of Doom* without recognizing it for the garbage it was? Maybe. That worried him. If he wanted a woman with whom he could talk, would he need a concubine? Peggol had one. Radnal wondered if the arrangement made him happy. Likely not—Peggol took a perverse pleasure in not enjoying anything.

Thinking of Wello brought Radnal's mind back to the two nights of excess he'd enjoyed with Evillia and Lofosa. He was sure he wouldn't want to marry a woman whose body was her only attraction, but he also doubted the wisdom of marrying one whose body didn't attract him. What he needed—

He snorted. *What I need is for a goddess to take flesh and fall in love with me . . . if she doesn't destroy my self-confidence by letting on she's a goddess.* Finding such a mate—especially for a bride price less than the annual budget of Tartesh—seemed unlikely. Maybe Wello would do after all.

"Are we going back by the same route we came?" Toglo zev Pamdal asked.

"I hadn't planned to," Radnal said. "I'd aimed to swing farther south on the way back, to give you the chance to see country you haven't been through before." He couldn't resist adding, "No matter how much the same some people find it."

Moblay Sopsirk's son looked innocent. "If you mean me, Radnal, I'm happy to discover new things. I just haven't come across that many here."

"Hmp," Toglo said. "I'm having a fine time here. I was glad to see the Night Demons' Retreat at last, and also to hear it. I can understand why our ancestors believed horrid creatures dwelt inside."

"I was thinking the same thing only a couple of hundred heartbeats ago," Radnal said.

"What a nice coincidence." A smile brightened her face. To Radnal's disappointment, she didn't stay cheerful long. She said, "This tour is so marvelous, I can't help thinking it would be finer still if Dokhnor of Kellef were still alive, or even if we knew who killed him."

"Yes," Radnal said. He'd spent much of the day glancing from one tourist to the next, trying to figure out who had broken the Morgaffo's neck. He'd even tried suspecting the Martoisi. He'd dismissed them before as too inept to murder anybody quietly. But what if their squawk and bluster only disguised devious purposes?

His laugh came out as dusty as Peggol vez Menk's. He couldn't believe it. Besides, Nocso and Eltsac were Tarteshans. They wouldn't want to see their country ruined. Or could they be paid enough to want to destroy it?

Nocso looked back toward the Night Demons' Retreat just as a koprit bird flew into one of the holes in the granite. "A demon! I saw a night demon!" she squalled.

Radnal laughed again. If Nocso was a spy and a saboteur, he was a humpless camel. "Come on," he called. "Time to head back."

As he'd promised, he took his charges to the lodge by a new route. Moblay Sopsirk's son remained unimpressed. "It may not be the same, but it isn't much different."

"Oh, rubbish!" Benter vez Maprab said. "The flora here

are quite distinct from those we observed this morning."

"Not to me," Moblay said stubbornly.

"Freeman vez Maprab, by your interest in plants of all sorts, were you by chance a scholar of botany?" Radnal asked.

"By the gods, no!" Benter whinnied laughter. "I ran a train of plant and flower shops until I retired."

"Oh. I see." Radnal did, too. With that practical experience, Benter might have learned as much about plants as any scholar of botany.

About a quarter of a daytenth later, the old man reined in his donkey and went behind another thornbush. "Sorry to hold everyone up," he said when he returned. "My kidneys aren't what they used to be."

Eltsac vez Martois guffawed. "Don't worry, Benter vez. A fellow like you knows you have to water the plants. Haw, haw!"

"You're a bigger jackass than your donkey," Benter snapped.

"Freemen, please!" Radnal got the two men calmed down and made sure they rode far from each other. He didn't care if they went at each other three heartbeats after they left Trench Park, but they were his responsibility till then.

"You earn your silver here, I'll say that for you," Peggol observed. "I see fools in my line of work, but I'm not obliged to stay polite to them." He lowered his voice. "When freeman vez Maprab went behind the bush now, he didn't just relieve himself. He also bent down and pulled something out of the ground. I happened to be off to one side."

"Did he? How interesting." Radnal doubted Benter was involved in the killing of Dokhnor of Kellef. But absconding with plants from Trench Park was also a crime, one the tour guide was better equipped to deal with than murder. "We won't do anything about it now.

After we get back to the lodge, why don't you have your men search Benter vez's belongings again?"

Amusement glinted in Peggol's eyes. "You're looking forward to this."

"Who, me? The only thing that could be better would be if it were Eltsac vez instead. But he hasn't a brain in his head or anywhere else about his person."

"Are you sure?" Peggol had been thinking along the same lines as Radnal. He'd probably started well before Radnal had, too. That was part of his job.

But Radnal came back strong: "If he had brains, would he have married Nocso zev?" That won a laugh which didn't sound dusty. He added, "Besides, all he knows about thornbushes is not to ride into them, and he's not certain of that."

"Malice agrees with you, Radnal vez."

By the time the lodge neared, Golobol was complaining along with Moblay. "Take away the Night Demons' Retreat, oh yes, and take away the cave cat we saw there, and what have you? Take away those two things and it is a nothing of a day."

"Freeman, if you insist on ignoring everything interesting that happens, you can turn any day dull," Toglo observed.

"Well said!" Being a tour guide kept Radnal from speaking his mind to the people he led. This time, Toglo had done it for him.

She smiled. "Why come see what the Bottomlands are like if he isn't happy with what he finds?"

"Toglo zev, some are like that in every group. It makes no sense to me, but there you are. If I had the money to see the Nine Iron Towers of Mashyak, I wouldn't whine because they aren't gold."

"That is a practical attitude," Toglo said. "We'd be better off if more people felt as you do."

"We'd be better off if—" Radnal shut up. *If we didn't fear a starbomb was buried somewhere around here* was how he'd been about to end the sentence. That wasn't smart. Not only would it frighten Toglo (or worry her; she didn't seem to frighten easily), but Peggol vez Menk would come down on him like he didn't know what, for breaching security.

All at once, he knew how Peggol would come down on him: like the Western Ocean, pouring into the Bottomlands over the broken mountains. He tried to laugh at himself; he didn't usually come up with such literary comparisons. Laughter failed. The simile was literary, but it might be literal as well.

"We'd be better off if what, Radnal vez?" Toglo asked. "What did you start to say?"

He couldn't tell her what he'd started to say. He wasn't glib enough to invent something smooth. To his dismay, what came out of his mouth was, "We'd be better off if more people were like you, Toglo zev, and didn't have fits at what they saw other people doing."

"Oh, that. Radnal vez, I didn't think anyone who was doing that was hurting anyone else. You all seemed to be enjoying yourselves. It's not something I'd care to do where other people might see, but I don't see I have any business getting upset about it."

"Oh." Radnal wasn't sure how to take Toglo's answer. He had, however, already pushed his luck past the point where it had any business going, so he kept quiet.

Something small skittered between spurges. Something larger bounded along in hot pursuit. The pursuit ended in a cloud of dust. Forestalling the inevitable chorus of *What's that?*, Radnal said, "Looks like a bladetooth just made a kill." The carnivorous rodent crouched over its prey; the tour guide pulled out a monocular for a closer look. "It's caught a fat sand rat."

"One of the animals you study?" Moblay said. "Are you going to blast it with your handcannon to take revenge?"

"*I* think you should," Nocso zev Martois declared.

"What a vicious brute, to harm a defenseless furry beast."

Radnal wondered if he should ask how she'd enjoyed her mutton last night, but doubted she would understand. He said, "Either carnivores eat meat or they starve. A bladetooth isn't as cuddly as a fat sand rat, but it has its place in the web of life, too."

The bladetooth was smaller than a fox, tan above and cream below. At first glance, it looked like any other jerboa, with hind legs adapted for jumping, big ears, and a long, tufted tail. But its muzzle was also long, and smeared with blood. The fat sand rat squirmed feebly. The bladetooth bit into its belly and started feeding nonetheless.

Nocso moaned. Radnal tried to figure out how her mind worked. She was eager to believe in night demons that worked all manner of evils, yet a little real predation turned her stomach. He gave up; some inconsistencies were too big for him to understand how anyone managed to hold both halves of them at once.

He said, "As I remarked a couple of days ago, the bladetooth does well in the Bottomlands because jerboas had already adapted to conditions close to these while this part of the world was still under water. Its herbivorous relatives extract the water they must have from leaves and seeds, while it uses the tissues of the animals it captures. Even during our rare rains, no bladetooth has ever been seen to drink."

"Disgusting." Nocso's plump body shook as she shuddered. Radnal wondered how long her carcass would give a bladetooth the fluids it needed. *A long time*, he thought.

Moblay Sopsirk's son whooped. "There's the lodge! Cold water, cold ale, cold wine—"

As they had the evening before, the Eyes and Ears and the militiamen came out to await the tour group's return. The closer the donkeys came, the better Radnal could see the faces of the men who had stayed behind. They all looked thoroughly grim.

This time he did not intend to spend a couple of daytenths wondering what was going on. He called, "Fer vez, Zosel vez, take charge of the tourists. I want to catch up on what's happened here."

"All right, Radnal vez," Fer answered. But his voice was no more cheerful than his expression.

Radnal dismounted and walked over to Liem vez Steries. He was not surprised when Peggol vez Menk fell into step with him. Their robes rustled as they came up to the militia subleader. Radnal asked, "What's the word, Liem vez?"

Liem's features might have been carved from stone. "The word is interrogation," he said quietly. "Tomorrow."

"By the gods." Radnal stared. "They're taking this seriously in Tarteshem."

"You'd best believe it." Liem wiped his sweaty face with his sleeve. "See those red cones past the cookpit? That's the landing site we laid out for the helo that's due in the morning."

"But—interrogation." Radnal shook his head. The Eyes and Ears' methods were anything but gentle. "If we interrogate foreigners, we're liable to touch off a war."

"Tarteshem knows this, Radnal vez," Liem said. "My objections are on the wire up there. I have been overruled."

"The Hereditary Tyrant and his advisors must think the risks and damages of war are less than what Tartesh would suffer if the starbomb performs as those who buried it hope," Peggol said.

"But what if it's not there, or if it is but none of the tourists knows about it?" Radnal said. "Then we'll have antagonized the Krepalgan Unity, Lissonland, and other countries as well, and for what? Nothing. Get on the radiophone, Peggol vez; see if they'll change their minds."

Peggol shook his head. "No, for two reasons. One is that this policy will have come down from a level far higher than I can influence. I am only a field agent; I have no say in grand strategy. The other is that your radiophone is too public. I do not want to alert anyone that he is about to be interrogated."

Radnal had to concede that made sense as far as security went. But he did not like it any better. Then something else occurred to him. He turned to Liem vez Steries. "Am I going to be, uh, interrogated, too? What about Zosel vez and Fer vez? And what about Toglo zev Pamdal? Are the interrogators going to work on one of the Hereditary Tyrant's relatives?"

"I don't know any of those answers," the militiaman said. "The people I spoke with in Tartesh wouldn't tell me." His eyes flicked to Peggol. "I suppose they didn't care to be too public, either."

"No doubt," Peggol said. "Now we have to act as normally as we can, not letting on that we'll have visitors in the morning."

"I'd have an easier time acting normal if I knew I wouldn't be wearing thumbscrews tomorrow," Radnal said.

"After such ordeals, the Hereditary Tyrant generously compensates innocents," Peggol said.

"The Hereditary Tyrant is generous." That was all Radnal could say while talking to an Eye and Ear. But silver, while it worked wonders, didn't fully make up for terror and pain and, sometimes, permanent injury. The tour guide preferred remaining as he was to riches and a limp.

Liem remarked, "Keeping things from the tourists won't be hard. Look what they're doing."

Radnal turned, looked, and snorted. His charges had turned the area marked off with red cones into a little game field. All of them except prim Golobol ran around throwing somebody's sponge-rubber ball back and forth and trying to tackle one another. If their sport had rules, Radnal couldn't figure them out.

Moblay Sopsirk's son, stubborn if unwise, kept his yen for Evillia and Lofosa. Careless of the abrasions to his nearly naked hide, he dragged Lofosa into the dirt. When she stood up, her tunic was missing some of its big gold buttons. She remained indifferent to the flesh she exposed. Moblay had got grit in his eyes and stayed on the ground a while.

Evillia lost buttons, too; Toglo zev Pamdal's belt broke, as did Nocso zev Martois's. Toglo capered with one hand holding her robes closed. Nocso didn't bother. Watching her jounce up and down the improvised pitch, Radnal wished she were modest and Toglo otherwise.

Fer vez Canthal asked, "Shall I get supper started?"

"Get the coals going, but wait for the rest," Radnal said. "They're having such a good time, they might as well enjoy themselves. They won't have any fun tomorrow."

"Neither will we," Fer answered. Radnal grimaced and nodded.

Benter vez Maprab tackled Eltsac vez Martois and stretched the bigger, younger man in the dust. Benter sprang to his feet, and swatted Evillia on the backside. She spun round in surprise.

"The old fellow has life in him yet," Peggol said, watching Eltsac rise, one hand pressed to a bloody nose.

"So he does." Radnal watched Benter. He might be old, but he was spry. Maybe he could have broken Dokhnor of Kellef's neck. Was losing a game of war reason enough? Or was he playing the same deeper game as Dokhnor?

Only when the sun slid behind the Barrier Mountains and dusk enfolded the lodge did the tourists give up their sport. The cones shone with a soft pink phosphorescent glow of their own. Toglo tossed the ball to Evillia, saying, "I'm glad you got this out, freelady. I haven't enjoyed myself so much—and so foolishly—in a long time."

"I thought it would be a good way for us to unwind after riding and sitting around," Evillia answered.

She had a point. If Radnal ever led tourists down here again—if the lodge wasn't buried under thousands of cubits of sea—he'd have to remember to bring along a ball himself. He frowned in self-reproach. He should have thought of that on his own instead of stealing the idea from someone in his group.

"If I was thirsty before, I'm drier than the desert now," Moblay boomed. "Where's that ale?"

"I'll open the refrigerator," Zosel vez Glesir said. "Who else wants something?" He cringed from the hot, sweaty tourists who dashed his way. "Come, my friends! If you squash me, who will get the drinks?"

"We'll manage somehow," Eltsac vez Martois said, the first sensible remark he'd made.

Fer vez Canthal had the coals in the fire pit glowing red. Zosel fetched a cut-up pig carcass and a slab of beef ribs. Radnal started to warn him about going through the stored food so prodigally but caught himself. If people fell into the interrogators' hands tomorrow, no need to worry about the rest of the tour.

Radnal ate heartily, and joined in songs after supper. He managed to forget for hundreds of heartbeats what awaited when morning came. But every so often, realization came flooding back. Once his voice faltered so suddenly that Toglo glanced over to see what had happened. He smiled sheepishly and tried to do better.

Then he looked at her. He couldn't imagine her being connected with the plot to flood the Bottomlands. He had trouble imagining Eyes and Ears interrogating her as they would anyone else. But he hadn't thought they would risk international incidents to question foreign tourists, either. Maybe that meant he didn't grasp how big the emergency was. If so, Toglo might be at as much risk as anyone.

Horken vez Sofana, the circumstances man from the Trench Park militia, came up to the tour guide. "I was told

you wanted Benter vez Maprab's saddlebags searched,
freeman vez Krobir. I found—these." He held out his hand.

"How interesting. Wait here, Senior Trooper vez
Sofana." Radnal walked over to where Benter was sitting,
and tapped him on the shoulder. "Would you please join
me, freeman?"

"What is it?" Benter growled, but he came back with
Radnal.

The tour guide said, "I'd like to hear how these red-
veined orchids"—he pointed to the plants in Horken vez
Sofana's upturned palm—"appeared in your saddlebags.
Removal of any plants or animals, especially rare varieties
like these, is punishable by fine, imprisonment, stripes,
or all three."

Benter vez Maprab's mouth opened and closed silently.
He tried again: "I—I would have raised them carefully,
freeman vez Krobir." He was so used to complaining
himself, he did not know how to react when someone
complained of him—and caught him in the wrong.

Triumph turned hollow for Radnal. What were a couple
of red-veined orchids when the whole Bottomlands might
drown? The tour guide said, "We'll confiscate these,
freeman vez Maprab. Your gear will be searched again
when you leave Trench Park. If we find no more contra-
band, we'll let this pass. Otherwise—I'm sure I need not
paint you a picture."

"Thank you—very kind." Benter fled.

Horken vez Sofana sent Radnal a disapproving look.
"You let him off too lightly."

"Maybe, but the interrogators will take charge of him
tomorrow."

"Hmm. Compared to everything else, stealing plants
isn't such a big thing."

"Just what I was thinking. Maybe we ought to give them
back to the old lemon-face so they'll be somewhere safe
if—well, you know the ifs."

"Yes." The circumstances man looked thoughtful. "If we gave them back now, he'd wonder why. We don't want that, either. Too bad, though."

"Yes." Discovering he worried about saving tiny pieces of Trench Park made Radnal realize he'd begun to believe in the starbomb.

The tourists began going off to their sleeping cubicles. Radnal envied their ignorance of what lay ahead. He hoped Evillia and Lofosa would visit him in the quiet darkness, and didn't care what the Eyes and Ears and militiamen thought. The body had its own sweet forgetfulness.

But the body had its own problems, too. Both women from Krepalga started trotting back and forth to the privy every quarter of a daytenth, sometimes even more than that. "It must have been something I ate," Evillia said, leaning wearily against the doorpost after her third trip. "Do you have a constipant?"

"The aid kit should have some." Radnal rummaged through it, found the orange pills he wanted. He brought them to her with a paper cup of water. "Here."

"Thank you." She popped the pills into her mouth, drained the cup, threw back her head to swallow. "I hope they help."

"So do I." Radnal had trouble keeping his voice casual. When she'd straightened to take the constipant, her left breast popped out of her tunic. "Freelady, I think you have fewer buttons than you did when the game ended."

Evillia covered herself again, an effort almost undermined when she shrugged. "I shouldn't be surprised. Most of those that didn't get pulled off took some yanks." She shrugged again. "It's only skin. Does it bother you?"

"You ought to know better than that," he said, almost angrily. "If you were feeling well—"

"If I were feeling well, I would enjoy feeling good," she agreed. "But as it is, Radnal vez—" At least she called him by his name and the polite particle. A grimace crossed her face. "As it is, I hope you will forgive me, but—" She hurried back out into the night.

When Lofosa made her next dash to the privy, Radnal had the pills waiting for her. She gulped them almost on the dead run. She'd lost some new buttons herself. Radnal felt guilty about thinking of such things when she was in distress.

After a game of war with Moblay that was almost as sloppy as their first, Radnal went into his cubicle. He didn't have anything to discuss with Liem or Peggol tonight; he knew what was coming. Somehow, he fell asleep anyway.

"Radnal vez." A quiet voice jerked him from slumber. It was neither Lofosa nor Evillia bending over him promising sensual delights. Peggol vez Menk stood in the entryway.

Radnal came fully awake. "What's gone wrong?" he demanded.

"Those two Highhead girls who don't believe in wearing clothes," Peggol answered.

"What about them?" Radnal asked, confused.

"They went off to the privy a while ago, and neither of them came back. My man on watch woke me before he went out to see if they were all right. They weren't there, either."

"Where could they have gone?" Radnal had had idiot tourists wander on their own, but never in the middle of the night. Then other possible meanings for their disappearance crossed his mind. He jumped up. "And why?"

"This also occurred to me," Peggol said grimly. "If they don't come back soon, it will have answered itself."

"They can't go far," Radnal said. "I doubt they'll have thought to get on donkeys. They could hardly tell one end of the beasts from the—" The tour guide stopped. If Evillia and Lofosa were other than they seemed, who could tell what they knew?

Peggol nodded. "We are thinking along the same lines."

He plucked at the tuft of hair under his mouth. "If this means what we fear, much will depend on you to track them down. You know the Bottomlands, and I do not."

"Our best tools are the helos," Radnal said. "When it's light, we'll sweep the desert floor a hundred times faster than we could on donkeyback."

He kept talking for another few words, but Peggol didn't hear him. He didn't hear himself, either, not over the sudden roar from outside. They dashed for the outer door. They pushed through the Eyes and Ears and militiamen who got there first. Tourists pushed them from behind.

Everyone stared at the blazing helos.

Radnal stood in disbelief and dismay for a couple of heartbeats. Peggol vez Menk's shout brought him to himself: "We have to call Tarteshem *right now!*" Radnal spun round, shoved and elbowed by the tourists in his way, and dashed for the radiophone.

The amber ready light didn't come on when he hit the switch. He ducked under the table to see if any connections were loose. "Hurry up!" Peggol yelled.

"The demon-cursed thing won't come on," Radnal yelled back. He picked up the radiophone itself. It rattled. It wasn't supposed to. "It's broken."

"It's *been* broken," Peggol declared.

"How could it have been broken, with Eyes and Ears and militiamen in the common room all the time?" the tour guide said, not so much disagreeing with Peggol as voicing his bewilderment to the world.

But Peggol had an answer: "If one of those Krepalgan tarts paraded through here without any clothes and they both ran back and forth all night—we might not have paid attention to what the other one was doing. Bang it . . . mmm, more likely reach under it with the right little tool . . . and you wouldn't need more than five heartbeats."

Radnal would have needed more than five heartbeats,

but he wasn't a saboteur. If Evillia and Lofosa were— He couldn't doubt it, but it left him sick inside. They'd used him, used their bodies to lull him into thinking they were the stupid doxies they pretended to be. And it had worked. . . . He wanted to wash himself over and over; he felt he'd never be clean again.

Liem vez Steries said, "We'd better make sure the donkeys are all right." He trotted out the door, ran around the crackling hulks of the flying machines. The stable door was closed against cave cats. The militiaman pulled it open. Through the crackle of the flames, Radnal heard a sharp report, saw a flash of light. Liem crashed to the ground. He lay there unmoving.

Radnal and Golobol, the physician, sprinted out to him. The firelight told them all they needed to know. Liem would not get up again, not with those dreadful wounds.

The tour guide went into the stables. He knew something was wrong, but needed a moment to realize what. Then the quiet hit him. The donkeys were not shifting in their stalls, nipping at the straw, or making any of their other usual small noises.

He looked into the stall by the broken door. The donkey there lay on its side. Its flanks neither rose nor fell. Radnal ran to the next, and the next. All the donkeys were dead— except for three, which were missing. *One for Evillia*, the tour guide thought, *one for Lofosa, and one for their supplies*.

No, they weren't fools. "I am," he said, and ran back to the lodge.

He gave the grim news to Peggol vez Menk. "We're in trouble, sure enough," Peggol said, shaking his head. "We'd be worse off, though, if the interrogation team weren't coming in under a daytenth. We can go after them in that helo. It has its own cannon, too; if they don't yield — goodbye. By the gods, I hope they don't."

"So do I." Radnal cocked his head to one side. A grin

split his face. "Isn't that the helo now? Why is it early?"

"I don't know," Peggol answered. "Wait a heartbeat, maybe I do. If Tarteshem called and got no answer, they might have decided something was wrong and sent the helo straightaway."

The racket of engine and rotors swelled. The pilot must have spotted the fires and put on full speed. Radnal hurried outside to greet the incoming Eyes and Ears. The helo's black silhouette spread huge across the sky; as Peggol had implied, this was a military machine, not just a utility flier. It made for the glowing cones that marked the landing area.

Radnal watched it settle toward the ground. He remembered Evillia and Lofosa running around in the landing zone, laughing, giggling, and . . . losing buttons. He waved his arms, dashed toward the cones. "No!" he screamed. "Wait!"

Too late. Dust rose in choking clouds as the helo touched the ground. The tour guide saw the flash under one skid, heard the report. The skid crumpled. The helo heeled over. A rotor blade dug into the ground, snapped, thrummed past Radnal's head. Had it touched him, his head would have gone with it.

The side panel of the helo came down on the Bottomlands floor. Another sharp report—and suddenly flames were everywhere. The Eyes and Ears trapped inside the helo screamed. Radnal tried to help them, but the heat would not let him approach. The screams soon stopped. He smelled the thick odor of charring flesh. The fire burned on.

Peggol vez Menk hurried out to Radnal. "I tried to stop them," the tour guide said brokenly.

"You came closer than I, a reproach I shall carry to my grave," Peggol answered. "I did not see that danger, much as I should have. Some of those men were my friends." He slammed a fist against his thigh. "What now, Radnal vez?"

Die when the waters come, was the first thought that crossed the tour guide's mind. Mechanically, he went through the obvious: "Wait till dawn. Try to find their trail. Pack as much water on our backs as we can and go after them afoot. Leave one man here for when another helo comes. Give the tourists as much water as they can carry and send them up the trail. Maybe they'll escape the flood."

"What you say sounds sensible. We'll try it," Peggol said. "Anything else?"

"Pray," Radnal told him. He grimaced, nodded, turned away.

Moblay Sopsirk's son got through the Eyes and Ears and trotted up to Radnal and Peggol. "Freeman vez Krobir—" he began.

Radnal rolled his eyes. He was about to wish a night demon on Moblay's head, but stopped. Instead, he said, "Wait a heartbeat. You named me properly." What should have been polite surprise came out as accusation.

"So I did." Something about Moblay had changed. In the light of the blazing helos, he looked . . . not like Peggol vez Menk, since he remained a short-nosed, brown-skinned Highhead, but of the same type as the Eye and Ear—tough and smart, not just lascivious and overfamiliar. He said, "Freeman vez Krobir, I apologize for irritating you, but I wanted to remain as ineffectual-seeming as I could. Names are one way of doing that. I am an aide to my Prince; I am one of his Silent Servants."

Peggol grunted. He evidently knew what that meant. Radnal didn't, but he could guess: something like an Eye and Ear. He cried, "Is there anyone in this cursed tour group not wearing a mask?"

"More to the point, why drop the mask now?" Peggol asked.

"Because my Prince, may the Lion God give him many years, does not want the Bottomlands flooded," Moblay said. "We wouldn't suffer as badly as Tartesh, of course; we own only a strip of the southernmost part. But the Prince fears the fighting that would follow."

"Who approached Lissonland with word of this?" Peggol said.

"We learned from Morgaf," Moblay answered. "The island king wanted us to join the attack on Tartesh after the flood. But the Morgaffos denied the plot was theirs, and would not tell us who had set the starbomb here. We suspected the Krepalgan Unity, but had no proof. That was one reason I kept sniffing around the Krepalgan women." He grinned. "Another should be obvious."

"Why Krepalga?" Peggol wondered aloud. "The Unity didn't join Morgaf against us in the last war. What could they want enough to make them risk a war with starbombs?"

Radnal remembered the lecture he'd given on how the Bottomlands came to be, remembered also his fretting about how far an unchecked flood might reach. "I know part of the answer to that, I think," he said. Peggol and Moblay both turned to him. He went on, "If the Bottomlands flood, the new central sea would stop about at Krepalga's western border. The Unity would have a whole new coastline, and be in a better position than either Tartesh or Lissonland to exploit the new sea."

"The flood wouldn't get to Krepalga for a long time," Moblay protested.

"True," Radnal said, "but can you imagine stopping it before it did?" He visualized the map again. "I don't think you could, not against that weight of water."

"I think you're right." Peggol nodded decisively. "That may not be all Krepalga has in mind, but it is in part. The Unity must have been planning this for years; they'll have looked at all the consequences they could."

"Let me help you now," Moblay said. "I heard freeman vez Krobir say the donkeys are dead, but what one walking man may do, I shall."

Radnal would have taken any ally who presented himself. But Peggol said, "No. I am grateful for your candor and suspect you are truthful now, but dare not take the chance. One walking man could do much harm as well as good. Being of the profession, I trust you understand."

Moblay bowed. "I feared you would say that. I do understand. May the Lion God go with you."

The three men walked back to the lodge. The tourists rained questions on Radnal. "No one has told us anything, not a single thing," Golobol complained. "What is going on? Why are helos exploding left and right? Tell me!"

Radnal told him—and everyone else. The stunned silence his words produced lasted perhaps five heartbeats. Then everybody started yelling. Nocso zev Martois's voice drowned all others: "Does this mean we don't get to finish the tour?"

More sensibly, Toglo zev Pamdal said, "Is there any way we can help you in your pursuit, Radnal vez?"

"Thank you, no. You'd need weapons; we haven't any to give you. Your best hope is to make for high ground. You ought to leave as soon as you load all the water you can carry. Lie up in the middle of the day when the sun is worst. With luck, you'll be up at the old continental shelf in, oh, a day and a half. If the flood's held off that long, you ought to be safe for a while there. And a helo may spot you as you travel."

"What if the flood comes when we're still down here?" Eltsac vez Martois demanded. "What then, freeman Know-It-All?"

"Then you have the consolation of knowing I drowned a few heartbeats before you. I hope you enjoy it," Radnal said. Eltsac stared at him. He went on. "That's all the stupidity I have time for now. Let's get you people moving. Peggol vez, we'll send a couple of Eyes and Ears back, too. Your men won't be much help traveling cross-country. Come to that, you—"

"No," Peggol said firmly. "My place is at the focus. I shan't lag, and I shoot straight. I'm not the worst tracker, either."

Radnal knew better than to argue. "All right."

The water bladders would have gone on the donkeys. Radnal filled them from the cistern while the militiamen and Eyes and Ears cut straps to fit them to human shoulders. The eastern sky was bright pink by the time they finished. Radnal tried to give no tourists loads of more than a third of their body weight: that was as much as anyone could carry without breaking down.

Nocso vez Martois said, "With all this water, how can we carry food?"

"You can't," Radnal snapped, tie stared at her. "You can live off yourself a while, but you can't live without water." Telling off his tourists was a new, heady pleasure. Since it might be his last, he enjoyed it while he could.

"I'll report your insolence," Nocso shrilled.

"That is the least of my worries." Radnal turned to the Eyes and Ears who were heading up the trail with the tourists. "Try to keep them together, try not to do too much at midday, make sure they all drink—and make sure you do, too. Gods be with you."

An Eye and Ear shook his head. "No, freeman vez Krobir, with *you*. If they watch you, we'll be all right. But if they neglect you, we all fail."

Radnal nodded. To the tourists, he said, "Good luck. If the gods are kind, I'll see you again at the top of Trench Park." He didn't mention what would happen if the gods bumbled along as usual.

Toglo said, "Radnal vez, if we see each other again, I will use whatever influence I have for you."

"Thanks," was all Radnal could say. Under other circumstances, getting patronage from the Hereditary

Tyrant's relative would have moved him to do great things. Even now, it was kindly meant, but of small weight when he first had to survive to gain it.

A sliver of red-gold crawled over the eastern horizon. The tourists and the Eyes and Ears trudged north. A koprit bird on the rooftop announced the day with a cry of *hig, hig, hig!*

Peggol ordered one of the remaining Eyes and Ears to stay at the lodge and send westward any helos that came. Then he said formally, "Freeman vez Krobir, I place myself and freeman vez Potos, my colleague here, under your authority. Command us."

"If that's how you want it," Radnal answered, shrugging. "You know what we'll do: march west until we catch the Krepalgans or drown, whichever comes first. Nothing fancy. Let's go."

Radnal, the two Eyes and Ears, the lodge attendants, and the surviving militiamen started from the stables. The morning light showed the tracks of three donkeys heading west. The tour guide took out his monocular, scanned the western horizon. No luck—dips and rises hid Evillia and Lofosa.

Fer vez Canthal said, "There's a high spot maybe three thousand cubits west of here. You ought to look from there."

"Maybe," Radnal said, "If we have a good trail, though, I'm likelier to rely on that. I begrudge wasting even a heartbeat's time, and spotting someone isn't easy even if he wants to be found. Remember that poor fellow who wandered off from his group four years ago? They used helos, dogs, everything, but they didn't find his corpse until a year later, and then by accident."

"Thank you for pumping up my hopes," Peggol said.

"Nothing wrong with hope," Radnal answered, "but you knew the odds were bad when you decided to stay."

The seven walkers formed a loose skirmish line, about five cubits apart from one another. Radnal, the best tracker, took the center; at his right was Horken vez Sofana, at his left Peggol. He figured they had the best chance of picking up the trail if he lost it.

That likelihood grew with every step. Evillia and Lofosa hadn't gone straight west. He quickly found that out. Instead, they'd jink northwest for a few hundred cubits, then southwest a few hundred more, in a deliberate effort to throw off pursuit. They also chose the hardest ground they could find, which made the donkeys' tracks tougher to follow.

Radnal's heart sank every time he had to cast about before they found the hoofprints again. His group lost ground with every step; the Krepalgans rode faster than they could walk.

"I have a question," said Horken vez Sofana: "Suppose the starbomb goes off and the mountains fall. How are these two women supposed to get away?"

Radnal shrugged; he had no idea. "Did you hear that, Peggol vez?" he asked.

"Yes," Peggol said. "Two possibilities spring to mind—"

"I might have guessed," Radnal said.

"Hush. As I was saying before you crassly interrupted, one is that the starbomb was supposed to have a delayed detonation, letting the perpetrators escape. The other is that these agents knew the mission was suicidal. Morgaf has used such personnel; so have we, once or twice. Krepalga might find such servants, however regrettable that prospect seems to us."

Horken gave a slow, deliberate nod. "What you say sounds convincing. They might have first planned a delay to let them escape, then shifted to sacrificing themselves when they found we were partway on to them."

"True," Peggol said. "And they may yet be planning to escape. If they somehow secreted away helium cylinders, for instance, they might inflate several prophylactics and float out of the Bottomlands."

Radnal wondered for a heartbeat if he was serious. Then the tour guide snorted. "I wish I could stay so cheerful at death's door."

"Death will find me whether I am cheerful or not," Peggol answered. "I will go forward as boldly and as long as I can."

Conversation flagged. The higher the sun rose, the hotter the desert became, the more anything but putting one foot in front of the other seemed more trouble than it was worth. Radnal wiped sweat from his eyes as he slogged along.

The water bladder on his back started out as heavy as any pack he'd ever toted. He wondered how long he could go on with such a big burden. But the bladder got lighter every time he refilled his canteen. He made himself keep drinking—not getting water in as fast as he sweated would be suicidal. Unlike the fanatic Morgaffos Peggol had mentioned, he wanted to live if he could.

He'd given everyone about two days' worth of water. If he didn't catch up to Lofosa and Evillia by the end of the second day . . . He shook his head. One way or another, it wouldn't matter after that.

As noon neared, he ordered the walkers into the shade of a limestone outcrop. "We'll rest a while," he said. "When we start again, it ought to be cooler."

"Not enough to help," Peggol said. But he sat down in the shade with a grateful sigh. He took off his stylish cap, sadly felt of it. "It'll make a dishrag after this—nothing better."

Radnal squatted beside him, too hot to talk. His heart pounded. It seemed so loud, he wondered if it would give out on him. Then he realized most of that beating rhythm came from outside. Fatigue fell away. He jumped up, doffed his own cap and waved it in the air. "A helo!"

The rest of the group also got up and waved and yelled. "It's seen us!" Zosel vez Glesir said. Nimble as a dragonfly, the helo shifted direction in midair and dashed straight towards them. It set down about fifty cubits from the ledge. Its rotors kept spinning; it was ready to take off again at any moment.

The pilot leaned out the window, bawled something in Radnal's direction. Through the racket, he had no idea what the fellow said. The pilot beckoned him over.

The din and dust were worse under the whirling rotor blades. Radnal had to lean on tiptoe against the helo's hot metal skin before he made out the pilot's words: "How far ahead are the cursed Krepalgans?"

"They had better than a daytenth's start, and they're on donkeyback. Say, up to thirty thousand cubits west of here." Radnal repeated himself several times, before the pilot nodded and ducked back into his machine.

"Wait!" Radnal screamed. The pilot stuck his head out again. Radnal asked, "Did you come across my group heading toward the trail up the old continental shelf?"

"Yes. Somebody ought to be picking them up right about now."

"Good," Radnal bellowed. The pilot tossed him a portable radiophone. He seized it; now he was no longer cut off from the rest of the search.

They sped. The helo shot into the air, heading westward. The tour guide knew relief; even if he drowned, the people he'd led would be safe.

"Now that this helo's here, do we need to go on?" asked Impac vez Potos, the Eye and Ear with Peggol.

"You'd best believe it, freeman." Radnal recounted the story of the lost tourist who'd stayed lost. "No matter how many helos search, they'll be covering a big area and trying to find people who don't want to be found. We stay in the hunt till it's over. By the way the Krepalgans fooled us all, they won't make things easy."

"Shall we keep resting, or head out now?" Peggol asked.

Radnal chewed on that for a few heartbeats. If the helo was here, that meant the people at Tarteshem knew from its radiophone how bad things were. And that meant helos would swarm here as fast as they could take off, which meant his group would probably be able to get supplied. But he didn't want to lose people to heatstroke, either, a risk that came with exertion in the desert.

"We'll give it another tenth of a daytenth," he said at last.

He was first up when the rest ended. The other six rose with enough groans and creaking joints for an army of invalids. "We'll loosen up as we get going," Fer vez Canthal said hopefully.

A little later, panic ran through Radnal when he lost the trail. He waved for Peggol and Horken vez Sofana. They scoured the ground on hands and knees, but found nothing. Rock-hard dirt stretched in all directions for a couple of hundred cubits. "If they pulled up a bush and swept away their tracks, we'll have a night demons' time picking them up again," Horken said.

"We won't try," Radnal declared. The rest of the searchers looked at him in surprise. He went on, "We're wasting time here, right?" No one disagreed. "So here is the last place we want to stay. We'll do a search spiral. Zosel vez, you stand here to mark this spot. Sooner or later, we'll find the trail again."

"You hope," Peggol said quietly.

"Yes, I do. If you have a better plan, I'll be grateful to hear it." The Eye and Ear shook his head and, a moment later, dropped his eyes.

While Zosel stood in place, the other searchers tramped in a widening spiral. After a hundred heartbeats, Impac vez Potos shouted: "I've found it!"

Radnal and Horken hurried to see what he'd come across. "Where?" Radnal asked. Impac pointed to a patch of ground softer than most in the area. Sure enough, it held marks. The more experienced men squatted to take a better look. They glanced up together; their eyes met. Radnal said, "Freeman vez Potos, those are the tracks of a bladetooth. If you look carefully, you can see where it dragged its tail in the dirt. Donkeys never do that."

"Oh," Impac said in a small, sad voice.

Radnal sighed. He hadn't bothered mentioning that the tracks were too small for donkeys' and didn't look like them, either. "Let's try once more," he said. The spiral resumed.

When Impac yelled again, Radnal wished he hadn't tried to salve his feelings. If he stopped them every hundred heartbeats, they'd never find anything. This time, Horken stayed where he was. Radnal stalked over to Impac. "Show me," he growled.

Impac pointed once more. Radnal filled his lungs to curse him for wasting their time. The curse remained unspoken. There at his feet lay the unmistakable tracks of three donkeys. "By the gods," he said.

"They are right this time?" Impac asked anxiously.

"Yes. Thank you, freeman." Radnal shouted to the other searchers. The seven headed southwest, following the recovered trail. Fer vez Canthal went up to Impac and slapped him on the back. Impac beamed as if he'd performed bravely in front of the Hereditary Tyrant. Considering the service he'd just done Tartesh, he'd earned the right.

He was also lucky, Radnal thought. But he'd needed courage to call out a second time after being ignominiously wrong the first, and sharp eyes to spot both sets of tracks, even if he couldn't tell what they were once he'd found them. So more than luck was involved. Radnal slapped Impac's back, too.

Sweat poured off Radnal. As it evaporated from his

robes, it cooled him a little, but not enough. Like a machine taking on fuel, he drank again and again from the bladder on his back.

Now the sun was in his face. He tugged his cap over his eyes, kept his head down, and tramped on. When the Krepalgans tried doubling back, he spotted the ruse instead of following the wrong trail and wasting hundreds of precious heartbeats.

By then, the western sky was full of helos. They roared about in all directions, sometimes low enough to kick up dust. Radnal wanted to strangle the pilots who flew that way; they might blow away the trail, too. He yelled into the radiophone. The low-flying helos moved higher.

A big transport helo set down a few hundred cubits in front of the walkers. A door in its side slid open. A squadron of soldiers jumped down and hurried west.

"Are they close or desperate?" Radnal wondered.

"Desperate, certainly," Peggol said. "As for close, we can hope. We haven't drowned yet. On the other hand"— he always thought of the other hand—"we haven't caught your two sluts, either."

"They weren't mine," Radnal said feebly. But he remembered their flesh sliding against his, the way their breath had caught, the sweat-salty taste of their skin.

Peggol read his face. "Aye, they used you, Radnal vez, and they fooled you. If it makes you feel better, they fooled me, too; I thought they kept their brains in their twats. They outsmarted me with the fornication books in their gear and the skin they showed. They used our prudishness against us—how could anyone who acts that way be dangerous? It's a ploy that won't work again."

"Once may have been plenty." Radnal wasn't ready to stop feeling guilty.

"If it was, you'll pay full atonement," Peggol said.

Radnal shook his head. Dying when the Bottomlands flooded wasn't atonement enough, not when that flood

would ruin his nation and might start an exchange of
starbombs that would wreck the world.

The ground shivered under his feet. Despite the furnace
heat of the desert floor, his sweat went cold. "Please, gods,
make it stop," he said, his first prayer in years.

It stopped. He breathed again. It was just a little quake;
he would have laughed at tourists for fretting over it. At
any other time, he would have ignored it. Now it nearly
scared him to death.

A koprit bird cocked its head, peered down at him from
a thornbush that held its larder. *Hig-hig-hig!* it said, and
fluttered to the ground. Radnal wondered if it could fly
fast enough or far enough to escape a flood.

The radiophone let out a burst of static. Radnal thumbed
it to let himself transmit: "Vez Krobir here."

"This is Combat Group Leader Turand vez Nital. I wish
to report that we have encountered the Krepalgan spies.
Both are deceased."

"That's wonderful!" Radnal relayed the news. His
companions raised a weary cheer. Then he remembered
again his nights with Evillia and Lofosa. And then he
realized Combat Group Leader vez Nital hadn't sounded
as overjoyed and relieved as he should have. Slowly, he
said, "What's wrong?"

"When encountered, the Krepalgans were moving
eastward."

"Eastw— Oh!"

"You see the predicament?" Turand said. "They appear
to have completed their work and to have been attempting
to escape. Now they are beyond questioning. Please keep
your transmission active so a helo can home in on you and
bring you here. You look to be Tartesh's best hope of
locating the bomb before its ignition. I repeat, please
maintain transmission."

Radnal obeyed. He looked at the Barrier Mountains.

They seemed taller now than they had when he set out. How long would they keep standing tall? The sun was sliding down toward them, too. How was he supposed to search after dark? He feared tomorrow morning was too late.

He passed on to his comrades what the officer had said. Horken vez Sofana made swimming motions. Radnal stooped for a pebble, threw it at him.

A helo soon landed beside the seven walkers. Someone inside opened the sliding door. "Come on!" he bawled. "Move it, move it!"

Moving it as fast as they could, Radnal and the rest scrambled into the helo. It went airborne before the fellow at the door had it fully closed. A couple of hundred heartbeats later, the helo touched down hard enough to rattle the tour guide's teeth. The crewman at the door undogged it and slid it open. "Out!" he yelled.

Out Radnal jumped. The others followed. A few cubits away stood a man in a uniform robe similar but not identical to the one the militia wore. "Who's freeman vez Krobir?" he said. "I'm Turand vez Nital."

"I'm vez Krobir. I—" Radnal broke off. Two bodies lay behind the Tarteshan soldier. Radnal gulped. He'd seen corpses on their funeral pyres, but never before sprawled out like animals waiting to be butchered. He said the first thing that popped into his head: "They don't look like you shot them."

"We didn't," the officer said. "When they saw they couldn't escape, they took poison."

"They were professionals," Peggol murmured.

"As may be," Turand growled. "This one"—he pointed at Evillia—"wasn't gone when we got to her. She said, 'You're too late,' and then died, may night demons gnaw her ghost forever."

"We'd better find that cursed bomb fast, then," Radnal said. "Can you take us to where the Krepalgans were cornered?"

"This very heartbeat," Turand said. "Come with me. It's only three or four hundred cubits from here." He moved at a trot that left the worn walkers gasping in his wake. At last he stopped and waited impatiently for them to catch up. "This is where we found them."

"And they were coming east, you said?" Radnal asked.

"That's right, though I don't know for how long," the officer answered. "Somewhere out there is the accursed starbomb. We're scouring the desert, but this is *your* park. Maybe your eye will fall on something they'd miss. If not—"

"You needn't go on," Radnal said. "I almost fouled my robe when we had that little tremor a while ago. I thought I'd wash ashore on the Krepalgan border, ten million cubits from here."

"If you're standing on a starbomb when it goes off, you needn't fear the floods afterwards," Turand said.

"Gak." Radnal hadn't thought of that. It would be quick, anyhow.

"Enough chatter," Horken vez Sofana said. "If we're to search, let us search."

"Search, and may the gods lend your sight wings," Turand said.

The seven walkers trudged west again. Radnal did his best to follow the donkey's trail, but the soldiers' footprints often obscured them. "How are we supposed to track in this confusion?" he cried. "They might as well have turned a herd of humpless camels loose here."

"It's not quite so bad as that," Horken said. Stooping low, he pointed to the ground. "Look, here's a track. Here's another, a few paces on. We can do it. We have to do it."

Radnal knew the senior trooper was right; he felt ashamed of his own outburst. He found the next hoofprint himself, and the one after that. Those two lay on opposite sides of a fault-line crack; when he saw that, he knew the starbomb couldn't rest too far away. But he felt time pressing hard on his shoulders.

"Maybe the soldiers will have found the starbomb by now," Fer vez Canthal said.

"We can't count on it. Look how long it took them to find the Krepalgans. We have to figure it's up to us." Radnal realized the weight on him wasn't just time. It was also responsibility. If he died now, he'd die knowing he'd failed.

And yet, while the searchers stirred through Trench Park, the animals in the Bottomlands kept living their usual lives; they could not know they might perish in the next heartbeat. A koprit bird skittered across the sand a few paces in front of Radnal. A clawed foot stabbed down.

"It's caught a shoveler skink," he said, as if the hot, worn men with him were members of his group.

The lizard thrashed, trying to get away. Sand flew every which way. But the koprit bird held on with its claws, tore at the skink with its beak, and smashed it against the ground until its writhing ceased. Then it flew to a nearby thornbush with its victim.

It impaled the skink on a long, stout thorn. The lizard was the latest addition to its larder, which also included two grasshoppers, a baby snake, and a jerboa. And, as koprit birds often did, this one used the thorn bush's spikes to display bright objects it had found. A yellow flower, now very dry, must have hung there since the last rains. And, not far from the lizard, the koprit bird had draped a couple of red-orange strings over a thorn.

Radnal's eyes came to them, passed by, snapped back. They weren't strings. He pointed. "Aren't those the necklaces Evillia and Lofosa wore yesterday?" he asked hoarsely.

"They are." Peggol and Horken said it together. They both had to notice and remember small details. They sounded positive.

When Peggol tried to take the necklaces off their thorn, the koprit bird furiously screeched *hig-hig!* Claws outstretched, it flew at his face. He staggered backwards, flailing his arms.

Radnal waved his cap as he walked up to the thornbush. That intimidated the bird enough to keep it from diving on him, though it kept shrieking. He grabbed the necklaces and got away from the larder as fast as he could.

The necklaces were heavier than he'd expected, too heavy for the cheap plastic he'd thought them to be. He turned one so he could look at it end-on. "It's got a copper core," he said, startled.

"Let me see that." Again, Peggol and Horken spoke together. They snatched a necklace apiece. Then Peggol broke the silence alone: "Detonator wire."

"Absolutely," Horken agreed.

"Never seen it with red insulator, though. Usually it would be brown or green for camouflage. This time, it was camouflaged as jewelry."

Radnal stared from Horken to Peggol. "You mean, these wires would be hooked to the cell that would send the charge to the starbomb when the timer went off?"

"That's just what we mean," Peggol said. Horken vez Sofana solemnly nodded.

"But they can't now, because they're here, not there." Fumbling for words, Radnal went on, "And they're here because the koprit bird thought they were pretty (or maybe it thought they were food—they're about the color of a shoveler skink's lure) and pulled them loose and flew away with them." Realization hit then: "That koprit bird just saved Tartesh!"

"The ugly thing almost put my eye out," Peggol grumbled. The rest of the group ignored him. One or two of them cheered. More, like Radnal, stood quietly, too tired and dry and stunned to show their joy.

The tour guide needed several heartbeats to remember he carried a radiophone. He clicked it on, waited for Turand vez Nital. "What do you have?" the officer barked. Radnal could hear his tension. He'd felt it too, till moments before.

"The detonator wires are off the starbomb," he said, giving the good news first. "I don't know where that is, but it won't go off without them."

After a static-punctuated silence, Turand said slowly, "Are you daft? How can you have the wires without the starbomb?"

"There was this koprit bird—"

"What?" Turand's roar made the radiophone vibrate in Radnal's hand. As best he could, he explained. More silence followed. At last, the soldier said, "You're certain this is detonator wire?"

"An Eye and Ear and the Trench Park circumstances man both say it is. If they don't recognize the stuff, who would?"

"You're right." Another pause from Turand, then: "A koprit bird, you say? Do you know that I never heard of koprit birds until just now?" His voice held wonder. But suddenly he sounded worried again, saying, "Can you be sure the wire wasn't left there to fool us one last time?"

"No." Fear knotted Radnal's gut again. Had he and his comrades come so far, done so much, only to fall for a final deception?

Horken let out a roar louder than Turand's had been. "I've found it!" he screamed from beside a spurge about twenty cubits away. Radnal hurried over. Horken said, "It couldn't have been far, because koprit birds have territories. So I kept searching, and—" He pointed down.

At the base of the spurge lay a small timer hooked to an electrical cell. The timer was upside down; the koprit bird must have had quite a fight tearing loose the wires it prized. Radnal stooped, turned the timer over. He almost dropped it—the needle that counted off the daytenths and heartbeats lay against the zero knob. "Will you look at that?" he said softly. Impac vez Potos peered over his shoulder. The junior Eye and Ear clicked his tongue between his teeth.

"A koprit bird," Horken said. He got down on hands and knees, poked around under every plant and stone within a couple of cubits of the spurge. Before a hundred heartbeats went by, he let out a sharp, wordless exclamation.

Radnal got down beside him. Horken had tipped over a chunk of sandstone about as big as his head. Under it was a crack in the earth that ran out to either side. From the crack protruded two drab brown wires.

"A koprit bird," Horken repeated. The helos and men would have been too late. But the koprit bird, hungry or out to draw females into its territory, had spotted something colorful, so—

Radnal took out the radiophone. "We've found the timer. It is separated from the wires which, we presume, lead to the starbomb. The koprit bird took away the wires the Krepalgans used to attach the timer."

"A koprit bird." Now Turand vez Nital said it. He sounded as dazed as any of the rest of them, but quickly pulled himself together again: "That's excellent news, as I needn't tell you. I'll send a crew to your location directly, to begin excavating the starbomb. Out."

Peggol vez Menk had been examining the timer, too. His gaze kept returning to the green needle bisecting the zero symbol. He said, "How deep do you suppose the bomb is buried?"

"It would have to be pretty deep, to trigger the fault," Radnal answered.

"I couldn't say how deep; I'm no savant of geology. But if Turand vez Nital thinks his crew will dig it up before nightfall, he'll have to think again."

"How could Krepalga have planted it here?" Impac vez Potos said. "Wouldn't you Trench Park people have noticed?"

"Trench Park is a big place," Radnal said.

"I know that. I ought to; I've walked enough of it," Impac said wearily. "Still—"

"People don't frequent this area, either," Radnal persisted. "I've never led a group anywhere near here. No doubt the Krepalgans took risks doing whatever they did, but not enormous risks."

Peggol said, "We shall have to ensure such deadly danger cannot return again. Whether we should expand the militia, base regular soldiers here, or set up a station for Eyes and Ears, that I don't know—we must determine which step offers the best security. But we will do something."

"You also have to consider which choice hurts Trench Park least," Radnal said.

"That will be a factor," Peggol said, "but probably a small one. Think, Radnal vez: if the Barrier Mountains fall and the Western Ocean pours down on the Bottomlands, how much will that hurt Trench Park?"

Radnal opened his mouth to argue more. Keeping the park in its natural state had always been vital to him. Man had despoiled so much of the Bottomlands; this was the best—almost the only—reminder of what they'd been like. But he'd just spent days wondering whether he'd drown in the next heartbeat, and all of today certain he would. And if he'd drowned, his country would have drowned with him. Set against that, a base for soldiers or Eyes and Ears suddenly seemed, a small thing. He said not another word.

Radnal hadn't been in Tarteshem for a long time, though Tartesh's capital wasn't far from Trench Park. He'd never been paraded through the city in an open-topped motor while people lined the sidewalks and cheered. He should have enjoyed it. Peggol vez Menk, who sat beside him in the motor, certainly did. Peggol smiled and waved as if he'd just been chosen high priest. After so long in the wide open spaces of the Bottomlands, though, and after so long in his own company or that of small tour groups, riding through the midst of so much tight-packed humanity more nearly overwhelmed than overjoyed Radnal. He looked nervously at the buildings towering over the avenue. It felt more as if he were passing through a canyon than anything man-made.

"Radnal, Radnal!" the crowds chanted, as if everybody knew him well enough to use his name in its most naked, intimate form. They had another cry, too: "Koprit bird! Koprit bird! The gods praise the koprit bird!"

That took away some of his nervousness. Seeing his grin, Peggol said, "Anyone would think they'd seen the artist's new work."

"You're right," Radnal answered. "Maybe it's too bad *the* koprit bird isn't here for the ceremony after all."

Peggol raised that eyebrow of his. "You talked them out of capturing it."

"I know. I did the right thing," Radnal said. Putting the koprit bird that stole the detonator wires in a cage didn't seem fitting. Trench Park existed to let its creatures live wild and free, with as little interference from mankind as possible. The koprit bird had made it possible for that to go on. Caging it afterwards struck Radnal as ungrateful.

The motor drove onto the grounds of the Hereditary Tyrant's palace. It pulled up in front of the gleaming building that housed Bortav vez Pamdal. A temporary stage and a podium stood on the lawn near the road. The folding chairs that faced it were full of dignitaries from Tartesh and other nations.

No Krepalgans sat in those chairs. The Hereditary Tyrant had sent the plenipo from the Krepalgan Unity home, ordered all Krepalgan citizens out of Tartesh, and sealed the border. So far, he'd done nothing more than that. Radnal both resented and approved of his caution. In an age of starbombs, even the attempted murder of a nation had to be dealt with cautiously, lest a successful double murder follow.

A man in a fancy robe came up to the motor, bowed low. "I am the protocol officer. If you will come with me, freemen—?"

Radnal and Peggol came. The protocol officer led them onto the platform, got them settled, and hurried away to see to the rest of the seven walkers, whose motors had parked behind the one from which the tour guide and the Eye and Ear had dismounted.

Peering at the important people who were examining him, Radnal got nervous again. He didn't belong in this kind of company. But there in the middle of the second row sat Toglo zev Pamdal, who smiled broadly and waved at him. Seeing someone he knew and liked made it easier for him to wait for the next part of the ceremony.

The Tarteshan national hymn blared out. Radnal couldn't just sit. He got up and put his hand over his heart until the hymn was done. The protocol officer stepped up to the podium and announced, "Freemen, freeladies, the Hereditary Tyrant."

Bortav vez Pamdal's features adorned silver, smiled down from public buildings, and were frequently on the screen. Radnal had never expected to see the Hereditary Tyrant in person, though. In the flesh, Bortav looked older than he did on his images, and not quite so firm and wise: like a man, in other words, not a demigod.

But his ringing baritone proved all his own. He spoke without notes for a quarter of a daytenth, praising Tartesh, condemning those who had tried to lay her low, and promising that danger would never come again. In short, it was a political speech. Since Radnal cared more about the kidneys of the fat sand rat than politics, he soon stopped paying attention.

He almost missed the Hereditary Tyrant calling out his name. He started and sprang up. Bortav vez Pamdal beckoned him to the podium. As if in a dream, he went.

Bortav put an arm around his shoulder. The Hereditary Tyrant was faintly perfumed. "Freemen, freeladies, I present Radnal vez Krobir, whose sharp eye spotted the evil wires which proved the gods had not deserted Tartesh. For his valiant efforts in preserving not only Trench Park, not only the Bottomlands, but all Tartesh, I award him five thousand units of silver and declare that he and all his heirs are henceforward recognized as members of our nation's aristocracy. Freeman vez Krobir!"

The dignitaries applauded. Bortav vez Pamdal nodded, first to the microphone, then to Radnal. Making a speech frightened him worse than almost anything he'd gone through in the Bottomlands. He tried to pretend it was a scientific paper: "Thank you, your excellency. You honor me beyond my worth. I will always cherish your kindness."

He stepped back. The dignitaries applauded again, perhaps because he'd been so brief. Away from the mike, the Hereditary Tyrant said, "Stay up here by me while I reward your colleagues. The other presentation for you is at the end."

Bortav called up the rest of the seven walkers, one by one. He raised Peggol to the aristocracy along with Radnal. The other five drew his praise and large sums of silver. That seemed unfair to Radnal. Without Horken, for instance, they wouldn't have found the electrical cell and timer. And Impac had picked up the trail when even Radnal lost it.

He couldn't very well protest. Even as the hero of the moment, he lacked the clout to make Bortav listen to him. Moreover, he guessed no one had informed the Hereditary Tyrant he'd been fornicating with Evillia and Lofosa a few days before they went out to detonate the buried starbomb. Bortav vez Pamdal was a staunch conservative about morals. He wouldn't have elevated Radnal if he'd known everything he did in Trench Park.

To salve his conscience, Radnal reminded himself that all seven walkers would have easier lives because of today's ceremony. It was true. He remained not quite convinced it was enough.

Zosel vez Glesir, last to be called to the podium, finished his thank-you and went back to his place. Bortav vez Pamdal reclaimed the microphone. As the applause for Zosel died away, the Tyrant said, "Our nation should never forget this near brush with disaster, nor the efforts of all those within Trench Park who turned it aside. To commemorate it, I here display for the first time the insigne Trench Park will bear henceforward."

The protocol officer carried a cloth-covered square of fiberboard, not quite two cubits on a side, over to Radnal. He murmured. "The veil unfastens from the top. Hold the emblem up so the crowd can see it as you lower the veil."

Radnal obeyed. The dignitaries clapped. Most of them smiled; a few even laughed. Radnal smiled, too. What better way to symbolize Trench Park than a koprit bird perching on a thornbush?

Bortav vez Pamdal waved him to the microphone once more. He said, "I thank you again, your excellency, now on behalf of all Trench Park staff. We shall bear this insigne proudly."

He stepped away from the microphone, then turned his head and hissed to the protocol officer, "What do I do with this thing?"

"Lean it against the side of the podium," the unflappable official answered. "We'll take care of it." As Radnal returned to his seat, the protocol officer announced, "Now we'll adjourn to the Grand Reception Hall for drinks and a luncheon."

Along with everyone else, Radnal found his way to the Grand Reception Hall. He took a glass of sparkling wine from a waiter with a silver tray, then stood around accepting

congratulations from important officials. It was like being
a tour guide: he knew most of what he should say, and
improvised new answers along old themes.

In a flash of insight, he realized the politicians and
bureaucrats were doing the same thing with him. The
whole affair was as formal as a figure dance. When he saw
that, his nervousness vanished for good.

Or so he thought, until Toglo came smiling up to him.
He dipped his head. "Hello, freelady, it's good to see you
again."

"If I was Toglo zev through danger in Trench Park, I
remain Toglo zev here safe in Tarteshem." She sounded
as if his formality disappointed her.

"Good," he said. Despite her pledge of patronage before
she hiked away from the lodge, plenty of people friendly
to Trench Park staff in the Bottomlands snubbed them
if they met in the city. He hadn't thought she was that type,
but better safe.

As if by magic, Bortav vez Pamdal appeared at Radnal's
elbow. The Hereditary Tyrant's cheeks were a little red;
he might have had more than one glass of sparkling wine.
He spoke as if reminding himself: "You already know my
niece, don't you, freeman vez Krobir?"

"Your—niece?" Radnal stared from Bortav to Toglo.
She'd called herself a distant collateral relation. *Niece* didn't
fit that definition.

"Hope you enjoy your stay here." Bortav slapped Radnal
on the shoulder, breathed wine into his face, and ambled
off to hobnob with other guests.

"You never said you were his niece," Radnal said. Now
that he was suddenly an aristocrat, he might have imagined
talking to the clanfather of the Hereditary Tyrant's distant
collateral relative. But to talk to Bortav vez Pamdal's
brother or sister-husband . . . impossible. Maybe that made
him sound peevish.

"I'm sorry," Toglo answered. Radnal studied her,

expecting the apology to be merely for form's sake. But she seemed to mean it. She said, "Bearing my clan name is hard enough anyway. It would be harder yet if I told everyone how close a relative of the Hereditary Tyrant's I am. People wouldn't treat me like a human being. Believe me, I know." By the bitterness in her voice, she did.

"Oh," Radnal said slowly. "I never thought of that, Toglo zev." Her smile, when he used her name with the polite particle, made him feel better.

"You should have," she told him. "When folk hear I'm from the Pamdal clan, they either act as if I'm made of glass and will shatter if they breathe on me too hard, or else they try to see how much they can get out of me. I don't care for either one. That's why I minimize the kinship."

"Oh," Radnal's snort of laughter was aimed mostly at himself. "I always imagined being attached to a rich and famous clan made life simpler and easier, not the other way around. I never thought anything bad might be mixed with that. I'm sorry, for not realizing it."

"You needn't be," she said. "I think you'd have treated me the same even if you'd known from the first heartbeat who my uncle happened to be. I don't find that often, so I treasure it."

Radnal said, "I'd be lying if I told you I didn't think about which family you belonged to."

"Well, of course, Radnal vez. You'd be stupid if you didn't think about it. I don't expect that; until the koprit bird, I thought the gods were done with miracles. But whatever you were thinking, you didn't let it get in the way."

"I tried to treat you as much like everyone else as I could," he said.

"I thought you did wonderfully," she answered. "That's why we became friends so fast down in Trench Park. It's also why I'd like us to stay friends now."

"I'd like that very much," Radnal said. "Provided you

don't think I'm saying so to try and take advantage of you."

"I don't think you'd do that." Though Toglo kept smiling, her eyes measured him. She'd said she'd had people try to take advantage of her before. Radnal doubted those people had come off well.

"Being who you are makes it harder for me to tell you I also liked you very much, down in the Bottomlands," he said.

"Yes, I can see that it might," Toglo said. "You don't want me to think you seek advantage." She studied Radnal again. This time, he studied her, too. Maybe the first person who'd tried to turn friendship to gain had succeeded; she was, he thought, a genuinely nice person. But he would have bet his five thousand units of silver that she'd sent the second such person packing. Being nice didn't make her a fool. He didn't like her less for that. Maybe Eltsac vez Martois was attracted to fools, but Eltsac was a fool himself. Radnal had called himself many names, but fool seldom. The last time he'd thought that about himself was when he found out what Lofosa and Evillia really were. Of course, when he made a mistake, he didn't do it halfway.

But he'd managed to redeem himself—with help from that koprit bird.

Toglo said, "If we do become true friends, Radnal vez, or perhaps even more than that"—a possibility he wouldn't have dared mention himself, but one far from displeasing—"promise me one thing."

"What?" he asked, suddenly wary. "I don't like friendship with conditions. It reminds me too much of our last treaty with Morgaf. We haven't fought the islanders in a while, but we don't trust them, or they us. We saw that in the Bottomlands, too."

She nodded. "True. Still, I hope my condition isn't too onerous."

"Go on." He sipped his sparkling wine.

"Well, then, Radnal vez Krobir, the next time I see you in a sleepsack with a couple of naked Highhead girls— or even Strongbrows—you will have to consider our friendship over."

Some of the wine went up his nose. That only made him choke worse. Dabbing at himself with a linen square gave him a few heartbeats to regain composure. "Toglo zev, you have a bargain," he said solemnly.

They clasped hands.